Two-Faced

High praise for Mandasue Heller's brilliant novels:

'Sexy and slick.' *Look*

'Powerful writing.' *Scotland on Sunday*

'A cracking page-turner.' *Manchester Evening News*

'Alarming . . . beguiling . . . exhilarating.' *Scotsman*

'A glamorous nightclub hides a seedy underworld that Heller knows only too well.' *Daily Express*

'Crammed with gangsters and glamour girls, this is a sassy take on the usual crime thriller.' *Woman*

'Mandasue has played a real blinder with this fantastic novel.' Martina Cole on *Forget Me Not*

By the same author

The Front
Forget Me Not
Tainted Lives
The Game
The Charmer
The Club
Shafted
Snatched

About the author

Mandasue Heller was born in Cheshire and moved to Manchester in 1982. There, she has found the inspiration for her novels: she spent ten years living in the infamous Hulme Crescents and has sung in cabaret and rock groups, seventies soul cover bands and blues jam bands. She still lives in the Manchester area with her musician partner.

MANDASUE HELLER

Two-Faced

First published in Great Britain in 2009 by Hodder & Stoughton
An Hachette UK company

First published in paperback in 2010

2

A CIP catalogue record for this title is available from the British Library

ISBN 978 0 340 95417 1

Typeset in Plantin Light by
Palimpsest Book Production Limited, Grangemouth, Stirlingshire

Printed and bound by Clays Ltd, St Ives plc

Hodder & Stoughton policy is to use papers that are natural, renewable and recyclable products and made from wood grown in sustainable forests. The logging and manufacturing processes are expected to conform to the environmental regulations of the country of origin.

Hodder & Stoughton Ltd
338 Euston Road
London NW1 3BH

www.hodder.co.uk

To my beautiful mum, Jean Heller – for everything you have been and still are to me.

Acknowledgements

As always, much love to my partner Wingrove Ward; and my children, Michael, Andrew, Azzura (& Michael), Marissa, Lariah, & bump; Ava, Amber, Martin, Jade, Reece & Kyro; Auntie Doreen, Pete, Lorna & Cliff, Chris & Glen; Mavis & Joseph, Val, Jascinth, Donna, Nats, Dan, Toni, & children – and the rest of our extended families, both here and in the USA.

Thanks to my editor, Carolyn Caughey, and everyone at Hodder; Nick Austin; and my agents, Cat Ledger, and Guy Rose.

Hi to Norman; Betty & Ronnie; Wayne; Martina – and the rest of our good friends everywhere.

Cheers to John Heaton, and Boss Model Management for the technical advice.

RIP Manchester legend Johnny Roadhouse.

Hello and thank you to all the readers and staff we met – and who made us so welcome – at the various venues we visited as part of the publicity events.

And, lastly, Hi to our Dakota band-mates (feel free to check us out at MySpace: Dakota ft Mandasue Heller)

Kim Delaney was alone when her waters broke. Alone in the sense that the baby's father wasn't there to bear the pain with her. But then he'd disappeared pretty much as soon as she'd told him she was pregnant, so it was no big loss. And there were plenty of onlookers to keep her company, it being a Monday and the favoured day for all the harassed mothers in the area to do their weekly Netto run.

Kim was on the last aisle when it happened, and had just spotted an empty till up ahead. Her basket was only a fraction as full as the trolleys being pushed around by the rest of the women who were dashing about grabbing bargains, but she was a month early so she hadn't expected to be stocking up on nappies and baby milk just yet. Quickening her pace, determined not to let anyone get to the till before her, she'd just reached down for a tin of deodorant off the bottom shelf when the hot liquid gushed out from between her fat thighs. Jerking upright, she crossed her legs to stem the flow. But there was no stopping nature.

Peering at the puddle around her feet, she cursed under her breath. She should have *known* something was wrong when she'd woken up with backache that morning. But she'd thought it was constipation, so she'd glugged some syrup of figs and downed a couple of paracetamol, then set off to do her shopping, thinking she had plenty of time to get everything done before the laxatives took effect.

She gasped when the first contraction seized her belly in

its iron grip and fell against one of the open-topped freezer cabinets, her face just inches from the frozen chips and peas.

Just as the pain began to subside, a small boy wandered around the corner. Eyes almost popping out of his head when he saw the mess at her feet, he yelled, '*Maaaam* . . . the lady's pissed herself!'

Kim tried to distance herself from the shameful pool that was spreading out across the tiled floor, but the second contraction slammed home before she'd taken two steps, and she sank to her knees.

The nosy boy's mother came hurtling around the corner just then. Skidding to a halt when she realised what was happening, she wrenched her son out of the way and shouted, 'Someone call an ambulance! There's a girl having a baby round here!'

That was all it took to fetch everyone and their mothers around into the last aisle, some dragging their loaded trolleys with them as they battled to get a better viewing position, others completely abandoning theirs.

Squatting now and panting like an animal as the pain tore through her, Kim squeezed her eyes tight shut, wishing that the gawpers would all just go away and give her a bit of privacy.

'Ambulance is on its way,' the store manager trilled, his voice squeaky with panic despite his desperate attempt to sound authoritative and calm. He clicked his fingers at one of his staff. 'You, fetch a mop before someone slips on . . .' Trailing off, his cheeks flared as he searched for words to describe the disgusting mess on the floor. 'The, um, the wetness,' he managed at last. Then, flapping his hands at the crowd, 'And can we all back off and give her some room, please?'

'She don't need room,' a gruff voice informed him knowingly. 'She needs a good big slug of gin, so bugger off ordering folk about and fetch a bottle. And get me some whisky while you're at it,' the speaker added, giving him a dig in his skinny ribs with her fat old cat-piss-stinking elbow.

'You tell him, Queenie!' one of the women in the crowd chuckled. 'But never mind whisky, shouldn't we be cracking champagne for a new babby?'

'Oh, now, I don't think we should be encouraging her to drink alcohol,' an elderly lady piped up disapprovingly. 'She doesn't look old enough.'

'Behave!' Queenie scoffed. 'She was old enough to open her legs, so she's old enough for a slug of the hard stuff.'

'For God's sake, will you all just get *lost*!' Kim grunted, her face turning an unnatural shade of puce as the pain intensified. She had an awful feeling that the laxatives were about to kick in, and the last thing she needed was to do a number two in front of this lot. It was bad enough that they'd already seen her piss herself – or as good as.

'Calm down, love,' a woman said soothingly. 'It'll all be over soon.' Squatting down beside Kim, she reached for her hand. 'There you go. You just squeeze on that if it helps.'

Kim was about to tell her to go to hell, but the next wave of pain washed over her like a tidal wave.

'*OOOWWW!*' the woman yelped, struggling to wrench her hand free as Kim squeezed it with all her might. 'Let go, you stupid cow! You're breaking my fingers!'

An ambulance pulled up outside. Ambling into the store as if they had all the time in the world, one of the male attendants proceeded to push the crowd back while the other went over to Kim.

'All right, sweetheart, cavalry's here,' he quipped, taking a quick feel of her stomach. 'What's your name?'

She opened her mouth to answer, but all that came out was a low, guttural moan of agony.

'I don't know her name,' someone in the crowd offered. 'But she lives near me on Claremont Road, if that's any help.'

'It's Kim,' she growled, twisting her head to see which of her neighbours was witnessing her humiliation. Then, feeling a cold draught on her thighs as the ambulance man tried to yank her legs apart, she clamped her knees together and shoved her skirt back down to cover her soiled knickers. 'Not here! Take me to hospital.'

'Doubt we'll have time for that,' he told her, pulling on a pair of latex gloves. 'I reckon this little one's well on its way.'

'It shouldn't be,' she groaned, her teeth clenched like a vice as a fresh contraction flared. 'I've got a month to go yet.'

'And you haven't had any pains before this? No signs that it might be coming early?'

'*No*! I mean, *yes*, this morning . . . bit of backache.' Remembering again about the laxatives, Kim clutched at his hand. 'Please, you've got to get me out of here. You don't understa— *aaagghhh*!'

Blood spurted out, soaking right through Kim's skirt and spreading out on the floor beneath her.

'Sorry, lovey, but you're going to have to let me take a look,' the ambulance man said, forcing her rigid knees apart. Pulling a pair of scissors from his breast pocket, he snipped straight through the seams of her knickers.

Kim wanted to shrivel up and die, but the pain outweighed the embarrassment, and she squeezed her eyes shut and held her breath when she felt an overwhelming urge to push.

Barking at her to stop it, the ambulance man waved his mate over. 'Head's engaged, but I don't think she's fully dilated yet.'

His worried tone alerted the watching crowd to drama, causing them to crane their necks to see what was happening between Kim's legs.

'I'll put a call out,' the second man said, heading for the door. 'See if there's a doctor nearby.'

'Monday's child, fair of face,' Queenie intoned, lounging

against the freezer cabinet and munching toothlessly on a chocolate biscuit she'd just liberated from a packet on the shelf behind her. 'Least it's not gonna take after its mum, eh, Kim.'

'Don't be tight,' someone scolded, with a snigger.

But Kim was beyond caring. This was her first baby, and the pain was worse than anything she'd ever experienced before in her life. And it wasn't just confined to her privates, which felt as if they were being ripped to shreds from the inside out; it was everywhere.

'It's moving,' someone yelped disgustedly as the slippery, blood-soaked head began to slide out. 'Oh my God, that is re*vol*ting!'

Just as the baby's shoulders began to slither into view, a doctor from the local surgery rushed in, along with a midwife who had been in the clinic at the time the call had been put out for assistance. Pushing the ambulance crew aside, she took control.

'It's a girl!' she announced seconds later, bringing cries of '*Aaahhh!*' from the crowd as she helped the squirming newborn into the light and gave it a quick look-over.

Kim's pain had momentarily eased, but when it started up again, even more intense than before, she screamed.

'It's only the placenta,' the midwife informed her matter-of factly – scaring the hell out of her, because she hadn't been to any of her antenatal classes and hadn't known that you gave birth to *that* as well.

'I don't think it is,' the ambulance man murmured, gesturing with a nod towards Kim's vagina. 'It looks like another one to me.'

Another gasp from the crowd – another excuse to stare at Kim's gaping hole. And there, amidst the blood and gore, was the unmistakable fluff of a second head of hair.

'Ooh, twins.' Queenie sucked an ominous breath in through her gums. 'You'll have double trouble now, eh, Kim?'

Kim wanted to tell her to shut the hell up, and to stop calling her by her name as if she knew her when she didn't. And she wanted to tell the ambulance man he'd made a mistake; that there couldn't possibly be two babies. But the words wouldn't come. Then, mercifully, the gawping faces began to dissolve as darkness descended.

Feeling herself drifting away, she caught snatches of words floating to her through the fog.

Haemorrhage . . .

Emergency . . .

State of all that blood . . .

Dead for sure . . .

But the screaming voice coming from inside her own head drowned them all out.

It couldn't be twins – it just *couldn't*! She wasn't even ready for one, so how the hell was she going to manage *two*?

PART ONE

I

'I need a fiver,' Mia said, hurtling through the living-room door and clicking her fingers expectantly.

'Yeah, and I need a rich man,' Kim replied, squinting at herself in the mirror through the smoke curling up from the cigarette clamped between her teeth. 'But I ain't getting one.'

'Mum, *please*.' Mia flapped her hands in exasperation. 'Me and Laura are going to the youthy; I need it.'

'It only costs fifty pence,' Kim reminded her, frowning at a fresh batch of grey hairs. Twirling one around her finger, she yanked it out – although she didn't know why she bothered, because it would only come back tomorrow with friends in tow.

'I can't go with fifty *pence*,' Mia scowled. 'Everyone will think I'm a right pauper. What about drinks?'

'I haven't got it,' Kim told her, reaching for her lipstick. 'Not enough to give you both a fiver, anyhow.'

'Who said anything about *her*?' Mia flicked a dismissive glance at her sister, Michelle, who was curled up on the chair by the window, reading. 'She's not even going.'

'If you are, so's she,' Kim informed her, stubbing her cigarette out and picking up the hairbrush. 'I'm off to bingo.'

'Aw, *mum*. I don't want her to come. No one even likes her.'

'Tough. She's not stopping in by herself – not with that peeping Tom still hanging about.'

'Like anyone's going to perv over a minger like *her*.'

'Do I have to go?' Michelle chipped in quietly, wishing they'd stop talking about her as if she wasn't even there.

'For God's *sake*!' Kim barked, slamming the brush down on the ledge. 'You're either both going, or you can both stop in – and that's that!'

Muttering a curse under her breath, Mia stomped out of the room.

'You'd better not have said what I think you just said, lady!' Kim bellowed after her, the threat in her voice diluted by the fact that she made no move to follow.

Tutting when a door slammed above, she lit another cigarette and glared at Michelle. 'Why are you still here?'

Reluctantly closing her book, Michelle made one last plea to be allowed to stay at home. Kim's reply was a warning stare; the kind that said *if you don't get your arse out of here right this minute . . .*

Heeding it, Michelle ran upstairs.

The house was a small run-down end-of-terrace in one of the few remaining streets in Moss Side which hadn't yet been earmarked for renovation. There were two bedrooms, one marginally larger than the other, but Kim had claimed that one for herself, so the girls had to share the remaining shoebox. And the older they got, the harder it became to manage the tiny space – although it wasn't from lack of trying on Michelle's part. She was constantly cleaning up after Mia, who was the complete opposite, and scattered her things around as if Michelle had no right to expect a share of the wardrobe, the drawers, or even the floor.

Coming into the room now and seeing Mia's clothes strewn about, and wads of dirty cotton-wool balls and unlidded tubes of make-up littering the dressing table, Michelle sighed.

'That better not have been aimed at me,' Mia warned, her eyes flashing spitefully in the mirror as she applied another coat of mascara.

Michelle knew that her sister was just looking for an excuse to start a fight so she kept her mouth shut and reached into the wardrobe for a cardigan.

Watching as she pulled the misshapen woolly on over the equally baggy jumper she was already wearing, Mia said, 'Er, I don't think so! You're not coming out in public dressed like that with *me*.'

'It's cold,' Michelle murmured, and climbed up onto her bunk, hoping to snatch a few more minutes of reading time before their mum turfed them out.

'I don't give a shit,' Mia retorted icily. 'Get changed, or you're dead.'

Ignoring her, Michelle propped her head on her hand and flipped the book open. But she hadn't read a word before Mia leapt up and set about her, tugging at her hair with one hand and punching her with the other.

'Why do you always have to go everywhere I go? You're like a smelly fucking dog I can't get rid of!'

'It's not my fault mum won't let me stay in,' Michelle protested. 'I don't even *want* to go.'

'She'd have let you stay if you weren't such a little mardy arse!'

'Stop it!' Michelle cried, her cheek stinging from a sharp slap.

'Or what? You'll burst into tears and get me *wet*?'

'I'll tell mum!'

'And what's *she* gonna do? She hates you as much as I do, you stupid bitch. *Everyone* does, or haven't you figured that out yet?'

Struggling to contain the tears, Michelle squeezed her eyes shut. There was no point arguing when Mia was in this kind of mood; she'd only get nastier.

Satisfied that her words had pierced the bubble of niceness that Michelle floated around in, Mia dropped back down to the floor. She despised her sister; resented that she was forced to share a bedroom with her, never mind a *face*.

Not that Michelle was anywhere near as pretty, because she wasn't. And that wasn't just Mia's opinion, all of her friends thought so, too. They were supposed to be identical, but having the same features didn't make you *look* the same. It was what you did with those features that made the difference, and Michelle didn't have a clue how to apply make-up or straighten her hair properly. Still, that was her lookout. If she spent more time reading fashion magazines instead of the soppy novels she borrowed from the library, she'd know that this was the twenty-first century, not the nineteenth. And these days, girls didn't sit around waiting for Mr Right to sweep them off their feet – they got their faces on and went out hunting for Mr *Wrong*, because that was the only way they were guaranteed to have a bit of fun. But with all the personality of a damp dishcloth, it wouldn't matter *what* Michelle looked like. She was never going to be as popular as Mia, and no boy was ever going to want her.

Downstairs, the doorbell rang, and their mum's voice floated up to them as she let the next-door neighbour in.

'All right, Pam, love; I'm just waiting on the girls.'

'They're not gonna be long are they?' Pam replied in her usual bellow, which echoed off the walls in the small hallway like a foghorn. 'Only the bus'll be here in five, and I don't want to miss getting me card for the national.'

'You hear that?' Kim yelled up. 'There's two thousand quid riding on this, so get moving!'

Smoothing her hair down as best she could with her hands, because Mia was using the brush and there was no way she would hand it over while she was being awkward, Michelle climbed off the bed and headed for the door.

'Er, where do you think you're going?' Mia demanded,

stepping in front of her. 'I thought I told you to get something decent on.'

Michelle gritted her teeth, pushed her sister out of the way and trotted down the stairs. She didn't see why Mia was so bothered about what she was wearing, anyway. It wasn't like they'd be *seen* together. Mia would disappear with her friends as soon as they got through the door.

'Mum, you'd best tell her!' Mia said, marching after her with her hands on her hips.

'Tell her what?' Kim asked, gathering up her keys and cigarettes and putting them into her handbag.

'That she's not coming out with *me* looking like *that*! She's a tramp!'

Glancing from Mia, with her immaculate make-up, short skirt, midriff-exposing top and stiletto heels, to Michelle, in her jumper, cardi, jeans and trainers, without so much as a hint of lip-gloss to brighten her pale face, Kim gave a little twist of her lip. 'You do look a bit of a mess, Shell.'

'Oh, leave her alone, there's nowt wrong with her,' Pam chipped in, sick of the way Mia and Kim always sided against Michelle. Gazing steadily back when Mia flashed a hateful look her way, she shrugged. 'Well, she's the double of you, so if she's a mess, what does that make you?'

'She looks *nothing* like me, and only an idiot would think she does,' Mia spat, giving Pam a dirty look before turning back to her mum. 'Make her get changed, or she's not coming.'

'Sorry, love, it's too late,' Kim said, pulling her coat on. 'I'm already pushing it.'

Making a strangled screaming sound, Mia stamped her foot. 'Why are you *doing* this to me? You're ruining my life!'

Kim ignored her and ushered them both out, saying, 'Don't bother coming back before ten, 'cos me and Pam are off into town after bingo. And Eric's got a job on, so he'll be a bit late.'

'Oh, right, so I've got to hang around in the cold like a dickhead,' Mia complained. 'Don't you think it's about time I had my own key?'

'When you're fifty, not fifteen,' Kim called back, already heading off towards the bus stop.

'What about my money?' Mia yelled after her.

Sighing, Kim stopped walking and took three pound coins out of her purse.

'What am I supposed to do with *that*?' Mia grumbled, snatching them. 'God, you're so tight.'

'Oi! Quit talking to your mam like that,' Pam scolded. 'And think yourself lucky, 'cos you'd get nowt but a slap if you were one of mine giving me that kind of lip.'

'It's got nothing to do with you,' Mia informed her tartly.

'Don't be trying your nonsense with me,' Pam warned. 'You might get away with it with your mam, but you ain't treating *me* like a divvy.'

Irritated with Pam for interfering, Kim took another pound out of her purse and pushed it into Mia's hand. 'There, now go.'

'Ooh, she's spoilt rotten, that one,' Pam chided, incensed by the sly grin that Mia flicked her as she walked away. 'And you wouldn't let the other one get away with it, so why do you put up with it from her?'

'Do I tell you how to bring your kids up?' Kim shot back huffily, setting off for the bus stop again.

'You're a born fool,' Pam grumbled, catching up with her just as the bus came around the corner. 'And you'll have no one but yourself to blame when she turns round and bites you in the arse.'

Drawling, 'Yeah, whatever,' Kim stuck her hand out.

Mia's friend Laura was waiting at the end of the road. Tutting when she saw Michelle, she said, 'What you bringing *her* for?'

'Had no choice,' Mia muttered, linking arms with her. 'But don't worry, she knows what she'll get if she doesn't stay out of my way.'

Michelle wrapped the cardigan tighter around herself and followed as they set off down the road. Hearing them whispering and sniggering, she guessed they were bitching about her – as usual. And she knew she shouldn't let it get to her, but it was hard not to sometimes. Identical twins were supposed to share some kind of supernatural bond, but she and Mia couldn't be more divided if they'd been born on different planets.

Still, you couldn't change who you were, and Michelle had long ago accepted that she was never going to be as beautiful or bubbly as her sister, so she got on with her own life as best she could, and left Mia to hers.

The youth club was already full when they got there, and distorted rap music was blasting out through the open doors. Spotting their friends on the far side of the hall, Mia and Laura quickly disappeared into the crowd. Knowing without having to check that none of *her* friends would be here, Michelle edged her way into a secluded corner.

Mia and Laura greeted their friends with hugs and air-kisses, then scanned the room for fit lads – the only reason any of them ever came here.

Clocking the group of lads to their left, Laura nudged Mia, whispering excitedly, 'Wow! Check who's here.'

Mia turned to look and inhaled sharply when she saw Darren Mitchell. He was absolutely gorgeous, and she'd fancied him for ages, but since he'd left school some months earlier he and his mate Stu hardly ever showed up here. Not that his being here made any difference, though, because she had no intention of going anywhere near him. Not when his psycho girlfriend, Sandra Bishop, was probably close by, waiting to knife any girl who so much as looked at him.

As it happened, Sandra was staying at her dad's new place in Wales that weekend, so Darren and Stu were heading into town to check out a strip club that had just opened. They'd only dropped in here so that Stu could give his cousin some weed, but the cousin hadn't arrived yet. Darren had been on the verge of telling Stu to sack it off, but he'd changed his mind when Mia had walked in.

Unlike the other tarts who'd been batting their eyelashes at him since he'd arrived, she was acting as if she hadn't even noticed him. And if there was one thing Darren liked, it was a challenge. Giving her a slow half-smile now, he pushed his mates out of the way and leaned against the wall beside her.

'So, where's your man?' he asked, giving her the full force of his baby blues.

'Haven't got one,' she replied, forcing herself to stay cool despite the butterflies dancing in her stomach. 'And I don't *want* one,' she added, letting him know that his charms weren't going to work on her.

'I don't believe you,' he drawled, taking a sip from his Coke can. 'No way would a gorgeous girl like you be single. Bet he hasn't got a car, though – whoever he is.'

Paranoid that Sandra might be watching, Mia folded her arms and gazed out at the dancers. 'No, but I suppose *you* have?'

'Too right,' Darren boasted. 'I'll take you for a drive sometime, if you want.'

Feigning lack of interest, she said, 'No, thanks,' although her heart was already racing at the thought of being seen in his car with him. None of her friends had boyfriends who owned their own cars. She'd be the envy of the entire *area* if she got off with him, never mind the school.

Not that she *was* going to get off with him, obviously.

'Bet you wouldn't say that if you saw it,' Darren said confidently. 'It was a bit of a shed when I first got it, but it looks *mint* since I put the alloys and fin on it. Only cost a grand so far, but it'll be worth about three by now.'

'*Wow!*' Mia exclaimed in a mocking tone designed to let him know that she wasn't impressed in the slightest. She actually didn't have a clue what alloys and fins were, but a grand was a hell of a lot of money, and she definitely was impressed by *that*.

'It's in the garage at the moment,' Darren was telling her now. 'I've just ordered a new exhaust, but it's custom-made so I've got to wait for it to get shipped over from the States. It'll be well worth it, though, 'cos it'll be faster than a Subaru once it's fitted.'

Sensing that he was losing her when her eyes began to glaze over, Darren glanced at his watch and decided to speed things along. Taking another sip of his drink, he said, 'So, you planning to go into modelling when you leave school, then?'

Her coolness faltering at the mention of her favourite subject – her looks – Mia glanced coyly up at him. 'What makes you say that?'

'It's obvious.' Shrugging, he peered down into her eyes. 'You're hardly going to waste yourself stacking shelves in some shitty shop when you look like Kate Moss, are you?'

'I don't look like her,' Mia scoffed, struggling to sound modest while her eyes gleamed with delight.

'Yeah, you do. Only when she was younger, obviously, 'cos she's a bit past it now. But you well remind me of her.'

Twiddling with the ends of her hair now, Mia pouted her glossy lips and fluttered her eyelashes. 'You really think so?'

'Wouldn't have said it if I didn't.' Darren gave her a sincere smile and offered her the can. 'Want some?'

Grateful, because she'd wanted to keep the rest of the money her mum had given her to buy cigarettes on the way home, Mia took a sip. Grimacing when it hit the back of her throat, she spluttered, 'Jeezus! What's *that*?'

'Vodka. Don't you like it?'

'Prefer whisky,' she lied, wiping her mouth on the back of her hand – and wishing she could wipe her tongue as well, to get rid of the bitter taste of almost neat alcohol.

'You're in luck,' Darren said smoothly. 'There's a full bottle of JD back at Stu's place. Fancy coming back for one?'

Thrilled that he'd invited her, but still wary of Sandra, Mia shook her head. 'Thanks, but I don't think that's a very good idea.'

'Course it is,' he insisted, grinning sexily. 'Unless you've got something better to do – which I doubt.'

Amused that he seemed to think he was such a catch – which he *was*, but she wasn't about to let *him* know that she thought so – Mia said, 'Don't think Sandra would be too happy if she could hear this, do you?'

'Aw, what you talking about *her* for?' Darren groaned, pulling a face.

'Er, 'cos she's your *girlfriend*.'

'No, she ain't.'

'Not what I heard.'

'Shouldn't believe everything you hear, then, should you?'

'Even if it's from the horse's mouth?' Mia looked him in the eye. 'Only I heard her in the loos at school today telling her mate about some necklace you gave her last night.'

'That was nothing,' Darren said dismissively. 'Just some piece of shit I found in the park.'

'Well, *she* seemed pretty chuffed with it. And why give it to her if you're not with her any more?'

Shrugging, Darren twisted his lip. 'Sort of like a finishing present, I suppose.'

'So you finished with her last night, did you? *After* you gave her the necklace.'

'Jeezus, don't you ever quit?' he muttered, glancing at his watch again. 'Anyway, shut up about her; she's history. Are you coming for that drink, or what? 'Cos if you're not, stop wasting my time.'

Mia bit her lip and mulled it over. Sandra was usually stuck to him like superglue, so the fact that she wasn't here tonight could mean that he was telling the truth. And even if he hadn't done it yet, he was obviously *intending* to end it, or he wouldn't be out on the pull – which Sandra could hardly blame Mia for.

'Can Laura come?' she asked. ''Cos I don't go anywhere without her.'

'I think she's already been invited,' Darren chuckled, nodding towards their friends, who had moved into a corner and looked deep in flirtatious conversation.

Mia watched as Laura did that funny flicky thing she always did with her fringe when she was trying to act shy and tutted softly under her breath. She wouldn't have minded, but Stu was a right ugly sod. Well, he was compared to Darren, who was big and muscly, with dark blond hair and sexy blue eyes.

And a car.

'All right,' she said, making it sound like she was doing him a favour. 'I suppose one drink won't hurt.'

'Cool.' Grinning, Darren drank the last of the vodka and dropped the can on the floor. 'Come on, then.'

'What, *now*?' Mia gasped. 'We've only just got here. And what about them?' She looked back at their friends who were kissing now.

Whistling through his teeth to attract Stu's attention, Darren jerked his head in a summoning gesture.

'Always get your own way, do you?' Mia teased when Stu immediately obeyed.

Winking at her, Darren planted his hand on the small of her back and pushed her on ahead of him.

Still in her corner, Michelle spotted Mia heading out of the door. Frowning when she saw who she was with, she followed them out into the entrance hall.

'Mia, wait! Where are you going?'

Mia groaned because she'd forgotten all about her stupid sister and told Darren to wait outside.

'Go home,' she hissed, dragging Michelle out of earshot. 'And if mum gets back before me, tell her I've gone round to Laura's to pick something up.'

'Where are you *really* going?' Michelle asked, casting a wary glance at Darren. She wasn't happy about Mia going off with him, because he was a troublemaker who had always been getting suspended for fighting when he'd still been at school. But it was his girlfriend who most worried Michelle. Gobby as Mia was, she was no match for Sandra Bishop.

'Mind your own business,' Mia snapped. 'And don't even think about trying to follow us.'

'We're supposed to stay together,' Michelle reminded her.

'Says who?' Mia retorted tartly. 'Mum only said you weren't allowed to stay in the house by yourself. She didn't say anything about me babysitting you.'

'What about Eric?' Michelle called when Mia flounced back to the waiting group.

'What about him?' Mia flipped back coldly. 'He's hardly going to try anything on with *you*, is he?'

Peering back at Michelle, Darren said, 'Who's that?'

'Her twin sister,' Laura informed him. 'Not that you'd think it to look at them, 'cos Mia's *well* prettier.'

'You're telling *me*,' he sneered. 'Beauty and the beast, or what!'

Tears of humiliation stinging her eyes when people started looking to see if he was right, Michelle put her head down and ran outside. It was already dark, and patches of ice were beginning to glisten in the puddles dotting the road. Shivering, she huddled deeper into her cardigan and headed for home – although she wasn't looking forward to being alone with her mum's boyfriend when she got there.

Eric had never actually done anything to her, but she just didn't like him. At six feet he towered over her mum, who was quite short. And where her mum was chubby, he was stick-thin, with a long miserable face and beady little rats' eyes. Appearances aside, what really pissed Michelle off was the fact that he had a key to their house when he didn't even live there. Well, not officially, anyway; he just stayed the night – most nights. And their mum might have told him only to use the key when it was dark in case someone reported her to the DSS, but he still shouldn't have it – and that was one of the rare things Michelle and Mia were in definite agreement about.

Not that their mum cared what *they* thought. If they complained, she just said it was her house, and if they didn't like it they knew what they could do – which was basically nothing, because they weren't old enough to leave. And they'd only met their real father once, so they couldn't go running to him. Mia had threatened to on more than a few occasions when she'd been sulking about something or other, but their mum had just laughed and told her to go for it, knowing full well that she wouldn't know where to start looking.

Still, creepy as Eric was, at least he wasn't violent like a few of her mum's exes had been. And he didn't spy on her and Mia, or barge into their bedroom in the hopes of catching them getting undressed, like the last one. So Michelle supposed she could tolerate him.

As long as he stayed away from her.

She reached Alexandra Road a few minutes later and was about to cross over to walk past the park when she spotted a gang of older girls from the estate hanging around at the gates. Knowing from experience that they would have a go at her if she walked past, she decided to go through the park instead. It might take twice as long, but it was better than getting her head kicked in.

She climbed through the broken fence and walked quickly, keeping an eye on the bushes as she skirted the inky waters of the lake. Hearing the sound of footsteps behind her a few seconds later, she glanced back, her heart lurching when she saw the shadowy figure of a man running towards her. But before she could even think about moving out of his way he barged into her, knocking her flat on her back.

Reaching down to help her up, he said, 'God, I'm sorry, love! I didn't see you there. Are you all right?'

Shrinking from his touch, Michelle pushed herself shakily to her feet and stared up at him. He was breathing hard, his face flushed and sweaty from running, and there were wisps of steam rising from his dark hair. He had a soft Irish accent which made him sound non-threatening, but without being able to see his eyes she couldn't be sure *what* he was thinking. All she knew was that she'd be powerless to defend herself if he went for her, because he was so much bigger than she was.

Fortunately for her, Liam Grant had never attacked a girl in his life – and he wasn't about to start now. Sickened by the fear in her eyes, because he'd seen it so many times in the eyes of his own mother, he raised his hands and stepped back.

'Don't worry, I'm not going to touch you. But there's plenty who would, so why the hell are you walking through here by yourself at this time of night? Don't you know how dangerous it is round here?'

Wiping her muddy hands on her jeans, Michelle muttered, 'I've lived here all my life, and nothing's ever happened to me.'

'*Yet*,' Liam countered, frowning at her. 'But you're only a girl; you shouldn't be out on your own in the dark.'

'*Only* a girl,' she repeated indignantly.

Tutting softly, he said, 'You know what I meant. Anyhow, come on . . . I'll walk you the rest of the way.'

Taken aback by the unexpected offer, Michelle stayed where she was when he began to walk on. Most of the lads round here didn't have the slightest sense of protectiveness towards the girls in their lives. Darren Mitchell, for example: it probably wouldn't even cross his mind to make sure that Mia got home safely from wherever he'd taken her tonight. He was the sort who would get what he wanted and then turf her out into the dark, forgetting all about her as soon as the door was shut. But here was a total stranger, showing genuine concern for a girl he'd never even met before.

'Are you coming, or what?'

Snapped out of her thoughts at the sound of his voice, Michelle gazed at him. 'Sorry?'

Walking backwards now, Liam flapped his hands. 'I said come on. I haven't got all night, you know.'

'It isn't really necessary,' Michelle said, already walking towards him.

'It's no bother,' Liam assured her, stuffing his hands into his pockets as she fell into step beside him. 'I'm going your way anyhow.'

'How do *you* know which way I'm going?' Blushing as soon as the words were out of her mouth, because it had sounded flirtatious and she hadn't intended it to, Michelle tried quickly to correct herself. 'Well, obviously you know I'm going *this* way, because this is the way I was walking when you bumped into me. I just meant . . .'

Amused when she trailed off, Liam glanced at her out of the corner of his eye. He already liked her voice, which was less aggressive than that of most of the girls he'd met since moving to Manchester. And now that he could see her more clearly as they neared the lit main road, he thought she was really pretty, too. Her fair hair contrasted sharply with the darkness of her eyes, and she had a small, cute nose, and lips that curved up ever so slightly at the corners, as if she were smiling a secret little smile. He couldn't make out much of her shape beneath the bulky cardigan, but her legs looked long and slim in her jeans, so he guessed she probably had a half-decent figure.

Unaware of his appraisal, Michelle walked on in silence. Relieved when they reached the road, she thanked him, and told him she'd be fine on her own from there.

'Take care, then,' he said. 'And don't let me catch you walking through there on your own in the dark again.'

Michelle pursed her lips when he followed this with a slow, teasing smile. 'Don't worry, you won't,' she muttered.

Darting across the Parkway now, she felt like a child as he followed her with his eyes. Because that was obviously what he thought she was: a silly little girl who didn't realise how dangerous a world this was. And it didn't help that he'd been so good-looking.

Not that that made any difference, because he obviously wasn't interested in her. Although she had no doubt that it would have been a different story if it had been Mia he'd run into. He'd probably have insisted on walking *her* the rest of the way home.

As she turned the corner Michelle's heart sank when she spotted Eric heading up the path. Her mum had said that he wouldn't be back till ten, and she'd prepared herself for a cold couple of hours on the doorstep. But he was here now, so she supposed she might as well go in. It was either that or go and sit in the park until Mia got home – and there was no way she was doing *that* after what had just happened.

Eric was just slotting his key into the lock. Hearing the gate squeak behind him, he snapped his head round, afraid that he was about to get jumped. 'Jeezus, Shell, you scared the shit out of me,' he gasped when he saw her. 'Where's Mee?'

Irritated by his use of the shortened versions of their names that only their mum ever used, Michelle told him that *Mia* had gone to Laura's and would be back soon.

When Eric opened the door, she rushed in and ran straight up to her room. Leaving the light off, she slipped her trainers and cardigan off and climbed up onto her bunk, pulling the quilt over herself and propping her chin on her arm to watch for Mia out of the window.

It was gone twelve when Mia and Laura left Stu's house. As she gave Darren a kiss on the doorstep, Mia gazed up at him coyly 'Promise you'll be there tomorrow?'

Smiling slyly, he slid his hand up under her top. 'I've said I will, so I will.'

'And you're definitely going to tell Sandra as soon as she gets home?'

'Definitely. Now *go*.'

'Okay, I can take a hint,' Mia snorted when he stopped groping her tit and gave her a little push. 'But you'd best not let me down. And don't forget to set up that meeting for me.'

'I'll get right onto it,' Darren lied, jerking his head at Stu.

When the door closed and the porch light went out, Laura shivered and pressed the button to illuminate the face of her watch.

'God, I'm in so much trouble. My mum's going to freak out.'

'Don't worry about it,' Mia flipped back breezily, heading off down the road. 'Just tell her you were helping me with some homework.'

'Like she's going to believe that when she knows we've been to the youthy. And what if she smells the booze on my breath?'

'How's she going to get close enough to do that? Unless you're planning on giving her a kiss goodnight – like an ickle-wickle baby?'

'Don't be disgusting! I haven't done that for years.'

'Chill out, then,' Mia said, sticking two fingers up as a car drove past and a couple of men leaned out and asked them if they were on a fuck hunt.

'Don't!' Laura hissed. 'What if they come back?'

'Let them. Darren would soon sort them out if they tried anything on.'

'You think so?'

'I *know* so.' Smiling secretively, Mia walked on as if she didn't have a care in the world.

Tottering along beside her on her too-high heels, Laura said, 'You won't tell anyone, will you?'

'What, about you and Stu getting jiggy?'

'We didn't go *that* far.'

'You went far enough, from what I heard,' Mia snorted. 'But don't worry, I won't say anything. As long as *you* don't go blabbing about me and Darren, 'cos he doesn't want anyone finding out until he's finished with Sandra.'

'God, no, I wouldn't say a word,' Laura agreed. 'But do you really think he'll do it?'

'Yeah, course. He's with me now, so why wouldn't he?'

'No reason,' Laura murmured, slowing down as they turned onto their road.

Mia really thought that Darren was being honest, but Laura wasn't so sure. There was something shady about the way he'd changed the subject whenever Mia had mentioned Sandra. And as for the so-called car he claimed was in the garage getting fixed up – Stu had backed him up in the end, but Laura was convinced that he hadn't known what she was talking about when she'd first asked him about it.

They reached Laura's house first. Mia said goodnight and

walked on to her own house at the other end of the road. Throwing a stone at the bedroom window, she hissed, 'It's me' when Michelle peered groggily out. 'Hurry up and let me in – it's bloody freezing out here.'

Almost falling off the bunk, Michelle staggered out onto the landing where the faint flickery glow of the portable TV was leaking out from under her mum's door. Unsure of the time, or if their mum had already come home, she tiptoed down.

Mia barged in without thanking her and headed straight up to their room. Coming quietly in after her, Michelle asked what time it was.

'Too late for you to be up,' Mia said, slipping her skirt off and kicking it into the corner.

'I *was* asleep.'

'Ah, diddums,' Mia drawled, turning her back to hide the lovebite on her breast. 'God, no wonder you stink,' she sniped when Michelle climbed back up onto her bunk. 'Aren't you even going to get undressed?'

Muttering 'I don't stink,' Michelle covered herself with the quilt and unbuttoned her jeans to slip them off.

'How come Laura asked why you don't wear deodorant, then?'

Pulling her jumper off now, Michelle punched the pillow into place and lay down.

'Oi, stinky,' Mia whispered, prodding her in the back. 'Guess who's the only virgin left in Manchester?'

'I hope you're not saying what I think you're saying?'

'I hope you're not saying what I think you're saying.'

'Why are you being such a bitch?' Michelle asked. 'It wasn't my fault mum made me go out with you. I even covered for you when Eric asked where you were – even though I didn't agree with what you were doing.'

'Have you got any idea how pathetic you sound?' Mia

sneered. 'Still, I don't suppose you can help being jealous, 'cos it can't be easy knowing that everybody loves me and hates you.'

Tears stinging her eyes, Michelle covered her ear with the quilt.

'Aw, you're not crying, are you?' Mia crooned, patting her on the shoulder as if she cared. 'Truth hurting, is it?'

Getting no response, she climbed into bed. Much as she enjoyed winding Michelle up, she had more important things to think about – things which, if Darren had been telling the truth, could send her life in an amazing new direction.

2

Wide awake, washed, and dressed by nine the next morning, Mia was all set to head off into town. The lads had promised to take them for a burger, and then on to the cinema, before heading back to Stu's place for another little party – and she couldn't wait.

Finding her mum flat out on the couch, her snoring mouth hanging slack, the cushion stained dark with dribble, Mia shook her roughly by the shoulder and asked where she'd put her handbag.

'Pack it in,' Kim growled, slapping her hand away. 'You're making me feel sick.'

'I need some money,' Mia told her, wrinkling her nose at the stench of stale alcohol, fags and sweat.

'What time is it?' Forcing a gummy eye open, Kim frowned when saw the quilt that was covering her. She didn't remember going upstairs last night. In fact, she didn't even remember getting home.

Hopping from foot to foot with impatience, Mia told her that it was nine o'clock.

'*Nine?*' Kim repeated, her head beginning to throb. 'What the hell are *you* doing up at this time? I can't usually drag you out of your pit till two in the flaming afternoon of a Saturday. It *is* Saturday, isn't it?'

'Oh, come on, mum, I've got things to do.'

'Get me some tablets.' Kim rubbed at her temples. 'My head's banging.'

In too much of a rush to argue, Mia darted into the kitchen, grabbed the tablets and poured a cup of water.

'Would it have killed you to make a brew?' Kim grumbled when she handed them to her.

'Money?' Mia held out her hand. 'Hurry up, mum, I've got to go.'

'Go where?' Kim sat up slowly.

'Out.'

'Out where?'

'Oh, for God's sake! Just *out*, okay? So, can I have some money, or what?'

'Or what. I told you last night, I'm skint.'

'Yeah, but that was before you went to the bingo. And you and Pam always win something between you, so you must have a couple of quid at least.'

Kim shook her head and popped the tablets into her mouth, grimacing at the taste.

'Right, forget it. I'll just go and sell my body on the corner.'

'You'd be better off going down the Range, love. You'll get loads more punters there.'

'Oh, ha ha, you're so funny,' Mia snarled, tugging on her jacket. 'All I'm asking for is a couple of lousy quid. And I shouldn't even have to ask, seeing as you get child benefit for me.'

'Oh, is that right?'

'Well, *duh*. Child benefit – *child*.'

'*Mother* of child. Payer of rent, buyer of food.'

'Yeah, with the money you get off the dole for me.'

Tiring of the cheek, Kim flashed her a warning look.

'It's the truth, isn't it?' Mia persisted self-righteously.

'Listen here, lady, *I*'m the adult in this house, and what I say—'

'*Goes*,' Mia finished for her in a mimicking tone. 'Yeah,

yeah, heard it all before. Sure you don't want to remind me how you nearly died giving birth to me while you're at it?'

'Shut up,' Kim groaned, the ache in her head worsening with every lippy comment. 'You're getting on my nerves now.'

Muttering a dismissive 'Whatever,' Mia folded her arms. 'Oh, by the way, in case you're *interested*, I've decided to be a model.'

'You what?'

'You heard. And there's no point trying to stop me, because I'm doing it whether you like it or not. Darren's cousin's a top model, and he reckons she's nowhere near as pretty as me. And he's going to set me up with her agent, and everything.'

'Who the hell's Darren when he's at home?'

'My boyfriend.'

'Since when?'

'Since last night. And I'm meeting him in town in a bit, so I'll need to tell him when I can get the money.'

'What money?' Kim couldn't keep up with this

Mia tutted irritably. 'Money for the photos for the portfolio I'll need. God, if I knew you were going to be this awkward about it I wouldn't have bothered telling you. I'd have got the money off Darren instead.'

'And how old is this Darren?' Kim demanded, instantly suspicious. ''Cos if I find out some old man's trying to pay you to strip off, I'll—'

'Don't be so stupid.' Mia cut her off tartly. 'He's *sixteen*, if you must know. And you can ask *her* if you don't believe me.' She jerked her head up towards the ceiling. 'Anyhow, are you going to get me the money or not? I'll need to let Darren know so he can tell his cousin to set up the meeting with her agent.'

'No,' Kim muttered, looking around for her cigarettes.

'Mum, I *need* it,' Mia moaned. 'And you'll get it back, 'cos

Darren reckons I'll make a fortune. And you can't say I'm not pretty enough, 'cos you know I am.'

'I never said you weren't.'

'Well, there you go then.'

Kim sighed wearily and looked up at her daughter. Mia *was* stunning, there was no denying that. And she had more than her fair share of personality, which, irritating as it could be when she was arguing the toss, was perversely one of the things that Kim was most proud of her for, because she recognised her younger feistier self in her. So, if she was serious about this, was there really any harm in giving it a go?

'How much is it going to cost for these photos?' she asked, trying to make it sound casual so that Mia wouldn't think she already had it in the bag.

Mia knew her too well. Grinning widely, she yelped, 'Thanks, mum! I *knew* you'd let me do it!'

'I'm only saying I'll *think* about it,' Kim told her. 'But don't rush me or I'll change my mind. And I'll want names and numbers before I make any decisions, 'cos I've heard about the scams these people pull on kids like you, and I'm having none of that. Not when it's my money getting used.'

Knowing full well that these were just words, Mia bounded across the room and kissed her mother, gushing, 'Thank you, thank you, you won't regret it.'

Forcing herself not to look as pleased as she actually felt by this rare show of affection, Kim said, 'I still need to know how much we're talking about.'

'Not much,' Mia said gleefully, oblivious to the instant look of horror on her mum's face when she added, 'Darren reckons it'll only be about three hundred.'

'God, that's a *lot*. How the hell am I supposed to get my hands on that kind of money?'

'You can't back out now you've said I can do it.' Mia's face darkened in a flash. 'I know it *sounds* like a lot, but it's not that much really. And I'll pay you back as soon as I get my first job.'

'That's not the point,' Kim countered reasonably. 'Honest to God, Mia, there's just no way I can afford it.'

'Oh, that's just great, that is,' Mia complained. 'You don't have any problem when you need booze and fags, do you? You just don't want to put yourself out for *me* – that's the truth of it.'

'That's not fair. You know I've always done my best by you.'

'So do *this* for me, then. You're always saying I'm way prettier than the girls on *America's Next Top Model*, and if they can do it, so can I – and *better*. A year from now you could be living in a mansion, with your own swimming pool and maids and everything.'

Kim flapped her hands and sighed. Mia was right; some of those top models earned a small fortune. She was always reading about them jetting about with their Prada shoes and their Gucci bags. And God knew none of *this* family was ever going to earn money from brainpower alone.

'All right, I'll try,' she said. 'But I'm not promising anything, 'cos it won't be easy. I'll have to get the Christmas Club money back off Pam for starters, and she's not going to like that.'

'Tough!' Mia snorted. 'It's our money, not hers, so she's got no say what we do with it.'

'I know, but you know what she's like. And don't you go saying anything to her and setting her off on one. Just let me deal with her.'

'How much have you paid in so far?' Mia asked, not in the least bothered that it was only a matter of weeks until Christmas and if her mum took the money back now there would be no way of replacing it in time.

'I haven't been writing it down, so I'm not positive,' Kim told her. 'But I reckon it should be about one-twenty or so by now.'

Grumbling that that was nowhere near enough, Mia thought about it for a moment, then said, 'How about Len Pritchard?'

'You must be joking!' Kim snorted. 'After what happened last time?'

Mia waved her hand dismissively and said, 'He'd never have cut your finger off really. He was just saying that to scare you into paying up.'

'Yeah, well, it worked. Anyway, he told me not to bother asking again, so I'm not.'

'Oh, right, so you're going to let pride get in the way of my future?'

'I never said that,' Kim murmured, rolling her eyes.

Squealing with excitement because it was a sure sign that her mum had caved in, Mia danced around the room, saying, 'I'm going to be a model! Yay! Wait till I tell Darren, he'll be well chuffed! And my mates will be *so* jealous.'

'Don't start running before you've even stood up in the cot,' Kim cautioned, trying to bring her daughter back down to earth before she got too carried away. 'It's not going to be that easy, you know.'

'Course it is,' Mia scoffed, sounding as confident as she felt as she skipped towards the door. 'I'm gorgeous – what more do I need? Oh, apart from some money to get to town.' She paused to give her mum a cheeky smile.

Tutting, Kim reached under the quilt in search of her handbag. Touching bare leg instead of the tights she'd been wearing the night before, she patted her way up her thigh and frowned when she discovered that she also wasn't wearing any knickers. She'd definitely had underwear on when she'd gone out, because bingo wasn't the kind of venue where she'd go commando. But then she'd gone to that club in town, and – if her memory served her right – Pam had persuaded her to go to some party in Salford with some blokes they'd met.

Oh, God!

Feeling sick now, wondering if she'd gone and shagged some stranger while she was pissed out of her head, she cleared her throat, and said, 'Have you, er, seen Eric this morning?'

'He didn't stay,' Mia told her. 'He left about half an hour after you got home last night.'

'What time was that?'

'About four, I think. And you were singing your head off, so it took me ages to get back to sleep.'

Ignoring the disapproving look that accompanied the words, Kim frowned. 'So when Eric came down, were we arguing, or anything?'

'*No*. He just came down, and then left about half an hour later. Now, can I have my money?'

Kim's frown turned into a scowl as realisation began to sink in. She hadn't done the dirty on Eric, *he*'d done the dirty *with* her while she was out of it – *again*. Just wait till she got her hands on him.

She yanked her squashed handbag out from beneath her backside and pulled out a five-pound note. Shaking her head when Mia snatched it from her hand and skipped out, she lifted the quilt to look for her knickers. She found them down at the other end of the couch and was tugging them back on when a sleepy-eyed Michelle wandered in and asked where Mia had gone.

'To meet her boyfriend,' Kim told her, lighting a cigarette. 'She's going to be a model, so he's setting up a meeting with his cousin's agent for her.'

'*Really?*' Michelle's eyebrows knitted together.

'Yes, really,' Kim replied waspishly. 'And what's with the face? At least she's got ambition. You'll never get further than the library at the end of the road, *you*.'

'You know I want to be a social worker,' Michelle reminded her, wondering what she'd done to upset her now. But then, you didn't really have to do anything to get into trouble in this house – unless your name was Mia, and then you couldn't do any wrong.

'Fat chance,' Kim grunted, puffing on her smoke. Pursing her lips as a sudden thought occurred to her, she peered up at Michelle through narrowed eyes. Her daughters were identical, so if one could be a model why couldn't the other?

As soon as she'd thought it, she visualised the girls standing side by side and dismissed it. Mia had that certain *some*thing about her that Michelle just didn't have; that sparkle that made people sit up and take notice. And Mia took pride in her appearance, whereas Michelle didn't seem to give a toss what she looked like.

'Make us a brew,' Kim said, her thoughts returning to Mia and this new career that she seemed so set on. 'Then get dressed, 'cos I need you to go and get my Club money back off Pam. Oh, and I'll need you to draw out your savings while you're at it.'

'*My* savings?' Michelle gasped.

'Yes, *your* savings,' Kim repeated tartly. 'Mee needs the money to get her pictures done. And I'm not asking, I'm telling – all *right*?'

'But I'm not supposed to touch them,' Michelle reminded her. 'My dad said—'

'Don't you *dare* quote that bastard to me,' Kim barked. 'And don't ever let me hear you calling him that again either, 'cos *I*'m the only dad you've ever had. Shows his face *once* when you're two flaming years old, and chucks a lousy fifty quid apiece at you out of guilt, and thinks that makes him a father? Don't make me *laugh*!'

'Sorry,' Michelle murmured, sloping into the kitchen to put the kettle on.

She leaned back miserably against the sink as she waited for it to boil and bit her lip to prevent the tears which were threatening to flow from spilling over. She hadn't meant to upset her mum; she knew how hard it had been for her to bring them up without help. But that money was *hers*, and she didn't see why she should have to hand it over just because Mia had decided that she needed it. And not just *her* money, but the Christmas money, too.

Their mum was constantly in debt of one kind or another; if it wasn't the gas or electric companies, it was the catalogue people sending threatening letters for non-payment, or one of the neighbours demanding back what she'd borrowed. Hiding behind the sofa when someone was banging on the front door was just a normal way of life in this house. But no matter how badly off she was, their mum *never* touched the Club money, because it was the only way they were guaranteed to have food and presents at Christmas.

And Michelle wouldn't have minded so much but this was the first mention she'd ever heard of Mia wanting to be a model. The only ambition Mia had ever had until now was to hook herself some rich footballer who would keep her in a life of undeserved luxury. But if she was calling Darren her boyfriend already, he'd obviously been filling her vain head with nonsense, so now they were all going to suffer. And there was nothing that Michelle could do about it, because her mum had made up her mind to scrape the money together and wouldn't take kindly to anyone questioning her about it. And Mia would only accuse her of being jealous if she voiced her objections.

Which she *wasn't*. She just didn't see why she should have

to go without Christmas *and* lose her savings for something which might very well not come to anything. And given how fast Mia changed her mind about everything else, it was all too likely that, a couple of weeks down the line, she would announce that she didn't want to do it after all.

Back in the living room, that same thought had already occurred to Kim. Not as blind to Mia's faults as everyone seemed to think, she was well aware of her daughter's habit of swapping and changing her mind at the drop of a hat. But this wasn't something trivial like a pair of shoes that she'd set her heart on; it was an opportunity for Mia to really make her mark on the world. And whatever it took, and whoever said what, Kim was determined to help her achieve it. But three hundred quid was a hell of a lot of money, and she had no intention of shelling out blindly. If they were going to do this, she would make sure that she was involved every step of the way – looking out for Mia, *and* guarding her investment.

On the phone with the yellow pages open on her lap when Michelle carried her tea through, Kim said, 'Oh, hello, is this Leece's photographers? I wonder if you can help me . . . My daughter's going to be a model, and I need to know how much it'll be to have one of them port-whatsits done.'

Michelle raised an eyebrow when her mum squawked '*How* much?' The quote was obviously higher than she'd expected, but if Michelle thought it would bring her to her senses and make her call the whole thing off she was disappointed when, moments later, Kim sighed, and said, 'Okay, fine. But we need it fast, so how soon can you book us in?'

Jotting down the date and time, Kim put the phone down and lit another cigarette off the butt of the last one.

'How much did they say?' Michelle asked after a few minutes of heavy silence.

Kim muttered an abrupt 'Never you mind,' stood up and

stalked over to the sideboard. Yanking the top drawer open, she rifled through it, asking, 'Have you seen that card with Len Pritchard's number on it?'

'Why do you want that?' Michelle frowned. 'I thought you weren't going near him again.'

Kim slammed her fist down so hard on the top of the unit that most of the ornaments that were standing on it fell over. 'Are you *determined* to make me lose my fucking temper? And I thought I told you to get dressed and go round to Pam's, so why are you still here?'

Knowing that her mum only ever said the f-word so vehemently when she was really close to the edge, Michelle ran upstairs, cursing Mia under her breath. Len Pritchard was the local loan shark, and he'd already proved that he wasn't a man to be messed with the last time her mum had borrowed from him. She'd only slipped up on one payment, but he'd kicked the back door practically off its hinges. Michelle still didn't know where her mum had found the money to pay him off, but she'd truly believed her when she'd promised never to go to him again. Yet here she was, searching for his number to do exactly that – and all because Mia wanted to be a flaming model.

Downstairs, Kim had found the card and made her call. Putting the phone down now, she chewed on her nails. Len hadn't been pleased to hear from her. In fact, he'd told her to go and fuck herself when she'd asked for a loan, forcing her to swallow her pride and beg – which hadn't come easy, but at least it had worked. He'd agreed to give her one hundred quid – but it would cost her extra in interest, and he'd warned that he wouldn't be as lenient as last time if she defaulted again.

If she'd felt sick before, Kim felt twice as bad now – and she still needed to find the rest of the money; although God only knew where she was going to get it at such short notice.

Even with the girls' savings added to Len's hundred, and the one-twenty from the Club, she was nowhere near the four-seventy-five that the photographers were asking for. But she didn't know anyone who could or *would* lend her the rest, and it was too late to ask for a crisis loan off the social because she'd booked the photographer for this coming Monday.

She could have kicked herself for going ahead and committing to that without making sure that she could afford it first. But she couldn't back out now, because the snotty bitch who'd made the booking had told her she'd be charged a cancellation fee. Anyway, she didn't want to go crawling back to them, because her pride was still smarting from the way the woman had sneered at her like she was some kind of pauper for baulking at the amount that she'd been quoted. Making out like four hundred and seventy-five quid was nothing; that it was a small price to pay – *if* she thought her daughter was worth investing in.

Well, yes, she bloody well did, *actually*!

Kim marched into the kitchen and came back with a large knife. Shoving the couch away from the wall, she got down on her hands and knees and set about slashing a large gash into the material at the back.

Walking in at that moment, Michelle gasped, 'Mum, what are you *doing*? Stop it – it's not worth it!'

'Oh, what, 'cos it's your sister I'm doing it for and not for you?' Kim snapped, shoving her hand through the gap she'd created and feeling around in the dust and accumulated junk in the base of the couch. 'Just piss off round to Pam's before you make me mad. And tell her it's urgent, so I don't want no messing about.'

Traipsing miserably down the short path from her house and up the neighbouring one, Michelle knocked on Pam's door.

'She can't do that,' Pam protested when she heard what Kim

had sent her for. 'I'll lose my commission. And what am I supposed to tell the collector when he sees I've got more written down than I've got in cash? He'll think I'm on the fiddle.'

'I'm really sorry,' Michelle apologised, fully understanding why Pam was so pissed off. 'But she says it's urgent.'

'I'll give her bloody urgent,' Pam grunted as she snatched a cardigan off the hook behind the door. Pushing Michelle ahead of her, she marched into Kim's house and demanded to know what she thought she was playing at.

Sucking on yet another cigarette, the floor around her littered with heaps of gunk she'd pulled out from the bowels of the couch, Kim said, 'Our Mee's going to be a model, and I need the money for her portfolio.'

'You're bang out of order,' Pam argued. 'And I wouldn't mind, but it's a pure waste of money.'

'You trying to say my daughter's not good enough?'

'Well, she ain't no fucking Jordan, is she?' Pam retorted scathingly, never one to shy away from telling it as she saw it. 'We all know you think the sun bounces off her backside, but she ain't nothing special, and you're a mug if you blow that kind of money on her. You might as well chuck it down the flaming grid!'

'It's got nowt to do with you,' Kim informed her angrily. 'It's my money, and I want it back. All one hundred and twenty of it.'

'In your dreams!' Pam snorted. 'You've only paid in eighty-five, so that's all you'll be getting back.'

'You bloody liar,' Kim gasped, staring up at her in disbelief. 'I've paid in regular as clockwork.'

'Yeah, and borrowed half back along the way for bingo and what have you,' Pam reminded her. 'I've got it all written down if you don't believe me.' Turning to Michelle now, she said, 'You're the only one around here with any sense – can't *you* talk her out of this?'

Michelle gave a helpless shrug.

'Oh, get out, you jealous bitch!' Kim barked, losing patience. 'Coming round here bad-mouthing my daughter, just 'cos *yours* are a load of speccy four-eyed little retards! Go on – piss off!'

'Don't worry, I'm going,' Pam spat. 'But that's me and you done for good, so don't come crying to me when you've spent all your money on that little trollop and can't even afford a tin of fucking beans!'

'Like I'd ask *you* for anything,' Kim yelled as Pam headed out of the room.

Wincing when Pam slammed the door, Michelle watched as her mum moved away from the couch and set about ripping open one of the chairs.

'Why are you still here?' Kim demanded. 'You know the post office shuts at twelve.'

Leaving her mother to her destruction of the furniture, Michelle went to her bedroom to get her savings book.

3

Mia was on cloud nine when she got to school on Monday. She'd had a brilliant weekend, and she was dying to tell her friends all about it. Well, not about her and Darren, obviously, because she hadn't spoken to him since Sunday morning and didn't know what had happened with Sandra yet. But she couldn't wait to see their faces when they heard about the modelling. They'd probably say she was lying to start with, but they'd soon know she was telling the truth when they saw the pictures she was getting done after school this evening.

She bundled them into the toilets now, leaving Laura as lookout, and perched on the loo to tell them her good news. But Lisa Holgate started talking before she had a chance.

'What happened with you and Darren Mitchell at the youthy the other night?' she asked. 'Don't think we didn't see you sneaking off with him. And you'd best watch yourself, 'cos Sandra will batter you if she finds out.'

'Like to see her try,' Mia snorted, snatching the cigarette that one of the others had just lit out of her hand. 'Anyway, it's none of her business, 'cos Darren will have finished with her by now. He was going to tell her when she got back from her dad's last night.'

'She didn't look upset when I saw her and Tina Molloy getting off the bus just now.'

'He probably hasn't had a chance to tell her yet,' Mia said, annoyed that Lisa wasn't letting her get on with her story.

'Anyway . . . I don't want to talk about *her*, I want to tell you about my photos.'

'What photos?' Jenny Marsh asked, watching the cigarette closely to make sure it didn't get finished before she'd had some.

'The ones I'm getting done after school tonight,' Mia announced. 'I'm going to be a model,' she elaborated, crossing her legs. 'So I'm getting my portfolio done – by a *professional* photographer.'

'What you going to do with them when you get them?' asked Lisa. 'Only I've heard you can end up paying loads of money out, and then no one ever sees them.'

'Not if you haven't got an agent,' Mia agreed. 'But Darren's setting me up with his cousin's one. She's only eighteen, but she's already got her own flat, and everything.'

'You what?' Lisa smirked. 'I hope you're not talking about Lorraine Braithwaite, 'cos there's only one reason *she*'s got all that shit, and it ain't what *I*'d call modelling.'

Mia narrowed her eyes and was about to demand to know what Lisa meant when Laura hissed that someone was coming. Dropping the cigarette into the toilet, she whispered that she'd tell them the rest later.

'Who's smoking in here?' Sandra Bishop shouted, banging on the door.

Cheeks flaming when her friends looked at her, Mia pretended that she thought it was a teacher and put a finger to her lips.

'Caught you!' Sandra barked, popping her head up over the cubicle divider. 'Give us a fag and I'll think about letting you off.'

'They're hers,' Mia said, pointing at Jenny.

Glaring at Mia for opening her big mouth, Jenny slid a cigarette out of her pocket and handed it up. Snatching it, Sandra jumped back down.

'God, I hate her,' Lisa muttered – quietly, in case Sandra heard. 'And how come you didn't tell her about you and—'

Hissing 'Shut your mouth!' Mia got up and yanked the door open.

Lisa followed her out into the corridor and said, 'I don't see what your problem is. I just reckon you should have told her – if you're so convinced Darren wants you instead of her.'

'It's not for me to tell her *any*thing,' Mia replied defensively. 'Darren wants to do it himself.'

'I bet,' Lisa snorted, voicing what they were all thinking: that Darren Mitchell had played her, and had no intention of chucking his girlfriend for her.

'He *will*,' Mia insisted. 'And anyone who thinks different can piss off, 'cos I don't need to listen to you talking shit about my boyfriend.'

'Boyfriend, my arse! He's using you, you stupid cow.'

'Who you calling stupid?'

'We're only looking out for you,' Jenny said calmly, sensing that Mia was getting upset.

'*I*'m not,' Lisa countered sharply. 'She shouldn't be doing the dirty on Sandra.'

'And when did *you* start being Sandra's best mate?' Mia demanded.

'I'm not,' Lisa retorted. 'Like I said, I hate her. But if you're going to brag about it, at least have the balls to tell *her*.' She jerked her thumb back towards the toilet door – just as Sandra walked out.

'Tell who about what?' Sandra asked.

'Nothing,' Lisa muttered.

Tutting, Sandra pushed them out of the way.

'Wow, you're brave,' Mia said sarcastically when she'd gone.

'Maybe I'm just not stupid enough to piss her off and get

my head kicked in,' Lisa spat. 'But if you want me to go and tell her what I was really talking about, just say the word.'

'No one's stopping you,' Mia said coolly, knowing that Lisa wouldn't dare.

'Oh, piss off.' Lisa jerked her chin up proudly. 'At least I'm not a slag who'd flash my tits for money.'

'Neither am I!'

'Oh, really? So how come you're hooking up with Lorraine Braithwaite's agent, 'cos that's the only so-called modelling she's ever done. And don't act all innocent, 'cos *everyone* knows what's she's like.'

'I'm not talking about *her*, so get your facts right,' Mia drawled. 'I'm talking about Darren's *cousin* Lorraine.'

'Lorraine Braithwaite *is* his cousin,' said Laura, shrugging guiltily when Mia glared at her. 'Sorry, I thought you knew.'

Mia hadn't known, and she was furious that Darren hadn't thought to mention it.

'I knew she was a whore from when she got caught giving that teacher a blow job and got expelled,' Lisa was saying now, a disapproving sneer on her face.

'Yeah, then I heard she got into porn,' another girl chipped in. 'But she picked up some disease that made her fanny go all manky and none of the men would shag her, so she had to go into Page Three instead.'

'Well, I don't care what *she* does,' Mia told them defensively. 'I'm going to be a proper model.'

'If you say so,' Lisa drawled. 'Won't hold my breath, though.'

Mia's eyes flashed with rage. Whatever they thought of Lorraine Braithwaite, they had no right to try and tar her with the same brush. Even if she wanted to get into something dirty like that – which she didn't – her mum probably wouldn't let her; and Darren *definitely* wouldn't. He probably hadn't even realised what his cousin really did for a living.

'You all right?' Laura asked softly as the bell rang and the girls started heading towards their first classes.

'Oh, yeah, I'm just fine,' Mia snapped. 'My mates think I'm a slag, and my so-called *best* mate couldn't even be bothered to warn me.'

'I'm sorry, but I honestly thought you knew,' Laura murmured. 'Anyway, Darren should have told you. It wasn't fair, getting your hopes up for nothing.'

'Who says it's for nothing?' Mia retorted proudly. 'Obviously I won't go to *that* agent now I know what he's about, but he's not the only one in the world. And soon as I've got those photos done, the others will be falling over themselves to sign me up – you watch.'

Sighing when Mia turned on her heel and marched off towards their first class, Laura set off after her. Mia was pretty, there was no denying that, but she was fooling herself if she believed that she was good enough to get into the big league.

Drifting through her lessons that morning, Mia barely heard a word that any of the teachers said. She was too busy mentally rehearsing her poses for the photo session and fantasising about being launched onto the world in a blaze of publicity.

If she'd been more alert, she might have picked up on the whispering that was going on all around her. But she didn't realise anything was wrong until it was too late to avoid it.

Noticing that people were giving her funny looks when she walked into the canteen at lunchtime, she assumed that Lisa must have been slagging her off about the Page Three crap. She knew she'd done nothing wrong so she held her head up and joined the slow-moving queue. Turning to see what was going on when she felt a charge of excitement in the air a few minutes later, her heart lurched when she saw Sandra

Bishop stalking in. She sensed that Sandra was coming for her and started pushing her way through the queue.

'Get back here, you little slag!' Sandra snarled. 'I want a word with you.'

Prevented from escaping when some girls shoved her back, Mia glanced helplessly around. As usual, there were no teachers or dinner ladies in sight and it was obvious from the excitement on their faces that none of the other pupils were going to step in.

'What's this I've been hearing about you saying you're seeing my boyfriend?' Sandra demanded, punching Mia in the chest and knocking her back against the counter.

Her face scarlet with humiliation as everyone crowded around, Mia tried to walk away. But Sandra grabbed her by the hair and kneed her in the stomach, taking her breath away.

'I'm still waiting to hear what you've got to say!' Sandra yelled, dragging her out into the open.

'I haven't done anything wrong!' Mia squealed. 'It's not my fault Darren's finished with you!'

'Don't even say his fucking *name*!' Sandra roared, landing a glancing punch off the side of Mia's head. 'And what do you mean, finished with me? Has he hell!'

Pushing her way forward, Laura said, 'It's not her fault, Sandra. He told her he wasn't with you any more; I heard him.'

'Oh, yeah?' Sandra spat, tugging the collar of her shirt aside to reveal a large fresh lovebite on her neck. 'So how come he give me this last night, then?'

Crying out when Sandra started laying into her again, Mia covered her face with her arms.

'What the *hell* is going on here?' Mr Ainsley, the deputy head barked, pushing his way through the crowd. 'Bishop! Pack that in!'

Forced to let go, Sandra aimed one last kick at Mia as she lay sobbing on the floor.

'Enough!' Mr Ainsley snapped, shoving her away. 'Go to my office. And you lot go and find something better to do,' he ordered, turning his glare on the onlookers.

Michelle walked in just as Sandra and her friend Tina reached the door. Stopping dead, Sandra frowned, wondering how the girl had got round there so fast – and why she didn't have a mark on her.

'I thought I told you to go to my office?' Mr Ainsley said, coming up behind her. 'Or would you rather I skipped the formalities and went straight to calling the police?'

Sucking her teeth, unimpressed by his threat, Sandra turned to give him a dirty look. But when she saw the face of the girl whose arm he was holding, she did a comical double take.

'They're twins,' Tina hissed, pulling on her arm. 'Come on, just leave it.'

'Fuckin' freaks,' Sandra spat.

'Get moving,' Mr Ainsley ordered. 'And if I hear any more bad language you'll be getting an extended suspension.'

Sandra muttered, 'Big *wow*!' and stomped off down the corridor.

'Take your sister to the nurse to get her checked over,' Mr Ainsley told Michelle, his mouth set in a tight line as he went after Sandra.

Instinctively reaching out to Mia when she saw the clumps of hair that had been dragged loose and the red marks on her throat, Michelle said, 'Are you all right?'

'Get off!' Mia hissed. 'And what have I told you about talking to me in public?'

'But you're hurt,' Michelle murmured.

'No, I'm not,' Mia sneered, linking arms with Laura.

Gazing after them as they walked away, Michelle clenched

her teeth when Lisa came over and said, 'She *well* deserved that. And she's lucky it wasn't me, 'cos I would have ripped her head off.'

'Good job it wasn't, then, isn't it?' Michelle retorted frostily, stalking out into the yard.

Ignoring her friends when they called out to her from the safe spot below the headmaster's office where they congregated at break times, Michelle sat down on the wet grass and hugged her knees to her chest. Mia had brought this on herself, because anyone would have reacted like Sandra just had if someone had nicked their boyfriend off them. But why had she had to go and pick on the hardest girl in school? That was just stupid. And, all right, so Darren Mitchell was good-looking, but he was a thug and an idiot, so he wasn't worth getting battered over.

Sitting there until the bell went, Michelle got up and dusted the back of her skirt down. But just as she was about to go inside she saw Mia coming out with the nurse.

'What's wrong?' she asked, running up to them as they headed towards the staff car park. 'Where are you going?'

Mia clutched at her ribs as if she was in agony and gave her sister a rare smile. 'It's okay, don't panic. Mrs Drake's just taking me home so I can get some painkillers.'

Presuming a closeness between the two girls that didn't exist, the nurse said, 'Don't fret, she's just a bit bruised, that's all. You can go home with her if you like. I'm sure Mr Ainsley won't mind.'

'*No!*' Mia blurted out. Then, tempering her tone, 'I'll be fine by myself. Anyway, you've got English this afternoon, and we all know how much you love English – eh, Shell?'

Frowning, Michelle slipped her hands into her pockets. Mia was still smiling, and Michelle would have loved to believe that it was genuine. But, sadly, she suspected that it was purely for the nurse's benefit.

Telling Michelle that she would see her when she got home, Mia continued slowly on to the car. Still standing where they'd left her when they drove past a minute later, Michelle sighed when Mia raised her hand as if to wave but stuck two fingers up instead.

Kim was lying on the couch watching Jerry Springer and she leapt up when she heard the car pulling up outside. Fearing that it would be the man from the gas board again, she peeped cautiously out through the nets. He'd already been twice this morning, making a holy show of her in front of the neighbours by shouting through the letter box about how he knew she was in, and how she'd better let him read the meter – or else. But she couldn't let him in – not while the meter was still rigged to go backwards.

Bloody Eric and his stupid ideas! But he hadn't shown his face since she'd had a go at him for having sex with her when she was out of it last Friday, so there was nothing she could do but wait for him to stop sulking and come round. Then he could put everything back the way it was supposed to be.

To her relief, it wasn't the gasman, it was Mia. But she wasn't alone, a strange woman was holding her arm as she hobbled slowly up the path.

'What's happened?' Kim demanded, rushing to the door.

Using the weak voice that she'd adopted on the journey over, having decided that she'd get more time off school if she made out like she was more badly hurt than she actually was, Mia said, 'I'm all right, mum.'

The nurse stepped forward and said, 'Let's get her inside, then I'll explain.'

'Who are you?' Kim asked.

'School nurse,' Mia told her, trying to convey with her expression not to kick up a fuss and delay Mrs Drake any longer than was necessary.

Kim rushed in ahead of them and kicked the overflowing ashtray beneath the couch. Telling Mia to lie down, she demanded to know what had happened.

'A fight?' she squawked when the nurse told her. 'Where?'

Wondering what the location had to do with anything, Mrs Drake said, 'I believe it was in the canteen.'

'So where were the teachers?' Kim wanted to know. 'I thought you lot were supposed to look after the kids to make sure this kind of thing can't happen?'

'I'm sorry, Mrs Delaney, but I wasn't actually there so I can't comment on that,' the nurse replied evenly. 'But I can assure you it won't go unpunished.'

'Too bloody right it won't,' Kim snapped, jabbing a finger in Mia's direction. 'This is no ordinary girl we're talking about here, you know. Her face is going to be her fortune, and if anything—'

'*Mum!*' Mia hissed, wanting to shut Kim up before she said too much. 'It's not her fault. And Mr Ainsley stopped it as soon as he realised what was happening.' Smiling at the nurse now, she rolled her eyes. 'Sorry, miss, but she can be a bit protective – as you can probably tell.'

Telling her not to worry about it, Mrs Drake took a form out of her bag and handed it to Kim. 'If you could just sign this to confirm that you've taken charge of her, I'll leave you to it.'

Kim snatched the form and looked around for a pen, muttering, 'I'll sign it to say she's home, but don't think the school's off the hook, because if I find out she's injured—'

'Just sign it,' Mia told her tersely.

Kim did as she was told and showed the nurse out. Coming back a few seconds later, she stopped in the doorway when she caught Mia leaping up.

'Oi, I thought you were supposed to be in agony?'

'I told you I was okay,' Mia reminded her, going to the window to check that the nurse had really gone.

'That's not how it looked to me; you could hardly walk when you came in. And what am I supposed to do now? We'll have to cancel the photographer, but he'll still want paying. And you know I can't afford to lose that money *and* book another session.'

'We're not cancelling anything,' Mia assured her, grinning slyly as she added, 'I just wanted to come home early so I'd have more time to get ready.'

'So you're not really hurt?'

'Well, yeah, a bit. But nowhere near as bad as *they* think. My mouth's a bit dry, though, so I wouldn't say no to a brew.'

Shaking her head, Kim lumbered through to the kitchen and filled the kettle. 'You might as well get a bath now you're here,' she called over her shoulder. 'Then you can try on them clothes I got you and do some poses. I want to make sure you've got them perfect, 'cos I can't afford for you to go into overtime – not with the money they charge.'

'I know what I'm doing,' Mia told her, coming into the kitchen and opening the cupboard. 'It probably won't even take one hour, never mind *three*, 'cos my pictures will be brilliant.'

'Bloody won't be if you keep stuffing your face like that,' Kim said, snatching the biscuit out of her daughter's hand. 'You'll be fat as a pig before you get anywhere near a camera at this rate.'

'It's only a biscuit,' Mia protested when Kim tossed it back into the cupboard. 'I didn't have any lunch.'

'It's your own fault for fighting when you should have been eating. And I suppose it had something to do with this stupid *boyfriend* you've gone and got yourself?'

'*He*'s not the stupid one, his *ex* is. She can't handle the fact that he's dumped her for me.'

‘Oh, well, that’s the end of him, then.’

‘It is not! Now she knows, she can get lost.’

‘No, *he* can get lost,’ Kim countered sharply, waving the teaspoon at Mia as she added, ‘and so can any other lad who comes sniffing round from now on. And don’t start pulling your face, because I’m saying this for your own good.’

‘I don’t see how.’

‘Boys are a distraction, that’s how. And I’m not having any randy little sod get in the way of your modelling, so there’ll be no more boys from now on. And no more fighting. And no more junk food, so you can quit staring at the cupboard or I’ll throw the whole lot in the bin.’

‘You’ve got to be joking!’ Mia gasped.

‘Do I *look* like I’m joking?’ Kim turned and gave her a deadpan look. ‘It’s for your own good,’ she repeated when Mia gazed moodily back at her. ‘You might not think so now, but you’ll thank me in the long run. And in case you think I don’t know what I’m talking about, I bought some magazines this morning to gen up on it, and I reckon you could really pull it off – as long as you do as you’re told.’

‘By *you*?’ Folding her arms, Mia gave her mother a scornful look. ‘You’re not an expert just ’cos you’ve read a couple of stupid magazines, you know.’

‘All right, so I might not know enough to be your manager,’ Kim conceded, stirring two sugars into her own tea and none into Mia’s. ‘But I know enough to keep an eye on what you eat and drink so you don’t go wrecking your skin. And I’ll be keeping a bloody close eye on your agent as well, ’cos I was reading about this girl who got in with a bad one, and she reckons they can really take the piss if you don’t let them know who’s boss from the off.’

‘God, you’re going to be so embarrassing,’ Mia complained. ‘I haven’t even started yet, and you’re already putting me off.’

‘Don’t even go there,’ Kim warned, handing her cup to her.

'I'm already up to my neck in it money-wise, and if you think I'm going to let you change your mind and leave me in debt, you've got another think coming.'

'I never said I wasn't going to do it,' Mia replied sulkily, sipping on the tea. '*Eew!* You forgot my sugar.'

'No, I didn't.' Kim ushered her out of the kitchen. 'You don't take it any more. Like you don't see boys any more, or—'

'Fight, or eat biscuits,' Mia finished for her, shooting her a resentful glare. 'So, is there anything I *am* allowed to do?'

'Earn money,' Kim said, grinning now. '*Loads* of money if the girls in that magazine are anything to go by, and you're way prettier than any of them. Anyhow, give me that agent's number while I'm thinking about it. I'll ring him while you're having your bath.'

'*Ah* . . .' Mia bit her lip sheepishly. 'I meant to tell you about that. Only I've heard he's probably not all that good.'

'Eh?' Already reaching for the telephone, Kim frowned. 'He's been the dog's doo-dahs all weekend, so what's changed?'

Fully prepared to jump to Darren's defence if her mum blamed him for trying to get her into *that* kind of modelling, Mia reluctantly admitted what she'd heard about Lorraine Braithwaite. But rather than go mad, as she'd expected, her mum just shrugged.

'Oh, well, at least we found out before we wasted time talking to him. We'll just ask the photographer to recommend someone more respectable. 'Cos they're all connected, you know. According to them magazines, it's a definite case of who you know, not *what* you know in this business.'

'God, you *have* been doing your homework, haven't you?'

Kim said that she wasn't as thick as people obviously thought she was, then craned her neck when she heard the gate squeaking. Seeing a young woman coming up the path tugging a small suitcase on wheels, she glanced at the clock. 'Christ, she's early.'

'Who?' Mia asked, reaching for the remote to flick through the TV channels.

'The beautician – or whatever she calls herself,' Kim said, snatching the remote out of her daughter's hand and shooing her into the hall. 'Get yourself in that bath – and be bloody quick about it, 'cos she's another one who charges by the hour, and I'm not having her sitting here clocking up air miles while you're lazing about in the bubbles.'

'I don't even *like* bubble bath,' Mia protested, trying desperately not to spill her tea as her mum pushed her towards the stairs.

'Well, *start* liking it,' Kim said breezily. ''Cos that's what models do, isn't it – lounge around in big bubbly baths, drinking cocktails while they're getting their pictures took.'

When Michelle got home from school later that day, she heard Mia complaining as she walked through the door. And when she saw the state of her, she understood why, because Mia looked like a clown.

'Trust me,' the beautician was saying, deftly backcombing Mia's usually sleek hair as if she were grooming a poodle. 'You *have* to exaggerate the make-up or it doesn't show up on the photos. And, believe me, I know what I'm talking about, because I've worked on *Coronation Street*.'

'Ooh, have you really?' Kim sounded impressed. 'So, do you do that Gail Platt's hair, then? It's ever so thick, isn't it?'

'Oh, she has *wonderful* hair,' the beautician gushed boastfully. 'And the thicker the better in my experience, because it stays exactly where you put it. Fine hair like this is the worst,' she added, pissing Mia off all over again. 'You spend hours fluffing it up, but it's flat as a pancake again in two minutes.

Not to worry, though. It'll take a Force Ten gale to shift it by the time I've finished.'

'You'd best not make it stick like *that*,' Mia protested, scowling at herself in the mirror. 'I look like a bleedin' drag queen.'

'Don't be rude,' Kim scolded.

Smiling, the beautician said, 'I've heard it all before. The younger girls always moan, and some of them try wiping it off as soon as my back's turned. But they regret it when they see how bad they look on film. Like little ghosts, they are . . . all pale and insignificant.'

'She won't be wiping nothing off,' Kim assured her, slapping Mia's hand when she tried to flatten her hair down

Leaving them to it, Michelle went upstairs to read in peace.

'Shell . . .' her mum called up the stairs some time later. 'We're off out. Come and put the bolts on, 'cos I don't want Eric letting himself in before I get back.'

Michelle watched through the window as Kim and Mia walked down the path with their noses in the air and climbed into the taxi that was waiting at the kerb. She thought it was odd how it was suddenly all right for her to stay in the house by herself, considering she hadn't been allowed to on Friday. Obviously the peeping Tom wasn't around any more. Or, more likely, her mum just wasn't bothered about him getting to Michelle any more, because she was too wrapped up in Mia to care about anything else.

She went downstairs, bolted the door and switched the TV on. At least she'd be able to watch what *she* wanted to for a change, because Mia always insisted on *Hollyoaks* or *The Simpsons* – or *any*thing other than what she knew Michelle would enjoy.

She found a local news channel and was just settling down to watch a report about a suspected arson attack in Hulme, where a baby had been dropped out of the window of a burning second-floor flat into the arms of a neighbour, when the phone started to ring. With half a horrified eye still on the screen, she reached for the handset.

'Hello?'

'Don't "hello" *me*, you slag!' Sandra Bishop snarled down her ear. 'My *boyfriend* wants a word with you. And be warned – I've got it on speakerphone so I can hear every word you say.' Obviously talking to Darren now, Sandra hissed, 'Go on, then – *tell* her.'

Michelle was already shaking and a chill ran down her spine when Darren came on the line.

'What d'y' think you're doing, spreading all them lies about me?' he demanded. 'Everyone knows you're a slag, so what makes you think *I'd* come anywhere near you? And where do you get off telling my bird I've finished with her for *you*? You're off your fuckin' head!'

'Hope you got that,' Sandra said as she came back on. ''Cos if I ever hear you've been telling anyone you're with my man again, you're dead!'

Shivering violently, Michelle put the phone down. Sandra had obviously confronted Darren about Mia and demanded that he make that call to prove the rumours weren't true. But he hadn't needed to be so nasty about it. And now she'd have to tell Mia, which wasn't going to be fun. But if she didn't, Mia would assume everything was all right and get herself into real lumber with Sandra.

Mia and Kim were on a high when they got home later that night. The session had gone fantastically, and Kim had been as proud as Punch watching Mia strut her stuff and pull all the poses she'd been rehearsing. And the photographer had given them the number of an agent, so it had all worked out brilliantly.

Home now, Kim just wanted to put her feet up and have a cup of tea. But before she'd had a chance to kick off her shoes, Michelle told Mia about the phone call and all hell broke loose.

'You *liar*!' Mia screamed, shoving her sister onto the couch. 'Darren wouldn't do that to me!'

'It's true,' Michelle insisted, struggling to get up before Mia jumped on her.

'You've always been the same,' Mia spat. 'You're just jealous 'cos I'm prettier than you! But it's not *my* fault you're ugly, so just get over it and stop trying to make out like I'm as sad as *you*!'

Pushing her off, Michelle stood up. 'I'm not jealous, I'm just trying to save you from getting hurt. Sandra was deadly serious. And if you'd heard the way Darren was talking to me, you'd have been devastated.'

'Yeah, well, like you just said, he was talking to *you*,' Mia shot back spitefully. 'There's no way he would have spoken to me like that.'

'He thought I *was* you,' Michelle reminded her.

Tutting when Mia started screaming at Michelle and tugging at her hair, Kim got up and pulled them apart. 'You'd best not be lying,' she told Michelle. ''Cos if this is your way of getting back at her because you're jealous about the modelling, I'll go mad.'

'It's true,' Michelle insisted, close to tears now.

Instinctively believing her, Kim nodded and turned to Mia. Seeing the tears in her eyes, she said, 'There's no point getting upset about it. I've already told you I don't want you messing about with lads, so it's just as well this one's shown his true colours before you got too involved.'

Mia scowled and flashed a hooded glance at Michelle, warning her to keep her mouth shut about how involved she already was.

Kim shooed Michelle towards the kitchen and waved her hand at the kettle, saying to Mia, 'Men are only out for what they can get, and they've got a nasty habit of trampling all over your dreams while they're getting it. So, we'll hear no more about this two-timing *Darren* – or whatever his name is. From now on, you'll concentrate on your career and nothing else. Got that?'

Pursing her lips tightly, reluctant to accept that Darren had two-timed her – albeit with his own girlfriend – Mia shrugged.

'Say it,' Kim demanded, wanting to make sure that they were on the same page now that she'd committed so much money to the project.

'All *right*,' Mia agreed huffily. 'But I'm not going back to school after this.'

'Don't talk rubbish,' Kim scoffed. 'You can't just stop going. It's against the law.'

'I don't care,' Mia shot back stubbornly. 'That bitch is only going to keep on hassling me. And you've already seen the bruises on my ribs from where she laid into me today, so what if she gets my face next time?'

Mulling the implications over, Kim decided that the risk was real enough to warrant concern. A damaged face would be the absolute end of the dream.

'All right,' she conceded. 'You've only got a few months left, so I don't suppose it really matters. But if you're going to miss your exams, you'd best be ready to put everything you've got into making a success of the modelling 'cos you'll stand no chance of getting a good job if it goes wrong.'

'I'll just have kids,' Mia retorted sarcastically. 'Then I'll get benefits, like you.'

'Don't make out like I had a choice,' Kim snapped. 'I had ambitions once, you know. But I made the mistake of getting involved with your flaming father. And what was I supposed to do when he left me with two kids to fetch up by myself?'

'All right, you don't have to go on with yourself,' Mia muttered, rolling her eyes. 'I was only joking.'

'Yeah, well, think before you start handing out your insults in future,' Kim warned her. 'And me agreeing to let you stay off school doesn't mean it's going to happen, by the way. If there's any trouble from the authorities, you'll be going back whether you like it or not, 'cos there's no way I'm going to court over it.'

'They can't force me to go back if I'm injured,' Mia reminded her. 'And the nurse thinks I'm much worse than I really am, so they can't say I'm faking it.'

'Yeah, well, make sure you don't tell anyone any different,' Kim told her firmly. 'From now on, you don't trust *no* one – and especially not your mates, 'cos they'll be the first to stab you in the back when they see you're doing better than them.' Reaching for the cup of tea that Michelle had just carried through for her from the kitchen, she added, 'And that goes for you, an' all. Anyone asks about her, you don't tell them nothing. Got that?'

'Don't worry, none of her friends ever talk to me anyway,' Michelle murmured, heading up to bed.

'God, she does my head in,' Mia sniped as soon as she'd gone. 'I don't see why she's always got to have a face on her.'

'She's just jealous of all the attention you're getting,' Kim said, gazing thoughtfully at the door. 'And that worries me, 'cos if she gets pissed off and says something, it'll be me who ends up copping for it.'

'She'd better not,' Mia retorted sharply. 'But if you're worried, just don't tell her anything. She can't tell what she doesn't know, can she?'

'Yeah, maybe you're right,' Kim agreed. 'Anyway, she doesn't need to know any of the details, 'cos she's not really involved, is she?'

'Not at all.' Mia smirked. 'We'll just keep it between you and me, eh, mum?'

Looking at her, Kim shook her head. 'You're a right one, you.'

'Yeah, but that's why I'm your favourite.'

'Oi, less of that,' Kim scolded quietly. 'And we'll have less of the arguing in future, an' all, and more concentrating on making you famous, eh?'

'Fine by me,' Mia said, slipping her shoes off and throwing her feet up onto her mum's lap. 'Give 'em a rub, then. It's hard work, this having your photo taken lark.'

'You're not a supermodel yet, lady, so don't be giving me your orders.'

'I will be when we get the pictures back, so I might as well get the practice in.'

Relieved that Mia already seemed to have forgotten about the boy, Kim smiled as she started massaging her daughter's feet.

4

Just over a month later, the cosy little scene of togetherness and optimism that Kim and Mia had shared that night was all but gone, and it was beginning to dawn on Kim that the future might not be quite as bright as she'd thought.

The portfolio had arrived a week after the session, and she'd been thrilled with the results – although, considering how much it had cost, she still didn't see why they had only been allowed to choose fifteen out of the hundreds of pictures that had been taken.

Still, they looked really professional in their faux-leather display case, and Mia looked absolutely stunning in them all, so Kim figured it had been worth it. Convinced now that it was just a matter of them being seen by the right people for Mia to be catapulted to instant fame and fortune, she'd wasted no time looking for an agent. Only not the one that the photographer had recommended, because he didn't even have a proper advert in the book. No, if Mia was going to be a star they would start as they meant to go on – at the top.

A month on, having visited every major agency in Manchester and chewed her nails to the quick waiting for the call-backs which still hadn't come, Kim decided that something must be wrong. While she could accept that *some* of the agencies might have decided that Mia wasn't right for them, they couldn't *all* be that stupid. There had to be an explanation – like maybe she'd given out the wrong phone number, or something.

Sure that this would turn out to be the case, she'd set about ringing them, only to find that she couldn't get through to any of the actual agents. Instead, she got the same dismissive message from each of the receptionists: 'Sorry, but we would have contacted you by now if we were interested. Please don't call again.'

Gobsmacked that they had all failed to realise that Mia had so much more to offer than any of the ugly anorexics whose pictures graced their office walls, Kim put the phone down after the last call and gazed helplessly out into the encroaching void of despair.

Finding her mother like this when she finally dragged herself out of bed and came downstairs, Mia gave her a funny look.

'I've got some bad news,' Kim told her, dreading her reaction. 'I've just rung the agencies, and they've all said no.'

'What, *all* of them? Even her from Quest?'

Nodding, Kim reached for her cigarettes.

'Two-faced *bitch*!' Mia spat. 'She was *well* making out like she was interested. I hope you told her about herself, wasting our time like that.'

'I would have if I could have got through to her,' Kim replied, exhaling a cloud of smoke into the room. 'But I couldn't get past them snotty cows on reception.' Mimicking them now, she said, '*Oh, no, our super-duper agents are* far *too important to talk to the likes of* you.'

Sucking her teeth, Mia said, 'Oh, well, I didn't want to work with that load of pretentious ponces anyway. They obviously don't know what they're doing.'

'Maybe not,' said Kim, wondering why Mia wasn't as upset as she'd expected her to be. 'But if they don't want you, what are we supposed to do now?'

'Nothing.' Shrugging, Mia went into the kitchen.

'What's that supposed to mean?' Kim asked, going after her. 'Anyone would think you don't care.'

'I don't,' Mia admitted, taking a biscuit out of the cupboard. 'To be honest, I'm fed up with all the bullshit. Might as well just sack it off and go back to looking for a rich boyfriend.'

Kim's mouth flapped open. 'You selfish little cow! What about *me*? I'm in a right mess because of you.'

'Don't blame me. No one told you to go and get yourself into debt over it.'

'You *begged* me to get the money for them photos. What was I supposed to do? Tell you to bugger off, and have you accuse me of depriving you?'

'God, why do you always have to have a shit fit about every little thing?' Mia muttered, folding her arms sulkily. '*I*'m the one who's had to put up with those idiots looking down their noses at me for the last month. So if I've changed my mind, it's *my* business.'

'No, it's bloody *not*!' Kim bellowed, slamming her fist down on the ledge. 'One lousy month you've given it, and that's *nothing*, so there's no way I'm letting you give up just like that. You'll damn well carry on until you get somewhere – even if I have to drag you round the agencies by your bloody *hair*!'

'*Pfft*,' Mia snorted. 'Don't see how, seeing as you reckon they've all turned me down.'

'Yeah, but they're not the only ones in the book,' Kim reminded her sharply. 'You might not be good enough for them, but *some*one will bloody well want you.'

Mia's face reddened as the barbed words sank in deep and she pursed her lips tightly. Exhaling loudly, Kim closed her eyes and clenched her fists.

'You know I didn't mean it like that, so don't try and put me on a guilt trip. I've been behind you a thousand per cent so far, but you've got to see this from my point of view. I've put everything into it, and I can't afford to let you give up just because you're pissed off about a few rejections. They're idiots if they can't see how good you are, but it'll be their loss when you make it. And you *will*. But you've got to do your part. Even if it means starting out smaller than we intended. So I'm going to give that agent the photographer told us about a call.'

'No way,' Mia protested, pride making her baulk at the idea. 'He's not even got a Yellow Pages advert, so he must be well crap.'

Saying 'Beggars can't be choosers,' Kim rooted through her handbag for the slip of paper she'd carelessly stuffed in there – the one she'd thought she would never need. Finding it, she reached for the phone. She could feel Mia's eyes boring into the back of her head as she tapped in the number, but she didn't care. This wasn't just about the money she already owed Len Pritchard, *or* what she owed the other loan shark she'd signed up with to get the rest of the money she'd needed; thanks to Eric, she was in the shit with the gas board as well.

She hadn't seen hide nor hair of him for weeks, and his phone had been switched off whenever she'd tried to ring him. So when he'd shown up out of the blue last week, she'd ignored the door and watched through the nets as he'd tried to get in with his key. Any normal man would have figured out that somebody must be in if the bolts were across. But not Eric. That thick bastard had stared at the door for a full five minutes, scratching his head, before going next door to ask Pam if *she* knew what was going on – and Kim had been furious to hear the devious bitch invite him in for a cup of tea.

And it must have been one bloody *big* cup, because he'd been there ever since.

Enraged afresh every time she heard them laughing or

having sex through the thin walls now, Kim had taken to turning the TV up to drown them out. She didn't even want him any more, she just wanted him to fix the meter, but they wouldn't answer the door when she knocked and she hadn't managed to catch them out on the street yet. And now the gas board had sent her a letter, telling her that they'd be coming round next Tuesday – and warning her that they'd be applying for a warrant if she didn't let them in.

So, yes, Mia might be upset about lowering her sights, but at least she wasn't facing jail.

'Hello, Mr Martin?' Kim said when the phone was answered at last. 'Sorry to disturb you, but I wondered if I could set up an appointment to see you . . .?'

Grimacing at the sound of her mum putting on the posh voice she'd been using at the agencies, Mia went back to bed. But just as she'd settled down, Kim ran in and yanked the quilt off her, saying, 'Get up and have a bath. And don't take all day about it, 'cos we've got to be at Sammy Martin's dead on six, and we need to set your hair and get your make up perfect.'

Michelle was exhausted as she traipsed up the path to her home that afternoon. The school netball team had been playing an away match in Altrincham and the minibus had broken down on the way back, so they'd been forced to sit and wait until the school sent another one out to get them. All she wanted to do was have her dinner and go to bed, but she had a load of homework to get through first and she had to go to the library before it closed as well.

'Where the hell have you been?' Kim demanded when she walked in.

'I had a netball match,' Michelle reminded her, sure that she'd told her about it that morning. 'But the coach broke down, so—'

'Oh, never mind,' Kim cut her off. 'You're lucky you're back or you'd have been locked out. Me and Mia have got an appointment, so make sure you keep the bolts on 'cos I'm sure that bastard tried to get in when I went to the shops earlier.'

'Maybe you should just give him his clothes back,' Michelle suggested, dropping her bag and slipping her blazer off. 'I'll drop them at Pam's if you don't want to see him. At least then he won't have any excuse to come round again.'

'And let him think he's got away with it?' Kim snorted angrily. 'I don't bloody think so!'

Sighing, Michelle began to pull her blazer back on.

'What you doing?' Kim demanded. 'The taxi will be here soon.'

'I've got to get some books for my art coursework,' Michelle told her. 'Mrs Hanson says it's got to be on her desk first thing or she'll want to know why. And if I have to see her she'll only start quizzing me about why Mia's not back in school yet.'

Kim pursed her lips and flapped her hand. 'Right, fine, go to the flaming library. But be quick, 'cos we can't hang about if the taxi comes.'

Promising to run there and back, Michelle dashed upstairs and grabbed her card and the books she needed to take back. Head down, she hurried up the road and around the corner. But just as she was passing the shops on the block before the library, a man came hurtling out of the off-licence and crashed into her, knocking the books right out of her arms.

'Shit, I'm sorry,' he apologised, squatting down to scoop them out of the puddle they'd landed in.

Their heads collided when they both reached for the same book and Michelle said, 'Leave it – *please*. I can manage.'

Glancing up at her when he heard her voice, Liam groaned. 'Oh, God, not *you* again. Are you determined to keep getting in my way, or what?'

'Ex*cuse* me?' Michelle gasped, jerking her head up. She blushed when she looked into his laughing eyes because she could see them more clearly than the last time, and they were the most beautiful shade of green. She quickly dropped her gaze, muttering, 'It's not me who keeps running round like an idiot.'

'Hey, I'm a busy man,' Liam quipped, grinning as he handed one of the books to her. 'And you're obviously blind as a bat.' Chuckling softly when she flashed him an indignant look, he held out his hands in a gesture of surrender. 'Okay, quit with the evils. It's my fault – I admit it.'

'Yes, it is,' Michelle agreed clippily, shaking water off the books. 'And it'll be your bill if I get charged for ruining these.'

Liam took them from her and wiped them on his jeans before handing them back. 'There you go, good as new – and if anyone says different, just tell them to talk to me about it.'

Saying, 'Fine, I'll do that,' Michelle sidestepped him and started to walk away. But she'd only gone a couple of steps when he called out her name. She stopped, turned and frowned at him.

Smiling, Liam held up her library card. 'It's got your name on it. Or did you think I've been following you around asking questions about you, or something?'

Blush deepening, Michelle marched back to him and snatched the card.

'You're welcome,' he drawled. 'And for future reference, my name's Liam – just so you know what to call me next time you go tripping me up.'

Aware that he was teasing her, Michelle pursed her lips. 'Thank you, *Liam*, but I'm not too fond of being knocked about, so I think it's probably best if we avoid each other from now on.'

'Shame,' he murmured, holding her gaze. 'I'm getting used

to picking you up. You're sort of becoming my good deed for the day.'

'Oh, so, now you're a Boy Scout?'

'Here to protect and serve.'

'Isn't that the police?'

'Probably, but a uniform's a uniform, and all that.'

Amused despite herself, Michelle shook her head and shifted the books to her other arm.

Tilting his head, Liam glanced at the titles. 'Please tell me you're not really into all that old romantic tosh.'

'Oh, and I suppose you're an expert on good literature, are you?' Michelle shot back, sure that he, like most of the lads she'd ever met, had never opened a book in his life unless it contained pictures of naked women.

'No expert, no. But if I'm going to give myself eye strain, it's got to have a bit more depth than *that*. Ever tried *Trainspotting*?'

'What, *literally*?' Michelle deadpanned. 'As in anoraks and binoculars?'

'Hey, that's pretty funny for a terminally serious girl like you,' Liam replied good-naturedly. Then, shrugging, he said, 'Just give it a try sometime, see what you think.'

Surprised to realise that he actually meant it, Michelle was impressed. Not only good-looking and considerate, but a reader, too – rare qualities indeed for a lad who lived around here.

Liam's phone started to ring. He took it out of his pocket and glanced at the screen. Not recognising the number, he answered with a light, 'Yo?'

Feeling awkward when his face darkened and he abruptly turned his back on her, Michelle decided to leave him to it.

Rigid with rage, Liam said, 'How did you get this number?'

'You seem to forget your Aunt Ruth's my sister,' his dad

reminded him, sounding his usual churlish, drunken self. 'And family don't keep secrets. But then, you wouldn't know about loyalty, would you? Stab me in the back as soon as look at me, you would. 'Cos you're just like your ma – no respect!'

'Don't you even *mention* her,' Liam snarled. 'In fact, why don't you do us all a favour and take one of them knives you were so fond of threatening her with and slice your own fucking throat open!'

'Aw, now don't be like that, son.' His father switched to a wounded tone now, as if he couldn't believe that his own child was rejecting him like this. 'You know I'd never have used it on her. But you know what she's like; she just pushes and pushes till I snap.'

'Don't you mean *pushed*?' Liam corrected him, his voice a low growl of rage and disgust. 'You can only *push* when you've still got breath in your lungs and blood in your veins. But she's got neither, because she's *dead* – and *you* killed her!'

'Aw, don't talk bollocks! If I was guilty, how come they let me off – tell me that, eh, smart-arse?'

'Just because she finished it doesn't mean you didn't start it. You made her life hell, and I'll never forgive you.'

'You don't mean that,' his father drawled. 'Me and your ma might have had our ups and downs, but we'd have been all right if she'd stayed in her place. Anyhow, that's all in the past, and it's time you let it go,' he went on, as if it were a perfectly reasonable thing to expect. 'You're my son, and I want you back home with me where you belong. And if it's going back to the old house where she topped herself that's putting you off, don't worry, 'cos they've already evicted me. But they've said they'll give me a new place if you agree to come back, 'cos obviously I'll be responsible for you when you're having the therapy, and that.'

Filled with utter contempt now that his father had revealed

his real reason for contacting him, Liam yelled, 'Next time I see you you'll be lying in a box, and I'll be spitting in your disgusting auld face!'

'Don't you feckin' *dare* talk to me like that!' his father yelled back. 'I'm your da, and you'll do as you're bastard well told!'

Disconnecting the call without another word, Liam ignored the phone when it immediately began to ring again. He'd known without having to ask that it would have been his aunt who'd given his number out. He'd only moved in with her because he'd still been a minor when his father had been arrested on suspicion of murdering his mother, and it had been a choice between her or going into care. And he'd opted for her, stupidly thinking that she'd abide by the social services recommendation to keep his whereabouts secret in order to let him rebuild his life without interference from his father. But now she'd betrayed him she could rot in hell, because he was out of there.

Remembering Michelle, Liam turned round to find her gone. Thinking that the least he owed her was an apology, he headed over to the library and leaned against the wall beside the door to wait for her.

Michelle rushed straight past him when she came out a few minutes later. Stopping in her tracks when he called out to her, she turned back, her books clutched tightly to her chest. 'Sorry, I didn't see you. Were you waiting for me?'

Shrugging, Liam stuffed his hands into his pockets. 'Just wanted to apologise in case you thought I was being rude back there. It was just a bit of an awkward call – family stuff, and that.'

Sensing that he didn't really want to discuss it, Michelle said, 'It's fine, really.'

Grateful that she wasn't going to hold it against him, Liam

glanced at her books. Grinning when he spotted the one he'd recommended, he said, 'Decided to give it a go, then?'

'Not because of you,' she blurted out, feeling the heat of yet another blush crawling up her neck. 'I just saw it and read the back, and thought it looked all right.'

'Hope you like it,' he teased, the light of amusement back in his eyes. Then, taking a deep breath, 'Look, say no if you don't want to, but I don't suppose you'd fancy coming out with me sometime, would you? To see a film, or something.'

Shocked, because this was the very last thing she'd expected him to say, Michelle glanced both ways along the road – sure that his mates must be hiding somewhere, because it *had* to be a joke. Gorgeous lads like him didn't ask girls like her out on dates.

Taking her hesitation as a sign that she wanted to refuse but was too polite, Liam felt a bit deflated – if not overly surprised. He'd only met her twice, but that was enough for him to know that she was the shy type.

'Sorry, I didn't mean to hit you over the head with it like that,' he apologised. 'I just thought it'd be nice to spend a bit of time with you, seeing as all I've done so far is knock you over.'

'It's all right,' Michelle assured him, wishing she could shake off the feeling that he was only doing this for a bet.

'All right as in you forgive me, but don't do it again?' Liam ventured, giving her a questioning smile. 'Or, all right, you'll think about it?'

Before Michelle had a chance to answer, a taxi pulled up to the kerb at the end of the path.

'Oi! I thought you were supposed to be coming straight back, so why are you still hanging about down here?'

Wishing the ground would open up and swallow her when Liam turned to see who was shouting at her, Michelle excused herself and rushed towards the car.

'Sorry,' she murmured, glad that the darkness was masking her flaming cheeks. 'I got talking and forgot the time.'

'Who's that?' Mia demanded, dipping her head to peer at Liam.

Murmuring, 'Just a friend,' Michelle's heart sank. If Mia could see Liam, then he could probably see her, and he'd be bound to lose whatever interest he'd had in Michelle.

'Never you mind about him,' Kim snapped at Mia. 'I've already told you you're off boys.' Yanking her keys out of her pocket now, she thrust them into Michelle's hand. 'Right, hurry up home and get the bolts on, 'cos I saw Pam nosying when we were getting in the cab.'

Nodding, Michelle slipped the keys into her pocket.

'Get going, then.'

Michelle cast a glance back at Liam and saw that he was on the phone again, his back turned. She really would have liked to say goodbye, but her mum was still looking at her expectantly. So, reluctantly, she set off for home.

Twisting her head when the taxi drove on, Mia stared back at Liam. She'd caught a glimpse of his face when they'd first pulled up, and she could have sworn he was really fit. But why would a fit lad be bothering with a dork like Michelle?

Facing the front again when they turned the corner, Mia pursed her lips thoughtfully. Michelle would have introduced him if he really was just a friend, but the fact that she hadn't indicated that she was scared he would fancy Mia. Smiling slyly to herself now that she'd solved the mystery, she settled back in her seat. So little Michelle thought she was keeping him to herself, did she? Well, they'd soon see about that.

Finishing his call, Liam turned to find both Michelle and the car gone. He frowned and looked out along the road. Spotting a dark figure receding in the distance, he called her name and set off after her at a run.

'Christ, how *fast* do you walk?' he gasped, breathless by the time he'd caught up with her.

'Sorry,' Michelle murmured. 'I've got to go home.'

'You never answered my question,' Liam said, peering into her eyes. 'About going out sometime?'

'Oh, right.' She bit her lip. 'You meant it, then?'

'Course I meant it.' He laughed. 'Or do you think I go round asking people out for fun? Well, obviously the intention *is* to have some fun once you actually *get* there,' he added quickly. 'But you know what I mean.'

Smiling shyly as her stomach did a little somersault, Michelle said, 'I suppose so.'

'So, is that a yes or a no?'

Gazing up at him, Michelle took a deep breath. This could be a wind-up, and his friends might well jump out of the bushes as soon as she opened her mouth. But if she didn't take this chance, she might never know.

'Okay,' she said, tensing for the piss-taking that she fully expected to follow.

But Liam didn't laugh. He tipped his head to one side, and said, 'Really?' as if he couldn't quite believe that she'd agreed. Then, grinning when she nodded, he said, 'Great. When?'

'I'm not sure,' she told him quietly, already wondering how she was going to manage it when her mum kept insisting that she stay in to guard the house.

'Tell you what, I'll give you my number,' Liam offered. 'Then you can ring when you're free.'

'I haven't got any credit,' she admitted – too embarrassed to add that she wasn't likely to get any top-ups any time soon, because her mum had been spending every spare penny on Mia lately.

'Okay, I'll take yours instead,' he suggested, taking his own phone out of his pocket.

Michelle rushed inside when she got home a few minutes later, leant back against the door and hugged the books tightly, slowly replaying in her mind what had just happened. She still couldn't believe that someone as gorgeous as Liam wanted to go out with her. But he really did, and he'd followed her not just once but *twice* in order to ask her.

The only problem now was how to make it happen without Mia finding out, because if Liam saw *her* he'd take one look and realise he'd picked the wrong sister.

But she wouldn't worry about that right now. She would just hold her secret close and wait for Liam to call – and pray that he didn't change his mind in the meantime.

Across town, Kim and Mia had just arrived at Sammy Martin's office. A far cry from the plush city-centre offices of the bigger agencies they'd visited so far, this was situated in the middle of a row of mostly boarded-up terraced houses on a gloomy backstreet off Ancoats. And if Mia had been reluctant before, she was positively determined not to even get out of the taxi now. But Kim was having none of it.

'Move,' she hissed, paying the driver and elbowing Mia out. 'And don't even think about making a show of me, or there'll be trouble.'

Kim straightened her clothes when the cab had gone, patted her hair to make sure it was still in place, then walked up to the door. Pressing the buzzer, she announced herself and waited for the door to be released. She pushed Mia into the dingy hallway, most of which was dominated by an uncarpeted staircase, stepped in behind her and waited for a receptionist. But a voice called down for them to make their own way up.

Hissing one last warning at Mia to behave herself, Kim held her head up and forced a smile onto her lips as she ascended the stairs and came face to face with Sammy Martin.

'Very nice to meet you,' Sammy said and pumped her hand. Then, turning to Mia: 'And hello to you, young lady.'

Getting a scowl and tightly folded arms in return, he waved them through to his office.

Sulkily following her mum, Mia flopped into one of the visitors' chairs and stared pointedly at the floor.

'Thank you so much for seeing us at such short notice,' Kim gushed, handing the portfolio across to Sammy as he took his own seat on the other side of the desk. 'I've been meaning to call you for ages, but we've been so busy I haven't had a chance.'

Smiling without comment, Sammy unzipped the faux-leather case and flipped it open. Nobody's fool, he knew that Kim would never have contacted him if she weren't desperate. It had been some five or six weeks since Tim Leece had rung to let him know that he'd recommended his agency to them – and having seen the expression on both their faces when they'd got their first sight of him just now, he'd bet they were wishing they hadn't bothered.

He couldn't really blame them, because in an industry where appearance was everything – whichever side of the camera you graced – Sammy was hardly the finest specimen of modelling manhood. But he was a self-confessed lazy bugger when it came to exercise, and the older he got, the more of a losing battle it became to even be bothered ironing a shirt in the mornings. And having reached the grand old age of fifty without learning how to cook – or sparing enough time to find a decent woman to do it for him – it was a case of junk food or no food.

It frustrated Sammy sometimes that he hadn't made more of an effort to play the image game, because he'd always had – and still did have – a keen eye for spotting undiscovered talent. But he'd long ago reconciled himself to the fact that top models would rather eat a proper dinner – and keep it all down – than be associated with a fat agent. Still, he'd managed to carve out a respectable niche in the middle market of catalogues and toilet-paper ads. And he had a great little stable of regular, reliable models – none of whom the big boys could be bothered to steal from him, because they had nothing remarkable enough about them to warrant it.

So, no, Sammy was under no illusions about his limitations. Any more than he was under any illusion about why Kim and Mia Delaney were sitting here now. And looking over the photographs, he could see exactly what the problem was.

Despite her mother's seeming conviction that she was the next Kate Moss in waiting, Mia didn't display that certain something that was essential for the catwalk. And her face was nowhere near quirky or outstandingly gorgeous enough for the high-fashion glossies.

Thanks to Tim Leece's wizardry, the pictures were of excellent technical quality, but even *he* couldn't magic *X-Factor* into a subject's eyes. That was born, not created, and Mia just didn't have it.

And she obviously found it hard to follow directions, too, because Tim would undoubtedly have told her how to stand, where to look, and what to do with her mouth, etc . . . and yet she had over-posed in every shot. And the self-satisfied *I'm-too-gorgeous-for-words* smile was bordering on sickening.

But Mia apparently thought she looked the business, because she'd tried to replicate the exact same look today – oblivious to the fact that harsh domestic bulbs didn't soften the effect like professional lighting did.

Glancing up at Mia now, only to see her still staring into space with a sullen expression on her over-painted face, Sammy sighed. Despite their only experience coming via the TV modelling shows they were all addicted to, these young girls all seemed to think that being a diva was the way to get ahead. But nobody in their right mind would waste time and money on a moody uncooperative novice when there were thousands of equally pretty girls to choose from.

Kim was beginning to fidget. They'd been here for almost twenty minutes now, and she'd been watching Sammy's face the whole time, desperately trying to read what he was thinking as he studied the photos. But his expression was giving absolutely nothing away. Unable to bear the heavy silence any longer, she cleared her throat loudly.

'So, what do you think?'

'They're okay,' Sammy replied, giving a tiny noncommittal shrug.

'*Okay?*' Kim repeated incredulously. 'Oh, come on, they're better than okay. She looks really pretty in them.'

'Pretty's not enough, I'm afraid.' Sitting back, Sammy looped his hands together on his belly. 'From what you told me when you rang, I gather you're expecting huge things for her. But if you want my honest opinion, she just hasn't got what it takes.'

Already irritated, having thought that a little backstreet agent like him would bite her hand off for the chance to represent an obvious star like Mia, Kim's nostrils flared.

'Look, she's bloody *gorgeous*, so don't be telling me she hasn't got it. And these cost a fortune, so you can't say *they*'re not good enough.' She jabbed her finger down on the photographs. 'So let's not waste any more time. You either want to be her agent, or you don't. And if you don't, just be honest and say it, 'cos there's plenty who'd jump at the chance.'

'Maybe so,' Sammy conceded. 'But I'm figuring you've already been turned down by all the good ones, so you've got to ask yourself if those who are left are the kind of people you'd want handling your daughter's career.'

'Yes!' Kim shot back without hesitation. 'At least I'd know

they had faith in her – like *I* have. But if you can't see what she's got to offer, it's your loss.'

Amused when she began to scoop the photographs together furiously, Sammy said, 'I'll tell you what, mum, she's lucky she's got you in her corner.'

'What's that supposed to mean?' Kim glared at him.

Nodding towards Mia, Sammy said, 'Be honest, is that the face of a girl who looks determined to do whatever it takes to make it? And if you say yes,' he added quickly, knowing that that was exactly what Kim was about to say, 'then you're either lying, or fooling yourself. In fact, if I had to hazard a guess, I'd say that *you* want it more than she does.'

'That's not true,' Kim shot back defensively. 'You want to do it, don't you, Mee? *Tell* him.'

Rolling her eyes as if she really couldn't give a toss, Mia issued a bored-sounding 'Mmmm.'

'Oh, well, you've got me convinced,' Sammy murmured.

'No, she really means it,' Kim insisted, tears of desperation beginning to glisten in her eyes. 'This was *her* idea, I swear to God.' Turning on Mia now, her voice shaky, she said, 'You know how much this means to me, so stop playing funny buggers.'

Glowering back at her mother, embarrassed that she was falling apart like this in front of a complete stranger, Mia hissed, 'I told you I didn't want to do it any more.'

'Only 'cos you've realised it's not going to be as easy as you thought,' Kim snapped back, her voice rising to a squawk as the anger and frustration overwhelmed her.

Feeling sorry for her, because it was obvious that she was really struggling to hold it together, Sammy cleared his throat to remind her that he was actually hearing all this. Smiling apologetically when she jerked her head around, he said, 'I hope you don't think I'm interfering, but do you really think there's any point trying to force her if she doesn't want to do it?'

Sensing that he was about to tell them that the interview was over, Kim's chin began to wobble uncontrollably. She'd come here with such high hopes, utterly convinced that Sammy Martin would sign Mia up without a second thought. But even he didn't want to know.

Sammy sighed when the tears that Kim had been struggling to hold back began to trickle slowly down her cheeks. He shoved his chair back and stood up.

'I'll make some coffee,' he said, lumbering around the desk and heading for the door. 'Then we'll have a chat, and I'll let you know what's wrong from my point of view.'

Grateful that he wasn't going to turf them out right this second, Kim pulled a tissue out of her pocket and blew her nose loudly.

'Do you have to?' Mia hissed when they were alone. 'Don't you think you've embarrassed me enough already without bursting into tears?'

'I can't help it,' Kim hissed back. 'You can't pick and choose when you start going through the change, you know.'

'*Ew!*' Grimacing, Mia shuddered exaggeratedly. 'Do you have to tell everyone about it?'

'You're not everyone,' Kim reminded her. 'And it'll happen to you one day, so I wouldn't be screwing my nose up if I was you.'

'*Pfft!*' Mia snorted, determined that she would never let herself go through something as disgusting as that.

A little more in control of herself now, Kim wiped her nose one last time and slotted the tissue back into her pocket. 'I'm doing my best for you,' she muttered. 'And you'd best get that slapped-arse look off your face before he comes back, 'cos you're lucky he hasn't already told us to sling it.'

'*Lucky*?' Mia repeated scathingly. 'Are you kidding me? This place is a *dump*. I bet he's not even a real agent.'

'Yes, he is,' Kim hissed, glancing nervously back at the door. 'That photographer wouldn't have given us his number otherwise. Anyway, just behave and let's hear him out. You've hardly got much choice, have you?'

Exhaling loudly, Mia swivelled her chair from side to side. Her mum could say what she liked, but Mia had no intention of listening to a word that Sammy fat baldy bastard Martin had to say.

Coming back just then, carrying a small tray bearing three steaming cups and a plate of biscuits, Sammy laid it down on the desk between them.

'Sorry, I've run out of coffee so it's tea, I'm afraid. And there's no milk. But I have got sugar and sweeteners, so take your pick. And help yourself to biccies.'

'No, thanks, we don't take sugar,' Kim lied, reaching for one of the cups.

Resisting the biscuits, even though the sight of them made her stomach grumble because she'd forgotten about dinner before they'd come out, she sat back in her seat and forced herself not to grimace when she took a sip of the hot bland liquid. She couldn't wait to get home for a fag and a lovely sweet cuppa. And then she'd be straight on the phone to order herself a kebab – but only when Mia had gone to bed, because she didn't want to go putting temptation in her way.

Looking serious now, Sammy said, 'Look, I've been having a good think about this, and I reckon there's a chance we could work something out.'

'Really?' Kim gasped, immediately cursing herself for sounding so grateful.

'*If*,' Sammy said, emphasising the word as he looked straight at Mia, '*you* can convince me you're willing to drop the attitude and really work at it.'

Arms still folded, Mia flicked him a *yeah, whatever* glance.

Giving her a chance to climb down off her high horse, Sammy sighed when she didn't do so after a few moments. He gave Kim a defeated shrug. 'Oh, well, I think we have our answer.'

Furious, Kim glared at Mia.

'*What?*' Mia said sullenly.

'You know bloody well what. He's offering us a chance here, you silly little cow. And if you blow it, that's it – you can forget about being famous.'

Shrugging as if she didn't give a toss, Mia scowled when Kim gave her a sharp prod in the arm.

'This isn't a game, lady, so sort yourself out, because this is important.'

'I don't see why,' Mia argued. 'He's hardly Mr Super-Cool, is he?'

'Let me guess,' Sammy interjected perceptively. 'You don't know why your mum's dragged you here, because you're obviously too good for me, and *I* obviously don't know anything about anything.' Taking the twitch of her eyebrows as affirmation that he'd hit the nail on the head, he smiled slowly. 'Did you see the silver car across the road when you got here?'

Wrinkling her nose, Mia said, 'Yeah – *so*?'

'It's a Bentley,' Sammy told her, not sounding in the least boastful. 'Now, I don't know if you've any idea how much they cost but they're not cheap. So, ask yourself this, if *you*'re so good, and *I*'m so bad, how come I've got one and you haven't?'

'Er, 'cos I'm only fifteen,' Mia reminded him sarcastically.

'And do you think you'll be any better off by the time you're my age?' Sammy persisted smoothly. 'Because I guarantee that you won't be if you carry on like this.'

'Says you.'

'Well, I won't knock your self-belief, my love, but I doubt you'd be here if Nemesis or Boss or any of the other agencies you've already seen had said any different.'

Licking her lips, sensing that Mia was on the verge of blowing their chances, Kim said, 'Look, Mr Martin, I admit we haven't had much success so far, but I still think she's got something special and we'll do whatever it takes to get her there. You said you thought we could work something out, so just tell us what we need to do and we'll do it – I promise.'

Sammy believed that she meant it and he nodded thoughtfully. Under normal circumstances, he'd have shown them the door by now, because, as he'd already said, there was no point trying to force someone to do something they blatantly didn't want to. But Mia must have wanted it to start with or she wouldn't have bothered posing for the photos, and he could only assume that her present truculence was due to the rejections she'd received so far. She was only young, after all, and rejection wasn't easy to swallow at any age.

Looking at Mia now, he said, 'All right, let's cut to the chase, young lady. We know how important this is for your mum, but I need to know if *you* want it as well – or are we just wasting our time? And before you answer,' he added quickly, 'let me just tell you about some of the models I represent. I take it you watch TV?'

'Oh, she does,' Kim blurted out. 'All the time.'

'So you'll have seen all the adverts for Slimma-Soup, with the young girl floating down the high street in a bubble? Well, she's one of mine. And the one about razor blades, with the young lad having his first shave before going on a date?'

Despite her determination to retain her scowl, a hint of interest flickered in Mia's eyes. She'd seen both those ads, but whereas she'd paid no heed to the Slimma-Soup one because she had no need of it, she'd *definitely* noticed the lad on the other ad.

Catching the shift in her demeanour, Sammy smiled. 'His name's Jonathon, he's just turned sixteen, and he's been with me for ten years. Although I doubt he'll be with me for too much longer, because this is his breakthrough job, and I imagine he'll be whipped out of my hands by one of the big boys any day now. But, hey ho.' He sighed resignedly and flapped his hands. 'Anyway, I can tell you've already noticed him, but I bet you can't tell me where you've seen him before, can you?'

Mia shrugged again, but Sammy noted that there was far less aggression in her expression now.

'Well, you might be surprised to hear that he's been in lots of TV ads. He was the Jelly-Tot tot, for example; and the Rainbow-Lite boy; and the kid who cut his knee falling over his dog and had to get plastered – pardon the pun – in those new padded Elastoplast strips.'

'Oh, I remember that one,' Kim exclaimed excitedly. 'But are you sure that was the same boy, 'cos he was an odd-looking little thing, and the lad in the shaving one is lovely.'

'My point exactly.' Sammy grinned. 'See, this is what I'm talking about, Mia. Jon's mum thought he was a superstar from the start but nobody else could see it back then. It takes time and experience to blossom, but they were willing to work their way up. And now it's beginning to pay off, because Jon could be in Hollywood this time next week. But where will *you* be?' Pausing for effect, he gazed at her steadily before adding, 'You can ignore my advice and stay exactly where you are, or admit that you're not as ready as you think you are and let me guide you. Your choice, but I know what I'd go for if I were you.'

Tilting her head to one side, Mia gave him a coy smile. 'Will I get to meet Jonathon?'

Laughing out loud, Sammy's fat belly wobbled. 'I'm sure it could be arranged. Although I'm not sure it'll get you anywhere, because he's just come out.'

'Out of what?'

'Never mind.' Sammy chuckled, shaking his head at Kim. He took a swig of his now-cold tea and glanced at his watch. 'Right, well, I think I've given you enough to ponder over for the time being, so why don't you go home and discuss it? Then your mum can ring when you know what you want to do. Okay?'

'We'll do it,' Kim blurted out without hesitation. 'And thank you so much, you don't know how much this means to me – *us*.'

Sammy extended his hand across the desk and said, 'My pleasure.' Then, turning to Mia, he gave her a questioning look. 'And what about you, young lady? Are you going to be a star?'

Mia shrugged again, but she was still smiling.

'The word you're looking for is *yes*,' Sammy told her, slapping his hand down on the desktop. Your mum believes you can do it; *I* believe you can do it. But do *you* believe you can do it?'

Caught up in his excitement at last, Mia grinned. 'I *know* I can do it.'

'Good girl!' Beaming, Sammy reached into a drawer and pulled out a pack of baby-wipes. 'Now go and wipe that muck off your face, because it looks ridiculous.'

Giving her mum a smug look, because the stupid make-up had been *her* idea, Mia got up and trotted obediently out to the toilet.

5

Sammy Martin was taking Mia and Kim out to a posh restaurant. It was Mia's first audition tomorrow and he wanted to have a good long talk with her in a more informal setting than his office; to make sure that she knew exactly what to do, and, more importantly, what *not* to do – like backchat the photographer, or start complaining.

More nervous about the audition than Mia was, Kim had been running around all day, bouncing from one task to another, and barking orders at Mia to hurry up and get in the bath, hurry up and get out again, hurry up and dry her hair, hurry up and set it . . .

Sick of listening to her mother, Mia was lounging on the chair by the window with her iPod earphones stuffed deep into her ears. She'd been ready for ages, and now she just wanted to go. Not that she was looking forward to seeing Sammy, because she knew she'd only get another brain-numbing lecture off him to top the ones she'd been getting off her mum all day. But it was the first time she'd ever been to a proper restaurant, and she wanted to see what it was like for when she was famous and eating out at posh places every night.

Feeling her phone vibrate in her pocket, she slipped it out. She saw Laura's name on the screen and ran into the kitchen to take the call in private.

'What you saying, girlfriend? Hope you've got good gossip for me.'

'Yeah, but you're not going to like it,' Laura told her. 'Lisa's been slagging you off all over the place, telling everyone you're not really sick, and that you're only staying off school 'cos you're scared of Sandra beating you up again.'

'She didn't even beat me up in the first place,' Mia scoffed. 'You saw me – there were hardly any marks on me, were there?'

'No, and that's what I told them when they started going on about it,' Laura assured her. 'Obviously I couldn't tell them why you're *really* staying off, 'cos you said I've got to keep it a secret. But I reckon they all know, anyhow, 'cos Lisa won't shut up about it.'

'She's such a jealous bitch,' Mia sneered.

'You know it was her who gave your number to Sandra, don't you?' Laura informed her. 'That night when Sandra rang and made Darren tell you to get lost.'

'I *knew* he hadn't given it to her!' Mia exclaimed triumphantly. 'He already had my mobile number, so if he'd meant it he would have just given her that instead of making her find out the landline number, wouldn't he?'

'Have you spoken to him since?' Laura asked – cautiously, because she had a bit of news of her own and wasn't sure how Mia would react when she heard.

'No, he's rung a few times but I was busy,' Mia lied, too proud to admit that he hadn't rung at all – and hadn't answered his phone when she'd tried to call him. 'I'm sure I'll catch up with him sooner or later,' she went on nonchalantly. 'But I don't know if I can be bothered with him any more, to be honest. You know I've got my first audition tomorrow?'

'Oh, yeah, you told me. So, how's it going? Are you ready?'

'Yeah, it's cool. My agent reckons I've got it in the bag.'

'Ooh, I can't wait to see you in a magazine,' Laura gushed. 'I'll be so proud of you. I'll be flashing it round all over the place, going, *look*, that's my best mate!'

'So long as you make sure Lisa and Sandra get a good long look at it,' Mia said, laughing softly. 'And just wait till I start getting in the papers for going to all the showbiz parties – that'll *really* rub it in.'

'I hope you won't forget about me when you're mixing with the stars.'

'Course I won't. Best mates are for life, not just Christmas, remember. Wherever I go, you'll be right there in the limo with me, swigging champagne, and—'

'You know the taxi will be here in a minute, don't you?' Kim interrupted, sticking her head around the door.

Flashing her an irritated look, Mia said, 'Sorry, Laura, got to go. I'll give you a ring tomorrow – let you know how it went.'

'I'd wish you luck, but I know you don't need it, 'cos you'll be brill.'

'I know! They won't know what's hit them when I walk in.'

Sighing, Laura told her friend that she wished she could be there. Then, just as she was about to say goodbye, she remembered what she'd meant to tell her.

'Oh, by the way,' she blurted out. 'You'll never guess who called *me* last night. *Stu!*' She answered her own question. 'I was going to call you after he got off the phone, but it was too late by then, 'cos he was on for ages. Anyhow, he asked me to go out with him this Saturday – can you *believe* that?'

Mia's lips were tightly pursed. 'And what did *you* say?'

Hesitant now because she sensed the dip in Mia's mood, Laura said, 'I told him I'd think about it – but I'm not going to. I mean, he hasn't bothered calling since all that stuff kicked off with you and Darren. And anyway, I wouldn't do that to you.'

'So how come you were on the phone so long?' Mia snapped accusingly. 'It only takes a second to say no, but you said he was on for ages.'

'Well, yeah, but only because he was trying to persuade me,' Laura murmured, wishing now that she hadn't told her. 'Anyway, why are you mad at me? *I* didn't ring *him*.'

'I'm not mad, I just don't see why you're acting so excited if you're not interested. Anyway, I've got to go, the taxi's here.'

Mia scowled as she cut the call. It didn't surprise her that they were all speculating about why she hadn't gone back to school, but it pissed her off that they thought she was scared of Sandra. She wished she'd never told Laura to keep it a secret that she wasn't really hurt, because at least then she could have set them all straight. But she couldn't risk any of the teachers finding out, or they'd be bound to try and force her to go back.

'Where's that necklace you said you were wearing?' Kim asked just then, interrupting her thoughts.

'Can't be bothered looking for it,' Mia muttered.

'You can't wear that dress without it,' Kim told her. 'You're showing too much boob, and you need the necklace to hide it. Go on – go and find it while you've still got time.'

In the bedroom, Michelle was running the hot-irons through her hair. Since her mum and Mia had met Sammy Martin, they were always whizzing in and out for meetings and coaching sessions. And while she didn't begrudge Mia her excitement as the first audition drew closer, she couldn't help but feel left out, because they were acting more like best friends than mother and daughter, forever discussing what Sammy had said, or giggling about the champagne lifestyle they would soon be living.

Michelle hadn't met Sammy, because she was never invited along to any of their meetings, but she figured he must be good if he'd managed to get Mia on side. And her mum seemed to have taken quite a shine to him as well, because she always seemed to be quoting him.

'Remember what Sammy said about this . . . Remember what Sammy said about that . . . Sammy said . . . Sammy said . . .'

Michelle actually suspected that her mum had a bit of a crush on the agent, because she'd started to take more pride in her appearance and she went into posh-voice overdrive whenever they spoke on the phone. But whether or not that was the reason, he seemed to be having a positive effect on her, because she'd started to pull up her socks in other areas of her life – like getting the gas meter sorted out.

Michelle didn't know how she'd done it but she was glad that she had, because it had been stressful hearing her fretting about being sent to prison. And, even better, now that she no longer needed Eric to put the meter back her mum had finally dropped her obsession with him and Pam.

Not enough to stop her from calling them all the bastards under the sun whenever she heard them moving about next door but enough to give Eric back his clothes – in return for her key.

The key which Michelle now possessed.

Not that it gave her the freedom to come and go as she pleased, because her mum was so convinced Eric had made a copy that she still insisted that Michelle put the bolts on whenever they went out. And usually Michelle did, but having fobbed Liam off so many times already with excuses about having too much homework or revision when he'd rung her about their date she'd finally agreed to meet up with him, fearing that he would lose interest if she didn't. And she'd chosen tonight, knowing that her mum and Mia were being taken out to some fancy restaurant, so they would be out for hours.

After rushing home from school this afternoon she'd done her homework and then jumped in the bath, her plan being to get ready while her mum and Mia were too preoccupied to notice. Then she would lie on her bed reading until they had gone.

Which was sound in theory, but Michelle should have known that Mia would smell a rat if she caught her making such an uncharacteristic effort with her appearance. And she didn't help herself by blushing guiltily when Mia barged into the bedroom now.

Instantly suspicious because Michelle *never* straightened her hair and she was wearing decent clothes for a change, Mia said, 'What are you getting tarted up for? You're not coming with me and mum.'

Blurting out the first thing that came into her mind, Michelle said, 'Sylvia's coming round. We've got some course-work to finish, so we thought we might as well do it together.'

'So why you getting tarted up for that?' Mia demanded. 'Unless you're a pair of lezzers now.'

'I'm only doing my hair,' Michelle muttered. 'And I'd have thought you'd be pleased, considering you're always telling me I look like a tramp.'

'I get it,' Mia hissed, remembering the boy she'd seen Michelle talking to at the library that night. 'You're going to see that lad, aren't you?'

Fronting it out, Michelle said, 'What lad?'

'Don't play dumb,' Mia spat, pursing her lips spitefully. 'You know exactly who I mean – that lad from the library . . . your so-called *friend*.'

Frowning as if she didn't know what Mia was talking about, Michelle tutted after a second and said, 'Oh, *him*. God, no, I haven't seen him in ages.'

'I know you're lying,' Mia retorted angrily. 'It's written all over your face. I bet you haven't told mum, though, have you?'

'You're wrong,' Michelle insisted, wishing that Mia would keep her voice down.

'We'll see about that!' Mia snatched up the necklace she'd come for and marched down the stairs, yelling, '*Mum* . . . guess what Michelle's doing!'

Michelle slammed the hot-irons down in despair and determinedly blinked back the tears that were stinging her eyes. Crying would only prove Mia right because they both knew that she wouldn't get upset if she'd been telling the truth about Sylvia coming round.

Inhaling deeply when her mum shouted for her a minute later, Michelle composed her face into an expression of innocence and made her way downstairs.

'What's this I hear about you thinking you're going out to see some lad?'

'I've already told Mia I'm not going anywhere. Sylvia's coming round, that's all. We're going to do—'

'Some coursework,' Kim finished for her. 'Yeah, she said you were going to say that.'

'It's true,' Michelle insisted. 'And you can ring Sylvia's mum if you don't believe me. I've got her number in my bag if you want me to get it.'

'Do I buggery,' Kim snorted. 'But if I find out you're lying, you've had it – so be warned.'

It had been a gamble, but Michelle had known that it would pay off because her mum would rather die than talk to any of her friends' parents. She thought they were all snobs who looked down their noses at her because she was a single mum living on benefits in a council house. Which was probably what they *would* have thought if they'd ever met her, but she'd never shown the slightest inclination to attend parents' evenings or any of the sports matches – let alone the various school plays – so it was highly unlikely that they ever would.

The taxi arrived. When she heard its horn Kim held the cigarette she'd just lit between her teeth and slipped her coat on. Then, picking up her handbag, she held out her hand. 'Give us your key – just in case you've got any funny ideas about sneaking out.'

Gritting her teeth to prevent herself from bursting into tears of frustration, Michelle glowered at Mia.

'No point giving me evils,' Mia smirked. 'If I'm not allowed to see boys, I don't see why you think *you* can.'

Reiterating that Sylvia was the only person she'd be seeing tonight, Michelle shrugged. 'But it's okay if you don't trust me, mum. Even *you* must get me mixed up with Mia sometimes.'

Astounded that this jibe had come from *Michelle* – who normally wouldn't say boo to a goose – Kim was unusually lost for words. But when the taxi horn hooted again, she tutted. 'Oh, forget it. I can't hang around all night waiting for you to go upstairs.' She herded an indignant Mia through the door and yelled back over her shoulder, 'Just make sure you keep the bolts on. And I want that Sylvia gone by the time we get back, 'cos I don't like the idea of your snotty friends nosing around my house.'

Michelle held her breath until she heard them getting into the car and driving away. Well, she'd got away with it – but only just. And Mia would be furious that their mum had sided with her just now, so life was probably going to be hell for a while. But Liam was worth it.

She ran back up to her room, finished doing her hair and looked herself over in the mirror. Her hair didn't look anywhere near as smooth or shiny as Mia managed to get hers, but it was all right. Taking a tube of lip gloss out of Mia's bulging make-up bag now, she slicked on a thin coating and then headed out.

Already nervous about the possibility of her mum doubling back and catching her on the street, Michelle pulled her hood up and kept her chin shoved down into her collar. When she reached the library five minutes later, she hesitated when she saw Liam surrounded by the local gang who hung out there. They were troublemakers who came here at night to drink alcohol and smoke weed – and to pick on anyone who strayed onto their turf. And knowing from the little that Liam had told her that he hadn't lived in Manchester for long, she dreaded to think what they were going to do to him.

Spotting her just then, Liam touched fists with the lads and walked towards her. Tipping his head to one side when he saw the fear in her eyes, he asked if everything was all right.

'Yeah, fine,' she murmured. 'I just thought they might be hassling you.'

'*Them?*' Liam glanced back. 'No way. We're cool.'

Hoping she hadn't offended him, she said, 'Sorry, I didn't realise you knew them. It's just that they're not exactly big on being friendly to strangers.'

Liam chuckled and said, 'Aw, you were worried about me. But there's no need, babe, I can handle myself. Anyway, they're not that bad when you get to know them. They might *think* they are, but they're smart enough to know who to mess with and who to leave alone.'

Sneaking a side glance at his handsome face as they set off towards the bus stop, Michelle wasn't sure she liked what he'd just said. It was almost as if he was implying that he was some sort of gangster – and that wasn't who she'd thought he was at all.

'You don't have to look at me like that,' Liam said quietly, making her jump because she hadn't realised that he'd seen her doing it. 'I'm not a thug, but I'm no idiot, either. It just makes life easier for me *and* them if we all know where we stand from the off – don't you think?'

Blushing when he looked straight at her, Michelle shrugged. 'I wouldn't know. I try not to get involved in things like that.'

'Which is precisely why I like you,' he said.

And it was true: he *did* like her – quite a lot as it happened. Having grown up with a master of deception, who could switch from despicable wife- and child-beater to caring husband and father in a nanosecond at the sniff of a uniform, Liam prided himself on being able to see through bullshit and suss people out on sight. He'd had Michelle down as a nice girl from the start, and after talking to her a few times over the phone he knew he'd been right. She was sweet-natured, intelligent, gorgeous, and classy. Like tonight, for example . . . he could tell she'd done something different to her hair, but unlike some of the other girls he'd dated who went over the top when they were going out she'd kept it subtle. Same with the lip gloss and the clothes – just that touch more special than usual, but still her.

When they reached the bus stop a few minutes later, Liam glanced down the road and, seeing no buses, sat down on the narrow plastic bench. He glanced up at Michelle when she stayed standing and patted the seat beside him.

Folding her arms, she perched at the other end of the bench.

'What's with the distance?' he teased. 'Scared I'm going to bite you?'

'No, course not.'

'Well, move up, then.'

Michelle held herself rigid and slid towards Liam, acutely conscious of their arms touching. She'd been dreaming about this moment for days but now that it was here she was terrified.

A taxi turned onto the road and drove slowly past. Amused when Michelle huddled even deeper into her jacket and followed the cab with her eyes, Liam said, 'What's up? Is someone after you?'

Taking a shaky breath when the car had passed with no sign of her mum having been inside it, Michelle shook her head.

'Well, you're not yourself,' Liam persisted. 'Is it me? Have I done something?'

Michelle bit her lip. She couldn't tell him that she was scared her mum would catch her, because then he'd think that she was a child who couldn't be trusted. So, instead, she lied, saying that she was just a bit tired.

'Must be all that school work you've been doing,' Liam said. 'And there was me thinking you were just making excuses not to come out with me.'

Smiling shyly, glad that he'd accepted her explanation, Michelle felt a sudden shift in his mood. Glancing round when he gazed past her, she saw a black Mercedes which had just driven past reversing back. The driver stopped at the kerb in front of them, slid the window down and jerked his head at Liam in a summoning gesture.

Liam made no move to get up and merely jerked his own head in reply.

'Don't play silly fuckers,' the man drawled, his dark eyes flicking casually over Michelle. 'You know if I was after you you'd already be on the floor with my foot up your arse. Get over here; I want a word.' Sucking on a spliff now, creating a halo of thick white smoke around his head, he added, 'In private.'

'Sorry about this, won't be a minute,' Liam murmured and strolled towards the car.

Davy Boyd, the Merc's driver, was his aunt's boyfriend, and Liam had no beef with him. But if there was going to be trouble over him walking out on her, Liam knew that he'd either have to stand and fight – in which case he'd end up dead. Or run – and he had too much pride to run from any man.

'Ruth's a bit upset with you,' Davy said when Liam squatted down beside the car.

'Not my problem,' Liam replied, shrugging.

'No, it's mine,' Davy retorted coolly. 'Seeing as I'm the fucker who's got to listen to her moaning about it. So be a good lad and get in the car, eh? I'll drop you round there and youse can sort it out.'

Liam sighed and shook his head. 'No offence, Davy, but she made her choice when she gave my old man my number, so there's nothing to sort.'

Davy peered silently back at him for several long moments, screwed up his mouth and shrugged. 'Oh, well, she can't say I didn't try. But if you're set on staying away, hurry up and get the rest of your gear, 'cos she's threatening to set fire to the whole fucking lot of it, and knowing her she'll do it when I'm in bed and fucking cremate me.'

Snorting softly, Liam said, ''Cos she's that upset about me leaving, eh?'

'She's a mad Irish bitch – what can I say?' Davy grinned. 'Anyhow, I didn't stop for that. I'm after Kedga. Seen anything of him?'

Shivering as warm air from the car circled his head, Liam said, 'Not lately. Why, what's up?'

'Alzheimer's,' Davy replied dryly. 'Keeps forgetting who he's dealing with. Walks off with two keys of my skunk, then thinks I'm gonna hang around like a pussy waiting for him to show up with my money.'

'I haven't seen him,' Liam said, standing up. 'But I'll keep an eye out for him, if you want.'

'Yeah, you do that,' Davy said and reached into his pocket. He took out his wallet, peeled some twenty-pound notes off the wad inside and held them out of the window. 'You've got my number; give us a bell when you find him, yeah?'

'Yeah, course,' Liam agreed, slipping his hands in his pockets. 'But I don't need paying for it.'

'Take it,' Davy insisted. 'I know you've been sleeping rough since you left Ruth's – I can smell you from here.'

It was a joke, and Liam took it as such. But he still didn't take the money.

'Honest, I don't need it. I've been kipping on my mate's couch, so I'm fine. And my social worker will be getting me into a hostel any day.'

Davy took another suck on his spliff and snorted softly. 'And that's what you want, is it? Do-gooders telling you what to do and checking on your every move?'

'Not really,' Liam admitted, hoping that Michelle couldn't hear any of this. He didn't want her to think he was a loser. 'But it's better than nothing. And I'm definitely not going back to Ruth's.'

'Can't say I blame you,' Davy chuckled. Then, peering up at him, he said, 'Actually, I might be able to help you out there.'

Liam kept his expression neutral but he was sure that whatever favour Davy was about to offer, there would be a catch. There usually was with guys like him.

'I've got a gaff for rent,' Davy went on. 'It's only a bedsit at the top of an old dump I've bought over in Longsight, but at least you'd be able to come and go without no fucker spying on you.' Grinning now, he nodded towards Michelle. 'Somewhere to take the honey for a bit of privacy.'

Liam smiled and shook his head. 'Cheers for the offer, but I think I'd best just go along with what the social worker's got planned for now. You know what they're like for asking questions, so you don't want them in your business as well.'

'Don't worry about me,' Davy countered unconcernedly. 'I bought the house to channel funds into something legit, so they can't touch me. You just tell them you found it on an ad in the newsagent's window, then sit back and leave them to set up your housing benefit and council tax. It'll be a doddle, and we'll both get what we want.'

Liam chewed his lip thoughtfully. He didn't really want to

be indebted to Davy, but he had to admit that the thought of having his own place was a damn sight more appealing than moving into a hostel. And at his age, with no job and no prospect of getting one any time soon that would earn him any kind of decent wage, a hostel was all he was likely to get.

'What about Ruth?' he asked.

'Nowt to do with her,' Davy assured him. 'Anyhow, I'll be passing by there in a minute, so why don't you come and take a look. I'll get you signed up and you can move straight in. And you'd be doing me a favour, 'cos I could do with having someone I trust in there to keep an eye on the place.'

'Why, is it empty?' Liam asked, thinking that he'd be acting as some kind of on-site security guard.

'I wish,' Davy snorted. 'The twats at the auction house conveniently forgot to mention the sitting tenants when I bought it. It's full of fuckin' junkies and alkies, and they've got *rights* so I can't turf 'em out.' Flashing a sly grin at the man sitting beside him now, he added, 'Not legally, anyhow, but we're working on it – eh, Faz?'

Nodding, the other man tapped his watch to remind Davy of the time.

Davy turned back to Liam and said, 'We've got to get moving. So what you saying?'

'I'm definitely interested,' Liam told him, glancing back at Michelle who was still huddled on the bench, looking thoroughly miserable now. 'But do you mind if we leave it till tomorrow? Only I'm supposed to be taking her to the pictures.'

'Nah, I've already got someone else in mind for it, so it's either tonight or forget it,' Davy told him. Then, grinning lewdly, he added, 'Bring her. There's a bed, so I'm sure she won't mind missing out on a film.'

Liam told him to wait a minute and went back to Michelle to explain the situation.

She cast a surreptitious glance at the men in the Merc when he asked if she wanted to come. They looked really sinister, and she *really* didn't want to be stuck in a car with them. Anyway, there was no telling how long it would take for them to get to wherever they were going and do what they had to do, and if she didn't get home before her mum and Mia there would be hell to pay.

'I'd best not,' she said. 'But you go. You need the flat.'

'Sure you don't mind?'

'Not at all.'

'And you'll be all right getting home by yourself?' When she nodded and said she'd be fine, Liam went to kiss her. Stopping himself in time, because he sensed that she would probably jump a mile, he shrugged and said, 'I'll give you a ring, then.'

Michelle watched as he got into the car. When they set off, she hunched her shoulders and headed for home, arriving just as the phone started ringing.

'Just making sure everything's all right,' her mum said when she answered – trying, Michelle thought, not to sound like she was checking up on her. 'You sound a bit breathless. What you been up to?'

'I was on the loo, so I had to run downstairs,' Michelle lied.

'Where's your mate?' her mum asked. 'I hope you haven't left her on her own and let her start rooting around?'

'She couldn't make it,' Michelle told her. 'Something came up, so we're just going to go over that coursework at school tomorrow instead.'

Sounding just the tiniest bit guilty now for having doubted her, her mum said, 'Okay, well, try not to fall asleep before we get back. Sammy's giving Mia some extra coaching so we might be a bit late, and I don't want to have to bang the door down.'

Michelle promised that she'd be up and put the phone down. She gazed at herself in the mirror. Despite the running, her cheeks were deathly pale, which made the freckles Mia despised stand out more sharply than usual. And the hood of her jacket had flattened her carefully straightened hair to her head, so she looked a fright. But at least she hadn't been caught.

This time.

6

Mia's first audition came and went without success.

Knowing her as well as he now did, and recognising a real diva in the making, Sammy had tried to prepare her for that eventuality, explaining that it was practically unheard of for *any* model to land the very first job they went after. He'd told her that she mustn't be disappointed when she didn't get it, because there would be plenty more opportunities in the future.

And Mia had listened to his advice with her usual dutifully attentive expression, although she hadn't believed for one second that she would fail. In fact, she'd been utterly convinced that she would prove to be the exception to the rule and land her first job with no trouble whatsoever. So when Sammy had told her the bad news, she'd been devastated. And it hadn't helped that the successful girl was also one of Sammy's clients – and a complete dog, in Mia's opinion.

But she'd hidden her disappointment well, too proud to allow anyone to see how badly it had affected her in case they thought that she was jealous of the dog – or something ridiculous like that.

Impressed that she'd handled her first rejection with such maturity – because he'd secretly dreaded that she would go into a major strop – Sammy had quickly lined up several more auditions, the last of which was for a TV ad along the same lines as Jonathon's teen-razor affair, only this time it concerned a girl waxing her legs for the first time because she was going on her first date.

He'd actually been a bit wary of putting her forward for that one, wondering if it might be too soon. But she'd insisted that she wanted a shot at it, and he'd let himself be persuaded.

Mia was ecstatic about the Wonder Wax audition, and the bitter taste of failure from the previous audition that was still so sour in her mouth just made her all the more determined to bag it. Using the intermediate audition as rehearsals, she soaked up the photographers' directions like a sponge and scrutinised the other models in order to analyse later what the ones who ultimately landed the jobs had over her.

Now, with just a week to go, she already felt like a pro, and so she really didn't appreciate her mum and Sammy constantly giving her last-minute tips. She never listened to a word her mum said, anyway, but Sammy was really getting on her nerves.

'The trick,' he was telling her on the phone now, for the third time today – and it wasn't even lunchtime yet! – 'is to *be*, not to *pose*. It's not enough to just sit there prettily tearing strips off your legs. You've got to really *believe* that you're going on your first date. So, *do* you believe it?'

'*Yes!*' Mia snapped, just about managing not to swear at him. 'Now will you just leave me alone and let me get on with it, or I'll be a nervous wreck by the time it happens!'

Much as Kim admired Sammy and understood what he was trying to do, even *she* thought that he was going a bit over the top with his constant coaching. Seeing how much it was pissing Mia off now, and fearing that her stubborn daughter might dig her heels in and make a mess of the audition if he didn't ease up on her, she snatched the phone out of Mia's hand.

'Hello, Sammy, it's Kim. Sorry she's so tetchy, but she's been practising all day and she's a bit kna— *tired*. Anyway,

I've been cracking the whip, so you don't have to worry.' She paused to listen to what the agent was saying and grimaced at Mia, mouthing, *'He's coming round.'*

'I'm not here!' Mia hissed. 'I'm going out!'

Gesturing to her to be quiet, Kim said, 'Yes, I'll be in, but I'm afraid Mia probably won't be by then. She's, er . . . she's got an appointment with the dentist.'

'He's doing my head in,' Mia complained when her mum came off the phone. 'Can't we find another agent?'

'No, we can't,' Kim told her firmly. 'I know he's a bit full-on, but it's only because he wants you to do well, so stop being disrespectful. He's a good man.'

'*Ew*,' Mia grunted, giving her mother a dirty look. 'You're starting to sound like you fancy him.'

'Don't be daft,' Kim scoffed, turning her head to hide the pinkness of her cheeks. 'Anyhow, hadn't you best get going? He said he'd only be ten minutes. He's dropping off some pictures he wants you to look through.'

'I'm not going anywhere,' Mia said, flopping down onto the couch and flicking through the TV channels.

'I thought you didn't want to see him?'

'I won't have to. You can go out to the car and get the pictures.'

'I can't not invite him in when he's gone to all that trouble; I'll have to at least offer him a coffee. Anyhow, you're the one who said you were going out.'

'I didn't mean it,' Mia grumbled. 'Anyway, there's nowhere *to* go. Laura's at school, and I'm not talking to anyone else.'

'Why don't you go into town, then?'

'Gonna give me some money?' Glancing up, Mia gave Kim a sly grin. 'Otherwise I might have to stay in and tell him you were lying about the dentist.'

'You're a cheeky cow, you,' Kim snorted. But she still reached for her purse – just as Mia had known that she would.

Shoving a twenty-pound note into her daughter's hand, she said, 'There, now piss off. And don't be telling Shell, 'cos I haven't got anything for her.'

'Like I ever talk to her anyway,' Mia drawled, snatching the money and skipping out into the hall. She slipped Michelle's jacket on because her own was upstairs and she couldn't be bothered going for it, shouted goodbye and let herself out of the house.

She walked around to the bus stop only to see a bus pulling away and leaned against the plexiglas shelter to wait for the next one. A few minutes later, daydreaming about the house she was going to buy far away from this dump when she landed the TV job and became mega-rich and famous, she glanced around irritably when the sound of an unfamiliar ringtone disturbed her thoughts. She frowned when she saw that there was nobody around, then patted her pockets when she realised the sound was coming from inside the jacket.

Pulling Michelle's phone out, her eyebrows puckered when she saw a love-heart symbol on the screen.

'Hello?' she said, answering. 'Who's that?'

'Me,' Liam said, chuckling softly. 'Don't tell me you've forgotten me already.'

'Depends who "me" is,' Mia replied dryly. 'You're not the only lad in the world, you know.'

'Liam,' he told her, a hint of uncertainty in his voice now. 'Sorry, I just thought you'd recognise my voice. But it's been a while since I called, so I guess I shouldn't have assumed.'

'Why haven't you called?' Mia asked, amused that Liam actually believed he was talking to Michelle.

'Long story,' he said. 'Remember when we were supposed to be going out that night, but then I got offered that flat so we couldn't go? Well, I took it, but I lost my phone while I was moving in so I couldn't call to let you know. And you haven't been at the library any of the times I've been round your way since, and I don't know your address, so . . .' Pausing, he exhaled loudly as if out of breath. 'Anyway, I've found my phone now – *obviously*. And you're the first person I've called. So, am I forgiven?'

Mia was smiling slyly. This was obviously the lad from the library and, as she'd suspected, he and Michelle were a lot more than friends – although why a man with as sexy a voice as this was interested in *her*, God only knew.

'I'll think about it,' she purred flirtatiously, wondering how best to turn this to her advantage. 'But you'll have an awful lot of making up to do first.'

'*Sorry?*' Liam murmured, taken aback because that was the last thing he'd have expected her to say. 'This *is* Michelle, isn't it? I haven't dialled the wrong number by mistake?'

For a split second it crossed Mia's mind to tell him that he *had* got the wrong number, because then he would probably delete it and wouldn't be able to get through to Michelle again. But she decided it would be much more fun to string him along for a while instead – maybe arrange to meet up with him. And if he was nice looking enough, maybe she would keep him for herself.

'It's the right number,' she told him now. 'Why, who did you think you were talking to?'

'I'm not sure,' he admitted, still sounding a little wary. 'Your voice sounds different.'

Remembering that Michelle had a wimpy little voice, Mia coughed for effect. Then, easily mimicking her, she said, 'Sorry, I've had a bit of a cold. Is that better?'

Sounding relieved, Liam said, 'Well, at least I can tell it's you now. You had me worried for a minute there. Anyway, I was wondering if we could try again – as long as you're up to it, obviously.'

'Try what again?'

'The *date*,' he said patiently. 'That film's still showing at

Cineworld if you fancy it. Or we could just meet up and go for a burger or something, if you've gone off the idea.'

'I haven't gone off it,' Mia assured him, thinking that she'd quite fancy a night out at the pictures – depending what was on, of course: knowing Michelle, it was probably one of those deathly boring foreign films. 'But can you remind me what we were going to see, only my head's been all over the place with this cold.'

'*Sceptic*,' Liam told her, amused that she'd forgotten the title of the film that *she*'d chosen. 'But if you're not that fussed,' he added hopefully, 'there's a new *Terminator* supposed to be coming out soon, so we could wait for that?'

'Oh, *yeah*!' Mia blurted out approvingly. 'I definitely want to see that.'

Laughing now, Liam said, 'God, you're a mystery, you are. There's no *way* I'd have thought you'd go for something like that – not with the stuff you like reading.'

'Yes, well, I'm not boring all the time,' Mia replied, taking a sly pop at Michelle.

'You're *never* boring,' he corrected her, unable to see the funny look his words brought to her face as she wondered how *anyone* could fail to see that her sister had all the personality of a bowl of cold porridge. 'Anyway, I'll go along with whatever you want to do. I know how busy you've been with your school work, so I wouldn't want to tire you out, or anything.'

Inhaling deeply when his soft teasing voice sent a little shiver through her body, Mia decided that she had to meet him. And what better time than now, with Michelle safely out of the way at school?

'I'm, er, not doing anything right now,' she told him. 'So we could meet up, if you want?'

'Really?' He sounded pleasantly surprised. 'Well, yeah, that would be great. I've just got a couple of things to do, but

I should be free in about half an hour. Should I meet you at the library?'

'No!' Mia blurted out. She didn't want him to come round to this area in case somebody saw them together and told him who she really was. 'Sorry,' she added quickly. 'I just . . . well, I was wondering if I could come to you instead, only I'd love to see the flat.'

Liam was surprised. He hadn't even thought to ask her round, because he'd assumed that she would think it too soon to be alone with him like that. And while he wouldn't have thought twice with any other girl, he'd already decided that he would let Michelle set the pace of this relationship.

'Are you sure?' he asked. 'I mean, you're welcome any time, but I don't want you to feel uncomfortable.'

'I'm sure,' Mia told him, taking his words as confirmation of what she'd already suspected: that prissy little Michelle hadn't got down and dirty with him yet.

Liam disconnected the call when he'd given Mia the address and whistled as he did a quick tidy-up to make sure there were no dirty underpants or socks lying around, or unwashed cups and plates stuffed under the bed or chair.

He liked living on his own, loved being able to chill out without his aunt constantly moaning at him to turn the music down or the lights off, or to get off the PlayStation because it was burning too much electric. Here he could do *what* he liked *when* he liked. And when he locked the door at the end of the day, nobody could barge in and disturb him unless he invited them to.

As it happened, his only invited-in visitors so far had been male – although it wasn't for lack of trying on the part of the two girls who lived in the room below. One or other of them was always at the door, using any excuse to talk to him and try to wheedle their way in. But Liam genuinely wasn't interested, because all he'd been doing lately was think about Michelle. He didn't know *what* it was about her, but she'd really got under his skin. And now she wanted to come round.

But only to see the flat, he reminded himself.

After straightening the bedspread and emptying the ashtray he lit a cigarette and stood at the window, praying that the guys who Davy was sending round would get here before she did, because he really didn't want her to know what he'd been doing for the past few weeks.

This was exactly why he hadn't wanted to be indebted to Davy, because he'd known that he would end up paying more than rent in the long run. Finding Kedga hadn't been a problem, because it was no skin off Liam's nose to ask a few questions and pass the info along. He had no idea what Davy had done with that information, and he didn't *want* to know, because he figured that Kedga and the other dealers who Davy had subsequently asked him to track down had brought whatever they'd got onto their own heads when they'd decided to bite the hand that supplied them. But he had to admit that the money Davy had paid him for those few jobs had come in really handy while he was getting his benefits sorted.

So, no, Liam hadn't minded those jobs. But he should have known that it wouldn't stop at that, and his involvement with Davy had quickly progressed from keeping an eye on the house to holding packages for his boys to collect. And having made the mistake of agreeing to do it once, it became a given, so now he was Davy's in-house distribution service – and there was no way of getting out of it without losing his home.

Still, the money was good, so Liam was able to save for a deposit to put down on a flat somewhere else. He had nothing against Davy; he was grateful to him for letting him stay, and he actually quite liked him now that they'd had a chance to get to know each other without Ruth's involvement. But he'd always vowed that he would never work to line any man's pockets but his own. And he might not yet have decided what line of business he wanted to go into, but whatever it was, he was determined that it would be legit.

Mia's taxi had just pulled up at the gap where the gate was supposed to stand. Getting out, she peered up at the house. It was a three-storey building, with rotten woodwork around every grimy window, huge chunks of plaster missing off the walls, and dark holes where tiles had fallen off or into the sagging roof. Still, she reminded herself; picking a careful course through the weeds and debris as she made her way up the path, it wasn't the outside she'd come to see – it was the man with the sexy Irish accent on the inside.

The front door was standing open, revealing a long, wide hallway which had a filthy tiled floor and peeling age-browned wallpaper. Mia wrinkled her nose at the stench of eons of neglect as she made her way to the stairs. An old man in stained jeans and jumper and with a huge pock-marked nose peered out at her from a doorway to her left. She scuttled past and rushed up to the first floor.

A red-headed girl was standing in another doorway up there, wearing a shirt tied in a knot beneath her braless breasts, and short shorts with the button undone to reveal flesh and a flash of red panties. She narrowed her eyes when Mia walked up the landing heading for the stairs to the top floor and darted swiftly into her path.

'Where do you think you're going?'

'What's it got to do with you?'

'I live here, *actually*. And you can't just walk in off the street and wander about. It's not an office block.'

'Piss off,' Mia sneered, taking her hands out of her pockets to push the bitch out of the way.

Before it could get to that, Liam appeared at the top of

the stairs and called down, 'It's all right, Gina. She's here to see me.'

When the girl stepped aside, Mia grinned victoriously and gave her a sly dig in the ribs as she passed.

Liam was waiting on the small square landing outside his attic bedsit. Mia's eyes widened when she got her first good look at his face and she just about managed not to let her mouth fall open. With his shiny black hair, long black eyelashes, and eyes as green as emeralds, he was absolutely drop-dead gorgeous. And that smile . . .

Oh, God! she complained to herself silently. *How the hell has Michelle managed to get this guy to fancy a minger like her? There's got to be something wrong with him mentally.*

'You were quick,' Liam said, waving her into his room and closing the door behind her.

'I got a taxi,' Mia told him, trying not to stare.

'You look great,' he commented, smiling down at her. 'But then, you always do. Anyway, take your coat off and make yourself comfortable. I've got coffee and tea, if you want one?'

Mia murmured, 'Coffee, please.' Her eyebrows puckered in disbelief. How could he think that Michelle always looked great? He really *must* be mental. Either that, or blind.

She slipped her jacket off, hung it over the back of the only chair and looked around as he filled the kettle at the minuscule sink. 'It's a nice room.'

'Yeah, it's all right, isn't it?' Liam agreed, reaching into the cupboard for cups. 'Not the greatest-looking house in the world from the outside, I know, but it's only temporary, so I'm happy with it. Sugar?'

Pleased that he didn't even know something as basic as whether his precious girlfriend took sugar in her coffee, Mia nodded. 'Two, please.' Then she sat down on his bed, crossed her legs and leaned back on her elbows. 'So how come it's taken you so long to invite me round?'

Taken aback by her uncharacteristic forwardness, Liam shrugged. 'To be honest, I didn't think you'd *want* to come just yet.'

'How would you know if you didn't ask?' Mia replied, biting her lip sexily.

Liam gave her a funny look. He hadn't seen her for weeks, and now that she was here there was something different about her. She'd never spoken to him like this before, for starters. But it wasn't just that. She was wearing mascara, which was unusual; and she'd covered her cute freckles with foundation. And unlike the touch of gloss she'd had on her lips when they'd been going out that night, she was wearing actual lipstick today. None of which could have been for his benefit, because there was no way she could have known that he'd phone her at that exact moment. So had her previous shyness been an act? he wondered. And was this more forward self the real her?

'Why are you looking at me like that?' Mia asked, still giving him the sexy eye.

'I don't know,' Liam murmured warily. 'You just don't seem the same.'

'In a good way or a bad way?' she pressed, confident that he would say *good*, because she was way more exciting than mousy little Michelle.

'I don't know,' he said again, not sure he liked this new flirtatious side to her. Not that he hadn't thought about how good it would be if she'd drop her barriers and let him get closer, because he had; but this just didn't seem genuine somehow.

Mia gave herself a mental kick when it occurred to her that she needed to *act* like Michelle as well as talk like her if she were to convince Liam that she *was* her. She quickly sat up and rearranged her face into the soppy pitiful-cum-guilty expression that Michelle always had on hers.

'I'm sorry. I was just so pleased when you rang, I guess I got a bit . . .' Trailing off, she shrugged. 'Well, you know – carried away.'

Liam immediately felt guilty. She'd obviously been making an effort, and now he'd embarrassed her.

'No, *I'm* sorry,' he said, passing her cup to her. 'And I *would* have asked you round earlier, only, like I said, I lost my phone. But you're here now – and it's really good to see you.'

Murmuring, 'You too,' Mia gazed at the floor as if she was too shy to look at him.

In actuality, she wasn't sure what to make of him. The lads she went out with were never this slow at coming on to her. If they fancied her, they made it blatantly obvious – and if she fancied them in return, she did the same. But this guy seemed to genuinely like her – or rather, to like *Michelle*. And that didn't make any sense, because he was way too good-looking for *her* – and surprisingly cool. But then, he looked older than most of the lads Mia knew; and he had an air of quiet masculinity which she found really, really sexy. She'd thought Darren was sophisticated, but he was an absolute child in comparison – and nowhere near as fit. In fact, Sandra Bishop was welcome to that muppet because, right now, Mia really wouldn't care if she never saw him again.

This had started out as a bit of fun to piss Michelle off, but now that she'd seen Liam up close Mia wanted him – and, whatever it took, she was determined to get him. But she would have to tread carefully, because she sensed that he was one of those rare ones who didn't believe in messing around behind their girlfriend's back. If she was to stand any chance of stealing him, she had to do it before he realised his mistake. Then it would be game over, because there was no way Michelle could compete with her. But first, she had to find a way of getting him to stop being so damn respectful.

And make sure that he couldn't get hold of Michelle again.

'By the way,' she said, looking up at him again. 'I've got a new number, so you'd best change the one you've got in your phone.'

Just as he'd finished replacing the old number with the new, a knock came at the door and Gina's voice sing-songed through the wood.

'Sorry to disturb you, hon, but I just caught a bloke walking in downstairs; reckons Davy sent him round. I thought I'd best check with you before I let him come up.'

Mia's eyes flashed jealously at the girl's familiar tone, but she forced herself to smile when Liam said, 'Sorry about this . . . won't be a minute.'

He put his cup down and rushed towards the door, pausing only to snatch a plastic bag from under the coffee table.

Mia caught the briefest glimpse of the tart from downstairs and directed an eyeful of venom at her before the door closed. How *dare* she call Liam 'hon'! Well, she'd best not show her face up here again when Mia was his girl, or she'd be dead!

'He's in the lobby,' Gina purred, grazing her breasts against Liam's chest as he squeezed past her. 'By the way,' she added, in a low tone, 'Kelly's nipped out for an hour, so if you want to pop down for a drink after you've finished we can have a chat – or whatever.'

'Nah, I'd best get straight back,' Liam muttered, and waved her ahead of him down the stairs. Walking on when she pushed open her own door, he went down to the hall, aware that she was still following him with her eyes.

He passed the bag over to the man who was waiting, took the money and quickly counted it before showing him out – all without a word. Then, after kicking the front door shut, he marched into the room to his right and snapped the light on.

'Oi!' he barked, glaring at the man who was huddled in a corner with a syringe full of blood in his filthy hand. 'Quit leaving the fucking door open. That's the third time this week someone's walked in off the street, and if it happens again I'm gonna knock you out!'

It infuriated Liam that the downstairs tenants couldn't remember a simple thing like keeping the front door shut. With it open, the police could walk in at any time and catch him unawares but at least he'd have a couple of minutes to get rid of the shit while they were trying to kick it down if it was locked.

Still, he wouldn't be here for much longer. He just hoped he managed to get out before Michelle realised that he wasn't the decent bloke she thought he was. And, judging by her reaction when he'd told her that he was mates with the gang at the library that time, and the look on her face when she'd seen Davy and his guys in the Mercedes, it was a safe bet that she wouldn't want to know him if she found out that he was just like them.

And he'd have been right – if it had been Michelle sitting in his room. But, fortunately for him, it was Mia. And she'd been doing a bit of snooping while he'd been downstairs.

Back on the bed when he came back in, she smiled. 'Everything all right?'

Liam slipped the money he'd just taken into a drawer and ran his hands through his hair. 'Yeah, sorry about that. My landlord left some paperwork for one of his new tenants, and they've just been to pick it up.'

'Oh, I see,' Mia murmured, smiling secretively to herself. She'd already taken a look in the other plastic bag that was under the table, so she knew *exactly* what he'd just been doing.

But he obviously didn't want prissy little Michelle to know, so she would play along for a while. But now that she knew what she was dealing with, she was more determined than ever to get him.

'I hope you don't think I was snooping,' she said innocently. 'But I couldn't help noticing *that*.' She pointed at a bottle of Jack Daniels that was standing on the ledge behind the TV. 'And I was just wondering what it tastes like?'

Glancing at it, Liam shrugged. 'Don't really know how to describe it. It's kind of got a taste of its own.'

Disappointed that he hadn't offered her some, Mia was forced to ask if she could try it. 'Just a sip,' she added quickly. 'To see what it's like.'

Liam was surprised, because he wouldn't have had her down as the type to drink. But then, he supposed he didn't really know her as well as he'd thought. Telling her to help herself now, he said, 'Be careful, though, 'cos it's strong.'

He excused himself again when the sound of the doorbell drifted up to them, grabbed the second bag and left her alone. Mia found a glass and poured a shot of the liquor into it. She drank it down in one, then waved her hand in front of her face when her eyes immediately began to water. She'd had JD that night at Stu's house but it had been mixed with Coke then, so it hadn't been half as potent. Still, it tasted nice, so she helped herself to another measure, thinking that it wouldn't hurt to be a little bit tipsy when Liam came back. Lads *always* liked it when girls got drunk, because it made it easier for them to get down to business. And, *boy*, did she want Liam to hurry up and get started. Just looking at him was driving her crazy.

When he came back a few minutes later, Liam found her coughing as if she was choking. 'God, are you all right?' he asked, rushing to pat her on the back. 'How much did you have?'

'Just a drop,' she croaked, indicating with her finger where she'd topped the glass up to.

'That's loads,' he gasped, peering down at her amusedly. 'Christ, you'll be wasted in a minute.'

Saying, 'Oops,' Mia bit her lip and gave a sheepish little smile. 'I see what you meant about it having a taste of its own. It's nice, isn't it?'

'If you like that kind of thing,' Liam chuckled. 'But I'm surprised *you* do.'

Mia pursed her lips and glanced up at him through her lashes. 'I might be shy, but that doesn't mean I don't want to have fun,' she told him, her voice soft and whispery. 'It just takes a while before I trust anyone enough to relax around them.'

'And you're relaxed with me?' Liam asked, squatting down beside her.

'Yeah, course,' she murmured, remembering to dip her gaze as if she were blushing – like Michelle probably would be in this situation. Not that Miss Goody Two-Shoes ever *would* be in this situation – more fool her.

'Glad to hear it,' Liam said softly, stroking her hair back from her face so that he could look into her eyes. 'Because you know how much I like you, don't you?'

Mia nodded quickly and parted her lips in anticipation of the kiss she felt sure was about to come.

Liam winked at her and stood up. 'I think I'd best get you another coffee to sober you up. But I've got to make a quick call first, so just give me a minute.' He took his mobile out of his pocket and headed towards the door. 'Bad signal in here.'

Mia tutted when he went out onto the landing. She reached for the bottle and took another swig straight from it. And then another. Sir Galahad was obviously intent on doing the honourable thing, so it looked like she was going to have to force things along. And if Liam liked Michelle as much as he claimed to, then he wasn't likely to knock her back and risk upsetting her again.

Lying down on his bed by the time he came back into the room, she purred, 'I think you were right about it being too strong. I'm feeling a bit . . .' She paused, and wafted her hand in a circle above her head. Then, patting the bed beside her, she said, 'Sit down, you're making the room look all wobbly.'

Liam laughed softly, then came and perched beside her. 'God, I should never have told you to help yourself. You're not feeling sick, are you?'

Mia shook her head and stared straight into his beautiful eyes. Then, breathing in deeply, as if this was one of the hardest things she'd ever done, she whispered, 'Will you please stop talking and kiss me.'

A frown flickered across Liam's brow and he said, 'I can't. Not like this. Sober up first, then if you still want to . . .'

'I will,' Mia insisted. 'I *do*. But if you make me get sober, I won't have the nerve to say it again.'

'Aw, don't do this to me,' Liam groaned when she reached for his hand and looped her fingers through his. 'You're making this really hard for me.'

'I hope so,' Mia murmured as she pulled him down and touched her lips to his.

Using his last reserves of resistance, Liam held himself back and gazed down at her. 'Are you really sure you want to do this?'

Whispering, 'Sshhh,' Mia closed her eyes, raised one hand to hold the back of his head and forced his mouth back down onto hers.

7

Kim was in a flap when the day of the TV ad audition came around, but Mia seemed totally unfazed. She'd been acting strangely for days, and Kim had actually begun to suspect that her daughter might be on drugs as she floated around the house with a dreamy smile on her lips. She'd confronted her about it the other night, but Mia had laughed it off, insisting that she was just happy with life. Without evidence to dispute this, Kim had been forced to give her the benefit of the doubt. But she prayed that this new-found happiness didn't distract Mia from putting maximum effort into her audition. And given that Mia hadn't mentioned it in the past few days, when normally it was *all* she talked about, that was a genuine concern. Added to which, Mia wasn't exactly in a rush to get ready now, even though she knew that Sammy would soon be here to pick them up.

In a desperate attempt to get Mia motivated without sending her into a strop today, Kim had run a bath for her and had ironed all the new clothes she'd bought for the occasion. Handing these to her when she came out of the bathroom, she told her to hurry up and get dressed.

'Yeah, yeah,' Mia said, and floated into her bedroom. Then, moments later, she yelled, '*Mum* . . . where's that deodorant you said you were going to get for me? And the tights? You know I can't wear this dress without tights!'

'Oh, damn, I forgot!' Kim muttered. Then, flapping her

hand at Michelle, she said, 'Put that book down and run to the shops. And hurry up!'

Reluctantly getting up to do as she was told, Michelle slipped her jacket on. She didn't object to running errands, but she *did* object to being disturbed in the middle of revision. That was why she'd been given the day off school, after all; which might not mean anything to her mum and Mia, considering they seemed to have forgotten the importance of exams, but it meant a lot to her.

At the shops, she got what she'd been sent for and was about to head home when a taxi pulled up in front of her.

'Hey, what you doing round here?' Liam asked, jumping out with a big smile on his face. 'I thought you were too busy to see me today. Why didn't you ring if you knew your plans had changed? You knew I'd want to see you.'

Confused, Michelle looked behind her, sure that he must be talking to someone else. But when, seconds later, he walked right up to her and tried to kiss her, she drew her head back, gasping, 'What are you *doing*?'

Liam gave her a quizzical smile and said, 'What's up with you? Don't tell me you've gone off me already?'

Heart beating so fast that she could barely breathe, Michelle prised his hands from around her waist and took two staggering steps back. Of course she hadn't gone off him: he was all she'd been thinking about for weeks. But he hadn't rung her in all that time, and she'd come to the conclusion that he wasn't interested any more, so she couldn't understand why he was acting like this now.

When he saw how pale she was, the smile slid from Liam's lips and a confused frown creased his brow. 'What's going on, Michelle? And don't say nothing, 'cos you were fine last night.'

'I don't know what you're talking about,' she murmured. 'I haven't seen you since we were supposed to go to the cinema that night.'

'Don't be daft,' Liam snorted, wondering if she was seriously trying to pretend that they hadn't seen each other since then. His eyes narrowed when it occurred to him that she might be guarding her words because she was being watched. He glanced around quickly, but there was nobody else in sight.

'You're confusing me,' he said.

'*You*'re confused?' Michelle blurted out. 'All I know is I haven't seen you in weeks, but you're standing here saying that you saw me last night. But I went straight home from school yesterday and didn't go out again.'

'Michelle, this is *me* you're talking to,' Liam said quietly. 'And I don't know why you're being like this, but whatever's going on in your head, it's not fair, because I haven't done anything you didn't want me to. You should have told me if you didn't like it, and I would have stopped – you *know* that.'

'Why are you saying this?' Michelle croaked as tears of confusion stung her eyes.

'Because it's *true*,' Liam replied adamantly. 'Christ, I can't believe you're doing this. You're making me feel like I forced myself on you, or something.'

A light suddenly flared to life in Michelle's head. Feeling faint, she took a deep breath. 'Are you saying that we . . .' She paused, and licked her lips before forcing the words out. 'Are you saying we *slept* together?'

'You know we did,' Liam shot back. 'But if you're regretting it, don't worry. I don't need telling twice.'

'It wasn't me,' Michelle told him, clenching her teeth as she felt her heart breaking to pieces.

'No, course it wasn't,' Liam retorted sarcastically. 'Must have been your twin sister, eh?'

'Yes,' she hissed. 'That's exactly who it must have been. But don't take *my* word for it – ask *her*.'

A scowl of frustration on his brow, Liam clenched his fists

as Michelle turned and ran away. He couldn't believe she'd just lied like that. After everything that had happened between them, and all the conversations that they'd had before it got physical, he'd really thought she was different from all the other girls he'd been out with. But whatever game she was playing, he deserved an explanation.

Michelle had already turned the corner of her road by the time Liam caught up with her. Still shaking, when he tried to get in front of her she swerved around him and continued on to her gate.

Right behind her, Liam followed her up the path. 'I'm not going away until you've told me what's going on, Michelle. And if I have to sit out here all night, I will.'

As she tried to slot her key into the lock, Michelle jerked her arm away when Liam reached out and put his hand over hers.

'Just tell me what I've done wrong,' he pleaded. 'Please, Michelle, I *love* you.'

'No, you don't!' she cried, the tears streaming down her cheeks now.

'Oh, baby, don't cry,' he said, reaching for her.

'Don't *touch* me!' she yelled, pushing him away. 'Just leave me alone!'

Hearing the commotion, Kim came storming out. When she saw Michelle in tears, she glared at Liam. 'What the hell have you done to her? And who the bloody hell *are* you, anyway?'

Liam didn't answer. He was too busy staring at Mia who had just come down the stairs and was standing behind her mother, a sheepish smile on her lips.

Turning to see what he was looking at, Michelle's eyes flashed with hatred as she glared at her sister's mock-guilty expression. 'You *bitch*,' she gasped. 'You did it on purpose, didn't you?'

'Did what?' Kim asked, looking from one to the other of them.

'Ask *her*,' Michelle blurted out, still staring at Mia. 'Well, go on, then – *tell* her. Tell us *all*.'

'Oh, chill out,' Mia drawled, as if Michelle was blowing it totally out of proportion. 'You'd have found out sooner or later, so what's the big deal?'

'Will someone *please* tell me what's going on?' Kim demanded, hands on hips now.

'Don't worry about it. I'll deal with this,' Mia said as she stepped outside and reached for Liam's arm.

'What the hell's going on?' Liam asked, looking from Mia to Michelle as if he didn't know which was the real one.

Gazing tearfully back at him and seeing the confusion in his eyes, Michelle said, 'It's not your fault, it's *hers*. She's my sister, in case you hadn't guessed, and she's obviously been lying to you. But it's too late to change anything. The damage is done.'

'Oh, stop being so dramatic,' Mia said scornfully. 'You must have known it wouldn't have worked out. Anyway, he's with me now, so you might as well go and crawl back into your boring books with your imaginary lovers – 'cos that's the only kind of man *you*'re ever going to get!'

Michelle bit her lip, fled up the stairs and locked herself in the bathroom.

'Oi!' Kim bellowed, thundering after her. 'Where's that deodorant and them tights I sent you for? Sammy's gonna be here any minute!'

Taking advantage of the fact that they were alone, Mia turned back to Liam and sighed. 'See what a lucky escape you had?'

'God, you're sick!' Liam hissed, stepping back towards the gate. 'That's your *sister*. How could you do something like that to her?'

'Oh, don't be mad at me,' Mia wheedled as she followed

him out onto the pavement. 'I was going to tell you, but I didn't get much chance 'cos we're always too busy kissing when I see you. But it's out now, so at least we won't have to sneak around any more.'

'What are you *talking* about?' Liam gasped, unable to believe that she seemed to think that they could carry on as normal. 'I don't even *know* you.'

'My name's Mia,' she told him, lowering her voice and glancing back to make sure that her mum wasn't at the door again, listening. 'And you *do* know me – a damn sight better than you ever knew *her*. I'm your girlfriend, remember?'

'*Girlfriend?*' Liam repeated incredulously, looking at Mia as if she was stark staring mad. 'I didn't even know you *existed*. I thought you were *Michelle*.'

'Yeah, well, now you know I'm not,' Mia purred. 'And we're in love, so nothing has to change.'

'Get off me,' Liam snarled when she reached for his hand, disgusted that she'd tricked him into bed and now seemed to think that they could just carry on as if they'd done nothing wrong.

Scared that she might have really blown it when he walked away, Mia was about to run after him when Sammy pulled up in his car.

'How's my star today?' Sammy asked, rolling the window down and beaming out at her. 'All set to knock their socks off?'

Mia sighed as Liam disappeared from view around the corner. He might be pissed off with her for the way she'd gone about it, but he couldn't deny that their relationship was already a thousand times better than anything he could ever have expected to have with Michelle. He was bound to forgive Mia when he'd cooled off. Especially if she got this job today, because only a fool would turn down the chance to have a TV star for a girlfriend. And Liam was no fool, she was sure of that.

She turned to Sammy and gave him a broad smile. 'Yeah, I'm ready. Just give me a minute to get my tights on.'

Still raging about what had just happened, Liam marched across the busy Princess Parkway without even pausing to check if it was safe to do so. But if he'd thought things were bad enough already, they were about to get a whole lot worse.

Snapping his head round when a car screeched to a halt just as he was about to step up onto the facing kerb, he glared at the driver.

'Fuckin' idiot!' the man yelled, baring an angry mouthful of gold and slamming both hands down on the steering wheel. 'Don't just fuckin' stand there – *MOVE!*'

Sitting in the back, Kedga Bull dipped his head to see who was causing the obstruction. When he recognised Liam his eyes glinted. He shoved his door open and leapt out.

'Yo!' he growled, stepping up to him so that they were nose to nose. 'I've been lookin' for you, you grass!'

'You'd best back the fuck up,' Liam warned him quietly, feeling the strange air of calmness which always descended over him before a storm erupted.

A flicker of uncertainty flashed through Kedga's dark eyes as he peered down into Liam's cold green ones. Davy Boyd and his boys had kicked the shit out of him after this cunt had worded them up where to find him, and he'd been laid up in the MRI for two days as a result. When, after getting out, he'd learnt that Liam had been behind it, he'd started gunning for him. But when no one had seen him around Kedga had figured that he must be lying low somewhere – shitting himself at the prospect of this confrontation. Now, though, he was standing here with this bad-ass look in his eyes, and that made Kedga nervous.

Kedga shook his gun down from his sleeve into his hand

as cars swerved around them and held it at groin level so that only Liam could see it.

'Get in the car, motherfucker.'

'That meant to scare me?' Liam sneered, already tensing for action.

'Nah, it's meant to tell you you're about to die,' Kedga told him. 'Now, move it!'

Swerving instinctively when Kedga tried to grab him, Liam brought his elbow down hard on the back of the man's neck. Stamping on his hand, he snatched up the gun and pointed it at Kedga's mates when they jumped out of the car – just as a police van came barrelling around the corner and screeched to a halt.

'It's all right,' he yelled, holding up his hands. 'It's not mine . . . I wasn't gonna use it!'

The cops were on him in a flash, some battering him down to the ground with their batons while others tried to blind him with pepper spray.

8

'You clever girl!' Sammy announced excitedly. 'You've only gone and got it!'

'Don't lie!' Mia squealed, clutching the phone to her ear. It had been two weeks since the audition and she'd been chewing her nails to the knuckle ever since, waiting for this call – desperately trying not to listen to the little voice of doubt that had been nagging away at her.

'Believe me, I'm as shocked as you are,' Sammy told her, chuckling throatily. 'But I assure you it's no lie. You are the Wonder Wax girl! They called just five minutes ago, and it's confirmed!'

Screaming down his ear, Mia started bouncing around the room like a lunatic. Kim snatched the phone off her before she ripped it clean out of the wall, cleared her throat, and said, 'Hello, Sammy, it's me. I take it we've got it, then?'

'We most certainly have, my dear!' Sammy said, and waited until she'd got all her own excited squeals out of the way. Then, giving her all the details – insisting that she wrote them down and repeated them back to him – he said, 'Make sure you're both ready at seven o'clock sharp tonight, because I'm taking you out for a celebratory dinner. This is the start of a wonderful career,' he went on, sounding every bit as thrilled as Kim and Mia were. 'And I've got to admit that there have been times when I've wondered if that young lady really had it in her. But, by God, she's done me proud – *and* you, I'm sure.'

'Oh, she certainly has,' Kim replied, beaming at Mia who had stopped bouncing and was grinning at her like a Cheshire cat, waiting to hear what was being said. 'Anyway, thanks for letting us know. And we'll see you tonight.'

'It *is* definite, isn't it?' Mia asked as soon as she put the phone down. 'Not just him *thinking* I've got it?'

'It's definite,' Kim assured her gleefully. 'They're faxing the contract over later tonight, so we've to go into the office in the morning to sign. And Sammy's taking us out to dinner to celebrate.'

'Oh my *God*!' Mia squawked, rushing over and hugging her tightly. 'I can't believe it!'

'Neither can I!' Kim exclaimed, jumping up and down with her now. Then, facing the wall that divided their house from Pam's, she yelled at the top of her voice, '*MY DAUGHTER'S GOING TO BE A TV STAR, SO STICK THAT IN YOUR PIPE AND SMOKE IT, YOU FAT COW!*'

On her way downstairs, Michelle heard what her mum said and guessed that Mia had clinched the TV ad. But if she was expecting congratulations, she'd be in for a long wait, because Michelle still hadn't forgiven her for what had happened with Liam. And it didn't make any difference that it had turned out exactly as she'd always feared it would, because Mia still shouldn't have done it.

Sidestepping her mum and Mia now, Michelle headed for the kitchen.

Tutting when she saw the morose look on her other daughter's face, Kim said, 'Come on, Shell, don't you think it's time to let bygones be bygones? Your sister's about to be a star, so get a smile on your gob and try telling her how well she's done!'

'Oh, leave her,' Mia sniped, giving Michelle a dirty look. 'It's her problem if she can't accept the truth.'

'*Truth?*' Michelle repeated incredulously. 'That's not what you told Liam, is it?'

'Yeah, well, he knows the truth *now*,' Mia retorted smugly. 'And he's still glad he's with me and not you, so there's no point pining over him, 'cos you've got no chance.'

It was a lie, but she wasn't about to admit that to Michelle. In fact, Mia hadn't seen or heard from Liam since he'd followed Michelle to the house that day, and his phone had been switched off whenever she'd tried to ring him. But that didn't mean that he wasn't *ever* going to come round again. They had shared something really special, and Mia was still convinced that when he'd calmed down and thought things through he'd realise that she'd been forced to do it that way and would forgive her. But until then, she had plenty to keep her occupied – like getting ready to be famous!

'When are we doing the shoot?' she asked her mum now, turning her back on Michelle.

'Three weeks,' Kim said, picking up the paper that she'd written it all down on to check. 'Fifteenth of April, ten a.m. start.'

Glancing at Michelle now and seeing the tears glistening in her eyes, Kim felt sorry for her. It was never easy losing a boyfriend, but she must have known that she couldn't compete with Mia. Although it had to be said that Mia really shouldn't have gone there. But, like they said, all was fair in love and war; and the boy was obviously serious about Mia if he was still seeing her after everything that had happened, so Michelle really ought to accept that she'd lost and let it go.

'Fancy coming out to dinner with us tonight, love?' Kim asked her now, hoping to raise her spirits a little. 'I'm sure Sammy won't mind an extra one at the table.'

'*Mum!*' Mia protested. 'This is *my* night, and I don't want *her* there! Anyway, she hasn't been interested in helping me so far, so why should she get to join in with the good bits?'

'Oh, don't worry, I don't want anything of yours,' Michelle told her.

'Good!' Mia retorted frostily. ''Cos you're not getting it.'

'Come on, girls,' Kim cajoled, looking from one to the other of them as they locked hostile stares. 'You're sisters, so don't you think it's about time you stopped all this fighting and arguing and made an effort to get along?'

'*No!*' they both said in unison. Then, sneering, Mia added, 'I hate her, and I wish you'd never had her! All she's ever done is creep around in my shadow like a stupid little dog.'

Sneering right back, Michelle said, 'Believe me, I wouldn't want to be *anything* like you.'

'Just as well,' Mia spat. ''Cos you could *never* be as good as me. You're way too ugly and thick, and that's exactly why Liam chose *me*!'

'More fool him,' Michelle murmured as she turned and marched back up to their room.

The atmosphere in the Delaney household plummeted to new depths over the next two weeks. Michelle and Mia still weren't speaking, and vicious eye-daggers flew between them whenever their paths crossed – which made Kim feel like she was stuck in the middle of one of those crazy Chinese films where everyone did somersaults and tried to kill each other. Giving up on trying to persuade the girls to make their peace, she took to keeping them apart as much as possible instead. Which, fortunately, wasn't too difficult: Michelle was at school during the day and spent the evenings reading in her room, while Mia had plenty to keep her occupied preparing for the impending TV shoot.

And it all seemed to be going so well – until the morning of the shoot, when everything suddenly turned upside down and inside out.

* * *

'Please tell me this is just nerves, and you haven't gone and caught a bug,' Kim groaned, her face a mask of worry when Mia limped out of the bathroom clutching at her stomach. 'That's the third time you've puked this morning.'

Turning a sickly shade of green, Mia turned right around and rushed back into the bathroom.

'It must have been something you had from the chippy last night,' Kim called through the door, grimacing at the sound of noisy vomiting. 'Then again, you had the same as me, and I'm all right. Did you get anything after that? You didn't eat any of that tuna I left in the fridge, did you? Only I thought it tasted a bit funny when I made that butty the other day.'

Her face pale and sweaty as she emerged once more from the bathroom, Mia shook her head. 'I didn't even finish my chips,' she murmured, sounding close to tears. 'I already felt a bit sick when you brought them in.'

'Well, it must be *some*thing,' Kim said, peering down at her worriedly. 'You didn't sneak any of my booze, did you?'

'*No*,' Mia croaked, feeling queasy again at the thought of it.

'You've only got three and a bit hours until the shoot,' Kim moaned, glancing at her watch. 'How about I run out and pick up some Alka Seltzer? That might settle you.'

Mia ran back into the bathroom and retched, but this time nothing came up. As she stood in the doorway watching her daughter heaving, Kim's jaw dropped as realisation hit home.

'Oh, my God, you're pregnant!'

'No, I'm not.'

'Well, when was your last period?'

'I don't know,' Mia admitted, looking up forlornly from where she was bent over the toilet.

'You stupid little *cow*!' Kim cried, wringing her hands. 'Oh God, what are we going to do *now*? You won't be able to film if you can't stop throwing up. And look at the state of you – you're *green*! They'll take one look at you and kick you out. And what the hell am I supposed to tell *Sammy*? Oh, Mia, how could you do this to me at a time like this?'

'It's not my fault,' Mia protested self-pityingly.

'Well, it sure as hell ain't *mine*,' Kim shot back lighting a cigarette, her hands shaking. 'And whose is it, anyway? And for God's sake don't tell me it's that lad you stole off Michelle. That'd be all we need.'

'He's the only one I've slept with,' Mia said, lying.

In actual fact, she had no idea if it was Liam's or Darren's because she didn't know how far on she was. But, given a choice, she'd go for Liam every time. She still hadn't seen him since the confrontation between Michelle, herself and him and he hadn't returned any of her calls. But now she had a legitimate excuse to go round to his flat and *make* him talk to her.

'Well, you can't have it, and that's a fact,' Kim said firmly, oblivious to the fanciful thoughts that were buzzing around her daughter's head. 'I'm going to ring the doctor and set up an appointment for an abortion.'

'*No!*' Mia crossed her arms protectively over her belly. 'I want to keep it.'

'Don't be ridiculous,' Kim replied flatly. 'How do you think you'll get work as a model when you're covered in stretch marks?'

'Kate Moss is a mum, and she still gets work.'

'Yeah, but she can afford all them fancy creams to make sure her skin doesn't turn to shit.' Kim sucked deeply on her cigarette and shook her head. 'No, it's impossible. Even if we wanted it, we can't afford it. And anyhow, there's no room in here for a baby.'

'We can apply to the council for a bigger house.'

'Oh, grow up!' Kim snapped. 'Look at Fat Slag next door.

She's brought up four kids in a two-bed, and she's been on the transfer list since the *first* one was born. And they've all left home now apart from speccy Graham, so she'll be stuck there for life. And so will we, 'cos there's only one way we're ever going to escape this hell-hole, and that's by you making a success of yourself and buying us out – which you *won't* be doing if you go saddling us with a baby! So, no, I'm sorry love, but it's got to go – whether you like it or not. And for God's sake don't tell Shell.'

Overcome by another rush of nausea, Mia staggered back to the toilet and dry-heaved for several minutes. Gasping for air when it had stopped, she said, 'How long will this last?'

'If you're anything like me, till you give birth,' Kim told her grimly. 'And then you'll have the pain of *that* – and believe me, it's the worst pain you'll ever feel in your entire life, 'cos it feels like you're being torn apart.' Sighing, she gazed down at her daughter's head. 'Sorry, love, but I'm calling the doctor. It's the only way.'

Too weak to fight, Mia got back up onto her knees and retched again.

Kim thundered down the stairs and was just about to reach for the phone when it started to ring. Snatching it up, all set to tell whoever it was that she couldn't talk right now, she grimaced when she heard Sammy's chirpy voice.

'Oh, good, you're up,' he said. 'I was only ringing to make sure you hadn't overslept. I'll be there to pick you up at nine forty-five on the dot, so make sure you're ready. And how's Mia this morning? Raring to go?'

'Er, yeah, she's good,' Kim lied, biting her lip.

'Good, good . . . well, I'll see you soon, then.'

Hanging up when he did, Kim cursed under her breath. What was she supposed to do now? She couldn't let Mia go ahead with the shoot in this condition. Even if Mia *wanted* to do it, she wouldn't be able to if she was throwing up every two minutes.

Michelle!

The thought popped into her head out of nowhere, but as soon as it came she seized it with both hands.

Of course! It was obvious – Michelle could take Mia's place and nobody would be any the wiser. They might have to do some extra work on her make-up to get her looking as good as her sister, but they were professionals so that shouldn't be a problem. And, while Sammy knew that Mia had a sister, no one had ever mentioned that they were twins, so he wouldn't ask any questions. It was the solution to everything!

'*Michelle* . . .' Kim yelled, rushing back upstairs. Bursting into the bedroom just as Michelle was laying her uniform out on the bed, she said, 'Put that away – you won't be going to school today . . .'

Sitting in the living room a few minutes later Michelle's face was a mask of horror as she listened to her mum's plan.

'I can't!' she gasped when Kim stopped speaking at last. 'I'm nowhere near as pretty as Mia. They'll know I'm not her as soon as they look at me.'

'*I'm* the only one who can really tell you apart just by looking at you,' Kim insisted, ignoring the *you've-got-to-be-kidding!* look that Mia aimed her way at the suggestion than anyone could possibly mistake Michelle for her. 'Anyway, you've *got* to do it. She's got a stomach bug.'

'I can't,' Michelle repeated lamely. 'I don't know the first thing about being a model.'

'Neither did Mia when she started out, but look at her now. Anyway, I'll tell you exactly what to do. And I'll be there the whole time, so I can give you tips if I think you're not getting it.'

'It's a stupid idea,' Mia piped up sulkily, lying on the couch with a quilt over her legs and a cup of milky tea beside her on the floor. 'She's an idiot – she'll cock it up.'

'Well, it's the only choice we've got,' Kim snapped at her. 'And you've only got yourself to blame,' she added, giving Mia a hooded look.

'I can't do it,' Michelle murmured, standing up and heading for the door. 'And she doesn't want me to, anyway.'

Glaring at Mia when Michelle had gone, Kim hissed, 'Are you trying to ruin everything? You'd better say something – and be quick about it, or you can forget everything you've been working towards.'

Mia really didn't want to have to beg, but she knew that her mum was right: Michelle was her only hope of salvaging her career. So, swallowing her pride, she took a deep breath and called, 'Michelle . . . can you come back a minute.' Adding, '*Please*,' when her mum gave her another glare, she clutched the quilt to her breast and sighed deeply.

'What?' Michelle said coolly, coming back and staring down at her.

As she met her sister's cold gaze, Mia's chin began to wobble and tears filled her eyes. In a small, guilt-ridden voice, she said, 'I'm so sorry, Shell, and I know I don't deserve it after everything that's happened, but if you'll just do this one thing for me I promise I'll make it up to you.'

Narrowing her own eyes with suspicion, Michelle pursed her lips but said nothing.

'I know you're still mad at me,' Mia went on, swiping at a tear that was trickling slowly down her cheek. 'And I don't blame you, 'cos I've been well out of order. But it's at times like this that you realise that blood really *is* thicker than water. Mum's been telling me that for ages, but I've been too stubborn to listen. But I get it now, honest. And I'll totally understand if you tell me to get lost, but I really, really need you to save this job for me, so I'm *begging* you to forgive me and help me.'

As she gazed down at her sister a flicker of uncertainty flashed through Michelle's eyes. Mia looked and sounded genuinely contrite, but was she really, or was it just a ploy to get what she wanted?

Rushing to the couch when Mia began to sob, Kim pulled her into her arms and gave Michelle an imploring look. 'Please, love, you can see how upset she is, and you know it won't have been easy for her to say what she just said, so give her a chance. And if you won't do it for her, do it for *me*.'

Michelle sighed and shrugged. 'Okay, I'll try. But don't blame me if I mess it up, because I won't have a clue what I'm doing.'

'Oh, thank you, love,' Kim gushed. Then, squeezing Mia, she crooned, 'See, everything's going to be all right now. Michelle will take your place until you're back on your feet.'

Mia nodded, then sniffed loudly. 'Thanks, Shell, you're a star.'

Moved by the emotion in her sister's voice, Michelle blinked back her own tears and went upstairs to get ready. It had been a terrible few weeks, but maybe this was what they needed to put things back on track between them. It still hurt that Mia had stolen Liam from her, but it was done, so there was no point holding on to the resentment. Anyway, this wasn't just about her and Mia, it was about their mum as well, and they had to pull together for all their sakes.

Downstairs, Mia had stopped crying as abruptly as she'd started. Giving her mum a slow smile, she whispered, 'And the Oscar for best actress goes to . . . *Mia Delaney!* Yay . . . !'

When Mia mimicked the sound of an audience cheering, Kim tutted and stood up, saying quietly, 'You'll be the bloody death of me with your play-acting, you. And you'd best not let madam hear you,' she added warningly. '*Or* find out why you're really sick. She only agreed to stand in for you because she thinks you're sorry for what you did, but if she finds out you're taking the piss she'll go right off on one.'

'Nah, she well thinks I meant it,' Mia scoffed unconcernedly.

'I hope so,' Kim muttered. 'Anyway, I'll ring the doctor and set up that appointment. And you hurry up and drink that brew before it gets cold.'

'Oh, did you have to?' Mia moaned, feeling nauseous again at the mention of the tepid tea she'd been trying to ignore.

'For God's sake get yourself upstairs if you're going to be sick,' Kim snapped, jumping back in fear of Mia projectile vomiting on her freshly washed clothes. 'And stay up there till we've gone, 'cos I don't want Sammy catching sight of you when he gets here and putting two and two together.'

Mia tossed the quilt aside, threw a hand across her mouth and dashed upstairs. Hammering on the bathroom door, just about remembering that she was supposed to have turned a new leaf, she said, 'Sorry, Shell, I just need the loo. I won't be a minute.'

Michelle came straight out and stood aside as Mia rushed past her and dived over the toilet. Feeling sorry for her sister as she retched and heaved, she asked, 'Is it food poisoning?'

'I think so,' Mia grunted, wiping her mouth. Then, smiling weakly up at Michelle, she said, 'Must be my punishment for doing the dirty on you, eh?'

'Don't say that,' Michelle murmured, feeling guilty now. 'We all make mistakes, but at least we're friends again.'

Friends? Mia thought scathingly, still smiling as she hobbled back to bed. *As if!* Let's see if Michelle still wanted to be friends when she realised that not only were Mia and Liam back together but they were about to have a baby.

Sammy arrived to collect Kim and Michelle a short time later. After watching from the bedroom window until the car had turned out of the street, Mia got dressed and rushed out to catch the bus to Liam's flat. She swallowed down the nausea that kept washing over her and made her way up the path. Knocking on the door, she stepped back so that Liam would see her if he looked out. But there was no sign of movement.

Getting no answer after several more attempts, she sat down on the filthy top step and hugged her knees to her chest. She was freezing, and she wished she could stop feeling so sick, but she supposed it was a small price to pay to get Liam back. And she would, she was sure, because he was far too decent to turn his back on his own child.

She jerked her head up at the sound of approaching footsteps and was disappointed to see Gina, the tart.

'What do you want?' Gina asked, giving Mia a dirty look as she climbed the steps.

'Liam, *obviously*,' Mia retorted icily, standing up and dusting herself down.

'Really?' Gina's eyebrows rose.

Folding her arms, Mia said, 'Well, I wouldn't be here for anyone else, would I?'

'So you were just going to sit and wait till he gets home, were you?'

'Not that it's any of your business, but yeah. 'Cos that's what you do when your boyfriend asks you to come round. He's just been held up, that's all.'

'I see,' Gina murmured, slotting her key into the lock. 'Well, you'll have a bloody long wait. Unless they've decided to let him out four years early – which I kind of doubt.'

'Yeah, whatever,' Mia snorted disbelievingly. 'We all know you're jealous 'cos you want him and I've got him, love, but that's a bit pathetic, don't you think?'

'I take it he didn't bother letting you know he'd been arrested?' Gina asked, pushing the door open.

Mia's eyes narrowed. 'You're lying,' she hissed, even though her instincts were beginning to tell her otherwise.

Sighing, Gina stepped aside and waved her through into the hall. 'Go and see for yourself if you don't believe me.'

Legs shaking, Mia raced up the stairs. When she reached the small landing she breathed in deeply, absorbing the lingering scents of Liam that she hadn't smelled in so long.

'Go in,' Gina said, coming up behind her. 'It's not locked.'

Mia pushed the door open and walked into the bedsit. It was even colder in here than it had been outside, and the undisturbed air smelled stale and damp.

'The police made a right mess,' Gina said wistfully, staying back in the doorway. 'I'm not sure what they thought they were going to find, but they ripped everything to shreds looking for it. I tried to tidy up in case he came back that night, but he didn't. And then it went to court, and he got four years.' She sighed, and gave Mia a sad little smile. 'Davy reckons he's going to keep the room for him, but I doubt he'll want to come back here. He'll probably go back to Ireland and make a fresh start.'

As the reality of the situation overcame her, Mia felt sick again and darted into the tiny bathroom. Watching from the doorway as she threw up, Gina said, 'Oh, God, you're not pregnant, are you? What are you going to do?'

'I don't know,' Mia admitted, reaching for Liam's towel which was still hanging on the small nail he'd hammered into the wall beside the sink. Clutching it to her face, she drank in the scent of him as the tears began to fall.

'Look, I know we never really hit it off,' Gina said softly. 'But I know how you're feeling, 'cos I miss him, too. Why don't you come down to my room and I'll make you a brew? It might make you feel better.'

Mia shook her head and said, 'Thanks, but I think I'd best just go.'

Worried about her, because she looked absolutely terrible, Gina said, 'Is it definitely his – the baby, I mean?'

Nodding, Mia bit her lip and swiped at the tears.

Gina peered at her thoughtfully for several moments, then reached into her bag and took out a photograph. 'You'd best take this.'

Mia's heart lurched when she glanced at it. It was a picture of Liam and a woman. He only looked about twelve, but he'd been every bit as handsome even then, with the same dark hair and twinkly green eyes that Mia had fallen for. And the woman was obviously his mother, because she looked so much like him.

'I know it's not very clear,' Gina said. 'But if the baby's not going to see its daddy for a few years, at least it'll know what he looks like.'

Mia thanked her, took the photograph and rushed out of the room. Galloping down the stairs, tears still streaming from her eyes, she brushed past the old drunk who was just coming in and ran outside.

The dream was shattered. She couldn't have this baby knowing that she'd be raising it alone for four years. Even if Liam didn't go back to Ireland as soon as he came out of jail, as Gina seemed to think he might, there was no guarantee that Mia would be able to find him. And even if she did, he might not believe that the child was his – and if it looked like Darren, he definitely wouldn't.

There was nothing else for it: she would have to get rid of the baby and concentrate on her career. At least that way she could offer Liam something to come back to.

Slotting the precious picture into her pocket, Mia cast one last glance back at the house, then set off for home.

Sammy's belly rumbled with anxiety as he hovered in the shadows at the back of the studio. Embarrassed, he glanced at Kim who was standing beside him, but she was too busy chewing on her nails to notice.

He didn't usually accompany his models to their jobs, but he'd taken a bit of a shine to Mia since she and her mum had burst into his life with their outrageously high expectations and he'd dedicated a lot of personal time and energy into sanding off her rough edges. Lately he'd begun to see flashes of the diamond that he believed lay hidden beneath the prickly exterior, but something was wrong today. She hadn't been her usual confident self when he'd picked them up this morning and she'd barely spoken a word on the drive here. If it had been anyone else he'd have assumed that it was just nerves, but Mia tended to get more fidgety and talkative when she was nervous, not less. It could just be that this was a TV shoot, he supposed, and she'd suddenly realised that her face would soon be seen in thousands of homes around the country. But, whatever it was, she'd best snap out of it, because she looked like a rabbit caught in headlights right now.

On set, Michelle's heart was racing so fast that she feared it might explode. The make-up women had taken ages to do her face and hair, but when they had told her to strip off so that they could paint the liquid foundation onto her body, she'd nearly died. They'd said that she'd best get used to it; that stripping off was part and parcel of being a model. But she wasn't a model, and had no intention of trying to become one, so it was just that step too far for her.

Glad that the women had eventually compromised and let her keep her bra and panties on for the foundation application, she'd slipped into the tiny vest top and matching knicker-like shorts and made her way out onto the set. Perched on the edge of a freezing cold bathtub now, in a three-sided mock-up of a bathroom, with what seemed like a warehouse full of people milling about in the shadows on the other side of the blazing lights and whirring cameras, Michelle was shaking from head to toe.

A woman with a set of headphones wrapped around her neck rushed over and thrust the wax into her hand, and then someone called for quiet on set.

Breaking out in goose bumps when a deathly hush fell over the room and what felt like a thousand hidden eyes bored into her, Michelle jumped as if she'd been electrocuted when a man barked 'Action!'

Desperately trying to copy the way she'd seen Mia rehearsing it, she raised her jelly-like leg and placed her foot on the lip of the bathtub. Then, trying to look as if she was dreaming about her upcoming date, she brought the applicator down onto her shin . . .

9

'I'm *so* sorry,' Kim mumbled, barely able to look Sammy in the eye as they made their way to his car. 'I think she might be coming down with a touch of flu, because she didn't sleep too well last night. I probably should have told you when you rang to ask how she was this morning, but I honestly thought she'd be okay.'

'Don't worry about it,' Sammy told her, helping Michelle onto the back seat. 'These things happen. No point beating yourself up about it.'

'No, but I still should have said something,' Kim repeated guiltily, climbing into the front seat. 'What'll happen now?' she asked when Sammy got in beside her.

'They'll contact their second choice and reschedule.'

'Can't they just wait until she's feeling better and let her try again?'

Sammy shook his head regretfully and glanced at Michelle in the rear-view mirror as he started the engine. He'd had his doubts about sending her for a TV job so early in her career but she'd convinced him that she could handle it and, given her quite staggering levels of self-confidence, he'd believed her. But that confidence had absolutely deserted her today, and right now she looked crushed.

'I don't think that's very fair,' Kim complained, tugging her seat belt on. 'It's not her fault she's ill. And I'm sure it wouldn't kill them to wait a week.'

'It would cost them thousands,' Sammy told her. 'They have to book the studio space in advance, and then there's the crew, and all the equipment . . .' Looking over his shoulder now as he manoeuvred the car out of the space, he added, 'Anyway, it's probably a good thing that we can use the illness as an excuse. TV is a lot more intense than magazine and catalogue shoots, and I really thought she was ready, but she's obviously not.'

'She *is*,' Kim insisted. 'Honestly, I've been watching how hard she's been working at it, and she's *more* than ready.'

'Kim, she's not,' Sammy said quietly. 'You saw her. She was absolutely terrified.'

'It was just a bad day,' Kim argued. '*Please* don't say you're going to set her back; she'll be devastated if I have to tell her that.'

Sammy thought it was odd that she was talking as if Mia wasn't in the car and hadn't already heard. He said, 'Look, we'll talk about it when she's feeling better.'

'But you're not going to drop her?' Kim asked, voicing her biggest fear.

'Why on earth would I do that?' Sammy replied without hesitation. 'I'm not saying she's no good, I'm just saying she's probably not ready for TV yet. No one becomes a star without suffering. Fainting, hysteria, tantrums – you name it, they all fall apart at some time or other. But the ones who go on to make it are the ones who learn from those early mistakes.' Glancing at Michelle now, he added, 'And Mia's a fast learner – aren't you, dear?'

Sammy pulled up outside their house ten minutes later and switched off the engine. Afraid that Mia might be downstairs and unaware that they were back, Kim unclipped her seat belt and jumped out, telling him not to trouble himself seeing them in.

Glancing at his watch, Sammy said, 'Well, actually, I'm a

bit early for a meeting, so I thought I might stick around for a coffee – if that's okay?'

Muttering that of course it was, Kim rushed in ahead of him. Relieved that Mia wasn't around, she told Sammy to make himself comfortable and put the kettle on. Then, telling Michelle to lie on the couch, she used the excuse that she was getting her a quilt to go upstairs and warn Mia not to come down.

Mia was curled up in bed. She hadn't been back from Liam's place for long and had cried herself to sleep. She groaned when her mum shook her, and said, 'Leave me alone.'

'We're back,' Kim told her in a whisper. 'You feeling any better?'

'A bit,' Mia lied, peering up at her mother through puffy eyes. 'What happened? Did she do all right? Did Sammy suss that anything was wrong?'

'He didn't suspect anything,' Kim told her, biting her lip before adding, 'But no, she didn't do all right.'

'What do you mean?' Mia jerked upright. 'What did she do?'

'Fainted,' Kim told her. 'But there's no point flying off the handle about it 'cos Sammy reckons it happens to the best of them. And it was her first time, don't forget.'

'I don't *care*!' Mia spat, her eyes flashing with fury. 'I *knew* she'd screw it up! I bet she did it on purpose to get back at me over Liam. I said we shouldn't let her do it. Why don't you ever listen to me?'

'*You*'re the one who should have listened,' Kim reminded her firmly. 'I told you to stay away from boys, but you had to go and flaming well sleep with one and get yourself up the duff, so if you want to blame anyone for this, blame yourself.'

'I'm not the one who sabotaged my job,' Mia pointed out angrily. 'And if she's messed up my career, I'll *kill* her.'

Kim told her to stop being so melodramatic and dragged the quilt down off Michelle's bed. 'And don't even think about coming down and picking a fight with her,' she warned, ''cos Sammy's stopping for a coffee. I'll let you know when the coast is clear.'

Mia glared at the door when she'd gone, flopped back against her pillow and beat the quilt with her fists. She should have known better than to agree to let the bitch take her place, because there was no way she could have got away with it. As she'd just proved, she didn't have the looks *or* the intelligence to pull it off. She was a stupid, pig-ugly *idiot*!

Downstairs, Kim had given Sammy his coffee and was now playing the concerned mother, fussing over Michelle, asking if she was comfortable, if she needed anything.

Sammy told her to sit down and have a smoke to calm herself, then said, 'Everything will be all right, I promise you. Mia's worked really hard over these last few weeks, and if we can just sand a bit more of that sassiness off her I reckon she'll be doing very well before too long.'

'*Sassiness?*' Kim gazed back at him through a cloud of cigarette smoke.

'Attitude,' Sammy explained, looking directly at Michelle now as he elaborated. 'Obviously you're not well today, but when you're back on your feet I want you to carry on being as polite as you were today, because that goes a long way with these people. You're usually huffing and puffing when someone gives you directions but you really behaved yourself today, and I was proud of you. Don't you agree, Kim?'

'Absolutely,' Kim said without hesitation, although, secretly, she couldn't help but think that Mia's *sassiness* – as Sammy had called it – was exactly what would eventually propel her into the spotlight. Never mind all this behaving-yourself stuff; controversy was what made you stand out from the crowd – Naomi Campbell was a living, breathing example of that.

Sammy's phone began to ring. As he pulled it out of his pocket, he rolled his eyes when he saw that it was the producer from the shoot they had just left. Excusing himself, because he was sure that he was about to get an earful for landing them with such an unsuitable model, he went into the kitchen to take the call in private.

Kim pursed her lips when he'd gone and glared at Michelle. 'You've done it this time, lady. Mia's after your flaming blood up there 'cos she thinks you did it on purpose to spite her. And if that's true you won't just have *her* to deal with, you'll have me an' all, 'cos you know damn well I was relying on that money.'

'I'm sorry,' Michelle murmured plaintively. 'I didn't mean to mess it up.'

'I'm not sure I believe you,' Kim retorted coldly. 'I know you're upset about that lad, but it's not her fault he wanted her instead of you, so there was no need to get back at her like this.'

Before Michelle could say anything to defend herself, Sammy came back into the room.

'Well, that was interesting,' he said, looking a little shell-shocked. 'That was the producer, ringing to make sure that Mia's all right. Apparently he's been having a look at the stills from before she conked out, and he thinks they show promise.'

'So, what are you saying?' Kim shuffled to the edge of her seat. 'Are they going to let her have another go at it?'

'No, they're not going that far,' Sammy told her. 'But he says he'd be happy to consider her for future projects – when she's got a bit more experience under her belt. Because – and I quote – the vulnerability in her eyes really stands out on film. Unfortunately, it's translating as terror at the moment, which isn't quite the image they want to portray with this particular product.'

He turned to Michelle and lowered his head, causing his

chins to treble. 'This is exactly what I meant about attitude. Anyone can have a pretty face, but it's a rare one who manages to capture you with their eyes. And if you're one of the few, then by *God* you'd better remember what was going on inside your head today, because that was what made you stand out and get noticed.'

Kim felt as if her heart would burst with pride when she showed Sammy out a short time later. She'd known that Mia was a star from the day she was born, and now the people who mattered were beginning to recognise it too.

It didn't even cross her mind that the comments had been made about Michelle and not about Mia.

In the same way that it also didn't cross Mia's mind when she flew down the stairs as soon as Sammy's car had driven away. She gave it to Michelle with both barrels, accusing her of trying to wreck her career out of spite, and warning her to stay the hell away from her from now on.

'You're just lucky your little trick didn't work,' she finished nastily. 'Because if you'd have destroyed my career you'd better believe I'd have destroyed *you*! And don't even think about talking to me again, because you're *dead* as far as I'm concerned.'

Heavy with guilt, Michelle took Mia's onslaught without a word. She'd warned them that she wouldn't be able to pull it off but they had begged her to try, and now they thought she'd screwed it up on purpose. Which she hadn't. At least, she didn't *think* so. But maybe they were right, and she really was that horrible jealous girl they had always said she was. And if she was and Liam had seen it in her, it was no wonder he'd chosen Mia over her.

Michelle got up when Mia turned her back, indicating that she'd said all she had to say, and wandered upstairs to wash off the heavy make-up.

'We need to sort out what we're going to do,' Kim whispered

when she'd gone. 'There's no worries about Sammy, because he's happy to carry on working with us. But he reckons you need more experience before he puts you forward for any more TV stuff.'

'That's not fair!' Mia protested. 'I worked really hard to get that job, and it wasn't me who screwed it up.'

'*We* know that,' Kim agreed. 'But they don't think you're ready, so you're just going to have to work even harder to prove them wrong. But first, I'm going to book you in for an appointment to get *that* sorted.' She nodded at Mia's stomach. 'But not a word to her upstairs, 'cos I'm booking you in under her name – make sure it doesn't bounce back when you're famous and ruin your reputation. So don't be forgetting when you get there and giving them your real name – okay?'

'Fine by me,' Mia said, thinking that it would serve Michelle right if *everybody* found out, because her sister would be horrified for anyone to think that she'd had *sex*, never mind an abortion.

PART TWO

10

The association hall was noisy as prisoners rushed to finish off discussions, arguments and games of pool and cards in the five remaining minutes before lock-up.

Sitting in the corner, from where he could keep an eye on both staircases for approaching officers, Liam leaned casually down as if tying his laces and slid the last neatly folded ten-pound note into the concealed slit on the underside of his trainer tongue.

He glanced up and sucked his teeth with irritation when a new prisoner sidled up and asked for a lay-on. The guy was shaking, and scratching like he had fleas, and if the officer who was on duty tonight spotted them talking he'd put two and two together and have Liam dragged off for an intimate search.

Hissing 'Get the fuck away from me' Liam got up and strolled down to his cell, glad that his cellmate wasn't back yet because that gave him time to stash his cash and the few small wraps of smack he had left without the other man seeing his hiding place.

Without a sniffer dog, the officers would never have found it. But Liam wasn't taking any chances with Darren Mitchell. In on an eighteen-monther for beating up his girlfriend, Darren had done all the usual posturing when he'd first arrived, reeling off his lengthy list of crimes to prove what a big bad fucker he'd been on the outside. His list included all the usual: fighting, stealing cars, shoplifting, drug dealing, et cetera . . . But it was Darren's seeming passion for burglary that had put Liam on his guard. To hear Darren talk about the places that he and his brother Pete had robbed between them, it was a wonder they hadn't been in prison a thousand times already. But the fact that they had perfected their art to such an extent that they had never been caught was a great source of pride to him.

That, and the fact that he had shagged Mia Delaney – the semi-famous model whose picture was plastered all over the wall beside his bed.

Like most of the dickheads who were banged up in here, Darren had his fair share of family snaps and nudes. But all those shots of Mia grinning out from the pages of the teen magazines that somebody kept sending in for Darren really wound Liam up. He had to admit – grudgingly – that she photographed well, but he still hated her.

It was two years now since he'd followed Michelle home to discover that Mia had tricked him into bed by posing as her sister, and the memory still rankled, because *she* was the reason he was serving time right now. If it hadn't been for her, he and Kedga Bull might never have crossed paths, and he wouldn't have been caught in possession of that gun – *or* the coke that the police had found in his bedsit after his arrest. He blamed Mia for all of that, and it didn't make it any easier to know that she was swanning about out there doing all right for herself.

In hindsight, Liam knew that he should have spotted the difference between them, because there was a coldness in Mia's eyes that he'd never seen in Michelle's – a greedy, grasping glint that spoke volumes about the personality which lay behind them.

But there was no sense in winding himself up about it, so, for the most part, he didn't think about it. And as much as he resented the presence of those pictures in his space, he knew that Darren would only put up new ones if he tore them down so he left them alone – refusing to give Darren the satisfaction of thinking that he'd vandalised them out of envy. And, given that Darren was already convinced that every man in here was jealous of him for being Mia's first, that was exactly what he *would* think.

Liam had better things to focus his mental energy on – like keeping his head down and building up his money so that he'd be properly set up when he got out.

He didn't particularly like dealing smack, but he'd decided early on that there was no point letting morals get in the way of his future plans. There were hundreds of hungry junkies in here, and loads of pushers only too happy to peddle them inferior shit – more often than not contaminated by *actual* faeces, coming in as it did via their girlfriends' arses or babies' nappies. But Liam had the edge over them all because he had Davy smuggling decent gear in for him, courtesy of a screw that Davy was paying.

Grateful that Liam had taken the full rap for the coke when lesser men would have thought nothing of grassing him up, Davy had vowed to see him right while he was inside. And so far he'd been true to his word. But if he thought he was buying Liam for life he was wrong, because Liam had no intention of continuing their agreement after he got out.

If he'd been determined to stay legit before, he was even more so now. He hated being locked up; despised the majority of the no-marks he was forced to share the rancid prison air with. So, no . . . soon as he got his feet back on that pavement out there, Liam Grant was never coming back through these doors.

And no woman would ever get under his skin deep enough to make him lose his head like that again – that was for *dead* sure.

11

'Please come with me,' Bruno begged, pouting at Mia in the mirror.

Mia frowned, and jabbed him in his flat belly with her elbow. 'Back off, lady-boy. Or are you deliberately disturbing me 'cos you want me to look like a dog's dinner?'

'Just say you'll come, and I'll leave you alone,' Bruno persisted. 'Please, please, please, plea—'

'All *right*!' Mia groaned, slamming the eyeliner pencil down on the cluttered worktop. 'Though why the hell *you* want to go to a place like that, I *do* not know.'

Bruno slapped her on the arm and hissed, 'Shut up! I've *got* to go. My dealer's threatening to cut my willy off if I don't bring his money.'

'Oh, great, so now you're trying to put *me* in danger?'

'There won't be any danger,' Bruno assured her, contradicting himself. 'Honest, he's cool. Soon as I pay up we'll be fine, and I'll be back in his good books.'

Giving him a doubting look, Mia said, 'I don't see how you can owe him that much in the first place. What have you been doing with it? Plastering the walls?'

'It's not all *me*,' Bruno reminded her indignantly. 'You've had your fair share.'

'Don't try and guilt-trip me,' Mia shot back. 'I didn't know you were putting yourself in debt for it.'

'No, 'cos it grows on trees, doesn't it?' Bruno gave her a sour look.

'Why don't you just cut your losses and ask Simone or Mark to get you something instead?' Mia suggested. 'They've always got something on them.'

'The shit *they* pass off as coke?' Bruno pulled a face. 'Do me a favour. I've had bigger hits off my baby nephew's bum powder!'

'So you'd rather traipse down to some skanky little dive in Levenshulme to get stuff off a madman?' Mia looked at him as if he was the world's biggest nutter, shook her head and reached for the blusher brush.

'He wouldn't hurt me really,' Bruno insisted. 'I used to go to school with him.'

'You just said he was threatening to chop off your willy.'

'Only if I don't pay up.' Bruno was getting exasperated now. 'Look, I've got to go – and you've got to come with me. You promised.'

Gordy, Bruno's paranoid boyfriend, came over just then to get his suit off the rack. As he heard the end of the conversation his eyes narrowed with suspicion. 'Come where?'

'To the *toilet*,' Bruno informed him huffily, giving him a dirty look before flouncing away.

Gordy watched him go, then glared at Mia in the mirror. 'I know that was a lie. Where are you really going?'

'Word of advice,' Mia said smoothly, stroking an extra layer of gloss over her lips. 'I've known Bruno a lot longer than you have, and if you don't stop quizzing him you're going to lose him.'

'I'm not quizzing him,' Gordy replied indignantly. 'But I think I've got a right to know where my boyfriend's going, and what he's doing.'

Mia shook her head, got up and stalked away. She'd met Bruno on a magazine shoot several months ago, and they had immediately clicked because he was as much of a bitch as she was. And their mutual passion for shopping had certainly helped to keep their friendship alive. But she neither liked nor gave a toss about his clingy boyfriend. She wouldn't have minded so much, but Gordy and Bruno had only met a few weeks ago at the casting for this show for which they were about to begin a week of rehearsals and their relationship was already on the rocks. But that was Gordy's problem. She'd warned him, but if he didn't want to listen there was nothing she could do – apart from sit back and laugh when Bruno dumped him.

'Everybody ready?' Arni Fabrizi called out, swooping down out of nowhere with the ridiculous collection of gold chains he wore around his fat neck clanking and jangling against his barrel chest.

He eyed his team with disgust and pointed at Anjeta, the gorgeous Polish girl, sneering, 'You are *way* too fucking fat for that dress. And *you*,' he turned on Simone, who looked like a young Cher, 'look more like a man than *him*!' He pointed at Bruno, who gave a gasp of mock indignation. 'And *you*,' he barked, spittle flying out of his mouth as he turned his wrath on Mia, 'aren't even fucking *dressed* yet! Do you think you've got all day, you stupid girl? You're supposed to be going on in a minute!'

Murmuring 'I'm *so* sorry, Arni, I got held up,' Mia tugged her outfit on and snapped her fingers at one of the two dressers to hurry up and fasten it.

Muttering curses under his breath, Fabrizi rolled his eyes and stormed away with his assistant Francie hot on his heels.

'Prick!' Bruno hissed unzipping his fly and waggling his surprisingly large penis at Fabrizi's back. 'Here, have a suck on this – you know you want to.'

Gordy gave him a filthy look, folded his arms and tapped his foot agitatedly.

Knowing it would wind him up, Mia couldn't resist reaching out and giving Bruno's dick a squeeze. 'Mmm, nice and hard. Just how we like 'em – eh, Simone?'

'Later,' Bruno scolded, slapping her hand away and zipping up his fly.

'What, both of us?' Simone teased. 'Sure you can handle it?'

Laughing, Mia pushed her team-mates on ahead of her when the call came for everybody to line up in the wings.

At eighteen, she had blossomed into a real beauty. But while her so-called identical twin was as unaware of her own attractiveness and as uninterested in her appearance as ever, preferring to concentrate on her college work in her quest to become a soppy social worker, Mia was *more* obsessed with herself than ever, and had spent every living moment of the last two years relentlessly pursuing her goal of becoming not just a model but a *super*model.

Despite Mia's hard work, the path to stardom had turned out to be much longer and tougher than either she or Sammy had anticipated, thanks mainly to shows like *Britain's Next Top Model*, which had brought girls who would previously never have dreamed they were pretty enough to model pouring out of the woodwork to snatch jobs which Mia just *knew* should have been hers. But those setbacks only served to strengthen her determination and she'd forged ahead, learning new and innovative ways in which to get herself noticed.

And if the other girls she'd met at the auditions she'd attended along the way feared her acid tongue and envied her effortless beauty, she didn't give a toss, because if there was one thing she'd learned about this business, it was that you either gave shit or took stick – and anyone who couldn't harden themselves to that fact wasn't cut out for modelling.

Fortunately for Mia, she was a fast learner so she was rarely out of work, the money from which allowed her to pursue her dreams without having to take on meaningless jobs to pay her bills and support herself – as so many struggling models were forced to. Although she was by no means earning as much as she believed she was worth yet. And having appeared in numerous catalogues and teen magazines, as well as co-fronting a couple of teen make-up campaigns, it frustrated her that she still hadn't achieved the one big break which would launch her into the stratosphere and see clients asking for her by name instead of type.

But she knew it would come eventually, and every cattle-market audition she attended, every lowly contract she won, Mia made sure she did something different from the other models in order to leave her mark.

Now, finally, she'd landed her first catwalk contract: modelling for one of an elite list of hot new designers who were showcasing their collections at the G-Mex Centre. They'd spent the whole of the previous week being fitted for the outfits they would each be wearing from their designers' collections, and now they were starting the week of dress rehearsals before the actual shows.

It was a five-day event, and the hype had already been incredible. London, Paris and Rome were all well-established fashion-show venues, but this kind of thing was relatively new to Manchester and the press were already covering it with fervour, speculating on everything from the clothes and their designers to which celebrities would be sitting on the front row each day seeking out the next big fashions in which to dazzle at the various parties and red-carpet events they would be gracing in the coming months.

Arni Fabrizi was one of the designers, and he dressed – and tried to act – like an LA gang-banger. Mia had loathed him from the moment she'd met him – him, *and* Francie, who seemed to spend her entire life trotting behind him with her tongue attached to his anus. From day one he'd thrown tantrums and had hysterical screaming matches with anybody and everybody, and he treated his models like shit, frequently reducing them to tears with his vicious putdowns. But this stinking attitude was exactly why Mia had jumped at the chance to be on his team, because it was already gaining him far more attention than he deserved. And, as they said, any press was good press, so she was happy to put up with the odious little fart if she got herself noticed because of him.

Unlike her fellow models who had mostly grown up in the 'nicer' suburbs of Manchester, Mia had been raised on the mean streets of Moss Side and knew *dangerous* when she saw it. And Fabrizi, for all his mouthing-off and cockiness, was about as dangerous as candyfloss, and nothing he said or did raised so much as a flicker of fear in her heart. But she understood how bullies operated, and she knew that while they got a kick out of terrorising people they tended to blank those who weren't fazed by them. So, determined that he wouldn't freeze her out and deprive her of her chance to shine, she'd been playing the game by his rules so far: pretending to be in awe of him, and quivering in his presence as if he scared the crap out of her. She resented having to do it, but it was a means to an end, and come the final show she intended to tell the sneering, supercilious little shit exactly what she thought of him.

Mia felt a surge of excitement pass down from the head of the line now as the house lights dimmed out front and the spots came on, followed by the pounding of the music to which they would be rehearsing all week. She took a deep breath. As the star of the show – in her own mind, if in nobody else's yet – she'd made damn sure that she was the final model in the line-up, ensuring that she would be the last to make her appearance on the catwalk on the final day – the one that the audience would *definitely* all remember.

'Well done, everybody!' Gloria Ford, the event organiser called out, drifting through the crowd of sweaty models backstage at the end of rehearsals in an almost visible cloud of Issy

Miyake perfume. 'That was magnificent! Now, be safe going home, rest well, and I'll see you all back here tomorrow!'

'God, I thought *I* was wearing a lot of slap,' Bruno muttered under his breath, slipping out of his suit trousers. 'You'd need a fucking hammer and chisel to find her face under that lot!'

'She's doing all right for seventy,' Simone quipped, pulling her top off over her head and exposing her breasts.

'Do you have to shove them in his face like that?' Gordy sniped, pushing roughly past her.

'You know what, he's really doing my head in!' Bruno complained to nobody in particular.

'What's everyone doing tonight?' Simone asked as she pulled on a T-shirt. 'Henry's taking me clubbing if anyone fancies joining us.'

'No, thanks, we're having a quiet night in,' Gordy informed her.

'Er, you might be, but *I'm* not,' Bruno corrected him tartly. 'Yes, thanks, Simmy, I'd love to.'

'Aren't you forgetting something?' Mia asked him quietly.

Waving his hand dismissively, Bruno said, 'We can do that first, then meet up with her later. *Any*thing but have a quiet night in with Doctor Death.'

Declaring that if Bruno was going, so was he, Gordy tugged his jacket on and looked pointedly at his watch.

'Waiting for something?' Bruno sniped.

'I thought we were supposed to be going for dinner,' Gordy reminded him.

'Oh, if I must,' Bruno moaned, rolling his eyes as if he couldn't think of anything worse. He leant towards Mia as Gordy set off and said, 'I'll pick you up at nine – make sure you're ready.'

'What was that about?' Simone asked, linking her arm through Mia's when they'd both finished dressing. 'Are you and Bruno going somewhere?'

'Nowhere special,' Mia told her evasively, waggling her

fingers at a couple of stunning heterosexual male models from one of the other teams as they made their way out. 'Christ, that Karl is *buff*! I wonder if he's free tonight. Where did you say we were going, and when?'

'Hexagon, eleven,' Simone told her. 'But you can't ask him to come – he's married.'

Ignoring her, Mia called, 'Hey, Karl – Hexagon tonight at eleven. Be there.'

She grinned when he winked at her. 'See, Simone, you're too conscientious for your own good. I'll be having a nice romp tonight while you're doing the same-old-same-old with your boyfriend. Let's guess who'll be having the most fun? Mmm . . . I think that will probably be *me*!'

Laughing, they emerged onto the broad steps fronting the G-Mex. Simone waved to her boyfriend Henry, who was parked on double yellow lines at the kerb ahead, air-kissed Mia and told her that she'd see her later.

Watching as Simone tripped lightly down the steps and climbed into the car, Mia smirked when Henry gave her the eye as he pulled out into the traffic. His name was a major turn-off, but he was quite cute, she supposed. And if Karl turned out to be a no-go and nobody else caught her eye tonight, she'd seriously consider him as an alternative.

Glancing at her watch now, and seeing that it was quarter to six, Mia set off down the steps in search of a cab.

12

It didn't look anything like a club from the outside. There were no windows, just graffiti-covered walls and a metal door in the centre of which was a spyhole. And there wasn't even a name sign, which made Mia wonder if it was just a boarded-up old house.

'Are you sure you've been here before?' she asked Bruno as the taxi drove away, leaving them alone on the dingy, badly lit street.

'At least once a week,' he told her, glancing nervously into the shadows which seemed to be pulsating out from every dark corner. 'Don't worry, it's not as bad inside.'

'So long as you don't get stabbed or shot before you *get* inside,' Mia muttered.

'Shut up!' Bruno scolded, grabbing her arm. 'Just don't leave me on my own, or you might never see me again.'

'Right now I'm wishing I'd never laid eyes on you in the *first* place,' Mia hissed, allowing him to drag her towards the door.

Bruno rapped his knuckles on the metal and waggled his fingers when there was a movement behind the peephole. Hearing the sound of several bolts being drawn back, Mia folded her arms when the door swung open. Her eyes widened when she found herself looking at a broad-shouldered, incredibly handsome black man and she decided that maybe it wouldn't be so bad after all.

'Hiya,' Bruno trilled 'Got room for two little ones?'

The man gave an upward jerk of his chin and stepped back to let them in. He swung the door shut behind them and held out his hand. Bruno shoved a twenty-pound note into it, grabbed Mia's arm and hauled her down a dark narrow hallway towards another black-painted door at the far end.

'You mean to tell me they've got the cheek to charge a tenner to get into this dive?' Mia complained.

Shushing her, Bruno hissed, 'It'll be worth it. Now, don't breathe in too hard, and for God's sake don't look at the stage or you'll turn to stone.'

Heavy instrumental soul music enveloped them when Bruno tugged open the door. As she stepped inside, Mia almost suffocated from the weed smoke that was hanging like a blanket in the air around their heads.

'My God, are you sure this is a club and not a blues?' she gasped, her eyes already watering.

'That's why I told you not to breathe in too deeply,' Bruno said, squinting around the dimly lit room.

Jumping when she felt a hand on her backside, Mia squawked, 'Do you *mind*!'

'Not if you don't,' the gaunt-faced old man on the other end of the hand replied, giving her a lustful grin.

'Fuck off!' she spat, balling her own hand into a fist, ready to punch him if he tried to touch her again.

Bruno dragged her away, saying, 'For God's sake don't start any trouble, or we're both dead.'

'*I* wasn't,' she informed him indignantly, yanking her arm free.

Bruno stopped dead and nodded towards a table at the far side of the room, where a young skinhead was sitting with his arms around two bored-looking women.

Glancing over, Mia's gaze skidded from the man to the stage, upon which a naked young girl with long glossy black hair was hanging upside down off a thin metal pole with her legs splayed.

'My *God*!' she spluttered. 'How the hell is she managing *that*?'

'Stop staring, you big lezzer,' Bruno hissed, shuddering as he added, 'Oh, gross! I think I just saw the insides of her *womb*!'

Telling him not to be so ridiculous, Mia dragged her eyes away from the woman and gave him a shove, urging him to hurry up and do what he had to do so they could get out of there.

'Keep an eye on me in case I need rescuing,' Bruno said nervously. 'Won't be a minute.'

Mia folded her arms protectively across her chest when she noticed several men giving her the same kind of lustful looks as the old man who'd groped her by the door. She glowered at them and walked over to the wall. It was definitely more like a blues here, given the amount of weed that was obviously being smoked, but, surprisingly, instead of young black guys the place seemed to be full of horrible old white men. And it was obvious what they had come for, given how many scantily dressed young girls were dotted around – some of whom seemed to be giving hand jobs under the tables.

Disgusted, Mia glanced over to see how Bruno was getting on. Frowning when she saw that he was leaning right over the table, aided by the skinhead's hand around his throat, she marched over.

Grabbing Bruno's arm with one hand, she seized the skinhead's wrist with the other and hissed, 'Let go, or I'm going to start screaming. And then I'm going to call the police and tell them you tried to rape me.'

Grinning, his face feral in the dim light, the skinhead said, 'I wouldn't try pulling any of that shit in here, darlin', 'less you wanna find yourself riding the train.'

Mia had absolutely no idea what that meant. But she was more concerned about freeing Bruno right now because his eyes were bulging and his face was purple.

'Look, I'm sure you've got your reasons for being pissed off,' she said, 'but if he's paid what he owes, just let him go before this gets out of hand.'

'Something wrong here?' a deep voice asked.

Glancing round, Mia was relieved to see the doorman standing behind her. But just as she was about to tell him that, yes, something *was* wrong, that this idiot was trying to kill her friend, the skinhead released Bruno and said, 'Nah, it's all cool, Vern. I was just having a quiet word with my mate – isn't that right, Bru?'

Bruno nodded quickly.

Casting a hooded glance at the two girls who, Mia noted, now looked terrified, Vern said, 'All right, but keep the noise down.' Then, instead of walking away, he turned to Mia, saying, 'The boss would like a word.'

'About what?' she asked, instantly on the defensive.

'You'll have to ask *him* that,' Vern said, gesturing with a nod towards the bar.

Turning, Mia saw two white men staring at her from the tall bar stools.

'Go see what he wants,' Bruno said quietly, giving her a little shove. 'I'll just sort out what I came for.'

'Are you mad?' she asked. 'After what he's just done to you?'

'We're fine now. Go. I can handle this.'

Flashing a warning glance at the skinhead, who grinned back at her and shrugged in a gesture of innocence, Mia pursed her lips and headed off to see what the so-called boss wanted with her.

Like Vern, both of the men at the bar appeared to be in their thirties, but while one was bald and really quite ugly the other was strikingly good-looking. His dark eyes had a slight

Oriental slant to them which she found quite sexy, and his nose had a tiny kink on the bridge, which she presumed to be from an old break – again, quite sexy. The only thing that let him down was his hair, which was tied back in a ponytail. That was really uncool, in her opinion, but she supposed that *his* generation probably considered it quite 'hip'.

'Your friend told me you wanted a word,' she said now, speaking directly to him.

He smiled, and jerked his head at the other man, who immediately climbed off his stool and walked away.

'No, you're all right,' Mia said when he gestured for her to sit down. 'I'm not staying.'

Pulling a disappointed face, he said, 'Surely you've got time for one little drink with a friend?'

'We're not friends.'

'Steve Dawson.' He held out his hand.

Sighing, because she really didn't see the point in introductions when she had no intention of staying, Mia unfolded her arms and shook his hand out of politeness.

'What, no name?'

'Mia Delaney,' she told him, sliding her hand out of his.

'Nice.' Steve smiled. 'And what does *Mia Delaney* like to drink?'

Feeling unusually flustered, Mia shifted her weight onto her other foot. 'Sorry, I really haven't got time.'

'Let me guess,' Steve said, as if she hadn't spoken. 'Rum and coke?'

Amused by his persistence, Mia said, 'Whisky and ginger, actually. But that doesn't mean I want one.'

It was too late. Steve had already clicked his fingers at the bar girl and ordered Mia a drink. Gesturing towards the vacant stool again, he said, 'You might as well sit down now you're staying. Unless you're planning on drinking and running – which would be a bit rude, don't you think?'

Glancing back and seeing that Bruno seemed to be deep in conversation with the skinhead, Mia sighed. 'Okay, but just *one*, because we'll be leaving as soon as my friend's . . .' Catching herself before she revealed the real reason for their visit here and got them thrown out or arrested, she blurted out the first thing that came into her head, 'We only dropped in so my friend could invite someone to a party.'

'Really?' Steve's gaze slid smoothly from Mia's face to her thighs as she sat down and crossed her legs. 'And will *you* be going to this party?'

'Er, no, it's not my kind of thing,' Mia muttered, surreptitiously tugging the hem of her skirt down. She was used to being in control when she met a man, but this one was making her nervous. It could just be that she was getting high off the smoke she'd been inhaling since they'd arrived, or the fact that he was older and more self-assured than the guys she usually got chatted up by. But, either way, his sexy eyes were doing funny things to her stomach. She cleared her throat to try and regain her composure and said, 'I thought you wanted a word about something?'

'Can't a man ask a beautiful woman to join him for a drink without needing an excuse?' Steve drawled, pushing her glass towards her when the bar girl served it. 'So, when are you free for dinner? Tomorrow's good for me.'

Mia took a sip, and coughed when it went down the wrong way. '*Sorry?*'

'I'll need an address,' Steve went on smoothly. 'So I know where to pick you up from. Seven-thirty all right?'

'I, er – no, not really.' Recovering, Mia shook her head. 'I'm working, and I don't get home till gone six.'

'Ah . . . and you'll need at least two hours to get ready if you're a typical woman. Why don't we say half-eight instead?'

Flattered that he seemed determined not to take no for an answer, Mia couldn't help but smile.

'Wow, that's a pretty sight,' Steve murmured. 'Ever thought of modelling?'

Coyly tilting her head to one side now, Mia said, 'I already do, actually.'

'Should have guessed,' he purred. 'Face like yours would be wasted on anything else. So, what are you working on at the moment?'

'Nothing special.' She shrugged, trying to appear modest in case he thought she was boasting. 'Just some catwalk thing.'

Narrowing his eyes, Steve said, 'Wouldn't happen to be that thing they're advertising at the G-Mex, would it?'

'Mmm.' Nodding, Mia sipped at her drink.

'Really?' Steve seemed genuinely impressed. 'So, I'm taking a bona-fide fashion model out for dinner. Can't be bad.'

Before Mia could remind him that she hadn't actually agreed to go out with him yet, she noticed Bruno waving at her from a few feet away. He had a *hurry up!* look on his face, and his body language said that he was desperate to get moving.

She said, 'Sorry, I've got to go,' finished her drink and reached for her handbag.

'Address?' Steve said, placing his hand over hers.

On her feet now, Mia looked at him thoughtfully. He really was quite sexy, and just because he managed a sleazy place that didn't mean he was a sleazy person. So could it really hurt to have dinner with him?

Impulsively, she took a pen out of her bag and scribbled her number on his hand. 'Call me. I'll let you know if I want to go out when I've had a chance to think about it.'

Steve winked at her and was smiling as she walked away.

'What the fuck are you playing at?' Bruno hissed when they got outside, sounding both angry and scared.

'What's your problem?' Mia demanded, irritated that he thought he had a right to talk to her like this.

'You and that man,' Bruno snapped, already setting off down the road. 'I told you to go and see what he wanted, not start drinking with him.'

'Oh, for God's sake, don't tell me you're jealous!' Mia snorted. 'Anyone would think I was your girlfriend and you'd just caught me cheating on you. Sorry, *boyfriend*,' she corrected herself sarcastically.

'What were you talking about, anyway?'

'Not that it's any of your business, but he asked me out to dinner,' Mia told him peevishly. 'Is that okay with you, or should I have waited to get your permission?'

'Mia, look around,' Bruno said, his own eyes darting nervously every which way. 'This is not the kind of place to go picking up men.'

'Oh, but it's all right for you to come here picking up drugs?'

'That's different. What you're doing is dangerous.'

'Don't make me laugh!' Mia snorted. '*You* nearly got strangled – *I* got asked out to dinner. Which sounds the most dangerous to you? Hmm . . . let me think!'

'I'm being serious,' Bruno snapped, relieved when they rounded the corner onto the well-lit main road. 'Look, you know I've got no problem with you shagging every man from here to Kingdom Come. Christ, I've even had a few of them myself when you've finished with them.'

'Don't be disgusting! I don't sleep with gay men.'

'Honey, you haven't got a clue.'

'All right, name them. Come on, I need to know in case I bump into any of them again and fancy a bit.'

Tutting, Bruno stuck out his arm when he saw a black cab. 'Jon, Neil, and Foxy – if you must know.'

'You *tart*!' Mia gasped, staring at him in disbelief as the cab pulled up. 'You know how much I liked Foxy.' Frowning now, she said, 'Which one was he again?'

'Oh, and *I*'m the tart?' Bruno scoffed, shoving her onto the back seat.

Giving him a funny look as he climbed in after her, Mia wondered if that was why he liked going out clubbing with her – so that he could pick up the men she'd discarded in order to console them in his own inimitable way.

After he'd told the driver where to take them, Bruno sat back and whispered, 'Anyway, you can't go out with Steve Dawson. He's dangerous. You know my friend back there at the club?'

'Didn't look like much of a friend to me,' Mia sniped. 'Friends don't generally try to strangle each other – tempting though it is in your case.'

'Oh, Robbo's a crack-head, and he flips out like that sometimes,' Bruno said, flapping his hand dismissively. 'As long as I get my baggy, I don't give a shit. Anyway, he saw you making eyes at Dawson and told me to warn you off.'

'I was *not* making eyes at him.'

'Bitch, you so were. You forget I know your M.O. Tilting head, gazing up through the lashes, twiddling with the hair . . .'

'*Ew*, have you been studying me, you strange little boy?'

'All right, make a joke of it if you must,' Bruno said huffily. 'But don't say I didn't warn you if you go ahead with this dinner and end up regretting it.'

'Oh, stop being such a drama queen,' Mia laughed softly. 'He's a nice man.'

'Honey, *nice* men don't own lap-dancing clubs and deal class A drugs.'

'Says the boy who *goes* to a lap-dancing club to *buy* his class A drugs.'

'Yes, well, you carry on thinking you're a bad-ass bitch who can handle anything and anyone,' Bruno retorted darkly.

'But think on this: that thing Robbo said about riding the train – he meant the *white-slave train*.'

Laughing out loud now, Mia said, 'Oh, now I know you're making it up. There were hardly *any* white girls in there – or didn't you notice?'

'Can't say I was looking that closely,' Bruno grunted, grimacing at the memory of the genitalia he'd been forced to view against his will tonight.

'Thanks for the concern,' Mia told him firmly. 'But I'm not stupid. If – and I do mean *if*, because I haven't agreed yet – I have dinner with him, I'll make my own mind up about what kind of man he is. Okay?'

She slid to the edge of the seat when the cab turned onto Oxford Street and waved when she saw Simone, Henry, and a couple of their fellow models standing outside the club.

Twisting his lip when he spotted Gordy hanging back from the others, Bruno muttered, 'Oh, goody, Doctor Death's here.'

'Why do you call him that?' Mia asked, smoothing her dress down.

'It's a euphemism for boring bastard who just lies there like a dead fish and waits to be fucked.'

'So dump him, and find someone more exciting.'

'What, and lose my pocket money?' Bruno squawked as he paid the driver. 'Do you know how long it's taken me to find a sucker with a rich mummy and daddy? Where do you think I got the money to pay Robbo off?'

'You're kidding me!' Shaking her own head when Bruno shook his, Mia said, 'Well, I'd stop giving him such a hard time if you want him to carry on lining your pockets, 'cos he looks like he's getting well and truly pissed off to me.'

'Honey, it's precisely *because* I give him such a hard time that he won't be going *no*where,' Bruno corrected her dramatically. 'He's a masochist; he loves being treated like shit. Oh, and having my nice big cock up his uptight arsehole obviously helps.'

'*Eughh!*' Mia grimaced. 'He's creepy enough already without me having to think about you and him at it.'

'So, don't think about it, then,' Bruno said, and opened the door. 'Oh, by the way,' he whispered before getting out. 'If he asks, we've been at a funeral parlour in Longsight viewing my dear old Aunt Lily's body.'

'*What?*'

'Well, I had to think of *some*thing to get him off my back. And I knew he wouldn't want to see a dead body, so I said I'd asked you instead – 'cos we all know *you* wouldn't be fazed by a stinking corpse.'

Unsure whether she'd just been insulted or complimented, Mia climbed out of the cab. Forgetting all about Steve Dawson, she glanced around to see if Karl the hunky married model had turned up. Not particularly bothered to see that he hadn't, she scanned the crowd and quickly earmarked a couple of very fanciable replacements.

13

'Mia, get up, there's a delivery for you,' Kim said grumpily, banging on the twins' bedroom door the following morning.

Groaning, Mia dragged the pillow over her head. 'Go away, I'm tired.'

'So am I – thanks to you keeping me up half the night. And that fella best not still be here!'

Reaching behind her, Mia patted the narrow mattress, relieved to find it empty. She hated waking up with men she'd picked up when she was pissed; they never looked as good through sober eyes.

'If he is, tell him to sling his hook,' Kim went on – loudly, for his benefit if he *was* there. 'It's bad enough your sister had to sleep on the couch because of him without me having to bump into him on me own flaming landing. And hurry up and get your arse downstairs, 'cos that delivery needs signing for.'

'Can't you do it?'

'No, he already knows I'm not you.'

'Well, tell *her* to do it, then.'

'Shell left for college hours ago.'

'*What?*' Mia jerked upright and brushed her mussed-up hair out of her eyes. 'What time is it?'

'Half-eleven.'

'Shit! Why didn't you wake me? I'm supposed to be at the G-Mex in half an hour.'

'Oh, 'cos I'm your personal alarm clock, me,' Kim grunted,

wrapping her dressing gown around herself and waddling towards her own bedroom. 'Oh, for God's *sake*!' she yelled when the bell rang again. 'Door, Mia! And put the kettle on while you're down there.'

'Er, are we still asleep, mother?' Mia yelled back. ''Cos that's the only reason you could be mistaking me for the slave daughter.'

'I'll bloody do it myself, then – as per usual!'

Mia got up, pulled on her dressing gown and padded down the stairs, frowning when she saw the enormous box that the delivery man was holding.

'What the hell's that?'

'Flowers,' he told her, passing it over.

Dropping it on the floor as if it had contaminated her hands, Mia glared at him. 'Since when have you had to sign for flowers? I've had a really hard night, and you're telling me you've just made me get up for *that*?'

'The sender requested a signature on delivery,' he informed her, trying not to stare at her nipples which were jutting sharply through the thin silk material.

Scowling, Mia scribbled something illegible on his electronic gadget and slammed the door in his face. Taking her anger out on the box for being the cause of her rude awakening, she kicked it ahead of her into the living room and tore the lid off. Snatching out the card, sure that it was probably just a 'congratulations for a great first rehearsal'-type thing from Gloria Ford's assistant, her eyes widened when she read the typed message.

Looking forward to dinner. See you at 8.30. S xxx

'*Miaaa!*' Kim yelled. 'Your flaming phone's ringing now. Come and get it before my head explodes!'

Angry with Bruno because, for all his words of warning, he must have told his friend Robbo where she lived and he in turn must have told Steve, Mia was still frowning as she went to answer the call.

'Morning, gorgeous,' Steve's smooth voice crooned down her ear. 'Did you like them?'

'They're lovely,' Mia said warily, wondering now if he was actually *spying* on her. 'But how did you know where to send them when I only gave you my number?'

'You know that saying, where there's a will there's a way? Well, I had a will, so I found a way.' Laughing softly now, he added, 'So, what . . . you're going to shoot me for wanting to get to know you better? Most women would be flattered.'

'I am, and thank you,' Mia said politely.

'You're welcome,' Steve replied. 'So, we're still on for tonight? Eight-thirty?'

'I kind of remember saying that I'd want to think about it first,' she reminded him. 'And I've hardly had much chance to do that, have I?'

'You've had all night,' he came back playfully 'Anyway, what's to think about? We've both got to eat, so why not do it together? And you never know, you might find that you actually like me when you give me a chance to show what a gentleman I can be.'

Mia couldn't help but smile. Steve Dawson was obviously used to getting his own way, but he certainly wasn't trying to heavy her into anything. And she vaguely remembered that he was really good-looking and sexy. So, again, she had to ask herself would there really be any harm in going for dinner with him? As he'd just said, she might find that she liked him. And, if not, well, she'd just let him down gently.

'Okay. Eight-thirty. I'll be ready.'

'Great.' Steve sounded genuinely pleased. 'Oh, and, break a leg at your show thingy today.'

Thanking him, Mia said goodbye and disconnected the call. After checking the time and realising that she was going to be late if she didn't get a move on, she booked herself a taxi. Washed and dressed by the time it arrived, she ran downstairs, calling back to her mum to find a vase for the flowers.

Mia was ten minutes late, and the rest of the models were already milling about in a state of undress in the warehouse-like space that was being used as a changing area. She pushed her way through to her own team station, grabbed Bruno and hauled him off into a quiet corner.

'Did you give that idiot Robbo my address?'

'Did I *fuck*!' Bruno protested indignantly. 'I don't know what you take me for, but I am *not* the sort of gobby poof you obviously think I am.'

'Yes, you are.'

'Oh, well, all right, I *can* be. But not when it comes to you. Anyway, why are you asking? Has something happened?' Bruno paused as something occurred to him and his eyes widened in horror. 'Oh, no . . . you haven't been burgled, have you?'

'No, I've been sent *flowers*,' Mia told him.

'*No!*' he gasped, throwing a hand over his mouth. 'Not *flowers*?'

'Stop taking the piss,' she scolded. 'I'm being serious.'

'Come off it,' Bruno scoffed. 'Robbo wouldn't send his own *mother* flowers if she was about to roll over and die.'

'They're not from him, they're from Steve Dawson. But *I* didn't give him my address, so you must have let it slip to that knob-head mate of yours.'

'I assure you that I did not.'

'Well, someone did,' Mia said, not sure if she believed him. Then, shrugging, she added, 'Not that it matters, I suppose, 'cos he rang straight after and I've agreed to have dinner with him tonight.'

'Are you sure that's wise?' Bruno asked. 'Given what you've just told me, I'd be running for the hills if I was you – 'cos it sounds like you might have landed yourself a stalker.'

Mia rolled her eyes when Fabrizi marched up behind her just then and demanded to know why they were standing around gossiping when they were supposed to be getting ready. Turning, she gave him a toadying smile.

'I'm *so*, so sorry, Arni . . . we were just talking about those gorgeous shoes you were wearing yesterday and we completely lost track of time.'

Smirking when the vain bastard just told her to hurry up and get dressed, she pushed Steve and the date to the back of her mind and immersed herself in her work for the rest of the day.

Mia borrowed a little of Bruno's coke when they'd finished that afternoon, just to give herself a boost if dinner turned out to be boring – although she doubted it would. Then she got changed and rushed out to get a cab.

Steve arrived at eight-thirty on the dot, and Mia had been ready for ages. Having already snorted the coke, she was impatient to get going and was agitatedly puffing on a cigarette and pacing the floor when the car pulled up. Glancing out to make sure it was him, her jaw dropped when she saw the gleaming black 7-series BMW. She'd known that he must have *some* money, but that was a seriously expensive set of wheels. And, to cap it all, he wasn't even driving himself – Vern, the gorgeous doorman, was *chauffeuring* him.

She stubbed out the cigarette, sprayed a thick cloud of Agent Provocateur perfume over herself and glanced nervously into the mirror. She'd thought that she looked fantastic until a few seconds ago. Now she was wondering if she looked classy enough to be seen in such a flash car.

Kim sat forward in her seat and craned her neck to see what kind of Adonis must be out there to have put the usually unflappable Mia in such a tizzy. 'Bloody hell!' she muttered when she spotted the car. Then, narrowing her eyes when she saw who was behind the wheel, she murmured, 'You never said he was black.'

Tutting, Mia gave her mother a frosty look of disapproval. 'Not that it's any of your business, but that's not him, so you can stop worrying.'

'Who said anything about being worried?' Kim asked, rising to her feet now. 'I wouldn't care if he was black, red or yellow so long as he treated you decent. I was just saying, that's all.'

'Yeah, well, now you know, you can relax and carry on watching your programme,' Mia told her, tugging a bolero jacket on over her sleeveless dress.

'I thought I'd come and say hello,' Kim said, walking towards the door.

'*Mother!*' Mia hissed, pushing her back into the room. 'It's the first time I've ever been out with him, so you don't really think he'll want to meet my flaming family, do you? And what's with the sudden interest, anyway? You usually can't stand any of the fellas I bring home.'

'Yeah, 'cos they're usually no good, like that rude bugger you had in last night,' Kim retorted disapprovingly. 'You'd have thought he could have kept the noise down, considering your mam was in the next room and your sister was right below.'

Reddening at the reminder of her one-night stand, which she'd sincerely have liked to forget about – and *really* didn't want her stupid mum mentioning in front of Steve – Mia snatched up her bag and headed out into the hall, saying, 'Don't wait up.'

'I won't,' Kim said, coming out after her.

Giving her a fierce look, Mia gritted her teeth and hissed, 'Get back inside, or I swear to God I'll never talk to you again.'

But it was too late. Steve was already out of the car. Strolling up the path, he extended his hand. 'Pleased to meet you, Mrs Delaney . . . Steve Dawson.'

'*Ms*,' Kim corrected him, taking an instant dislike to him. He was way too old for Mia, and there was something really smooth and cocky about him.

Smiling as if he hadn't noticed the distinct coolness in her eyes, Steve placed a hand on Mia's waist. 'Well, it was nice to meet you, and I'm sure we'll be seeing more of each other. But, if you'll forgive me, we're on a bit of a tight schedule, so . . .'

'He means we've got to go,' Mia explained, smiling tightly.

Folding her arms in case he took it into his head to try and hug her, like most of these poncey city types seemed to think they had to do whenever they said hello or goodbye, Kim said, 'Off you go, then.' Then, giving Mia a hooded look, she added, 'Just you be careful, you.'

Ushering Mia onto the car's spacious back seat, Steve climbed in beside her. He held his smile as he waved to Kim, who was still scowling at them from the step, and said, 'I don't think she likes me.'

Laughing, relieved to be getting away from the shame of her humble home, Mia said, 'However did you guess?'

'Oh, I don't know,' Steve drawled, turning to her as they pulled out into the road. 'Something to do with the dirty looks she was giving me, like I'd just crawled out from under a stone?' Chuckling, he shook his head. 'Jeezus, I thought I'd left all that having to be nice to my girlfriend's-parents shit *way* behind.'

'That's what you get for asking a younger girl out on a date,' Mia quipped, glad that she'd decided to come out with him now because he was even more handsome than she'd remembered – and obviously a damn sight richer than she'd thought.

'Hey, I'm not that old,' he protested. 'Anyway, I thought you young girls liked your men older?'

Assuring him that they did, Mia thought it best not to

mention that she had always personally preferred the younger fitter model boys.

'Glad to hear it,' Steve said, settling back in his seat. 'Why did she tell you to be careful, by the way? Does she think I'm a serial killer who's going to kidnap you and chop you into little bits?'

'*God* only knows what goes through that woman's mind,' Mia snorted disloyally. Then, giving him a knowing smile, she said, 'She's probably taken one look at your car and at Vern, and decided you must be a major drug dealer. And I didn't mean that the way it probably sounded, Vern,' she added quickly. 'It's got nothing to do with you being black. It's just the whole minder thing.'

'I've heard worse,' Vern replied, flashing a hooded look at Steve in the rear-view mirror.

Catching it, Mia glanced at Steve and felt a flutter of apprehension when she found him peering intensely back at her. She'd thrown the comment in to let him know that she knew about him and didn't care, but now she was wondering if she might not have been a little hasty. It was only the second time they had met, after all, and dealers were notoriously paranoid about people knowing their business.

Steve's eyes narrowed when he noticed the tiny trace of white powder below Mia's nose. He gave a slow smile and, reaching out, wiped it off. 'I take it that's why you came to the club last night? And I also take it that Robbo's been opening his big mouth about me?'

Nervous now, because if Steve went after Robbo for telling her Robbo would go after Bruno, Mia bit her lip. 'I'm sorry. It's none of my business. I shouldn't have said anything.'

'Relax.' Steve reached for her hand. 'You haven't done anything wrong. Robbo should know better, that's all. Anyway, if we're going to be seeing as much of each other as I have a feeling we are, you'd have found out sooner or later.'

'Please don't tell him I told you,' she implored. 'He already tried to strangle my friend.'

'The queer you were with last night?'

'Well, he prefers poof, but yeah – him. And I'd hate it if he got hurt because of me.'

Drawing his head back, Steve gave her a mock-wounded look. 'Come now . . . do I look like the kind of man who gets his kicks out of stirring up shit? Don't you worry about Robbo, I'll make sure he leaves your friend alone.'

Mia's eyebrows knitted together in worry. She hoped for Bruno's sake that Steve meant what he'd just said.

'About the coke,' Steve said quietly. 'Don't go to Robbo again. If you want anything in future, come to me – okay?'

Nodding, Mia glanced out of the window as Vern drove into the car park of the Lowry Hotel. As handsome, sexy, and rich as Steve undoubtedly was, just now she'd sensed something dark below the surface which made her nervous. But he must think she was pretty special to bring her to such an expensive place for their first date when he'd already sent those beautiful flowers. And he'd told her to come to him when she wanted coke in the future, which, she presumed, meant that she wouldn't have to pay for it.

After parking up, Vern opened Steve's door before coming round to open Mia's. Smiling when he winked at her as if to say *You're one of us now, we'll look after you*, she took Steve's arm and strolled into the hotel between them, feeling ridiculously proud when people turned to look at them as they were shown through to the restaurant. *Oh*, yes . . . she could definitely get used to this.

14

The next two weeks flew by, and before Mia knew what had hit her the day of the final show was upon her.

Since meeting Steve, she hadn't slept in her own bed once, only going home after work in order to get ready to go out with him, then returning in the morning only to get changed to go back to work. She'd always been a party animal, liking nothing better than to go out with her friends for a night of drinking, dancing, drugs and casual sex. But Steve's world was that touch darker and more exciting than anything she'd ever experienced before, and she was really enjoying being involved in it all, from the expensive restaurants to the clubs and casinos, to his enormous bed in his Quayside apartment. She even loved going to his own club, because it was a whole different experience to go there as the boss's woman, being given unlimited drinks – and coke – and treated like the lady of the manor by the staff and customers alike.

Tonight, however, she'd be sleeping alone, because there was a VIP end-of-show party being thrown at a nightclub in town, and it was a strictly no partners or uninvited guests affair.

All the other models were buzzing about the party, dying for today to be over so they could really let their hair down. But Mia was dreading the thought of waking up in the morning with no more shows to look forward to. From the moment she'd stepped out onto the catwalk for the first show proper and seen real faces packed into the previously empty seats she'd been in heaven: the heavy music seeming to vibrate through her body, the spotlights beaming onto her from every direction making her feel like the brightest star in the sky. She'd found her true niche, and now that it was about to end she didn't know if she was ever going to feel that same kind of rush again.

So far today, everything had been going smoothly. There were journalists and photographers from all the major magazines and newspapers, and three separate TV crews out front, plus a host of specially invited mega-celebrities who were lending an added air of glamour and excitement.

Backstage, after two weeks of working together as harmoniously as a bunch of self-obsessed divas could, the models had suddenly revealed their true competitive colours and, as if their masks had been stripped away, the petty bitching which had been going on throughout had suddenly flared into outright backstabbing and vicious slanging matches. While onstage, they desperately tried to outshine each other, hoping that it would be their face shown on the news bulletins that evening and splashed all over the front pages tomorrow.

When the finale finally came around – the last big parade in which they would each take their final stroll down the runway, wearing their designers' most outlandish and eye-catching creations – they were all crackling with nervous energy as their dressers manhandled them, and make-up artists and hairstylists struggled to add their finishing touches where they stood.

With the madness going on all around, Mia smiled serenely to herself as she was prodded and pushed and dusted and painted. There had only ever been one outfit in Fabrizi's collection that she actually rated and she was thrilled to be wearing it now, because it was certain to capture the attention of the press. Made of shimmering gold material, it had a halter neck that plunged down to just about cover each breast, and the front was split at crotch level, fanning out to reveal a flash of gold panties beneath. The sleeves, which hung in soft pleats when the arms were down, flared out like exotic wings when they were extended. At the lower back the skirt flowed out in a long train, while the upper back consisted of almost invisible wisp-thin laces, which criss-crossed like a golden spider's web and ended at the base of the spine.

Mia had had her heart set on that dress from the start, and had shamelessly sucked up to Fabrizi in order to make sure that she was the model he chose to wear it in the finale. And, sickening as it had been to have to kiss his fat arse, it had worked. So now she was standing in line with the rest of her team, looking like a golden goddess as they waited for the final call.

With tension running so high, the designers had been in a frenzy all day. Fabrizi, however, had been relatively calm – which Mia had thought quite strange. But he'd obviously been saving his biggest tantrum until the very last moment because, with just minutes to go before they were due to go out for the final walk, he suddenly went on the rampage – swearing at his models, insulting them, and physically pushing them around. But when he made the mistake of calling Mia a fish-faced tramp who ought to be stacking shelves at Aldi, she snapped. It was time somebody taught the jumped-up little shit a lesson, and as this was the last time she was ever going to work with him she didn't see why *she* shouldn't get the pleasure.

Still smiling now, she stood in line, waiting for the final call to move into the wings. When at last it came, she waited until her team began to move forward before she darted behind one of the clothes racks.

Running to catch up with her team when she re-emerged, safe in the knowledge that as last in line nobody would see what she had done until it was too late, Mia composed her face into her trademark ice-goddess expression. Then, relaxing her shoulders, she jutted out her hips, and strolled out onto the catwalk.

An audible gasp went up in the audience, and cameras began to flash like crazy. Maintaining her composure, with the skirt-tail draped over her left arm and her right 'wing' extended, Mia pranced gracefully down the catwalk as if she wasn't aware that most of the cameras were now focused squarely on her.

'Oh, my good fucking *God*!' Fabrizi's hysterical voice rang out from the shadows behind her. 'It's back to front! *IT'S BACK TO FUCKING FROOONT!*'

Sensing that something was happening behind them, Mia's team-mates glanced at her out of the corners of their eyes as they made their turnarounds at the end of the runway. Momentarily losing concentration, Bruno's eyes widened and his step faltered, causing Anjeta, who was right on his heels, to crash into him.

'You're *crazy*!' Simone spluttered, clutching at Mia's arm when they came off stage and started jostling their way to their station. 'You nearly made me fall flat on my face!'

Eyebrows raised in innocence as Anjeta fled past in tears, Mia said, 'What . . . ? Did I do something wrong?'

'I just can't *believe* you!' Simone laughed, her eyes dancing with envy and excitement. 'There was no *way* you had that dress on the wrong way round when we set off. But how the hell did you manage to turn it round without breaking something?'

Thundering up with Francie hot on his heels came Fabrizi. His fat cheeks wobbled with fury as he jabbed a finger at Mia's face. 'You *she*-devil!' he screeched. 'I made you my golden lady, and you turned me into a fucking laughing stock!'

'Oh, chill out,' Mia drawled, her breasts still clearly on

display through the spider's web which should have been adorning her slender back. 'I made sure it got noticed, didn't I?'

'*Chill out?*' Fabrizi repeated in a strangled tone, glancing around to make sure that everybody was listening. 'Did you all *hear* the stupid slut? She dares to tell *Arni Fabrizi* to chill the fuck *out*!' Glaring at Mia again now, spittle flew from his lips as he hissed, 'You are finished . . . *fin-ished*!'

'Get over yourself,' Mia jeered, gazing down at him with fearless eyes. It was done now; there was nothing to gain from pretending that she gave a shit what he thought.

'Take it off!' he snarled through clenched teeth. 'You're not fit to *look* at it, let alone wear it!'

Still holding his gaze, Mia slowly snapped the straps and let the dress slide to the floor. Then, stepping out of it, she kicked it aside as if it were worthless.

'There you go, *Arnold*. But before you start congratulating yourself when you see it splashed all over the front pages tomorrow, remember that *I*'m the only reason it's getting talked about.'

'*I* designed it!' Fabrizi squawked, pounding his chest with a fistful of gold rings. '*I*'m the talent here! *You* – you are *nothing*!'

'You're *shite*, and everyone knows it,' Mia told him bluntly. 'And in case you hadn't noticed, everyone was talking about *Nanito* before I did what I just did, so you should be kissing my feet, never mind having a go at me. And as for me being finished, I don't *think* so.'

Almost breathing fire now, Fabrizi clenched and unclenched his fists. He had never wanted to punch anybody so much in his entire life, but the thought of the adverse publicity and the inevitable lawsuit stayed his hand. That, and the glint in Mia's eyes which told him that she would probably retaliate – and possibly get the better of him.

'You're wanted out front,' Francie hissed at him just then, clicking her little radio receiver off. 'The press are asking for you.'

Saved the indignity of having to climb down to an unknown model whom he would normally be smearing across the floor right now, Fabrizi raised his chin proudly.

'Sorry, *who* do they want to interview?' he crowed smugly, cupping a hand to his ear and turning in a circle as if listening. 'Is that *her* name they're calling?' He waved his hand at Mia in a dismissive gesture. Then, immediately answering his own question, 'No! Because they do not want *her*, they want *me*!'

Snapping his fingers at Francie now, barking at her to pick up his dress, he turned on his heel and strode away.

'That was *terrifying*,' Simone gasped when he'd gone. 'I thought he was going to go absolutely mental on you.'

'He wouldn't dare,' Mia sneered, snatching up her T-shirt and pulling it over her head. 'Guys like him think they're tough, but they're *nothing* compared with the guys I grew up with.'

'I wish I could stand up for myself like that,' Simone sighed, gazing at her with respect. 'I'm a gibbering wreck when he shouts at me. Guess I should stick with you in future, huh? Let you be my bodyguard.'

'Wonderful show, everybody,' Gloria Ford called out just then, her shrill voice easily carrying over the noise. 'And to show our appreciation for your magnificent contributions, we have goody bags for you all, which my assistant will be handing out as you leave.' Holding up her hands now when the excited models began to speculate about what could possibly be in them, she added, 'The party will begin at ten, but you may arrive at any time after nine. Don't forget or lose your tickets, because you won't get in without them – no exceptions. And, as you already know, no partners or friends are allowed!' Finishing, she said, 'Be safe going home, and I look forward to seeing you all later. And, again, thank you all so very much!'

Turning now as some the models applauded, Gloria scanned the faces. Locating Mia, she cocked a finger at her before turning and walking back the way she'd come.

'Oh, dear!' Bruno said grimly, stepping out of his suit trousers. 'Looks like Mizz *Thang*'s about to get her ass whupped!'

'Oh, so what!' Mia scoffed, as if she couldn't care less. She stared at Bruno's penis as she slipped into her skinny jeans and said, 'You got a licence to have that out without a muzzle?'

'Ex*cuse* me!' Gordy squawked possessively.

'Hey, if he didn't want anyone to see it, he wouldn't whip it out every chance he gets,' Mia told him bluntly. 'But don't worry, I'm not trying to steal him off you.'

'Oh, believe me, I'm not worried about *you*,' Gordy retorted, flashing a hooded glance in the direction of a young Dutch model on a nearby team.

'What's that supposed to mean?' Bruno demanded, puffing his skinny chest out as if he was getting set to fight.

'You know *exactly* what it means,' Gordy snapped. 'Or do I have to spell it out?'

Mia smirked at Simone when they started bickering and snatched up her handbag and jacket. 'See you all at the party,' she said, setting off after Gloria.

'If they don't bar you!' Bruno called after her, momentarily forgetting his argument. Turning back to the others when she'd gone, he shook his head. 'Fabrizi's gonna sue her ass, for sure.'

Hearing this, Mia felt sick as it occurred to her that that might be what Gloria wanted to see her about. Managing to smile despite the apprehension, she kept her composure as she made her way out of the changing area. A few of the other models congratulated her as she passed, but most flicked dirty looks her way – a sure sign, in her mind, that they were all as jealous as hell that they hadn't thought of doing what she'd just done.

Although they might not be quite so jealous in a few minutes, depending on what Gloria had to say.

For a woman of such meticulous personal appearance, Gloria's makeshift office was an absolute mess. Seated at the desk now, sifting through a ton of paperwork, she waved her hand when Mia walked in, gesturing for her to take a seat.

Thoroughly clued-up on the correct etiquette of such occasions, Mia did the exact opposite and sat sideways-on to the desk instead of the more formal straight-on, with her legs crossed and her arm draped casually over the back of the chair. She might just have made the biggest mistake of her life, but she was damned if she was going down with fear in her eyes.

When she didn't find what she'd been looking for, Gloria tutted, clasped her hands together on the desktop and looked at Mia. 'That was quite some stunt you pulled back there, young lady. May I ask if it was spontaneous or planned?'

'Spur of the moment,' Mia admitted, shrugging as she added, 'I just thought the dress needed a bit of spicing up.'

'Indeed,' Gloria murmured, her tone giving nothing away. 'And did it not occur to you that your actions could cost you dearly were word to spread that you sabotaged your designer?'

Wondering where this was headed, because Gloria was neither an agent with a vested interest in keeping Mia in work nor a potential client who might have been considering hiring her in the future, Mia gazed coolly back at her. They couldn't refuse to pay her, because, apart from the finale, she hadn't put a foot out of line in the entire five days. And if Fabrizi intended to sue, it would be between him, Sammy Martin, and their respective solicitors.

'Fortunately,' Gloria went on, 'it seems that your reckless behaviour may actually have drawn dividends for you, because

I've just been approached by one of the designers, requesting your agent's contact details.'

'*Really?*' Mia blurted out, sounding every bit as surprised as she actually was.

'Yes, *really*,' Gloria affirmed patronisingly. 'Which is quite remarkable, considering you almost caused a disaster. Think yourself lucky there were only a few minor stumbles because, believe me, if any of the models had fallen off the runway and hurt either themselves or an audience member, I would have held you entirely responsible.'

Feeling like a child being reprimanded by the head for disrupting class, Mia shifted in her seat and pursed her lips sulkily.

Gloria shook her head, but a faint trace of a smile had appeared on her lips.

'You, Mia Delaney, are what is commonly known as a loose cannon. But remember that bravado can be a gift or a curse. Allowed to run free, it will sink you without trace. Used wisely, however, and kept *rigorously* under control, it has the potential to carry one to great heights.'

A frown of confusion flickered across Mia's brow. Was she in trouble, or wasn't she? And had Gloria just insulted or praised her? Either way, Gloria knew her name – which was incredible, considering she hadn't called *any* of the models by their own names all week, referring to them instead as *Fabrizi's girl*, or *Nanito's boy*, or whatever. Mistake or not, at least her actions had got her noticed.

'Anyway, I do have everybody's details, but as you can see –' Gloria gestured with a nod towards the heap of papers '– it would take hours to locate any in particular. So, if you could just give me your agent's name, I'll pass it along to the interested party.'

'Er, Sammy Martin.' Clearing her throat, Mia sat up a little straighter. 'I've got his number, if you want it.'

'Sammy Martin?' Gloria repeated quietly, writing it down. 'I don't think I know him. Who does he work for?'

'He doesn't work for anyone,' Mia told her. 'He runs his own agency.'

'Really?' Glancing up, Gloria frowned. Then, 'Ah, yes, of course. Sammy. I've met him several times; decent chap. Although, I have to admit I'm surprised he managed to get you included in this show, because he's very small and we usually only deal with the majors.'

Shifting uncomfortably in her seat when Gloria peered at her as if waiting for an explanation, Mia said, 'I, er, think he might have mentioned having a contact on the committee.'

'I see,' Gloria murmured. Then, after raising and lowering her eyebrows, she shrugged and said, 'Oh, well, I shall pass the information along. But if I were you, I would seriously consider changing.'

'Sorry?'

'Agents, my dear. You're young, you need somebody more cutting-edge to represent you.'

Simone was waiting at the end of the corridor when Mia came out of Gloria's office a short time later. Whispering, 'I nicked you one,' she thrust one of the two fancy red goody bags she was carrying into Mia's hands. 'Just in case they decided not to let you have one.'

'Why wouldn't they?' Mia asked distractedly, still reeling from the conversation she'd just had with Gloria. It was great that a designer had asked for her agent's details, but it didn't necessarily mean that anything would come of it. And, right now, she was more concerned about the loose-cannon reference, and Gloria's inference that her actions might be viewed as sabotage. In which case, she might very well have just shot herself firmly in the foot.

'None of us knew what was happening,' Simone said,

linking arms with her as they made their way out into the entrance hall. 'And Bruno reckons Fabrizi will sue you for damaging his reputation.'

'So I heard,' Mia muttered. 'But he's forgetting that the little shit didn't *have* a reputation before I came along. Well, not for his designs, anyway. And if he tries to sue me, my agent will have him straight in court.'

'What did Gloria want you for if you're not in trouble?' Simone asked, looking at her quizzically.

'Nothing, really,' Mia lied, unwilling to discuss what had really been said, because she needed to get it straight in her own head first. 'She was just, um, warning me about the press.'

'What about them?' Simone's eyes widened. 'Is something happening? They haven't asked to interview you, have they? Oh, God, you're so lucky!'

'I don't know what's going on,' Mia told her irritably. 'I wasn't really listening. Anyway, I don't want to think about it right now.'

Sure that Mia would tell her everything later, Simone let go of her arm and waved to Henry when they got outside. Then, whispering, as if she thought he might actually be able to hear what she was saying from that distance, she said, 'I'm so glad we're not allowed to take partners tonight. There's bound to be loads of really fit guys there, and it's been absolutely ages since I shagged someone famous.'

'Dirty bitch,' Mia laughed.

'Takes one to know one,' Simone retorted, struggling to keep a grip on her bags as a gust of wind whipped her hair across her eyes. 'Anyway, can we meet up and go in together tonight? Anjeta's just asked me to go with her, but her breath stinks like dog shit.'

'I know, it's *rank*,' Mia agreed, wrinkling her nose as she buttoned her jacket up. 'I had to hold my breath every time she walked past me today in case I puked.'

'And we don't want to be doing *that* in public, do we, dear?'

'No, we do *not*.'

Laughing, they arranged what time they would meet up outside the club. Then, waving over her shoulder, Simone skipped down the steps and hopped into the car while Mia went off in the opposite direction and flagged down a black cab. She gave the driver the address of the dress agency she wanted to go to and told him to put his foot down.

It was a tiny shop tucked away on a backstreet in Didsbury, but it stocked some of the most fantastic reasonably priced vintage designer gear that Mia had ever seen. She'd been going there for a while now, but nobody else on the circuit seemed to have discovered it – which was great, because it meant that she never had to admit how little she acually spent on clothes. And she was always guaranteed to be original, which was important if you wanted to stand out from the crowd – especially so tonight, when Mia suspected that the rest of the lame-brain models would turn up sporting the cast-offs they had scrounged off their designers today. And if it turned out that she *had* signed and sealed her modelling death warrant with her actions today, she intended to go out in fine style.

Kim had the catalogue open on her knee when Mia arrived home. She smiled and turned the list she'd been making face down so that Mia wouldn't see all the stuff she was about to order and have a go at her about wasting money again.

'How did it go?'

'Okay,' Mia said, slinging her jacket and bags onto the chair and carefully hanging the dress bag on the door frame. 'It was absolutely packed, and there were loads of press there.

Sooo . . .' she added, unable to stop herself from grinning as she walked into the kitchen, 'expect to see plenty of pictures of *me* in the papers tomorrow!'

'Why, what happened?' Kim asked, following her.

Mia took a bottle of water out of the fridge before giving her mother a brief account of the stunt she'd pulled.

'Oh, you didn't!' Kim gasped.

'I did! And it was worth it just to see the look on Fabrizi's ugly face. He had an absolute *fit*. But like I told him, at least it got his stupid dress noticed. And he's lucky, because they were all raving about this other designer before that.'

'What exactly did you do?' Kim was greedy for detail.

'Turned the dress back to front,' Mia told her. 'Then walked to the top of the runway and back as if I didn't even know. The cameras were all flashing like crazy, so it'll definitely be me they're all talking about tomorrow.'

'Ooh, you are clever,' Kim said proudly. Then, sighing wistfully, she added, 'But I wish I'd been there to see it; it's been ages since I've seen you working. Which reminds me . . . I was talking to Sammy earlier, and he reckons you should have had a special ticket for me.'

'I did,' Mia admitted, leaning back against the ledge. 'But I didn't want you there, so I didn't tell you.'

'Eh?' Kim's face wrinkled up quizzically. 'Why not?'

'Why do you *think*?' Mia took a sip of the water and looked her mother up and down.

'Oh, I see. You're ashamed of me because I'm a bit overweight – is that it?'

'A *bit*? Have you actually *looked* in a mirror lately?'

'Oi, there's no need for that. You know it's harder to shift when you're going through the change.'

'Not that old excuse again. You've been using that one for years; can't you come up with something more original?'

Kim tutted, then folded her arms and changed the subject.

'By the way, Sammy mentioned something about another catwalk thingy in Prague.'

'Oh yeah?'

'Well, you don't have to sound so excited about it. Sammy was practically having kittens.'

'He'd get excited about an extra slice of bread in his loaf,' Mia retorted dryly. 'But there's no point *you* getting your hopes up, because, whatever it is, you won't be going.'

Kim frowned deeply and said, 'Oh yes, I will. I'm not letting you go to a foreign country on your own. It's too dangerous.'

'Like to see how you'd get on the plane without a passport,' Mia reminded her smugly, determined that Kim would *not* be going.

'That's easily sorted,' Kim argued, equally determined that she damn well *would*. 'It only took a few weeks for yours to come through, so it's just a matter of finding the money. Which reminds me . . . I need your keeps.'

'Sorry, I'm broke,' Mia lied, heading for the door. 'You'll have to wait till Sammy releases the money from this job.'

'Mia, that could take weeks, and I need it *now*,' Kim complained as she followed her. 'You must have *some*thing. You haven't given me anything in the last three weeks, and you can't have spent all the money you got off that last job, because it was more than two grand.'

'Course I haven't,' Mia lied, knowing exactly how badly her mum would react if she realised that she had blown most of that money on clubbing and clothes. Since meeting Steve she'd hardly had to pay for anything, so she'd had a couple of hundred left in the bank this morning. But she'd just spent one-forty of that on the dress and shoes, and she couldn't hand over the sixty she had left, because, without Steve, she needed that for taxi fares and whatever.

'I've only got one cig left,' Kim told her. 'And there's nothing in for dinner, so you'll either have to go to the bank or give me your card and I'll go.'

'I don't *think* so!' Mia snorted, snatching up her handbag when she saw her mum's eyes drifting towards it. 'It's *my* account, and I'm not having you dipping into it whenever you feel like it.'

Incensed, Kim said, 'Who the hell do you think you're talking to, Mia? You might think you're the bee's knees, swanning about with your fancy man in his flash car, but you're not too old for a flaming good slap! And I wouldn't mind, but you wouldn't even *have* anything in that account if it wasn't for me bankrupting myself. So either hand the card over, or get your arse down to the bank, but either way I want my money!'

'Oh, chill out before you give yourself a hernia,' Mia drawled. 'I'll go. But is it all right if I have a bath first?'

'So long as you don't take too long about it,' Kim grumbled.

Mia snatched her bags and marched upstairs. She was eighteen, not eight, and considering she was the only one who was earning any kind of decent money around here, her mum had a damn cheek trying to lay down the law about when, where, and on what she could spend it. She was just glad that she had full control over her earnings now, because if that fat greedy cow could still get her hands on it she'd have blown the lot by now on bingo, booze, and all that cheap shit she was so fond of ordering out of the catalogue and thought Mia didn't know about.

Mia put her bags down on her bed and was heading across the landing to set the bath running when she heard the phone ringing below.

'Mia, it's Sammy,' Kim yelled up. 'He wants a quick word.'

'Tell him I'm busy,' she called back.

'He says it's important. Something to do with one of the

designers from the show wanting to set up a meeting. And he's talking about that Prague thing again.'

Mia closed the bathroom door without answering and punched the air in silent victory. *Oh, yes!* It looked like Gloria might have been right and this was going to turn out to Mia's advantage, after all. But she wouldn't spoil it by making herself appear too eager. If they wanted her badly enough to come looking for her, then they could wait until she was good and ready to get back to them.

Kim apologised to Sammy, explaining that Mia was exhausted and had gone for a lie-down, and promised that she would have her call him back as soon as she was fit to talk.

Michelle walked in just as she put the phone down. Venting her frustration on the easy target, Kim said, 'Why are you back so late? College finished hours ago.'

'I called in at the nursing home on my way home,' Michelle told her, slipping her coat off.

Sniffing exaggeratedly, Kim muttered, 'Yeah, I can smell you from here. Can't they put nappies on them, or something?'

'They can't help being incontinent,' Michelle murmured as she went into the kitchen and looked in the fridge. Sighing when she saw that it was empty of everything except margarine, milk, and several bottles of the water Mia seemed to exist on, she asked what was for dinner.

'Nothing,' Kim told her. 'Mia's not given me her keeps, so you'll have to get yourself something from the chippy.'

Michelle tutted softly. Mia might not have handed over *her* keeps, but Michelle had, and the least she expected in return was food. But now she was expected to try and scrape together the money for dinner from her EMA, even though her mum had already taken half of it, and the rest had been swallowed up on bus fares to and from college.

Deciding that maybe it wouldn't hurt to go hungry tonight, she filled the kettle instead.

'Mia's going out,' Kim said when Michelle handed her a cup of tea and headed for the door. 'And you know what she's like when you get in her way, so stop down here till she's out of the bath and ready to go.'

'I need to get changed,' Michelle protested. 'I've got to be back at the centre in a couple of hours to help out at the barn dance.'

'Something else you won't be getting paid for, no doubt?' Kim grumbled. 'And if you've got that much free time on your hands, I don't see why you don't get a proper job and fetch some money in. It's not like we couldn't do with it.'

'I'm doing it for the experience,' Michelle reminded her, wishing she didn't always have to be so condemnatory. 'And my tutor thinks I'll easily get a job there when my course finishes.'

'If there's one going – which there *won't* be,' Kim retorted bluntly. 'I mean, why are they going to suddenly start paying you to do what you've been doing all year for free? You need to start wising up, lady.'

A little offended by the insinuation that nobody valued her efforts, Michelle slumped down on the chair by the window and sipped at her tea. No matter how hard she tried, she always seemed to end up facing this same brick wall. Mia could do no wrong, Michelle could do no right. Mia could do as she pleased, Michelle must do as she was told. Michelle could go hungry, because Mia had *yet again* got away with not paying her keeps. And now Michelle couldn't even go to her own bedroom to get changed, because she'd be getting in *Mia*'s way.

Not that she particularly *wanted* to see Mia, because the hatred her sister felt for her was as ripe as ever. If anything, it was even more intense. But she'd apologised a thousand times to no avail for screwing that TV ad up, so now she just stayed out of her way – which, fortunately, wasn't too difficult, given that Mia spent so much time out of the house, either working, or partying with her new boyfriend.

It was almost an hour before Mia came downstairs, dressed like a film star and drenched in the expensive perfume that Steve had bought her a few days earlier. Blanking Michelle, she snatched up the phone and booked herself a cab.

'Er, what do you think you're doing?' Kim demanded, hearing her tell the operator that she would be going into town. 'You've got to go to the bank first.'

'Sorry, it completely slipped my mind,' Mia lied. 'And I can't go now or I'll be late.'

'That's your own fault for taking so bloody long to get ready,' Kim pointed out. Then, narrowing her eyes, she looked Mia up and down. 'I haven't seen them clothes before. Or them shoes.'

'So?' Mia replied shortly, taking her cigarettes out of her bag and lighting up.

Kim's eyebrows shot up in indignation and she snapped her fingers. 'Er, I'll have one of them, seeing as you're offering. And then you can explain where you got the money to be splashing out on fancy clobber when you reckon you can't afford to pay your keeps.'

Mia tossed a cigarette to her and said, 'I didn't pay for it, if you must know. Steve did.'

'Oh, and I suppose he's stumping up for the taxi you've just booked, an' all, is he – even though he's not even here?'

Flicking her a dirty look, Mia stalked to the window without answering and yanked the curtain aside.

'You're taking the piss,' Kim snapped. 'You must have some change, and I don't see why I should sit here gasping for a fag all night while you're off out again, so hand it over.'

'Oh, what, like *you* used to hand it over whenever *I* asked for something when I was a kid?' Mia sniped, dropping the curtain when she saw the cab turning onto the road.

Jaw dropping, Kim gaped up at her. 'You liar! I *always* gave you money when you asked for it.'

'Only after you'd made me beg.'

'Don't talk to mum like that,' Michelle said quietly, pushing herself to her feet. 'She hardly ever had money when we were kids, but you *always* got what you asked for.'

'Was anyone talking to you?' Mia sneered, looking at her sister as if she'd just crawled out of a tramp's backside. Sucking her teeth when the horn hooted, she pulled out a five-pound note and tossed it into Kim's lap. 'There! Now you know how you used to make *me* feel.'

'I'll bloody swing for her one of these days,' Kim hissed when Mia flounced out, slamming the door behind her. Then, balling the money up, she threw it to Michelle, telling her to nip down to the shops and get some cigs.

'I'm already going to be late,' Michelle reminded her wearily.

'So two more minutes won't make any difference, then, will it?' Kim barked. 'Christ, anyone would think I never did anything, but I've spent my entire *life* running round after youse two. I'm like a bleedin' skivvy in me own house, and what thanks do I get . . . ?'

Sighing, Michelle picked up the money.

15

There was a long Joe Public queue to the left of the doors when Mia arrived at Shalimar that night, and a shorter VIP queue to the right. Stepping out of the cab, she smiled when Simone spotted her and rushed over.

'You look *amazing*!' Simone gushed, looking her up and down. 'Is that a Dior?'

'Vintage,' Mia affirmed, giving a little twirl in the short beaded dress with its shimmering purple and green hues, plunging neckline and non-existent back.

'And please don't tell me they're Rossi?' Simone was breathless with envy now as she gazed at the strappy shoes on Mia's feet. 'I saw them in Milan a few years ago, and they cost an absolute *fortune*!'

'Uh-huh,' Mia lied, preening herself for the benefit of the people who were already looking their way. Simone was an idiot if she couldn't tell the difference between originals and copies – but that was precisely why she was never going to make it to the big time, in Mia's opinion.

Mia felt excited as she took her invitation out of her tiny beaded handbag. She'd been here several times in the past but had never managed to get into the VIP area before, so this was a special night. Especially so because she was about to share airspace with some pretty famous people – like the two premiership footballers who were climbing out of the limo which had just pulled up a short distance from where she and Simone were standing.

Two premiership footballers minus their wives or girlfriends!

Simone spotted them at the same time and clutched at Mia's arm. 'Anton McCready! Oh, my God, I *love* him!'

'It's Ant*wo*n,' Mia corrected her, having religiously genned up on footballers in her pre-modelling days. 'And stop drooling, it's unattractive.'

Mia took a deep breath and strolled towards the queue. As fit as Antwon undoubtedly was, she was far more interested in his friend, Jay King. With his dark hair and green eyes, he really reminded her of Liam. And it might have been years since she'd seen Liam but her heart *still* raced whenever she thought she saw him on the street or in a club.

Deliberately brushing against Jay as she passed him now, she reached out and lightly touched his arm. 'Sorry, babe. I wasn't looking where I was going.'

Jay peered round at her and gave her a slow smile. 'No worries, darlin'.'

Just as Mia was about to ask if he was going to the same party, as a means of striking up a conversation, somebody yelled out her name. Glancing irritably around, she frowned when she spotted Laura Peel waving at her from the end of the other queue. Pissed off when she looked back to see Jay and Antwon disappearing inside, her nostrils flared when Laura called her again.

Knowing that it was obvious she must have seen her, and that she would therefore look like a bitch if she ignored her – which wasn't the best of images to give to your public when you were about to need their support – Mia told Simone she'd be back in a minute.

'Oh, wow, it's fantastic to see you!' Laura gushed, throwing her arms around her. 'It's been absolutely *ages*! What have you been doing with yourself?'

Disentangling herself, Mia stroked her hair back into place. 'Catwalk at the G-Mex,' she said – casually, so the people who were eavesdropping wouldn't think she was being big-headed.

'God, really? That's brilliant,' Laura exclaimed, sounding genuinely proud of her. 'Always said you'd make it big, didn't I?'

'Mmm,' Mia murmured, remembering all too well that Laura, along with the rest of their loser friends, had never believed for one minute that she would make it. But she'd certainly shown them.

'You remember Stu, don't you?' Laura asked now, dragging the guy who was standing behind her into better view.

Nodding, Stu Quigley gave her a sheepish smile. 'All right, Mia. You're looking good.'

'Thanks,' Mia said, her smile staying firmly on her lips and out of her eyes. 'Right, well it was nice to see you, Laura, but I'd best—'

'We were talking about you only the other day – weren't we, Stu?' Laura blurted out, seemingly oblivious to the fact that Mia was trying to get away. 'Darren's always asking after you.' She paused after she'd said this and gave Mia a conspiratorial smile, as if she thought that Mia ought to be flattered by this information. 'You know he's in Strangeways, don't you?' she went on after a moment, mercifully lowering her voice as she added, 'He got eighteen months for *supposedly* beating Sandra Bishop up. And I say supposedly, because he did do it, but only after she went for him with a knife, so she kind of asked for it.' She sighed, and shook her head. 'Anyway, he's coming out on the fifteenth, and I know he'd give *anything* to see you again, so if you're free you should come to the party Stu's organising.'

The words *Are you fucking crazy?* sprang to the tip of Mia's tongue. Smiling, she said, 'Sorry, I think I'm busy on the fifteenth. Work commitments.'

'We could rearrange it,' Laura offered, glancing at Stu

for confirmation. 'I'm sure Darren wouldn't mind if it meant seeing you. You're all he ever talks about these days, and he's always asking us to send in new pictures for his cell.'

Shuddering at an image of Darren lying on his bed playing with himself while she smiled down at him, Mia said, 'Yeah, well, I'll have to get back to you on that. But I've really got to go now – end-of-show party.'

'Any chance of getting us in?' Stu piped up hopefully. 'Us being mates, and that.'

'Er, no, sorry. I would if I could, but it's invitation only, I'm afraid.' Slipping her phone out of her bag when it beeped, Mia deleted her mum's message without reading it. Then, using it as an excuse, she said, 'Sorry, best go. My boyfriend's wondering where I've got to.'

'Anyone we know?' Laura asked, smiling conspiratorially. 'Or should I say, know *of*? Like the footballer you were talking to at the door just now.' Whispering now, to preserve what she presumed was supposed to be a secret – although it was obvious that everybody around had heard, because they were all gaping at Mia, waiting to hear her answer, she said, 'What's his name again, Stu?'

'Jay King.'

'Yeah, him – it's not, is it?'

Blinking slowly, as if to say, *Damn, you got me!* Mia smiled, and said, 'I've really got to go.'

'I'll call you,' Laura called after Mia as she strolled back to Simone. 'Then we can have a proper catch-up – without anybody listening in on stuff they don't need to know!'

Mia waved over her shoulder without answering.

'Friend?' Simone asked.

'Not really,' Mia said, handing her invitation to the doorman, eager to get inside before anyone else tried to delay her. 'Just someone I used to know at school.'

'Ah, that's nice. And it's good that she recognised you. I'm not sure anyone would recognise *me* if I hadn't seen them in ages. But I suppose I'm lucky, because I still see most of my old friends – when I get a chance between jobs.'

'Must be nice to see so much of them,' Mia commented smoothly.

A shadow flitted across Simone's eyes as she wondered if Mia had just had a dig at her. It kind of felt like it, but Mia was still smiling, so maybe not.

Simone handed her own invitation over and said, 'I still can't believe how easily you got Antwon's friend to talk to you.'

'Believe me, if I get my way we'll be doing a damn sight more than *talking* before the night's over,' Mia laughed.

'You've got a boyfriend,' Simone reminded her in a mock-scolding tone.

'He's not my boyfriend, we're just dating. Anyway, you've got room to talk. What was that you said earlier about how you're glad Henry couldn't come because you're dying to shag someone fit and famous?'

'That's different. I've been with him for two years, so it's obvious I'll get bored now and then. But you've only been seeing Steve for two *weeks*, so you've got no excuse.'

'Who needs an excuse to get laid?' Mia quipped, her four inch stilettos sinking into the carpet as they headed up the narrow staircase to the VIP lounge.

Glancing around as they made their way in, she saw Antwon and Jay and a couple of their footballer pals at the end of the bar, slapping each other on the back, no doubt congratulating each other for whatever goals they'd managed to score lately – or whatever birds they'd managed to score *with*. Beyond them, some soap stars were lounging on two semicircular couches, probably gossiping about rival soaps and boasting about their crappy upcoming storylines. To their right, a couple of American R'n'B singers and their entourages had already taken over a corner, and between there and the bar a trio of ageing 'zany' TV presenters were making a lot of whooping noises as they endeavoured to attract the attention they still craved but no longer got.

Making a mental note to avoid them – because she could tell that they would get pissed in record time, then spend the rest of the night dad-dancing and trying to chat up girls young enough to be their granddaughters – she looked around when Simone nudged her. Bruno and Gordy had arrived – and judging by their body language they were still arguing. Noting how cute Bruno looked in his skintight white pants and electric-blue T-shirt emblazoned with the words *Bitch Boy!* in sparkling diamante, Mia scooped a glass of champagne off the bar and said, 'Let's go say hello before it gets too packed and we can't hear each other.'

Aware that Jay was watching her, she smiled to herself as she slinked across to greet the boys. She was *so* going to have him – but she wasn't about to let him know it yet. No doubt he was used to girls throwing themselves at his feet, but she was going to make him work for her attention. Mia wasn't sure if he was still married, because she'd seen it written somewhere that he might be going through a divorce. But, either way, it didn't really matter.

Relieved and delighted to see her, Bruno threw his arms around her. 'Oh, baby, I thought I was never going to see you again! Did Gloria hurt you? Did she pin you down while Fabrizi stamped on your head and skewered your innocent little heart with his wicked tongue?'

'You're such an idiot,' Mia laughed, kissing his baby-smooth cheek.

'That may be true,' he declared, lowering his voice to a surprisingly masculine pitch and placing a hand on his boyish chest. 'But this here idiot *cares* for ya, baby!'

'Oh God, why are all the good men gay?' she teased, resting her head against his shoulder.

'Oh, *he*'s not gay,' Gordy sniped, flashing a tell-tale look of disapproval at Bruno. 'Least, not in *public*, anyway.'

'Oh, will you just shut *up*,' Bruno groaned. Then, rolling his eyes at Mia, he said, 'He's only being like this 'cos I wouldn't hold his hand when we got out of the cab.'

'Oh, believe me, it's got nothing to do with that,' Gordy corrected him tartly. 'But if I'd known I was going to be your dirty little secret, I'd have gone for someone like Ricardo instead. At least *he* wouldn't keep me dangling like an insignificant little piece of fluff!'

'*Ricardo?*' Bruno drew his pretty head back. 'Oh, so it's like that, is it?'

'No worse than you making eyes at that Dutch boy,' Gordy retorted piously. 'Or did you think I hadn't noticed?'

'How could I *not* notice,' Bruno spat back. 'You're like a fucking stalker – watching my every little move, and sucking in every breath I exhale!'

'Now, now, boys,' Mia chided, aware that people were beginning to notice. 'Let's not do this here.' Grabbing Bruno's hand to separate them, she said, 'Come on, you, let's go dance. And *you* –' she gave Gordy a school-marmish look as she shoved her bag and drink into Simone's hands, '– go find us a table. And lose that look you've got on your face before I get back, or I'll slap it off!'

'He's doing my box in,' Bruno griped. 'He's a jealous nutter, and I've a good mind to shag someone right under his stupid nose!'

'How about him?' Mia suggested, giving a surreptitious nod in Jay's direction.

'Ooh, don't tempt me,' Bruno groaned lustfully. 'Mind you, second thoughts, have you seen how big his mates are? They'll probably tie me up and chuck me in the canal if they find out I'm a poof.'

'You're not *that* obvious,' Mia lied. 'But you could always throw them off the scent by making out like you're with me, if it makes you feel better.'

'*You?*' Bruno pulled an incredulous face. 'You'd eat me up for breakfast and spit me out for lunch!'

Laughing, Mia threw her head back and started dancing, not in the least fazed at being the first to brave the empty dance floor. It gave her the perfect stage to show off without anyone else to distract the eyes of whoever was watching. And Jay King definitely was.

As more people began to arrive, the dance floor gradually filled up. Aware that Jay probably couldn't see her any longer, Mia told Bruno that she needed a drink.

Several of their friends had arrived by the time they reached their table, and everyone was chattering loudly about the show, and what each thought of the others' performances. Saying their hellos, Mia and Bruno collapsed into their seats and snatched up their drinks.

'Here,' Simone whispered, passing a small mirror to Mia under the table. 'I saved you some.'

Mia still had plenty of the coke that Steve had given her the night before, but she wasn't about to waste her own when someone else was offering. So, draining her glass, she reached for the rolled-up twenty-pound note and dipped her head to snort the line. This was the first time in two weeks that she'd partied as a single woman, and she intended to make the most of it.

High as a kite by eleven, she was happily exchanging increasingly suggestive glances with Jay King when the committee bigwigs and designers deigned to put in an appearance, effectively stopping the party.

Bored when the music stopped and the speeches started, Mia sneaked off to the loo for a top-up of her own much cleaner and stronger coke. Tripping back out some minutes later, only to bump straight into Fabrizi on his way to the gents, her happy smile turned into a vicious smirk when he gave her a thunderous glare.

'Something wrong, Arni?' she asked, her tone viperish. 'You look like you didn't expect to see me. Not disappointed, are you?'

'You don't deserve to be here,' he snarled back at her. 'They should have kicked you into the gutter where you belong.'

'Now that's not a very nice way to talk to the girl who made you famous,' Mia purred. ''Cos let's face it, there's no way the press would have wanted to talk to *you* if it wasn't for *me*.'

'You are *filth*,' Fabrizi spat. 'Fat, ugly, stupid, *filth*!'

Jay King came up behind him in time to catch this, tapped him on the shoulder, and said, 'Apologise to the lady.'

'*Lady?*' Fabrizi squawked. 'I assure you this *slut* is no lady, my friend!'

Losing the vicious smile, Mia placed a hand on her throat and blinked nervously up at Jay as if she'd been truly scared.

'And you're no friend of mine,' Jay told him, the quiet tone of his voice at odds with the anger that was flashing in his eyes. 'But *she* is,' he added, nodding towards Mia. 'And if I ever catch you talking to her like that again, I'll rip your fucking liver out and feed it to you in a drip – got that?'

Almost crying with fear, like a typical bully who crumpled in the face of real strength, Fabrizi spluttered something unintelligible and flapped his hands. Guessing that he wouldn't be causing any more trouble, Jay jerked his head at him in a *piss off* gesture. Blushing fiercely, Fabrizi lurched into the gents.

'You okay?' Jay asked Mia.

Nodding, she exhaled nervously. 'Thanks for that. I didn't know what he was going to do.' Thinking how gorgeous Jay was up close, she said, 'He's a designer I've been modelling for all week, but I messed something up today and he thinks I did it on purpose, so now he's got it in for me.'

'Guys like him are just dicks,' Jay said dismissively. 'But you know where I am if you need me. My name's Jay, by the way.'

Gazing up at him coquettishly through her lashes, Mia told him her own name in a soft little voice, sensing that, like most heroes, he probably preferred feminine girly-girls.

'Your people in there are still going on with themselves, so I won't keep you,' Jay said. 'But feel free to come and join me for a drink when it's done, yeah?'

Murmuring, 'Thanks, I might just do that,' Mia inhaled deeply when he winked at her before walking away. If she hadn't been determined before, now she was *definitely* ending the night in that man's bed.

Glancing at the door to the gents when Jay had gone, she contemplated waiting for Fabrizi so she could finish him off. She'd been looking forward to this confrontation all day, relishing the thought of getting into a verbal spat with him, because she'd seen him at his worst and knew that he was no match for a bad bitch like her. But she decided to leave it, knowing that if it really kicked off Jay would soon realise that she hadn't really needed rescuing. Anyway, Fabrizi still had the agony of seeing her all over the papers abusing his beautiful creation to come – and that was going to hurt a lot more and for a lot longer than a few nasty words.

Back at the table when the music came back on at last, Mia shook her head when Bruno asked if she wanted to dance.

'Sorry, but I've promised myself to a straight man.'

Drawing his head back as she reached for her handbag, Bruno pursed his lips and demanded to know who. His jaw dropped when she nodded in Jay's direction, and he gasped, 'You sneaky bitch! You knew he was top of my list.'

'Your *wish* list,' she quipped, leaning down to kiss him.

'Face it, bitch boy, some men need a *real* woman, not a pretend one.'

Waggling his head in mock-indignation, Bruno said warningly, 'Watch your back, girlfriend, 'cos some *other* man might think he's already got exclusive rights.'

Knowing that he was referring to Steve, Mia gave a nonchalant shrug. 'Well, some *other* man best get a grip, 'cos Mia Delaney don't belong to no one but her own sweet self!'

'You got plans?' Jay asked fifteen minutes later, his face so close to Mia's as they gazed into each other's eyes that she could almost taste the alcohol on his breath.

'Yes,' she murmured, rubbing her knee against his inner thigh. 'I take it you're staying at a hotel tonight?'

'Uh-huh.'

'So why are we still sitting here?' Finishing the second drink she'd had since joining him, she whispered. 'Get a cab and wait at the corner.'

Smiling, because she obviously wasn't some kiss-and-tell tart – not that it would have stopped him, because he was hot for her – Jay said, 'See you in five.'

Leaving him to make his excuses to his boys, Mia went back to her friends with a weary look on her face.

'What's up?' Simone asked. 'You look really fed up. Didn't it work out with him?'

'No, he's an idiot,' Mia lied. 'All he talks about is football, and I'm *so* not interested.' Shrugging now, she added, 'I'm pretty knackered, anyway, so I wouldn't have been much use to him. I think I'll just go home and get my head down.'

'Aw, you can't go,' Simone moaned, clutching at her hand. 'There's hours to go yet, and I might not see you again for ages.'

Smiling regretfully, Mia said, 'Sorry, babe, my head's banging. I need some fresh air.'

Looking as if she was about to cry, Simone threw her arms around Mia, gushing, 'We've *definitely* got to stay in touch. I've got your number, so I'll give you a ring and we'll meet up – soon. Okay?'

Nodding, Mia disentangled herself. Looking around for Bruno to tell him she was going, she smiled when she spotted him flirting with a pretty-boy waiter. She told Simone to kiss him goodbye for her, blew kisses to the rest of the models and made a hasty exit.

She spotted the taxi down at the corner and hurried towards it – unaware that Robbo was watching from the shadows of a shop doorway across the road.

16

Mia was smiling contentedly when the taxi pulled up behind Sammy's Bentley the following lunchtime. Net curtains twitched at windows all along the street as she stepped out, and chinks appeared in blinds. Tossing her head back, she strolled up the path like a movie star.

Kim barrelled out into the hall and said, 'Where have you *been*? We've been worried sick about you.'

'Why?' Mia asked, kicking off her heels.

'Because you disappeared, and no one knew where the hell you'd gone,' Kim told her, following her into the front room. 'The phone's not stopped ringing all morning and I had no idea what to tell people. I rang all your friends, but that Laura was the only one who'd seen you, and she reckoned you'd gone off with some footballer. So then I was *really* worried, 'cos for all I knew he could have had you locked up in some hotel being – what do they call it – *roasted*.'

'What the hell do *you* know about stuff like that, mother?'

'Hey, I read the papers, I know what goes on out there. Anyway, I'm not the only one who thought something bad might have happened, 'cos Sammy was worried, an' all – weren't you, Sammy?'

Guessing from Mia's clothes and the shadows circling her eyes that she'd spent the night partying and was probably exhausted, Sammy said, 'We were starting to wonder. Maybe you could have rung your mum to let her know you were okay.'

'Or answered my flaming messages,' Kim added reproachfully. 'I sent enough, so you must have known I was tearing my hair out.'

'I had my phone switched off,' Mia told her truthfully, perching on the arm of the chair. 'I don't see why you're so worked up, though. I've stayed out loads of times before, and you haven't been worried about me.'

'This is different.' Snatching up the pile of newspapers that Sammy had brought with him, Kim shoved them under her nose. 'Any weirdo could have grabbed you after seeing this lot!'

'They only came out this morning,' Mia reminded her, glancing at the picture on the front page of the *Mirror*. She'd seen them all already, having studied them in detail over breakfast in bed with Jay. But it gave her a buzz to see them again.

'Let's not dwell on that now,' Sammy suggested, sensing that Kim was about to start ranting again – and he'd already had a good hour of it, so his ears needed a rest. 'You're back, and you're obviously all right, so if we can just have a quick talk about where we go from here I'll leave you in peace.'

Shuffling forward on the couch, he reached for his briefcase and took out a sheaf of papers.

'I've had several enquiries since the show yesterday, but we'll discuss them in a minute. First, I just want you to take a quick look at the contract that was faxed over from Prague. It's six months away but they like to have these things signed and sealed well in advance so, if you're happy with the terms, we should get that sent back a.s.a.p.'

'You don't usually ask if I'm happy with the terms,' Mia reminded him.

'You're not usually in as much demand as you are right now,' Sammy came back smoothly. 'Which puts us in the rather fortunate position of being able to raise the fee-bar somewhat.'

'It's 'cos of the papers,' Kim chipped in excitedly. 'Sammy reckons he can pretty much dictate how much they've got to pay now your name's getting known.'

'I understood without you spelling it out, thank you very much,' Mia said brusquely as she walked into the kitchen.

Close on her heels, Kim slammed the newspapers down onto the ledge. 'Don't you be copping attitude with me, lady! If it wasn't for me, you wouldn't be where you are right now.'

'I think you'll find it's my *face* that's got me to where I am right now,' Mia pointed out dismissively.

'The face I grew in *here*,' Kim reminded her, slapping a hand down on her own fat belly. 'So don't be making out like you popped out of nowhere and did this all by yourself.'

'Well, I sure as hell didn't get my looks from *you*,' Mia said, snatching a bottle of water out of the fridge.

Mortified that Sammy was witnessing this display of rudeness, Kim followed her back into the other room. 'I think you should apologise for making Sammy feel uncomfortable. And then you can apologise to *me* for talking to me like that.'

'I don't *think* so.'

Breathing in deeply in an attempt to control the anger which was making her body shake, Kim gritted her teeth. 'You're one ungrateful little cow at times, Mia! Me and Sammy have done our best, and now you've got the cheek to walk in here and make out like we've done nothing.'

'You haven't,' Mia replied, with all the arrogance of one who believed that her ship had not only come in but was well and truly docked. 'I'm the one who's done all the work. All *you* had to do was get a bit of money together for my first pictures. And all he's done –' she pointed at Sammy '– is make a few phone calls and negotiate a few contracts. And you've *both* done very bloody nicely out of me for the past two years, so don't say *I*'m ungrateful. Oh, and, seeing as we're on the subject . . .' She turned to face Sammy now. 'You might as well know that I've decided to get a new agent.'

'You *what*?' Kim squawked. 'Don't talk rubbish, you stupid girl! You can't just get rid of him.'

'I can, and I am. And we haven't got a contract, so there's nothing you can do to stop me.'

Looking at her, Sammy saw the same glint of stubbornness in her eyes that had been there back when her mum had first dragged her into his office. He'd thought they had developed a pretty good rapport since then, and he'd certainly become more involved with her than he usually did with his models. She'd obviously been biding her time, waiting for her moment to break free. But while she'd undeniably caused a stir and earned herself some useful press coverage, without the correct guidance the opportunities which arose from it would potentially be wasted. This was when the serious work should begin; when they should put their heads together and decide how to build upon what could very easily turn out to be a flash in the pan.

Watching as they stared at each other – the thoughts that were racing through Sammy's eyes unreadable, the determination in Mia's all too clear – Kim felt as if her world was spinning out of control. If Mia dropped Sammy, her new agent would probably be one of those snotty bastards they'd met when they'd first started out – and there was no way they would want Kim around. But how could she allow herself to be pushed out of Mia's life when Mia *was* her life?

Kim swallowed loudly, sounding as scared as she felt when she said, 'She can't really do this, can she, Sammy?'

Knowing that this would be more of a blow to her than it was to him, because he still had his other models to work with, Sammy sighed. 'I'm afraid so, although I really wouldn't advise it at this early stage.' To Mia now, he added, 'It's your decision, but I think you should be very cautious, because it can be a pretty nasty business when you're out there on your own.'

'You *would* say that,' Mia retorted smugly, taking his eagerness to hold onto her as an affirmation that he knew she was going to be huge and didn't want to lose out. 'But I wouldn't be on my own. I'd have my new agent behind me.'

'I'm saying this out of concern for you, not myself,' Sammy assured her. 'You're young and relatively inexperienced, and there are people out there who would manipulate you for their own ends without giving it a second thought.'

Sighing, Mia shook her head. 'Oh, Sammy, you're so wrong. You only think I'm young because *you*'re so old, but you obviously haven't noticed that I'm a *woman* now. And I've been working solidly for two years, so I'd hardly describe myself as inexperienced. But if that's how you see me, then you're leaving me with no option, because all you're going to do is hold me back.'

'I assure you that's the last thing I'd *ever* want to do,' Sammy told her sincerely, gathering his papers together. 'But you're old enough to make your own decisions, so I'll respect whatever choice you make.'

Thanking him for his understanding, Mia eyed the contract. 'Er, you can leave that. I'll get my new agent to look it over.'

'Sorry, it doesn't work like that,' Sammy told her, slotting the contract into his case. 'It's been drawn up naming me as your agent, so it can't just be handed over to someone else.'

'That's not fair,' Mia protested. 'It's me they're booking, not the agent, so what difference does it make whose name's on it?'

'Nothing's been signed, so you're welcome to get your new representative to approach them about having a new one drawn up,' Sammy said, getting to his feet now. 'But don't leave it too long, or they might fill your spot.' Turning to Kim now, he held out his hand. 'It's been a pleasure, my dear, and you know where I am if you need me.'

Tears glistening in her eyes, Kim begged Mia to change her mind. 'This isn't right, not after everything he's done for us.'

Annoyed with Sammy for refusing to hand the contract over, Mia sucked her teeth and looked away.

'I don't know what's got into her,' Kim wailed as she let Sammy out. 'All I can think is that she must be knackered. She'll bite your head off as soon as look at you when she's tired, but she never means it.'

'If she goes, she goes,' Sammy said simply. 'And that's not to say I *want* her to, because I don't. But there's no point fretting about it. You just be proud that you have such a beautiful, strong-minded daughter, because I'm sure she'll be fine – whatever she decides.'

Kim bit her lip to keep her tears at bay as Sammy climbed into his car. He'd been her closest friend for two years – well, maybe *friend* was too strong a word, because they'd hardly had what could be described as a personal relationship; but she'd spent more time chatting to him on the phone than she'd talked to anyone else in that entire time. And he seemed to genuinely like her, which was nice – even if it wasn't as much as she'd once hoped for, because he'd never so much as looked at her as if he saw her as a woman and not just the mother of his little star.

Watching from the step as he drove away, she didn't hear Pam's front door opening. But Pam saw her.

Grinning nastily as she dropped a rubbish bag into the wheelie bin, she said, 'I see your Mia's taken to stripping now. You must be *so* proud.'

Eyes flashing, Kim snapped her head around. 'Too right I'm proud. But for your information it's not called stripping, it's called modelling. And she's so bloody good at it she's on all the front pages today, *and* the phone's been ringing off the hook with people begging to book her – so swivel on *that*, you jealous auld cow!'

'I'm not the jealous one round here,' Pam shot back – loudly, for the benefit of some neighbours from further down who'd come out onto their steps to listen. '*You* are, 'cos you just can't accept that Eric and me are still together after he dumped you. But that just shows how pathetic you are.'

'Is that right?' Kim had a savage smile on her lips. 'Well, if I want him so badly, how come I haven't taken him back any of the times he's come round begging for a second chance?'

'Yeah, right,' Pam scoffed, not believing a word of it. 'Like he'd want *you* when he's got *me* to look after him.'

'And that makes you feel good, does it? Knowing he's only with you 'cos you're stupid enough to do his washing and cooking?'

'And the rest. Don't think he hasn't told me how crap you were in bed.'

'Couldn't have been that bad, or he wouldn't keep sneaking round whenever your back's turned.' Smirking when she saw the doubt flash through Pam's eyes, Kim said, 'If you don't believe me, just watch when you're supposed to be at bingo tonight.'

'Meaning?' Pam came up the path and stood in front of Kim with her fists on her hips.

'*Meaning*,' Kim lowered her face to within inches of her former friend's, 'that you'll see for yourself if I'm lying. Only try and keep your gob buttoned, 'cos if you go telling him what I just said he ain't gonna do it. My back gate – eight o'clock.' Turning on her heel, she marched back into the house.

Watching through the window as Pam waved her arms about, yelling to whoever was listening that people like Kim and her slaggy daughter shouldn't be allowed to live among decent folk, Mia demanded to know what the argument had been about.

'Nowt for you to concern yourself with,' Kim told her.

'Anything to do with Eric concerns me,' Mia retorted angrily. 'And you'd better have been lying to Fat Slag about him sneaking in here behind her back.'

'Excuse me, but this is *my* house,' Kim reminded her indignantly. 'And I'll have whoever I want in!'

'So you *have* been seeing him!'

'No. He's been sniffing round, but I've told him I'm not interested. Anyhow, it's none of your business.'

'Oh, I see, so you don't think I should have a say what goes on here, but you still expect me to pay all the bills?'

'*All* the bills?' Kim repeated incredulously. 'Don't make me laugh! You haven't given me nothing for weeks.'

'Maybe not, but when I *do* pay up I hand over way more than that stupid cow ever has to,' Mia shot back angrily.

'Michelle only gets thirty quid a week.'

'*So?* It's her problem if she's too lazy to get a job and earn proper money like me.'

'Oh, just belt up and get off your flaming high horse,' Kim yelled. 'And quit trying to change the subject, 'cos I want to talk about that rubbish you just pulled on Sammy. I've never been so humiliated in my entire life. After everything he's done, I don't know how you've got the nerve to try and sack him like that!'

'For your information, I was *advised* to.'

'By who? Some snotty little tart of a model who thinks she knows it all?'

'No, by Gloria Ford – the fashion-show organiser, *actually*.' Watching as this information hit home, Mia gave her mother a smug smile. 'Thought that would make you see things differently.'

Frowning, Kim sat down heavily. 'She actually told you to get rid of Sammy?'

'She said he's small-time, and considering they only deal with the major agencies she didn't know how he'd managed to get me onto the show in the first place.'

'They're not trying to get out of paying you, are they?'

'No, they can't do that.'

'Thank God for that.' Tapping her nails on the arm of her chair for several moments, thinking everything over and weighing up the options, Kim finally said, 'I think you should stick with him. He mightn't be as flash as some of the others but at least he cares, and you know you can trust him. That Gloria might not rate him, but someone on the committee obviously does or they wouldn't have got you on the show as a favour to him, would they?'

Mia tutted softly and shook her head. 'You're a right one, you. You'd do anything to keep him around, wouldn't you?'

'Don't be daft,' Kim protested, blushing because she knew exactly what Mia was getting at. 'I just think he's a decent bloke, that's all. And like they say, it's better the devil you know.'

Mia narrowed her eyes thoughtfully and said, 'I'll make you a deal. I'll stick with Sammy if you promise not to see Eric again.'

'Deal!' Kim said without hesitation.

'You're barking,' Mia drawled, laughing now. 'Sammy's fat and ugly, and he's never shown the slightest bit of interest in you. But if you're stupid enough to waste your life hankering after him . . .' Leaving the rest unsaid, she yawned and glanced at the clock. 'Right, I'm going for a nap. Wake me up in a couple of hours, 'cos I want to have a bath before I go out.'

'Where are you going?' Kim asked. 'I thought we could nip over to Sammy's and get that contract signed.'

'Not now.' Smiling, Mia headed for the door. 'Steve's taking me out for dinner.'

'What about the footballer you were with last night?'

'You need to stop listening to gossip. Especially when it comes from a stupid cow like Laura, who I haven't even seen in months.'

'So if you didn't go off with a footballer, where were you?'

'Booked myself into a hotel,' Mia said, taking her phone out of her bag and switching it back on. 'I knew it would go through the roof when the papers came out, so I thought I'd treat myself.'

The phone began to ring at the exact same time as the doorbell. Smiling when she saw Steve's name on the screen, Mia answered them at the same time.

'Hi, lover . . .' she said, laughing softly when she saw the same flower-delivery man on the step with an even bigger box than the first one. 'I take it you've seen the papers, then?'

Tutting when the delivery man grinned and nodded, she gave him a dirty look. 'Not *you*, pervert!' She gestured at him to put the box down, signed the gadget and shut the door. 'God, the way people look at you when you're famous. You'd think they'd just been touched by royalty, or something.'

'Guess I'll have to keep a closer eye on you from now on, won't I?' Steve chuckled. 'Can't have anyone trying to muscle in and steal you away from me.'

'As if,' Mia snorted, shivering as a vision of Jay King's muscular legs flashed through her mind. Steve was in good shape, but there was no way he could compete with a twenty-something footballer. Not that she'd be seeing Jay again, because he'd told her that he was being transferred to Real Madrid in a few weeks.

'Right, well, get some rest and I'll see you later,' Steve said. 'Oh, and I've got a surprise for you, so make sure you're looking sexy.'

Reminding him that she always looked sexy, Mia disconnected

the call. Shouting, 'Mum, there's some flowers out here, can you deal with them?' she tripped happily up the stairs.

'How's my little superstar?' Steve drawled, hugging Mia when he picked her up later that evening.

'Absolutely exhausted,' she told him, feeling like a princess as she climbed into the back of the car, because loads of the neighbours were actually watching from their steps tonight instead of peeping through their curtains as they usually did. 'I need a nice pick-me-up,' she added pointedly as he got in beside her.

'Already?' He gave her a funny look. 'I gave you three grams the night before last. Don't tell me you've done it all.'

Mia pulled a little-girl expression and pursed her lips. 'Sorry. I got a bit carried away with all the excitement yesterday.'

Shaking his head fondly, Steve said, 'I think I'm going to have to keep an eye on you in more ways than one. The rate you're going, I'll have nothing left to give to my dealers by the end of the week.'

Smiling coyly, because she knew he was only playing, Mia said, 'It *is* the end of the week, silly.'

'Still got tonight and Sunday to get through yet,' he reminded her. 'I could be homeless come Monday morning, thanks to you.'

'I'm not that bad.'

'Only messing, babe. You know you can have whatever you want – what's mine is yours, and all that. Subject of, try this.' Taking a small bag of coke out of his pocket, Steve passed it to her. 'It's just come in, and I think it's a bit special.'

Mia leant over and kissed him before turning her attention to the bag. Moistening her little finger, she dipped the tip into the powder and coated it, then licked it off greedily.

'Wow!' she murmured, closing her eyes as a rush of pleasure coursed through her body.

'Thought you'd like it,' Steve said, watching her face closely.

'I tried it in a spliff, and it's even better. Try it and let me know what you think.' He took a ready-rolled one out of his pocket, lit it and passed it to her.

Sucking on it, Mia said, 'Oh, yeah, that is good.' Several deep pulls later, her eyes began to roll.

Watching as she melted into her seat, Steve plucked the spliff from her fingers and dropped it out of the window. No longer smiling, he exchanged a glance with Vern in the rear-view, and Vern immediately changed course and headed towards the club instead of the restaurant Mia had thought they were taking her to.

As soon as the car had gone, Kim had got straight on the phone to tell Sammy the good news. Sounding as relieved and delighted as she'd thought he would, he said, 'Great, I'll come straight back. The sooner we get that contract signed and faxed back, the happier I'll be.'

'Sorry, it'll have to wait till tomorrow,' Kim told him. '*He*'s just picked her up and whisked her off out for dinner again.' Exhaling noisily through her teeth, she said, 'I just hope she can drag herself away from him for long enough to get on with her work now it's picking up, 'cos I'll bloody swing for him if he gets in the way.'

'I'm sure she won't let that happen,' Sammy assured her. 'Anyway, who knows . . . if he's doing as well for himself as you say he is, he may be just the kind of stabilising influence she needs right now.'

'I suppose so,' Kim conceded grudgingly. 'But I still don't like the look of him.'

Chuckling softly, Sammy said, 'She's your child; no one will ever be good enough for her in your eyes. But you're obviously forgetting what a stubborn little madam she is. Believe me, no man is going to steer that girl off course unless she wants to be steered.'

Thanking him for letting her sound off at him, Kim said goodnight. Telling herself that he was right, that Steve Dawson probably *was* a perfectly decent sort who would prove to be a good influence on Mia, she pushed the negative thoughts to the back of her mind and settled on the couch to watch TV. But before the opening music of her chosen programme had finished, she jumped half out of her skin when a terrific crashing sound coming from the back yard shook the house.

She jumped up as Michelle ran downstairs to see what was going on and rushed into the kitchen where she grabbed the baseball bat that she kept in the broom cupboard. Telling Michelle to get ready to call the police, she flicked on the outside light, all set to whack any intruders who might be out there.

It was Eric, and he was already getting whacked by Pam, who had a tight grip on his T-shirt with one hand while she smacked him around the head the other, screaming, 'You lying little shit! You said you was going to your mother's!'

'I was!' Eric protested, shielding his head with his skinny arms. 'I *am*! I just needed to borrow some money for the bus!'

'Off *her*?' Pam screeched, pointing at Kim, who had put the bat down and was leaning against the door frame, watching. 'And I suppose she just guessed that you'd be needing it at this precise fucking moment, did she?'

'I don't know what you're talking about!' Eric yelled, struggling to get free of her. 'You're off your fuckin' head, woman!'

'Yeah, I fuckin' *must* be for believing a dirty little smackhead like *you*!'

'Oh, don't tell me he's on the brown now?' Kim gave a disapproving tut.

'You can shut your mouth,' Pam bellowed at her. 'And don't make out like you didn't know, 'cos you must have if he's been coming round here shagging you behind my back!'

'Who said anything about shagging?' Kim lied. 'I only said he'd been coming round begging me to take him back. And like I told you, just like I've told *him* every time, I'm *not interested*.'

'Don't listen to her,' Eric piped up, sensing that it would be safer to keep on Pam's good side right now, because she was the one who posed the most immediate threat.

'Believe what you want, but just remember who told you the time and the place,' Kim said. 'Now, if you don't mind, I've got better things to do than waste my energy arguing over a worthless little scab like him. So get him out of my yard – and try and keep him out this time!'

Kim went back into the house and rubbed her hands together as if she was dusting the last remnants of Eric off them. Well, she'd kept her side of the bargain. Now as long as Mia played her part and stayed with Sammy and got on with making a success of herself, life was sure to get a whole lot better around here.

Watching her mother, Michelle shook her head and went back up to her room. Everyone was crazy round here, and she sometimes thought she was the only sane person left on the planet. Or maybe she was just boring, like Mia had always said. But, if so, she was glad, because she couldn't be doing with this constant drama.

Waking up gradually, Mia struggled to open her eyes. When she did, it took a while before she could focus. Squinting, she gazed confusedly around. She was lying on a bed, so this was obviously a bedroom. But there didn't seem to be a wardrobe or dressing table, or anything to say *whose* bedroom it was.

Twisting her head when she heard the sound of heavy breathing, she tried to smile when she saw Steve sitting on a chair beside the bed. But her face felt numb, and she wasn't sure if her lips actually moved.

'I must have fallen asleep,' she croaked, her voice sounding distant and odd to her ears. 'Where . . . where are we?'

'That doesn't matter,' Steve told her quietly, his voice sounding even odder because it had an edge to it that she'd never heard before. 'All you need to know is it's not the hotel room you were in last night.'

Blinking rapidly to try and clear her head as goose bumps of fear began to spring up all over her body, Mia licked her lips and tried to think how he could have known about that. Remembering that she'd told her mum that she'd booked herself into a hotel to treat herself in anticipation of the boost to her career, she exhaled nervously, presuming that she'd probably told him the same thing.

'Oh, yeah . . .' She tried to smile again. 'I decided to treat myself after the party. Thought I might as well get some proper sleep seeing as I wasn't going to see you.'

The slap was sudden, unexpected, and sharp as hell. Clutching her cheek as the sting flared across her face like fire, she squawked, 'What the hell was *that* for?' She scrambled up in the bed, feeling nauseous as the room swayed around her.

'You ever lie to me like that again and I won't just slap you, I'll *kill* you,' Steve warned, his voice low and dark. 'You seem to forget I've got eyes and ears *every*where. So, do you want to tell me again about this room you booked yourself?'

Mia's nostrils flared with indignation. He'd obviously found out about her spending the night with Jay, but that didn't give him the right to hit her. Throwing off the blanket that was covering her, she swung her legs over the edge of the mattress.

'Did I say you could go?' Steve shoved her back down.

'How dare you!' Eyes blazing, Mia glared up at him. 'We're only dating; you don't *own* me! And you can't treat me like this. I'm not one of your hookers!'

'I didn't think so,' Steve agreed, his own eyes glowing with barely suppressed anger. 'But now I'm not so sure. And was he worth it? Hmm? Was his cock as good as mine? Did he make you come like I do?'

Genuinely scared now, because she could see how close he was to losing it, Mia edged away from him.

'*TELL ME!*' he roared, baring his clenched teeth.

Resorting to the age-old trick of bursting into tears, Mia buried her face in her hands. 'I'm sorry . . . I didn't mean to do it, but I had a horrible argument with my designer, and he – he defended me.'

'Like the good little defender he is, eh?' Steve growled. 'How very appropriate.'

'It meant nothing,' Mia cried. 'I swear to God, I was so high and pissed I didn't know what I was doing. One minute I was fighting, the next I was in a cab . . . I didn't even know where I was when I woke up this morning.'

Peering at her intensely, Steve breathed hard as he struggled to bring his emotions under control. Seeming to calm down at last, he said, 'You're lucky he's leaving the country soon or, believe me, he'd be dead by now. But if you *ever* make the mistake of thinking you can disrespect me like that again, I promise you'll regret it for the rest of your life – do you understand me?'

Mia nodded mutely and stared up at him wide-eyed.

'Here.' Tossing a small wrap onto the bed, Steve stood up. 'Sort yourself out, then get a wash. We've got a table booked in twenty minutes.'

Mia gasped for breath when he flicked a light on and left the room. Her hand shook violently as she reached for the wrap. She couldn't believe he'd just treated her like that. They'd only been dating for two weeks, and that was *nothing*. But he was acting like they'd been married for twenty years and she'd just broken his heart.

Well, she would be breaking it soon, let there be no mistake about that. She'd play along with him for now, because she didn't want to risk him going off on her again. But just wait till he dropped her back at home tomorrow, because that would be the last time he would ever see her!

17

Mia felt more in control after snorting a fat line of the coke Steve had tossed onto the bed for her. And Steve was back to his usual charming self when she came out of the strange bedroom and walked down the stairs to find herself in the club. Kissing her, and telling her that she looked beautiful, he escorted her out to the car as if nothing had happened.

Still bristling about the slap, she played it cool on the ride across town, letting him know that she wasn't pleased with him. But she soon perked up when she saw that he'd brought her back to the scene of their first date. And, five minutes later, the argument a distant memory as she sipped on the champagne which had been waiting on ice for them at their table – a table for two, this time, instead of the usual three to accommodate the ever-present Vern – she bit her lip when Steve told her to close her eyes and hold out her hand.

'Can I look?' she asked when she felt the velvet of the box brush against her palm seconds later.

'I suppose you'd better,' he said, laughing softly at the excitement on her face.

Opening her eyes, she said, 'Oh,' when she saw that it was a long box, and not the small square one she'd expected. Then, smiling slyly, thinking that he'd probably done it on purpose to trick her, she eased the lid up, sure that the ring would be in there.

'Like it?' Steve asked when she gazed down at the diamonds twinkling like ice in the candle-glow.

Recovering quickly, Mia nodded. 'It's gorgeous. Thank you.'

Saying, 'My pleasure,' Steve reached for the bracelet and looped it around her wrist. 'The least you deserve for putting up with me for so long.'

'Don't be daft,' she said softly, twisting her arm to admire the bracelet. 'It's only been two weeks.'

His eyes suddenly serious, Steve reached for her hand. 'I know, and that's why I'm apologising. I was completely out of order earlier, and you had every right to be angry. But I can't help it if I've fallen for you.' Raising her hand to his lips now, he kissed it before continuing. 'I thought you felt the same, but I guess I forgot how young you are. I've been there; I know how hard it is to take anything seriously. You made a mistake and let yourself get smooth-talked into bed, but I need to know if you meant it when you said you regretted it?'

Feeling guilty now, because he obviously cared about her and she'd hurt him, Mia nodded. She'd been excusing her behaviour by classing their relationship as dating, but she knew that wasn't entirely true, or fair. Since they'd met, they'd spent every night apart from last night together, and if the shoe were on the other foot and he'd cheated on her, she would be going just as berserk as he had.

'I'm sorry,' she said, smiling apologetically. 'You're right, I *am* young, and I'll probably make loads more mistakes before I'm as sorted as you are. But I honestly didn't mean to hurt you, and I won't do it again.'

Saying, 'That's good enough for me,' Steve winked at her and reached for the menu. 'So what do you fancy? How about lobster, for a change?'

Wrinkling her nose, Mia said, 'Never tried it, and I'm not sure I like the sound of it.'

Assuring her that she'd love it, Steve called the waiter over. He straightened the bracelet on her wrist when he'd made their order and said, 'Why don't you bore me with all the details of your show yesterday? But before you start,' he added, giving her a mock-disapproving look, 'let it be known that I was *not* very happy to walk into my club this morning to find my staff perving over my lady's breasts – gorgeous as they are.'

Laughing, because she knew he was just teasing, Mia told him all about Arni Fabrizi, and how he'd pissed her off just one time too many, bringing out the reckless devil in her.

'I didn't even think about what would happen afterwards,' she admitted. 'But it seems to have worked out all right, because I've definitely dominated all the headlines today, and my agent's had loads of people calling about booking me. And tomorrow I'll be signing a contract for a catwalk show in Prague – which is incredible, because that's bound to lead to New York, or Paris, or something fantastic like that.'

'You've done well,' Steve said softly.

'I *know*!' she gushed. 'And that probably sounds like I'm bragging, but I don't mean to. I'm just so excited about it all.'

'So you should be,' Steve said, sitting back when their starters arrived. 'Eat up, and when we've finished we'll go and celebrate properly.'

Celebrating properly, Mia soon learned, meant splashing obscene amounts of cash on the roulette table at Steve's favourite casino in Chinatown, followed by a trip to a nightclub where she danced and drank copious amounts of champagne before floating back to his apartment to drink more champagne and snort heaps of coke before falling into bed and having wild sex until the sun began to rise.

And the celebrations didn't end that night, or the next. In fact, they just carried on happening, as Steve, obviously still trying to make up for having lost his temper with her, went on a complete charm offensive. Nothing was too much trouble, or too expensive. Whatever she wanted, she could have – and the more she got, the more she wanted.

Slipping easily into the role of Steve Dawson's little woman, Mia smiled like the trophy-dolly she had become as he paraded her around over the next few months. Vern was always there, but he was so unobtrusive that Mia barely noticed him. And the faces of the other men who drifted in and out of their company all seemed to merge into one, so she was never sure if he was talking to one of Steve's men or to one of his numerous mysterious business contacts. But she didn't care. As long as she was being treated like a princess and lavished with gifts, coke and champagne, nothing else mattered.

Life was as near perfect as it could possibly be. She had the provider of her dreams, if not exactly the man. And, under Sammy's careful control, her modelling was really starting to take off like she'd always known that it would. She'd secured all the offers that had been tabled after the near-disaster of the G-Mex publicity, and she was just a few months away from the Prague catwalk show, which was bound to catapult her to the next level.

But the little bubble of contentment she was floating around in was just about to burst.

Since they'd got together and he'd taken it upon himself to be her protector, Steve had drummed two important tips for survival into Mia's head: one, she couldn't trust anybody except him; and, two, under no circumstances should she do coke in a public place.

Given that she spent most of her time with him, the first was easy to follow, because she didn't have the time or the inclination to confide in anybody else, anyway. And she did so much coke before they went out at night, and more after they got back, that she hardly ever needed a top-up. But on the rare occasions when she did feel like a quick boost, she made sure the toilets were empty before she did it.

The trouble started when Steve decided to take her to Shalimar one Saturday night. Mia hadn't been there since the VIP party, and she really didn't want to go now in case it sparked an argument. Steve hadn't mentioned Jay King since their fight, but she knew it still played on his mind, because she'd catch him sometimes, watching her with a dark, brooding look on his face. And knowing that distrust and insecurity still festered below the charming façade, she didn't want to go anywhere or do anything to spark him off.

Unfortunately, she couldn't tell him why she didn't want to go to Shalimar this night without raising his suspicions and, as he'd already arranged to meet someone there, she had no choice but to go with him. And just as she'd feared would happen, fate stepped in and created a situation that was guaranteed to end in tears.

Just like last time, Laura and Stu were standing in the queue. But this time Darren was with them – looking just as buff as ever, and even more muscular, having dedicated a lot of time to his physique in the prison gym.

Glad that Steve wasn't the kind of man to be made to queue, Mia tried to pretend that she hadn't seen them as they walked up to the door. But, as if they were in some crazy time loop, Laura spotted her and yelled out her name.

'Someone you know?' Steve asked, immediately putting his arm around her waist and ushering her inside.

Shaking her head, not giving a toss this time if anyone thought she was being ignorant, Mia said, 'No. Probably just someone who's recognised me from the papers.'

They went inside only to be told that the VIP lounge had been temporarily closed because of a leak and Mia was dismayed when they were shown to a sectioned-off area in the main clubroom. Heading for a corner table, she jumped into the seat that was closest to the wall and hid herself in the shadows.

But it didn't take Laura long to find her. Wandering around while Stu and Darren went to the bar, she spotted Mia and waved to her from the other side of the barrier.

Pretending not to have noticed, Mia sipped at her drink and gazed at the floor. But Steve nudged her, saying, 'That girl definitely looks like she thinks she knows you. Are you sure you don't know her?'

Forced to look, at which point Laura grinned and raised her hands in an *at last!* gesture, Mia said, 'Oh, yeah. I went to school with her.'

'Invite her over for a drink,' Steve suggested. Immediately amending this when he spotted the men he was meeting as they walked through the door, he said, 'Second thoughts . . . take this and buy her one.' Pulling a couple of twenties out of his wallet, he pushed them into her hand.

Mia snatched up her bag and rose reluctantly to her feet. She didn't usually mind being shunted off while Steve talked business, because they were usually at his club when it happened and she could wander about playing queen of the castle. But if she went and talked to Laura now, it was inevitable that Darren would find them. And, while she had no doubt that she could put him in his place without too much fuss, she dreaded the thought of Steve seeing them together and guessing that they had a past.

'I thought you were never going to notice me,' Laura exclaimed when Mia came over to the barrier. Reaching across, she gave her a hug. 'Amazing, huh? Second time I've seen you in months, and both times it's been here.'

'Mmm, amazing,' Mia agreed, her gaze darting nervously out over Laura's shoulder. 'You must come here a lot.'

'Every weekend,' Laura admitted, rolling her eyes. 'Stu's

cousin is the DJ, so he won't go anywhere else. Anyway, look at *you* looking even more gorgeous than last time,' she went on, giving her a playful nudge as she added, 'I could have killed you after those pictures came out. Stu wouldn't stop gawping at them, and I was that jealous! But he's been behaving since Darren got out. Doesn't care if *I* object to him lusting after you, but God forbid *Darren* should catch him at it. Talking of who,' she went on, grinning slyly. 'He's here, and he's dying to see you. Why don't you come and say hello. They're around somewhere – probably checking out the talent, knowing them.'

'Ah,' Mia murmured, casting a quick look back at the table. 'That might be a bit awkward. I'm with my fella.'

Glancing over, Laura's eyebrows rose. 'Wow, he's *gorgeous*.'

'The white one,' Mia told her, guessing that she was lusting over Vern. Then, clarifying which white man, because the two men who'd just joined them were also white, she said, 'The one who looks a bit Chinese.'

'Not bad,' Laura said, nodding her approval.

Blanching when she saw Stu and Darren heading their way, Mia said, 'I, er, just need to go to the loo.'

'I'll come with you,' Laura offered annoyingly. Linking arms with her when she cocked her leg over the barrier, she said, 'Just like old times, eh? Remember how we used to meet up in the loos at school for a fag and a gossip. Subject of . . . I saw Lisa Holgate the other day, and she's *fat*, man. She's got a kid now – and by the looks of her, another on the way. She swears she's not pregnant again, though, so I suppose we'll just have to wait and see. She was with Jenny. You know she's at uni in Sheffield now, studying law? Always was the brainbox, though, wasn't she? And you'll never guess who she's seeing? Only that lad who—'

'Laura, *please*,' Mia interrupted, a pained expression on

her face as she pushed her way towards the toilets. 'I'm *so* not interested.'

'How could you not be interested in the old gang?' Laura asked, giving her a disbelieving smile. 'We're the BFLC crew: best friends for *life*, not just Christmas – remember?'

Mia gave her a withering look. 'We were fifteen, Laura. And now we're not. At least, *I'm* not,' she added scathingly.

Narrowing her eyes, Laura said, 'You being funny?'

'*No*,' Mia drawled sarcastically.

'You are,' Laura replied coolly, giving her a look that was a mixture of confusion and hurt. 'Stu said you were being funny last time, but I didn't believe him. He reckons you think you're too good for me, but I told him we're too much like sisters for that. And, all right, so I haven't seen you for a while, but I thought we were the kind of mates who can just pick up where we left off even if we haven't seen each other for years.'

Realising that it was going to take bluntness to shake this girl of the belief that they were as close as they had once been, Mia had just opened her mouth to tell her to get a life when Darren and Stu turned up.

Darren was staring at her as if in awe, and he had a smile of what Mia could only describe as shyness on the lips that she still remembered kissing.

'Told you,' Stu said, grinning as he nudged him. 'Looks well good, don't she? Way sexier than all them piccies you've been fantasising over for so long, eh?'

Flashing him a *Shut your stupid mouth!* look, Darren said, 'All right, Mia. Long time no see. How's it going?'

He looked even better up close than in the glimpse she'd had of him in the queue outside, and he seemed to have matured, because he wasn't giving it with the cocky *I am* that he used to be so full of. But Mia hadn't forgotten the way he'd finished with her, talking to her like she was a piece of dirt in order to keep his bitch happy. And it didn't matter that it had been Michelle who'd actually taken the shit, he'd intended it for her ears – and hadn't made any effort to contact her afterwards to tell her that he hadn't meant it. So he could stand here now, giving her goo-goo eyes because she was gorgeous and famous and he felt like they had something to talk about because he'd taken her virginity, but he *so* wasn't getting a piece of her.

'Don't bother, Darren,' Laura said sharply, folding her arms. 'She's made it quite clear she thinks she's better than us.'

'Laura, I never said that,' Mia told her wearily, sensing that this would turn into a scene if she didn't put a stop to it now. 'I just said I wasn't interested in what Lisa and Jenny were up to. You can't seriously think I'd still want to be mates with them after the way they turned against me at school when . . .' Trailing off because she'd been about to mention the time when Sandra Bishop had attacked her, she shrugged. 'Well, you know what I'm talking about.'

'If it's only them you've got a problem with,' Laura said quietly, 'how come you never return my calls? I know it's the right number, 'cos your mum gave it to me when she called that day asking if I'd seen you.'

Lips tightening, furious with her mum for giving out her number without asking permission, Mia said, 'She must have given you my work number, but I hardly ever check that 'cos my agent deals with everything.'

Murmuring a disbelieving, 'Mmm,' Laura said, 'So why haven't you bothered trying to get in touch with me? You know where I am, and you knew I wanted to hook up with you. Or couldn't you be bothered, 'cos I'm not one of your posh model mates?'

'Laura, have you any idea how busy I've been?' Mia protested. 'I'm working all the time. Christ, I hardly get a minute to talk to my own *mum*.'

'Quit interrogating her, man,' Darren said, irritated with Laura for ruining his reunion. 'She's busy; you can't expect her to drop everything to run round after you.'

'I'm not,' Laura shot back. 'I just don't see why she thinks she's too good to even call me to say hello.'

'Oh, believe what you want,' Mia snapped, fed up with the schoolgirl farce this was descending into. 'I've got better things to think about. Nice to see you again, Darren. Hope you and Sandra have managed to patch things up, 'cos she was always the one you really loved.'

Reaching out as Mia turned to go into the toilets, Darren grabbed her arm. 'Wait, you're wrong. Me and Sandra are history.'

Yanking her arm free, Mia said, 'Oh, *great*!' when her bag fell to the floor and the contents spilled out at their feet. Squatting down to help her pick them up, Darren gave her a questioning look when he picked up the small plastic bag of coke. Snatching it, she shoved it back into her bag.

Vern came around the corner at that exact moment. Seeing the way her and the boy's eyes seemed to be locked, he grabbed the back of Darren's jacket and hauled him to his feet, slamming him up against the wall.

'What the *fuck* . . . ?' Darren roared, trying to shove him off. 'Who d'y' think you're messing with, dickhead?'

Holding him easily with one huge hand on his chest, Vern looked at Mia. 'You know this clown?'

Face drained of colour, Mia instinctively shook her head, praying that Darren would have the sense not to contradict her. She'd always known that Vern must be hard, but this was the first time she'd ever actually seen him in physical action, and Darren was obviously no match for him. And Stu wasn't helping; he was too busy whispering to Laura – probably telling her to go and round up some mates before he attempted to help out his friend.

Shaking now, she said, 'It's okay, Vern, you can let him go. I dropped my bag and he was helping me pick my stuff up, that's all.'

Inclining his head towards Darren, Vern spoke to him so quietly that only Darren could hear what was being said before dropping him. Flashing him a glance of resentment, Darren straightened his shirt and jacket and jerked his head at Stu.

'Steve's ready to get off,' Vern told Mia when they had gone, as calmly as if nothing had happened.

Nodding, she bit her lip, wondering if she ought to ask him not to mention what had just happened. Deciding against it, figuring that it would only make her look guilty, she said, 'Won't be a minute. I just need the loo.'

Scuttling into the ladies, she rushed into the empty cubicle at the far end of the block and locked the door. Hands shaking violently, she took out the coke and rooted for her small compact mirror. Realising that it must have skidded across the tiled floor when she'd dropped her stuff, she tore a wad of toilet roll off the dispenser and wiped the top of the cistern before sprinkling out a thick line. Hesitating when she heard the main door swing open, she held her breath. Seconds later, it opened again and some chattering girls entered. Relaxing, knowing that their noise would drown out hers as cubicle doors slammed shut and the sound of pissing and singing rang out, Mia quickly rolled up one of the twenty-pound notes Steve had given her and snorted the line. Closing her eyes, she leaned her head right back as the rush enveloped her – oblivious to the mobile phone filming her over the cubicle divider.

Steve's face was stormy when Mia joined him by the club's front door. Grabbing her roughly by the arm, he marched her down the road and around the corner into the side street where the car was parked.

'Where's Vern?' she asked, trying to act as if she hadn't realised that anything was wrong in order to defuse whatever was going on in his head.

'Dealing with something,' Steve snarled, using his own key-fob to unlock the car doors. Yanking the back door open, he shoved her in before jumping into the driver's seat and starting the engine.

'What's going on, babe?' Mia asked nervously, clinging to the sides of her seat as he pulled furiously away from the kerb. 'Please don't tell me this has got anything to do with that guy Vern gripped just now. 'Cos I've already told him what was happening. I dropped my bag, and he was helping me pick up my stuff, that's all.'

Ignoring her, Steve drove around the block and screeched to a halt when he spotted Vern. Hopping in, Vern reached into the glove compartment and took out a wad of tissues as they set off again.

Mia felt sick when she noticed that he was wiping blood off his knuckles. She dug her nails into her palms and cast longing glances out of the window as they sped out of town, wishing she could leap out and roll to freedom on the grey pavements that were whizzing by.

Still furious when he parked up at the back of the club, Steve shoved Mia inside. Staying outside to have a hushed conversation with Vern, he came in a few minutes later and lashed her across the face with the back of his hand, sending her sprawling across the floor.

Crying out, she looked to Vern for help, but he just calmly locked the door and walked through to the club.

'Who was he?' Steve demanded, his face livid as he stood over her. 'And before you open your mouth, just remember what I told you last time – lie, and I'll *kill* you.'

Weeping now, Mia cowered back into the corner. There was no sense in lying; Vern had obviously got that blood on his hand from beating Darren up, so Darren would have had no option but to tell him exactly who he was. But he might at least have had the sense not to mention that Mia and he had slept together.

'He's – he's just an old friend.'

'*Friend?*' Steve repeated caustically, swinging his foot back and slamming it into her thigh. 'Try again, sweetheart!'

Mouth wide, barely able to speak for the pain, Mia clutched at her leg. 'All right! I went out with him! But I was only fifteen . . . we were just kids.'

Squatting down beside her, Steve grabbed her by the throat and slammed her head back against the wall. Teeth gritted, he said, 'So why did you lie to Vern and say you didn't know him?'

'Because I knew you'd be like this if you found out,' Mia sobbed, truly terrified now.

'And that girl you pretended not to notice,' Steve went on, putting two and two together. 'She was with him, wasn't she?'

'Yes,' Mia admitted, blinded by tears as she clutched at his wrist to prevent him from strangling her. 'But I knew it would end up in trouble, that's why I didn't want to see her. But you *made* me go and talk to her. You *made* me!'

'Stop making so much fucking noise,' Steve hissed, banging her head off the wall again. 'Did you arrange to meet up with them there? When I said that was where we were going, did you get straight on your phone and set it all up so you could see your old fucking boyfriend again?'

'*NO!*' Mia sobbed. 'I didn't even want to go, 'cos I saw her there last time and didn't want to risk bumping into her again.'

'Did you now,' Steve growled, his eyes flashing dangerously. 'So this is the *second* time you've seen him and thought you could get away with not telling me?'

'No!' Mia squawked. 'He was in prison that time – I swear

to God! She kept going on about how much he wanted to see me when he got out, but I told her I wasn't interested. And tonight I told her I was with you and didn't want to see him, but he caught up with us outside the loos. I was telling him to get lost when I dropped my bag, and that's when Vern came round and gripped him up.'

Staring into her eyes for several long moments, Steve said, 'You know how lucky you are that your ex-dick told Vern the same story? If there had been one thing that had been remotely different, it wouldn't just be *him* on his way to hospital right now – you understand me?'

Biting her lip, Mia squeezed her eyes shut and nodded.

Reaching for her handbag now, Steve said, 'Let's just check your phone, eh? Make sure you haven't been taking numbers behind my back.'

Tipping the bag up, he was about to reach for her phone when he noticed the edge of a photograph sticking out of her purse. Pulling it out, he stared at it intently. Then, a light of recognition sparking in his eyes, he glared at her. 'What the *fuck* are you doing with a picture of that dickhead footballer?'

Guessing that he'd mistaken Liam's dark hair and green eyes for those of Jay King, Mia shook her head and blurted out the first thing that came into her head. 'It's not him, babe . . . I swear it's not. It's m-my dad and my grandma. It's the only picture my mum had of him, and I took it 'cos she was going to throw it away. I've been carrying it round for years.'

'He ain't blond,' Steve pointed out, looking from the picture to her.

'No, but my mum is,' Mia reminded him. 'Please, Steve, it's my dad. You can ask her. She hates his guts, but she'll tell you.'

Still holding her gaze to see her reaction, Steve slowly tore the photograph down the middle. Seeing genuine pain in her eyes, he decided that maybe she had been telling the truth. He knew for a fact that she'd had no contact with the footballer, so it wouldn't hurt her if that had been his picture. Anyway, she'd have been more likely to be carrying one of the pro shots of the dickhead in his footballing prime than one of him as a snotty kid.

Letting go of her throat now, Steve stood up and dusted himself down. Then, reaching for her hand, he pulled her to her feet and took her in his arms.

'You know you're my girl, don't you,' he murmured, stroking her hair. 'And I don't like hurting you, but I just can't stand being lied to. Steal my money, smash up my car, call my mother a whore – *any*thing but lie. 'Cos if I can't trust you, then there's no point to any of this, is there?'

Mia shook her head and buried her face in his chest, glad that he was holding her up because her legs were shaking so badly that she'd probably have collapsed otherwise. She wanted to get away from Steve, but they always spent the night together and if she tried to change the routine now he'd get even more paranoid. But there was no way she was staying with him after this. This was the second time he'd hit her, and it had been way worse than the first. At least then she'd been kind of anaesthetised by that really strong new coke he'd given her which had knocked her out. But this time he'd really gone for her, and she dreaded to think what he might have done if she hadn't told him the same thing that Darren had told Vern.

'Let's go get a drink,' Steve said now, gently wiping her tears away. 'I think we could both do with one, couldn't we?'

Nodding, Mia forced herself to smile.

Kissing her softly on the lips, Steve peered into her eyes. 'That picture really your dad?'

'It doesn't matter.'

'Yeah, it does.' Reaching down, Steve scooped up the two halves. 'I'll get it fixed up for you tomorrow.'

Having no intention of being here tomorrow, Mia took the pieces from him, saying, 'It's okay. I'll just sellotape it. It'll be fine.'

Glad of the dim lights to hide her tears and bruises as he walked her into the club, Mia went through the motions of drinking and chatting as usual until it was time to leave. But beneath the smile, she was just praying for the night to end so that she could go home and shut Steve out of her life for ever.

18

Kim was woken by the phone.

'Sorry for disturbing you,' Sammy apologised when she picked it up, his tone grimmer than she'd ever heard it. 'Ordinarily I'd have waited and rung back later if I caught you in bed, but this can't wait.'

'It's okay,' she assured him. 'Has something happened?'

'Mia's in the paper. Is she there?'

'No, why?'

'I've had a couple of journalists on the phone already,' Sammy told her. 'It's not good, and we need to get hold of her.'

'What's going on?' Kim asked worriedly.

'I'll tell you when I get there,' Sammy said. 'And if anyone knocks or rings in the meantime, don't answer any questions.'

Seriously concerned now, Kim put the phone down and ran upstairs to get dressed. Chain-smoking and pacing the floor when Sammy arrived fifteen minutes later, she practically dragged him inside.

Sammy plonked himself down on the couch and handed her the newspaper he was carrying. 'Read that.'

Eyes widening when she saw the front page, Kim slumped down beside him. There were two pictures of Mia, both grainy, and obviously taken from above. The first showed her with a rolled-up banknote up her nose snorting a line of white powder off the top of what appeared to be a toilet cistern; the other clearly showed her face, with her head thrown back, her eyes closed, and a tiny smile of ecstasy on her half-open lips.

FAME TO SHAME IN ONE STRAIGHT LINE!

As Kim speed-read the snatch of story below the headline – which apparently continued on pages four and five – her frown deepened into a valley as she learned that Mia, who, the paper claimed, had seemed poised to become Britain's next big thing on the catwalk, had been caught last night snorting cocaine in a nightclub toilet.

'Did you know she was on drugs?' Sammy asked when she'd finished reading.

'Did I hell! Don't you think I would have stopped her if I had?'

'Of course you would, that was a stupid thing to say,' Sammy said as he reached out and patted her hand. 'Do you know where she is now?'

'No, but I'll bet she's with that flaming Steve.' Casting an accusing look at Sammy now, she added, 'You know – the man *you* reckoned was going to be such a good influence on her. He's got to be behind this, 'cos she never touched drugs till she got involved with him. I've a mind to ring the police and have him arrested for corrupting her!'

'Let's not jump to conclusions,' Sammy urged. 'We don't know how long she's been doing it, or who's been supplying her. But we do know that she needs help before it gets any worse.'

'How can it get any worse?' Kim wailed. 'She's ruined.'

'Not necessarily,' Sammy said thoughtfully. 'This is the first negative press she's had, so I reckon if we put our heads together we should be able to come up with a genuine-sounding statement of contrition.'

'You what?' Screwing her face up, Kim looked at him as if he'd spoken in Latin.

Before he could explain, Michelle walked in. Blushing,

because she'd avoided Sammy like the plague since the abortive TV shoot where she'd fooled him into thinking that she was Mia, she said, 'Sorry, mum, I saw this when I was on my way to town, and thought I'd best show you before you found out off someone else.'

Seeing that she was holding the same newspaper that Sammy had already brought round, Kim told Michelle that she was a bit late. 'You stopping in, or going straight back out?' she asked then. 'Only, you can put the kettle on if you've got a minute. I haven't even offered Sammy a brew yet.'

Frowning when she scuttled into the kitchen, Sammy called her straight back in. 'Don't you think there are more important things on the agenda right now than coffee, young lady?'

'Oh, no, that's not Mia,' Kim told him quickly. 'That's . . .' Trailing off when she remembered what had been happening the last and only time that Michelle and Sammy had ever met, she blushed. Then, hoping that he didn't put two and two together, she murmured, 'This is Michelle.'

Staring at the girl, Sammy said, 'Good grief. How remarkable. I'm sorry, I had no idea that you and Mia were twins or I'd never have snapped at you like that.'

Murmuring, 'It's okay,' Michelle cast a hooded glance of relief at her mum. He obviously hadn't clicked.

'They're identical,' Kim told him. 'Sorry, I thought I'd mentioned it.'

'No, I don't think so,' Sammy said as Michelle went back into the kitchen. 'You just said you had another daughter. And I'm sure you said she was younger than Mia.'

'Well, she is, by a couple of minutes. Anyway, what was that you were saying about a statement?'

'Basically, when you get caught out – as Mia just has – and there's no denying that it's you in the picture, it helps if you make a statement saying how sorry you are,' Sammy explained. 'You say it was the first time you ever tried it, and you know it was stupid, but you promise never to do it again – that sort of thing.'

'Me?' Kim looked horrified. '*I* haven't done anything.'

'No, not *you*,' Sammy said patiently, remembering that Kim was the kind of woman who took things very literally. 'The one who's been discredited – in this case, Mia.' Smiling up at Michelle when she brought his coffee in, he said, 'Excuse my staring, but it's such a shocking likeness.'

'Mia's prettier,' Michelle murmured, trotting out the mantra that she'd spent her entire life hearing and saying.

'Come now, there's not the slightest difference,' Sammy argued. 'I see that you don't wear make-up, and your hair's different, but everything else is identical.' Chuckling softly now, he added, 'If only I'd known, I could have had you *both* on my books. That would have turned some industry heads, I can tell you.'

Almost choking on her tea, Kim said, 'She's not interested in modelling – are you, Shell? She's the bookworm of the family.'

When she heard a car pull up outside just then, Kim was on her feet and at the window in an instant. Eyes narrowing, she slammed her cup down on the table and shoved her sleeves up as if she was preparing for a fight.

'Right, let's see what the bastard's got to say for himself!'

'Kim, wait,' Sammy said firmly. 'We don't know if he's involved in this, so you can't go accusing him of anything. We need to speak to Mia and get her side of the story first.'

'He's right, mum,' Michelle chipped in quietly. 'Anyway, if it *has* got anything to do with her boyfriend and you go off on him, she'll only defend him and fall out with you – you know what she's like.'

It was this that made Kim stay put. She knew Mia better than Mia thought she did, and Kim knew that if it came to her having to choose between her fat old mum and her big-bucks boyfriend, the greedy mare would follow the money every time.

'All right, I won't say owt,' she conceded, folding her arms. 'But if I find out that it *was* him who got her on it, I'll have him.'

Mia practically fell through the door. Slamming it shut, she threw the bolts across and pressed her eye up against the spyhole to make sure that Steve wasn't coming after her. She'd been acting as if everything was all right, but there was no telling if he believed her, because you never knew what crazy thoughts were going through his head until he acted on them.

Coming out to see what was keeping her, Kim grabbed her and yelled, 'No point hiding out here, lady! Get yourself in there – we want a word with you.'

Shushing her, Mia said, 'Just wait till he's gone, can't you? If he hears your big gob, he'll come knocking to make sure I'm all right.'

'What you talking about?'

'*Him*,' Mia snarled, taking another peek. Exhaling loudly when she saw the car pulling away, she muttered, 'Yeah, go on – piss off, you fucking nutter!'

'Will you tell me what the hell's going on?' Kim asked again.

'I've finished with him – if it's any of your business,' Mia told her, turning to go upstairs. 'So if he calls in future, I'm not here – okay?'

'Oh, yeah, that's fine by me,' Kim agreed. 'At least that's one thing sorted. But there's worse stuff to deal with yet, lady, so get in there and start expl—'

Stopping abruptly when she noticed the ring-like shadow around Mia's neck, her eyes narrowed to slits. Taking her by the arm, she pulled her into the living room to get a closer look by the light from the window. 'Oh, my good *Jeezus*!' she cried when she saw the bruise in all its glory. 'Don't tell me you tried to hang yourself because of them pictures? Oh God, *no*!'

Frowning at her as if she'd gone stark staring mad, Mia flashed Sammy a questioning look.

Guessing that she hadn't seen the paper yet, Sammy handed it to her and watched her face as she looked at the incriminating pictures.

'Oh, Mia,' Michelle gasped, throwing a hand over her mouth when she noticed the enormous bruise on her sister's thigh, which was clearly visible beneath the short skirt she was wearing. 'What the hell's happened to you? Have you been attacked?'

Ignoring her, Mia slumped down on the couch, still staring at the pictures, trying to figure out who could possibly have taken them without her having seen them.

'Mia,' Sammy said quietly. 'Do you need help?'

'Of course she does,' Kim blurted out. 'It's bloody obvious.'

'I'm asking,' Sammy said calmly, 'because I'm trying to assess the depth of the problem. The nature of addiction is such that the ones who need the most help are the very ones who deny it. So, again, Mia . . . do you need help?'

'Please, Mia,' Michelle urged when her sister didn't respond. 'He cares about you. We *all* do.'

Lip curling into a sneer, Mia's head shot up. 'Shut your mouth, you stupid cow. You're not in one of your counselling sessions now.'

Bushy eyebrows puckering together as he glanced from one to the other of the girls, Sammy noticed for the first time just how thin Mia was, and it shocked him. Gradual weight loss was easy to miss when you had nothing to compare the person to. But these girls were supposed to be identical and, compared with Michelle who looked fit, healthy and a perfectly normal weight for her height, Mia was sallow and unhealthy-looking; her collarbone, wrists and knees jutted out painfully, and her cheekbones were much more sharply defined than her sister's.

Switching her defiant gaze onto him as she felt him staring at her, Mia said, 'You don't have to look at me like that. So I do coke now and then – it's no big deal. And I'm perfectly capable of looking after myself, thank you. Always have been, always will be.'

'Oh, yeah, 'cos it's no big deal getting caught sniffing drugs, is it?' Kim snapped.

'It's called snorting, *actually*,' Mia corrected her smugly. 'And don't pretend you know anything about it when you can't even say it right.'

'I know enough to know that you've put your career on the flaming line over it,' Kim countered angrily. 'Or do you think nobody's going to think anything of it, and you'll just carry on as normal?'

'Didn't do Kate Moss any harm,' Mia reminded her nonchalantly.

'You're winding me up now,' Kim bellowed. 'You really think you're on a par with the likes of her? Get a grip! You've only just started out. Who's going to want you after this?'

Staring back at her mother, Mia tightened her lips. She knew that Kim and Sammy were right, that this wasn't just going to go away. But right now, with them pecking at her head the way they were, they were just making her want a snort more than ever. At least coke made her feel good about herself, but these idiots were just trying to make her feel bad. Steve had been right; she couldn't trust anybody – him included. They all claimed to have her best interests at heart, but really they were just using her for their own selfish purposes. Steve liked having her on his arm because it gave him kudos with his stupid friends and business colleagues. And her mum and Sammy just wanted her to do as they said and stay in line, because she was their meal ticket. As for Michelle, *she* was only acting concerned to prove what a saint she was. But none of them really cared how Mia felt. None of them gave a damn that it was because of the pressure they'd put her under that she *needed* the coke.

'I'm going out.' She stood up abruptly. 'And don't bother trying to stop me,' she added, seeing her mum getting ready to stand in her way. 'Because I'm old enough to do what I want.'

'So you'd rather just throw in the towel and lose everything because you've been caught out?' Sammy asked calmly.

'If it means I don't have to listen to you lecturing me, yeah,' Mia replied coldly. 'Anyway, she's already made it clear that I've blown it, so what's the point of stressing about it? There's no going back, so I might as well accept it and start living my life the way I want to.'

'Which means giving up your independence and being a kept woman?' Sammy persisted. 'Forget your dreams; forget the fame, the money?'

'At least I'll be having fun.'

'Yeah, it really looks like fun, an' all,' Kim chipped in darkly. 'Covered in fucking bruises – excuse my language, Sammy – and skinny as a rake. You're going to kill yourself if you carry on like this – if somebody doesn't do it for you.'

'She's right,' Sammy said, trying not to wince when he noticed the angry bruise that Michelle had pointed out on her sister's thigh. 'Somebody's already hurt you, and if you let them think it's all right they're bound to do it again. You're not stupid; you know how these things work.'

'I told you I should have called the police,' Kim muttered. Then, pointing her cigarette at Mia, she said, 'And I swear to God, if you leave this house and go running back to that bastard after this that's exactly what I'm going to do.'

'Don't be stupid,' Mia spat, her eyes flashing with anger. 'I just told you, I'm finished with him.'

'I should think so too!' Kim snarled, the fury at the thought of that man laying his dirty hands on her child making her want to tear him apart. 'Just wait and see what happens if he dares show his face round here again; I'll bloody *kill* him! In fact . . .' Glancing around as a thought popped into her head, she located Mia's handbag and pounced on it. 'I'm gonna ring him; *tell* him to come round.'

'Don't you dare!' Mia screeched, leaping forward and trying to wrestle the bag off her. 'Mum, I mean it! *Don't!* You don't know what you're messing with!'

Hearing the panic in Mia's voice, Kim peered into her eyes. 'Right, lady, I want the truth. Did he do that to you?'

Instinctively covering her bruised throat, Mia said, 'Yes, but he was pissed off with me for talking to another lad.'

'You *what*? You talk to another lad and he thinks he's got the right to strangle you over it?'

'You don't understand,' Mia said defensively, making another grab for the bag. 'He's just a bit possessive, that's all. He's fine if I stick to the rules.'

'*Rules?*' Kim glanced at Sammy. 'Have you ever heard anything like it in your life?' Back to Mia now, she said, 'So were you coming on to this other lad, or what?'

'*No.*'

'But Steve *thought* you were, so he punished you?' Kim shook her head angrily. '*No* man's got the right to knock you about – I thought I'd taught you that much, at least. But if you won't let me deal with him, the police can, 'cos there's no way he's getting away with this.'

'She's right, Mia,' Sammy agreed. 'You can't expect the people who care about you to sit back and do nothing when they can see you're being hurt.'

'Why don't you just keep your fucking nose out?' Mia

screamed, furious with him for interfering. 'This has got nothing to do with you. *Or* you,' she added, turning on her mum again with clenched teeth. 'So give me my bag back, or it'll be *me* calling the police.'

Guessing from her desperation to get the bag that Mia was carrying something in it that she didn't want them to see, Kim tipped it out onto the couch. Picking up the small plastic bag of coke, she looked at Mia accusingly.

'Give it to me,' Mia demanded, her voice low and menacing.

'Where did you get it?' Kim asked, unfazed by Mia's attempt at acting fierce.

'None of your business.'

'Oh, I think you'll find it is,' Kim growled, pushing her down onto the couch and standing over her. 'This is *my* house, and that gives me the right to say what comes into it. And now I've got this –' she waggled the bag in front of Mia's eyes '– I'm going to call the police and tell them all about your drug-pushing boyfriend.'

'It's got nothing to do with Steve,' Mia insisted, terrified of what would happen if the police searched his club or apartment, because he would know for sure that she'd had something to do with it.

Saying, 'I don't believe you,' Kim reached for the phone.

'Mum, *don't*!' Mia cried, tears spurting from her eyes now. 'You don't know what he's like. He'll come after me.'

'He won't be able to if he's in prison,' Kim replied firmly, Mia's obvious fear of the man making her all the more determined to get the scumbag out of her daughter's life.

'I'll do anything you want,' Mia sobbed, knowing that she'd lost the battle. 'But please don't tell the police.'

'Anything?' Hesitating with her hand on the phone, Kim peered back at her.

Arms wrapped around her skinny stomach, Mia nodded, rocking backwards and forwards on the edge of her seat.

Shuffling forward, Sammy put an arm around her and pulled her towards him, saying, 'Everything's going to be all right, Mia. Trust us. We've been behind you all the way because we know you're worth so much more than this. And, whatever happens, we'll always be here for you – you know that, don't you?'

Feeling strangely safe in his big warm arms, Mia nodded.

'If this is all because we've been putting you under too much pressure, then it stops here,' Sammy went on. 'Soon as I get back to the office, I'll cancel the outstanding contracts. You won't have to do anything but relax and get better.'

'No!' Mia spluttered, looking up at him tearfully. 'I don't want to give up modelling. I know I've messed up, but I *need* it. There must be *some*thing I can do to put things right?'

Heartily relieved that Mia was showing that she still had passion for something other than drugs and her destructive relationship, Sammy said, 'Your mum and I were talking before you came in, and I think there's a possibility we could turn this around. But it'll mean you throwing yourself on the mercy of the press and admitting that you've made a mistake. Are you prepared to do that?'

'Can't I just say it wasn't me?' Mia suggested lamely. 'They can't prove it.'

'Don't be ridiculous, it's obvious it's you,' Kim said irritably. 'Christ, you've had your picture in the papers often enough lately, anyone with eyes will recognise you from that.'

'She's right,' Sammy said quietly. 'And someone obviously knew it *was* you or they wouldn't have bothered following you into the toilets to take those pictures.'

'I know *exactly* who it was,' Mia muttered, pure hate in her voice as she remembered the way Stu had been whispering to her so-called friend, obviously setting her up to do what she'd done. 'It was Laura. She was trying to get me to talk to Darren, and just 'cos I said I wasn't interested, she went off at me.'

'*Darren?*' Kim repeated. 'That nasty bugger you went out with when you were at school? What were you talking to *him* for?'

'I just told you, I wasn't,' Mia repeated impatiently. 'But now I know it was her, I'll deny it. I'll just say she's faked the pictures from old ones she already had of me.'

'They can do tests to prove if they're fakes,' Sammy warned her. 'And there's CCTV footage at the club for them to go on as well, don't forget. No. The best bet is the statement.'

'Would they believe her?' Kim asked. 'I mean, she looks bloody awful, so it's obvious she's been on it for some time. If *I* saw her in the paper saying it was her first time, I'd be the first to call her a liar.'

Telling her that it was a risk they were just going to have to take, Sammy explained that if Mia denied it and was proved to be lying, the press would make it their mission to dig up whatever dirt they could on her. Likewise if she chose to get away with making no comment when questioned, because then they would label her as arrogant. All bad publicity, which would inevitably lead to clients with whom she had outstanding contracts retracting them, and potential new clients finding 'cleaner' models to associate themselves with.

'To put it bluntly,' Sammy finished. 'Mia's by no means well-known enough to merit anybody turning a blind eye to this. If she's to stand any chance of turning it around, she'll have to admit it and promise never to do it again. *And*,' he added, speaking directly to Mia now, 'the police may want to question you to find out where you got it.'

'No!' Mia shook her head adamantly. 'I can't tell them about Steve. And before you start,' she said to her mum, 'this isn't a game, and you need to stay out of it. If I've got to make the stupid statement, I will. But there's no way I'm dragging Steve into it, or he'll kill me.'

'If you tell them what you know, he'll be in prison,' Kim pointed out again. 'He won't be able to touch you.'

'Are you stupid?' Mia shot back. 'If *he* can't get to me, somebody else will do it for him. Why do you think I put the bolts on when I came in? Look what he did to me just for *talking* to someone. He's already going to kick off when he realises I've finished with him, but if I grass him up as *well* . . .'

She left the rest unsaid, but they all knew what she meant.

Michelle had been sitting listening to all this in silence. Clearing her throat now, she said, 'There is one way we could do this without involving him.'

As one, their heads snapped round to face her, each of them desperate for a solution.

'You say Mia's got to make that statement or she'll probably lose everything . . . What if *I* make it in her place? At least that way they might believe it was her first time, 'cos it's obvious I've never touched drugs.'

'Oh, 'cos you're *far* too much of a goody-two-shoes for that,' Mia sniped, resenting what she took as Michelle having a pop at her.

Saying, 'Shut your mouth, you,' Kim slapped her on the shoulder. 'Go on, Shell.'

'Don't tell me to shut up,' Mia yelled before Michelle had a chance to speak. 'My career's on the line here, and after the mess she made the last time she pretended to be me, losing me that TV advert and making me have to work twice as hard to get my credibility back, I'm not having her anywhere near this.'

Kim glared at Mia, but it was too late: Sammy had already picked up on what had been said.

'Could you just run that by me again?' he asked quietly. 'Are you telling me that it was *Michelle* at that Wonder Wax shoot and not *Mia*?'

'It's not their fault,' Michelle blurted out, her cheeks flaming.

'I'm sorry for lying, Sammy, but Mia was really sick that day with food poisoning, and my mum didn't want to let you down, so I offered to take her place. I did try, but I'm not like her, and I couldn't pull it off.'

'Good lord.' Sammy shook his head bemusedly. 'I knew Mia wasn't herself that day, but I never imagined that she literally *wasn't* herself. How inventive.'

'Yeah, well, now you know, so you understand why she can't take my place again,' Mia said.

'It wouldn't make that much difference anyway,' Kim said gloomily. 'If Sammy's right, the police might still question you about the coke. And if this Steve's as bad as you say, you can't tell them about him. So we're back to square one.'

Casting a sly glance at Michelle, Mia said, 'What if we say it was *her* in the picture?'

'Don't be daft. Everyone knows Shell wouldn't touch drugs.'

'*You* didn't even know *I* was doing it,' Mia reminded her. 'And you see me every day. We're identical, don't forget. If we say it was her instead of me, they'll believe it.'

'Yeah, and then they'll put the two of you together and see which one looks rough as a dog,' Kim said bluntly. 'And, let's be honest, it ain't *her*.'

'But if we swap them round,' Sammy mused, 'the *new* Mia would still look healthy, and her career would remain unblemished.'

'But mine wouldn't,' Michelle protested. 'I could get kicked off my course if they thought I was doing drugs.'

'Oh, don't be so selfish,' Kim scolded. 'This is Mia's *career* we're talking about, and that's a damn sight more important than a flaming college course. Anyway, everyone knows that students take drugs when they're under pressure, so it won't come as any surprise to anyone.'

'No, Michelle's right, we're asking too much of her,' Sammy

murmured guiltily. 'She's done nothing wrong, and we can't expect her to tarnish her own reputation to save Mia's.'

'Yes, we can,' Mia piped up. 'I'm a *star* – I could be earning millions this time next year. *She*'s only going to be a stupid social worker, and she probably won't even be able to hack that, 'cos she's too much of a wuss.'

'Mia's got a point,' Kim said quietly. 'You know you're a soft touch, Shell. Think what it'll be like when they start sending you round to people's houses to take their kids off 'em and you come up against some gobby bitch like her next door. They'd eat you for breakfast.'

'And spit you out for lunch,' Mia added, smirking as the phrase Bruno had used about *her* not so long ago popped into her head.

Mia's mobile phone began to ring. Still holding it, Kim's face paled when she glanced at the screen. 'It's him!' she hissed, as if he could hear her.

'I can't talk to him,' Mia squawked.

His mind whirring into action, Sammy said, 'Pass it to me.'

'Why, what you gonna do?' Kim asked, doing as she was told.

Motioning at her to be quiet, Sammy took a deep breath and, cupping his hand around the mouthpiece as if he didn't want anybody to hear him, answered the call in a hushed, pompous tone.

'Mr Dawson, please don't hang up . . . My name is Leonard Golborne, and I am Miss Delaney's solicitor. I'm sure you're aware by now of the story in today's newspaper concerning Miss Delaney. We're currently awaiting interview at the police station, and I was about to call you because she was concerned that you may be feeling – shall we say – *apprehensive* about the matter. She wishes me to assure you that you need *not* be concerned, but requests that you do not try to contact her again after today, as she doesn't wish for you to become the focus of any of the media interest or police investigations which will undoubtedly arise from this unfortunate incident . . .'

'Finished?' Steve said quietly when Sammy finally stopped talking. 'Right, well, pass my regards to *Miss Delaney* for a speedy recovery, and thank her for her consideration. But give her a message from me, yeah? Tell her foolish talk costs lives . . . You got that?'

A rare flash of anger sparking in his eyes at the blatant threat behind the softly spoken words, Sammy said, 'She's an intelligent girl, Mr Dawson, and I'm sure that she won't say anything which she may later regret. As she herself told me, she got herself into this mess, so she's just going to hold her hands up and accept the consequences – alone.'

Gaping at him in disbelief when he disconnected the call, Mia said, 'Oh, my God, you're such a major *liar*!'

'Never mind liar,' Kim chipped in, laughing with amazement. 'You should be a flaming actor. You didn't sound anything like yourself.'

'Good,' Sammy said, exhaling nervously as he pulled his handkerchief out of his pocket and mopped his sweaty head. 'I'd hate to bump into him down some dark alley one day and have him recognise my voice. That was *not* a pleasant experience, and I hope never to have to do anything like that again.'

Relaying what Steve had said to him, he gave Kim a worried look. 'I don't know about you, but I'm thinking it might be a good idea if the three of you stayed somewhere else for the next few days. And the sooner we get that statement drafted and presented to the press the better. Once Dawson sees it and realises that she's not implicating him, he might be more inclined to disassociate himself from her.'

'Whatever that means,' Kim muttered, wishing that he'd speak in plain English.

'It means he'll leave her alone when he knows she hasn't grassed him up,' Michelle explained. 'Because he won't want to risk being seen with her if she's being watched by the police.'

'Exactly,' Sammy said, giving her a respectful smile. It was refreshing in his line of work to meet a young, beautiful, obviously intelligent girl who was neither vain nor arrogant. Mia had come a long way in the two years he'd known her, but she'd be a damn sight further ahead by now if she'd possessed a little of her sister's composure, he was sure.

'So, what you're saying is that we need to stay somewhere else for a bit,' Kim said, getting it straight in her own mind. 'Because he might be a danger till he knows she's kept him out of it? But Mia still has to give a statement that could wreck her career and get her in trouble with the police – while he gets off scot-free?'

'Either that, or risk him coming after her,' Sammy replied. 'And, after speaking to him just now, I'd have to say that I think Mia's probably right about him.'

'I am right,' Mia said adamantly. 'He's okay most of the time, but when he turns, he's a psycho.'

Quietly mulling everything over as they talked, Michelle came to a decision. While she vehemently disagreed that her chosen career was any less important than Mia's, it was true that she had far less to lose by taking the blame for Mia's latest mess. The most that would probably happen to her would be a lecture about the stupidity of letting herself and the college down, followed by a couple of counselling sessions. But as she wasn't actually in a bad state of health either physically or mentally, it wouldn't take long to persuade her tutors that she had learned her lesson and was fit to resume her training. And while it would be a major embarrassment to have people whom she respected think that she was a drug user, that was a lot less damaging than the consequences to Mia. Even if it didn't destroy her career, she would carry the stigma for the rest of her life, and the press would bring it up again whenever anything newsworthy happened to her.

'I'll do it,' she said suddenly. 'I'll say it was me in that club last night.'

Frowning, Mia tipped her head to one side and gazed at her sister questioningly. 'You'd do that for me?'

Exhaling wearily, Michelle shrugged. 'You're my sister, and you need my help. *Our* help,' she corrected herself quickly, sensing that Mia would respond better if this wasn't just about the two of them. 'But if I do this and you go back to that man after he put those bruises on you, I swear I'll never speak to you or do anything for you again.'

Mia bit her lip to stop it quivering. 'I can't believe you're being so nice after I've been such an absolute bitch to you.'

Smiling sympathetically, Michelle said, 'I don't blame *you*, Mee. I know about addiction; it dictates your moods and masks your real emotions. And it makes you lash out at the ones who are closest to you, because they're the ones who most want to stop you from doing it. We do that because we love you, but you think we're just trying to deprive you of your pleasure.'

Eyes still glittering with tears, Mia had a contrite expression on her face as Michelle made her speech, but she was thinking, *What a crock of utter bollocks!*

'This is brilliant,' Kim said, a beaming smile on her face. 'So, what happens now?'

Looking at Michelle, Sammy asked if she was absolutely sure about this; had she really thought about the impact it was going to have on her status at college? When she said yes, he said, 'Well, I guess we just need to draft a statement and get the ball rolling, then. But *you*, young lady,' he turned and gave Mia a stern look, 'are coming off the drugs – and no arguments. Your sister's doing you an enormous favour by agreeing to present herself as you but, as we already know, we can't risk her taking on your modelling work. There are a couple of minor jobs scheduled which I can cancel, but we need you fit before we lose anything major.'

'I will be,' Mia insisted, really meaning it.

Sighing, Sammy glanced at his watch. 'Right, well, get together whatever you all need. You're coming to stay with me.'

'Oh no, we couldn't,' Kim objected. 'Seriously, Sammy, you've done enough already. And you've got no idea what a pain it is living with these two.'

Smiling fondly at the girls, Sammy said, 'My dear, I've lived alone for most of my adult life. Believe me, it will be a *pleasure* to have you around.'

Muttering, 'I bet you won't be saying that by the end of the week,' Kim couldn't help but grin as she gestured to the girls to go and get their stuff.

19

Sitting in a small tea shop just a five-minute walk from Sammy's house in Alderley Edge later that evening, Michelle was nervous as she prepared to give the statement that Sammy had prepared to the journalist from the *Evening News*.

He'd chosen that paper deliberately, knowing that the majors would sensationalise it and Mia could come out looking as if she was trying to promote herself. But keeping it low-key like this would add pathos. And, having met Rebecca Dunne on a few occasions, he knew that she would handle the story sensitively.

He'd thought this through in minute detail, even getting Kim to take Michelle to Mia's hairdresser for an emergency make-over. Now, with her hair cut in Mia's style, and having had Mia apply her make-up exactly as she did her own, Michelle endured a torturous five-minute photograph session before Rebecca switched on the Dictaphone she'd brought along.

Smiling, Rebecca said, 'Just relax, Mia, and say it in your own words.'

Taking a deep breath, Michelle nodded.

'This isn't a pleasant thing to have to discuss in public,' she started. 'And I'm not doing it to save myself, I'm doing it help someone very dear to me. You see, it wasn't me in those photographs which appeared in the newspaper today, it was my twin sister, Michelle.

'It saddens us as a family to have to admit that one of our

own has succumbed to such a destructive addiction,' she went on. 'But I feel particularly guilty, because if it wasn't for my job making *me* of interest to the press she would never have been humiliated like this.

'My sister's a beautiful, caring woman, and we all love her dearly. She and I share an immensely strong bond, and I feel her pain as if it were my own – just as I feel her shame over this. But now that her secret is out, we have to forget about ourselves and do whatever we can to help Michelle get better. And I hope that we will be allowed to do this without further intrusion – *please*.'

Switching the machine off when she'd finished, Rebecca gave Michelle a reassuring smile and patted her hand in a gesture of support.

'That was very moving, Mia. This is obviously distressing for you, but many of our readers will know at first hand what you're going through right now, so I'm sure they'll respect your wishes and leave you to deal with this in private. And I'll do whatever *I* can to put the need for that across.'

'Thank you,' Michelle murmured, feeling sick for having lied to Rebecca, because she was being so nice.

Flopping back in her seat when Sammy walked Rebecca out to her car a short time later, Michelle held her hands over her face, cringing with disgust and embarrassment.

'You did really well,' Sammy told her when he came back. 'She really warmed to you, and that was exactly what we needed.'

After paying the bill he helped Michelle up from her seat and, putting a fatherly arm around her, set off on the short walk home.

'If this doesn't give Mia a kick up the backside, nothing will,' he said, chuckling as he added, 'Still, if she buggers about and doesn't get herself in shape for Prague, I've always got *you* to send in her place, eh?'

'God, no!' Michelle squawked, horrified by the prospect. 'You saw how bad I was last time.'

'Don't worry, my dear, I was only joking,' Sammy said, squeezing her shoulder. 'I know it's not your bag, and I wouldn't dream of asking you to put yourself in that position. Let's just keep our fingers crossed that your sister has an ounce of the sense that *you* were obviously born with.'

'Oh, she has,' Michelle said loyally. 'She really wants this, and I think she'll do her best to kick the drugs and make a go of it. She might be stubborn, but she's not stupid.'

Winking at her as they reached his house, Sammy pushed open the gate and ushered her in ahead of him. She was right: Mia wasn't stupid, and she wanted to be successful more than even *she* had probably realised until she'd almost lost it.

20

The first week at Sammy's house had quickly run into two, and then three. And Kim would probably have stayed for ever if she could have, because she'd relished the unfamiliar peace and quiet. But by the end of the third week, even she had to admit that they were outstaying their welcome. Sammy had said nothing to indicate that they were getting in his way, but Mia had put on weight and was looking fit and healthy again, and Michelle was desperate to get back to college, so there was really no excuse not to go home.

Which was absolute music to Mia's ears, because she'd been going out of her mind with boredom since day one.

She'd spent her entire life in the inner city, only ever passing through the countryside on various modelling shoots, but she'd paid no attention to the locations on those occasions because she'd been far too busy admiring herself – and bitchily scrutinising her rivals.

Compared with their own tiny terraced house, Sammy's place was a mansion with its five beds, two baths, massive kitchen, and gardens front and back. But any illusions they'd had of grandeur when they'd got their first look at it had evaporated as soon as they'd stepped through the front door. Sammy had bought it for a song some years earlier, imagining that it would be a retreat from the pressures of his work life. But work *was* his life, and he'd found that he rarely got back there in time to do anything other than eat whatever crap food he'd picked up on the way home and go to bed.

Consequently, it was shabby and unloved, with a thick layer of dust coating everything from the unstylish furniture to the cooker he'd never used to the fridge, which served only as a glorified milk cooler for the constant cups of coffee that he drank. In fact, the most used item was the kitchen bin, which was overflowing with stale take-out cartons and pizza boxes.

Saint Michelle of OCD had soon got to grips with cleaning it up, though. Unable to go to college now that everybody knew she was a secret junkie, she'd moped around like a ghost, scrubbing, polishing, dusting and redusting everything in sight, until it was so clean that they could have eaten out of the toilet, never mind off the floor.

Mia, in the meantime, had prowled like a caged animal. For years she'd fantasised about becoming rich enough to leave Moss Side, but now that she was no longer there she missed the everyday drama of life in the area: the random gunshots, the screaming and arguing of neighbours at war, the roar of engines and the blaring of sirens as the police chased stolen cars through the streets in the dead of night . . . Those sounds were such an inherent part of her life that she'd barely registered them when she was surrounded by them. But here the *lack* of them made the silence thunder in her ears. And the stench of cow dung disgusted her.

Sammy had initially wanted to send her to some stupid rehab place that he'd read about, but Mia had flat-out refused. They'd been convinced that her so-called 'addiction' was something terrible and life-threatening which required the intervention of professionals, but she knew better. Coke wasn't like smack or crack; they were a need, but coke was a desire. And since she'd realised that she desired the fame she'd almost lost more than she craved the buzz of coke, it was relatively easy to stop. But that didn't stop her mum, Sammy and Michelle from watching her like a hawk – which pissed her off so much that it made her want to do it just to spite them.

And she'd been sorely tempted when, the day after the *Evening News* article had appeared, Steve, obviously thinking it was safe to contact her now that he knew the police weren't watching her, rang to ask when he would be seeing her again.

She'd only answered the call out of curiosity, to gauge his mood, to see if she was safe or if he intended to come after her. But he'd sounded so much like his usual loving self that she'd actually found herself contemplating giving him another chance, and had almost asked him to come and pick her up. But the bruises had quickly brought her to her senses. They were still so vivid, and Mia had known that if she went back it would undoubtedly happen again – and probably be worse next time. So, taking advantage of the fact that he was calm, she'd taken the bull by the horns and told him that, much as she'd enjoyed their time together, she thought it best if they called it quits.

To Mia's relief and amazement, Steve had accepted this without a fight – almost, she thought, as if he'd been expecting it. And after he'd wished her well and said goodbye, she hadn't heard from him again.

The police hadn't been able to press charges, because for all they knew the white substance in the photographs could have been sugar. Safe now, all Mia had to do was wait until Michelle's supposed rehab was complete, and then she could get back to work.

And there was plenty of work *to* get back to, because, just as Sammy had hoped would happen, the interview casting her as the concerned sister of the real culprit had caused a resurgence of interest. Mia Delaney was no longer just that model who'd shocked the fashion world when she'd gone out on the catwalk wearing her dress the wrong way round; she was the model with the enormous heart, who had put her blossoming career on hold in order to support her beloved sister. And she couldn't wait to get back out there and start soaking up the new-found adulation.

Driving them home on his way to the office that morning, Sammy said he would call in later to see how they were settling back in.

Left to readjust to the confines of their own tiny house when he'd gone, Kim immediately switched on the TV and flopped down on the couch, while Michelle set about cleaning the dust which had accumulated in their absence. Mia, however, had other, more pressing things on her mind.

'Where are you going?' Kim wanted to know when she declared that she was nipping out, immediately worried that she was going in search of drugs.

'To see Laura,' Mia told her in a dark tone. 'See what the bitch has got to say for herself for trying to drop me in the shit like that.'

Sneering at the mention of *that* girl, Kim said, 'Right, well, make sure there's no witnesses before you do anything. And tell her from me, I'd best not catch her walking down this end of the road or she's in for a slap.'

Saying, 'Don't worry, she won't be in any hurry to come near here again after I've finished with her,' Mia marched out.

Hurrying down the road with her head down, she didn't notice Robbo sitting in a car in the side-street opposite her house. But he noticed her. Sucking deeply on his roll-up, he flipped his phone open.

'Yo, she's on the move . . . Yeah, I'm sure it's her.' Craning forward, he watched as Mia turned into a gate further along the road and hammered on the door of the house.

Just then, a movement across the road caught his eye. Glancing over, he narrowed his eyes when he saw Mia's double come out of the house he'd been watching for days.

'Second thoughts, I could be wrong,' he murmured. 'No, hang about . . . yep, the first one's definitely her.'

'What the fuck are you talking about?' Steve blasted him.

'One came out and took off down the road,' Robbo explained. 'Now the other one's come out to put some rubbish in the bin, and I wasn't sure which was which. But I figure bins ain't the kind of thing your bitch would dirty her hands on. Oh, and now she's stroking a cat,' he added with a chuckle. 'Can't see Mia doing that, somehow; she's more likely to kick it up its arse.'

Telling him to keep an eye on the first one, Steve disconnected the call.

Getting no answer at Laura's house, Mia waited on the step for a good ten minutes before it occurred to her that the bitch was probably hiding out at Stu's. So she set off for there instead – just as Steve's car rolled up silently alongside Robbo's.

After pointing her out, Robbo grinned when Steve tossed a little bag through the window and told him to disappear. Reversing with a squeal of tyre rubber, he did a quick three-point turn and roared off to get to his crack pipe, leaving Steve and Vern to deal with Mia.

As she took short cuts into Rusholme, Mia didn't notice Steve's car following at a distance. But when she decided to cut down a long alley that ran between two blocks of terraced houses, she soon realised her mistake. Halfway down, she stopped in her tracks when the car pulled across the other end, effectively blocking it off. Heart in her mouth when Vern stared out at her, she turned, all set to run back the way she'd come. But Steve was right behind her.

'Going somewhere?' A snake-like smile on his lips, he put his arms around her – looking, to anyone who might be watching from any of the overlooking windows, like someone greeting their lover.

'*Ow!*' Mia cried, twisting her ankle on the cobbles when he jerked her tight up against him. 'Stop it, Steve – you're hurting me.'

'We've got unfinished business,' he told her, his eyes laughing maliciously as he peered down into hers.

'No, we haven't,' she retorted, trying to push him away, angry that he seemed to think he could still behave as if they were together. 'We're finished, Steve, so just leave me alone, or I swear I'll tell the police.'

As soon as the words were out, she knew she'd made a huge mistake.

Prodding her in the stomach with the tip of the blade he'd pulled out of his pocket, Steve increased his grip on her, and whispered, 'Scream, and you'll be dead in two seconds. Now, put your arm around me, and act like you love me.'

'Please don't,' she gasped, finding it hard to breathe now. 'I'm sorry, I shouldn't have threatened you. But I can't keep seeing you, Steve. I've got to stay clean or I'll lose everything.'

'You really thought you could finish with me and I'd just walk away?' he replied softly. 'After the money I've spent on you?'

'If it's about the money, I'll pay you back,' Mia promised, tears of pain and fear glistening in her eyes. 'But please just let me go home.'

'Hasn't it sunk in yet that I *own* you?' Steve informed her coldly. 'I bought you, so you're mine until *I* say different. Now, *move*!'

Jelly legs barely supporting her, Mia stumbled up the alley with his steel-band arm around her waist. Tears streaming down her cheeks now, she flashed desperate glances up at the windows of the houses, praying that somebody would notice what was happening and call the police.

Reaching the car, Steve shoved her onto the back seat and leapt in beside her.

'Where are you taking me?' she asked, sounding as scared as she felt when Vern centrally locked the doors and set off.

Reaching out, Steve wiped her tears with the back of his finger. 'Shhh . . .'

Licking her lips nervously, Mia glanced at him. He seemed to be calming down, but knowing how quickly his moods changed she figured she should probably try to win him round now, while he wasn't as agitated.

'Steve,' she murmured, using the little-girl voice she always used when he'd given her a gift or she was hinting about something she wanted. 'I'm sorry for saying we should call it quits. I wasn't thinking straight. It was just all that stuff in the papers, it did my head in. And the police . . . they kept on and on at me, wanting to know who my dealer was. I didn't tell them anything, I swear, but they said they'd be watching me from now on, so I thought it would be fairer if I stopped seeing you – to keep you out of it. But I didn't mean to hurt you – you do know that, don't you? You know I still love you.'

Holding her gaze the whole time she was speaking, Steve had the faintest of smiles on his lips. 'Finished?' he asked when she'd stopped.

Nodding, she fiddled nervously with her fingers. The back-handed slap came out of nowhere, making her eyes water and her nose bleed.

Seizing her by the throat, Steve dragged her towards him so that their faces were less than an inch apart and, gritted teeth bared, hissed, 'What you seem to have forgotten, you lying whore, is that I *saw* the paper, and I know you wormed your way out of it by saying it wasn't you. Which means that you're *not* being watched by the police, so I'm not in any danger – *am* I?'

'I thought you were,' she sobbed. 'Honest, Steve, I was so paranoid, I thought I was being followed all over the place, and I was desperate not to land you in any trouble. You don't know what it's been like for me these past few weeks, not to be able to see you or talk to you.'

'Well, you're seeing me and talking to me now,' Steve reminded her coldly. 'But all you've done so far is lie, so I suggest you shut your mouth and save your energy.'

Slumping back in the seat when he released her, Mia dabbed at her bloody nose with her sleeve. She was *really* scared now. He'd always warned her not to lie, and now he'd caught her out he would definitely punish her. And going by experience, whatever he did was bound to be far worse than the last time.

After pulling into the yard at the back of the club a short time later, Vern unlocked the doors and marched Mia inside. Right behind them, Steve took a set of keys out of his pocket and unlocked an internal door, pushing Mia ahead of him up the narrow staircase beyond.

This was only the second time Mia had been up to the first floor of the club, but she'd felt so disorientated the last time that she only had a vague recollection of the bedroom she'd been in and of these stairs which had led her back down to the club. She hadn't noticed if there were any more rooms up here, but when she reached the top of the stairs now she saw a long corridor with several closed doors leading off it.

Opening the first door now, Steve flicked the light on and threw Mia inside. She landed heavily on the bed and scrambled to sit up as he followed her in. Edging nervously back towards the headboard as he came towards her, she said, 'Look, I know you're going to hit me, but please don't do anything stupid . . . I've still got to go to work, and you left me with some really bad bruises last time . . . I-I've got loads of jobs coming up, and people will start asking questions.'

'Quit . . . fucking . . . *whining*,' Steve said – slowly, as if the sound of her voice was jangling his nerve endings.

'Please, Steve,' she whimpered, the blood draining from her face when he took a loaded syringe out of a box. 'My m-mum will probably call the police if I'm not home soon . . . Steve, please . . . *PLEASE* . . .'

Steve punched her in the face, straddled her and gripped her arm firmly, squeezing it to bring up the vein. He didn't have time to waste on fooling her into smoking the white heroin that she'd thought was coke the last time. Anyway, he wanted her good and out of it, and this was the only way to guarantee how much went into her system.

'I gave you everything,' he told her quietly as he calmly sank the needle into her vein. 'And you took it all as if you'd *earned* it. And now you think you can discard me like a piece of shit and go back to your own life as if I don't exist? I don't think so! I'm not finished with you, sweetheart. I've got big plans for you. You want to be a *star* . . . ? Well, as of tonight, Miss Mia I'm-a-fucking-supermodel Delaney, that's exactly what you're going to be!'

21

When there was no sign of Mia after a couple of hours Kim began to get nervous. Pacing the floor, she ran to the window every time somebody walked past outside. But it was never her. By five, when Mia still hadn't returned and her phone had been switched off for hours, Kim's nervousness turned to anger, and she marched down to Laura's house, thinking that they'd probably kissed and made up and Mia was busy blabbing all their secrets to the back-stabbing cow.

But Laura hadn't seen Mia. According to her mum, she and Laura had been out all day, so nobody would have been in when she'd called round.

Letting Sammy in when he arrived a little later, Kim felt sick as she prepared to deliver the bad news. But Sammy had news of his own, and he started talking first.

'Where's my girl? I've got something to tell her, and she is going to *love* it.' Flopping down onto the couch, he smiled up at Kim expectantly.

Perching on her chair, she said, 'She's, er, not here. She nipped out earlier, and—'

'Oh, well, let's hope she's back soon, because I can't wait to see her face when she hears this,' Sammy jumped back in. 'Have you heard of Blaze Cosmetics?'

Vaguely remembering having seen an advert in one of her magazines, Kim nodded. 'I think so.'

'New American company,' Sammy went on excitedly. 'All set to smash onto the market and give Max Factor and Rimmel a run for their money. Well, I had a call from them when I got to the office this morning . . . Seems they're holding auditions to find the face for their UK campaign, and they've invited *Mia* along! So what do you think about *that*?'

'It's brilliant,' Kim said, still feeling sick. 'But I think we might have a problem.'

'*Oh?*' Sammy's eyebrows crept together. Everything had been fine when he'd dropped Kim and her daughters off that morning, so he didn't see how there could be a problem now.

Taking a deep breath, Kim briefly explained what had happened.

'You're joking!' he groaned. 'Have you spoken to Laura? You know what these girls are like – worst of enemies one minute, best of friends the next.'

'That's what I thought,' Kim said. 'But she's been out with her mum all day. And Kath's not the kind to lie, so I know it's true.' Exhaling loudly now, she said, 'To be honest, I don't think Mia had any intention of going there in the first place. I think she only said it so she could get out of the house without me suspecting her. I reckon she's gone back to *him*.'

'Surely not,' Sammy murmured disappointedly. 'Not after everything we've done to get her back on track.'

'Oh, she won't be bothered about us,' Kim told him bluntly. 'She'll only be thinking about herself – as usual.'

'But she seemed so positive about getting back to work. I can't believe she'd throw it all away again.'

'*I* can. Anyhow, knowing her, she won't think she's throwing anything away. She'll come waltzing back in when she's ready, thinking everything's hunky-dory.'

Sammy shook his head and glanced at his watch. 'Well, it's almost seven now. If she's not back by ten, maybe we should think about calling the police and reporting her missing?'

'They won't do nothing,' Kim told him gloomily. 'They'll just say she's an adult, and she's entitled to leave if she wants to.'

'Not if we tell them we have genuine concerns for her safety,' Sammy pointed out logically. 'Surely if they knew the kind of danger she might be facing they'd have to look for her.'

'And you don't think they might want details?' Kim asked pointedly, wondering why it was that really intelligent people like Sammy seemed to have no common sense.

'Ah . . . in which case, it wouldn't be long before they realised that it *had* been her in those photographs, and we'd be right back where we started.'

'Exactly.' Wringing her hands in a gesture of hopelessness, Kim said, 'Anything we do will just make it worse. We don't know where Steve hangs out, so we can't go looking for her there. And even if we did manage to find her, the chances are she'd tell us to bugger off. We've got to face it . . . if she wants to be with him, we don't stand a cat in hell's chance of getting her away until she wants to.'

'But he beat her black and blue,' Sammy reminded her worriedly. 'And what about all that stuff she said about never going back to him?'

A little ashamed to have to admit it, Kim said, 'She's greedy, Sammy. She likes money, and he's *got* money. She won't walk away from that just because they've had a fight. Anyway, she probably thinks she's punished him enough just by staying away for so long.' Giving a derisive snort now, she added, 'Knowing her, she'll have made him grovel, and he'll have bunged a load of cash at her, and she'll be shopping as we speak.'

'But why would she take money from that animal when she knows she'll be earning plenty of her own before too long?'

'Because she don't like waiting. When she wants something, she wants it *now*. You ought to know; you've seen her in action enough times.'

'So we do nothing?'

'Nothing we *can* do, except wait till she comes back. And that's *if* she comes back, 'cos I've got a feeling she's thinking we've forced her to choose between him and us.'

'Well, if you're right I hope she comes to her senses soon,' Sammy said worriedly. 'We've got several contracts in hand, and I'd hate to have to cancel them. But if we can't get hold of her I'll have no option.'

'Are they important?' Kim asked.

'They're *all* important,' Sammy told her. 'But I thought I'd start her off with a couple of the less taxing ones, to see how she coped before easing her back into the more high-profile things that are in the pipeline. This Blaze thing couldn't have come at a worse time, but it was too good an opportunity to turn down.' He sighed. 'It's my own fault. I should have said something when I first heard about it, because it might have made her think twice about taking off. But I didn't want to build her hopes up in case it didn't come to anything.'

'What are you talking about?' Kim asked. 'I thought you said they only rang this morning.'

'Yes, to invite her to audition,' Sammy replied. 'But they first contacted me a couple of weeks back, asking to see her portfolio, after their scout spotted her – sorry, *Michelle* – in the *Evening News*.'

'You're joking!' Kim gasped.

'Afraid not.' Sammy shook his head. 'It would have been amazing for her, because they're planning a nationwide saturation campaign. But there's no use harping on about it, because I'm definitely going to have to cancel it.'

'Please don't,' Kim begged, terrified that Mia was about to lose out on her biggest chance yet. 'I know I've been moaning about her, but I'm just pissed off with her for staying out so long. She'll be back soon, I know she will. Let's just give her a bit more time.'

'Kim, this is too important to play around with,' Sammy told her wearily. 'If she comes back tonight, or even tomorrow morning, and she can prove she hasn't been doing drugs – fine, I won't cancel. But if she *has* done something, we both know she'll be a mess again in no time. And I couldn't let her to go ahead with the audition, because these Americans don't mess around. If she won the contract and screwed it up they wouldn't just terminate it, they'd sue the backsides off us.'

Chewing on her nails now, Kim peered at him thoughtfully for several long moments before saying, 'I still don't think you should cancel it.' She held up her hand when he opened his mouth to argue and said, 'Hear me out before you say anything . . . Right, let's say we're wrong, and she's just met up with a mate and lost track of time. Then tomorrow she comes back all bright and breezy, only to hear that we've cancelled the audition because we don't trust her. How's she going to react to that, do you think?'

'But what if we're right, and she *has* gone back on the drugs?' Sammy countered. 'I don't cancel, and she doesn't turn up because, like you said, she's chosen her boyfriend over us, and we can't get hold of her to tell her about it. Or, worse, she *does* turn up and *gets* the job, then goes rapidly downhill and they can't use any of the pictures. Both of our reputations go down the pan, and we get sued to boot.'

'Maybe not,' Kim said quietly. 'I'm sure she'd quit the drugs if she had something important like this to look forward to.'

Giving her a doubtful look, Sammy said, 'Come on, Kim, you don't really believe that. How long has she been away from drugs while you were at my house? And how long did it take when I brought you back before she took off? I think we both know what that signifies.'

'I know,' Kim admitted gloomily. 'But if this Blaze thing is as big as you say, we can't just give up on her without a fight.'

'You can't fight for somebody who isn't here to be saved,' Sammy reminded her simply.

Sitting in silence for several minutes, Kim lit a cigarette and quietly thought things over.

'There's always our Michelle,' she said after a while.

'Oh no, I don't think so.' Sammy shook his head. 'We both know she's not cut out for the modelling life.'

'But this would be different from the last time,' Kim persisted. 'I mean, she had to try and *act* then, but she wouldn't really have to do anything this time, apart from smile and let them put make-up on her.'

'You know there's much more to it than that.'

'Maybe so,' Kim conceded. 'But we're only talking ifs here, don't forget. *If* Mia doesn't turn up, Shell can stand in for her. And if she gets the job, Mia would be so made up that she'd be bound to pull her socks up and get on with it. If she didn't get it, we wouldn't really have lost anything. And at least they couldn't say that Mia just hadn't bothered turning up.'

'I don't know,' Sammy murmured doubtfully, still thinking it would be best to just cancel.

'Well, I think it's worth considering,' Kim said firmly. '*You* didn't know the difference last time Shell stood in for her. And you know how good she looks since she got her hair done like Mia's. And how amazing was it when Mia did her make-up for her that time? Even *I* would have had a job telling them apart if I hadn't been there to see it all. *And*,' she added, hitting him with her biggest gun, 'it was *her* that the scout noticed in the first place, so she obviously takes a good picture.'

Sammy couldn't deny the truth of this, but he still thought it would be a huge mistake to put a complete novice forward for such a high-profile campaign.

'I'll think about it,' he said. 'But we'll need to speak to

Michelle about it before we make any decisions, because we've asked a lot of her already and I don't want her to feel as if she's being coerced into it.'

'I'm sure she'll do it when she realises what a massive opportunity it is for Mia,' Kim said – sure that she could persuade her into it. 'Anyway, we're still only talking ifs here. For all we know, Mia could be on her way home as we speak.'

'I sincerely hope so,' Sammy said. 'I really do.'

Mia didn't come home that night, or the next morning. And when she still hadn't shown up the day after that, Kim resigned herself to the fact that she'd definitely done a runner.

Less well-versed in the selfishness of teenage girls, Sammy was convinced that something must have happened to her, because *surely* she wouldn't just stay away without at least letting them know that she was all right. Humouring him, even though she knew that it was pointless, Kim rang around the local hospitals to see if Mia had had an accident and been rushed in – which, of course, she hadn't. And she'd even agreed to call the police, telling them that she was concerned because Mia had been under a lot of pressure lately. But, as she'd told Sammy from the start, they said that, as an adult, Mia was perfectly entitled to leave home without telling anybody. And, yes, they would keep a general eye out for her, and they would certainly inform Kim if any bodies matching her description turned up. But that was as far as they were willing to go. There would be no search, because, frankly, there was no reason to suspect that Mia was in any kind of danger.

Michelle agreed with her mum. Mia was fine; she'd just done her usual trick of making a mess and walking away from it, leaving them to pick up the pieces. She was furious with Mia for that, because she'd already sacrificed so much to help her. Michelle's reputation was in tatters, and she'd had the humiliation of having to try and convince her tutors that the coke incident was a one-off which would never be repeated, only for them to inform her that she couldn't come straight back to college without first undergoing a course of counselling to ensure that she was mentally fit enough to continue.

Yet, despite knowing that it was Mia who had put her in that position, Michelle still couldn't completely condemn her sister. Mia was an addict, and addiction was no laughing matter. Nor was it something that could be as easily fixed as her mum and Sammy had seemed to think. She had fooled them all into thinking that she was 'cured' after that extended stay at Sammy's, but, in hindsight, Michelle knew that she should have known better. She'd covered addiction at college, and the general consensus seemed to be that you couldn't help an addict until the addict was ready to accept help. Until then, they would do whatever it took, and tell you whatever they thought you wanted to hear, in order to get you off their backs so they could get out and score their next hit.

Feeling guilty for not saying any of this to her mum and Sammy, which might have put them on their guard and prevented this latest disaster, Michelle agreed to stand in for Mia at the Blaze audition. She was truly dreading it, but she figured that she had to do *some*thing to bring Mia to her senses and get her firmly back on track. And if something as big as this potentially was didn't do it, nothing would.

22

The audition was being held in London, in a private function room at the Hilton where the New York-based Blaze executives were staying.

They already had a specific idea in mind of the kind of girl who would ultimately front their campaign, so they had sent their scout out a few weeks ahead of time to find as many likely candidates as possible who fitted their criteria. Then, after poring over each of the proposed girls' portfolios, they had cherry-picked the best ten and invited them along to the audition.

To the untrained eye, the waiting area seemed to be filled with the same girl in different clothes. But to Sammy's finely honed eye, there was only one who posed any real threat to Mia – or, rather, to *Michelle*. And he'd have liked to have been able to reassure Michelle of this but the poor girl was too tense for conversation.

Sitting beside him now, she was struggling just to stay seated. As far as she was concerned, every one of the other girls was gorgeous and deserved to be here, but she, Michelle, was an impostor. And it didn't matter how many times her mum tried to remind her that it had been *her* picture that the scout had originally spotted, as far as she was concerned that wasn't her, that was her imitating Mia – the girl they really wanted; the one who had earned the right to be here after working her socks off for two long years. And now Michelle was walking in and stealing her thunder.

Or *not*, because there was no way she was going to get this job. Not with all these gorgeous *proper* models to compete against.

The make-up artists began to call the girls through to a side room to get them ready. The products that they would be using would all be Blaze ones, to make sure that the girls' skin-types suited the new range – because the last thing they needed was to choose a girl who immediately broke out in an unsightly rash. Once ready, each girl would then go through to face the panel, where they would be viewed in person for the first time and photographed before a final decision was made.

Leaving Michelle, because this was the part of the torturous journey that she really would have to face alone, Sammy went out to collect Kim from the hotel foyer. He took her for a coffee and a bite to eat, holding a confident smile in place as he told her what had been happening so far, and what was probably happening now.

Beneath the jovial words, Sammy was actually a nervous wreck. Michelle was just about holding it together, and if she performed anything like the last time she could well be coming out on a stretcher in a very short space of time. But still, he had to give her credit for putting herself through this. She owed Mia nothing, and yet, once again, she'd stepped in to try and salvage something from the mess that Mia seemed to be determined to make of her life.

He couldn't deny that he was fond of Mia, having spent so much of the last two years championing her with a dedication that she probably didn't deserve. But he'd always thought that she had something about her that was worth the effort. She was a beautiful girl and he'd excused her often bad attitude as high spirits, telling himself that when she matured she would have the potential to really make something of herself. But since this latest episode the scales had begun to fall from his eyes and he'd realised that she was never going to change. If anything, her attitude would get worse – and he'd already had a taste of that when she'd threatened to sack him at the first taste of success.

If only Mia were more like her sister, he believed that she could truly have the world at her feet. Michelle was every bit as beautiful – even if neither of the girls could see it. But she was also polite, reasonable, and intelligent – qualities that were sadly lacking in Mia. The only problem being that Michelle just didn't have the same vain urge to be famous; and she was so insecure about herself that she was unlikely to do well at this audition – if she got through it at all.

Back in the waiting area, Michelle had been made up and was waiting her turn to face the panel. Three girls had been in already, and had all come out within minutes with tears streaking their cheeks – which didn't help Michelle's nerves, because if *they* had been rejected she stood even less chance of getting through than she'd thought.

Taking a deep breath when the girl sitting next to her was called in, Michelle stared at the floor and gave herself a talking to. All right, she already knew that she wasn't going to win, so there was no point letting it tie her up in knots. Sammy had told her just to do her best – and not to worry if she failed because at least she'd turned up, so nobody could say that Mia was unreliable. She looked the part, thanks to the make-up artist's wizardry, so now she had to stop thinking of herself as shy, plain Michelle and make-believe that she was Mia. It would be a struggle, but she could do it – she *had* to do it.

'Mia Delaney, please . . . Mia Delaney?'

Snapping her head up at the sound of the voice, Michelle swallowed nervously. She'd been in a world of her own and hadn't realised that the last girl had already come back out. It was her turn.

There were two men and a woman sitting on a long leather couch in the audition room. A photographer and his assistant were standing in the corner, the camera facing a stool which was standing in front of a plain backdrop.

The woman told Michelle to come and stand in front of them. She stared at her long and hard before having a hushed discussion with her colleagues. Then she wrote something down on the notepad she was holding and gestured with her pen towards the stool, saying, 'Go sit in the light so we can get a better look at you.'

Feeling a little like a horse gone to market, Michelle sat down elegantly. The woman had sounded so dismissive that they must surely be wondering what she was doing here. But she *was* here, so she had to see it through to the end.

Michelle raised her face towards the light when instructed to do so by the photographer, and relaxed exactly as Sammy had told her to. She gazed into the camera lens, silently telling herself that she was Mia Delaney . . . the beautiful, already successful model who had been doing this for years.

Back on the couch, the Blaze people whispered among themselves as the photographer snapped numerous shots of Michelle. Then, getting up when he'd finished at last, they came over to view the results on his laptop.

Glad that the torture was almost over, and sure that they were about to send her out with a flea in her ear, Michelle was already half off the stool in preparation for a quick exit. So when the woman smiled at her after several minutes and asked her to wait outside, she was confused. None of the other girls had waited; they'd rushed straight out and hadn't come back. So why were they asking *her* to wait?

Unless . . .

Oh, no! What if they'd realised that she wasn't really Mia? Could she get into trouble for impersonating her and wasting their time?

As Michelle made her way outside, she felt even more nervous than before she'd gone in. Oblivious to the sly looks that the remaining girls were casting her way as they too wondered why she hadn't been sent home, she sat down and concentrated on breathing evenly, wishing that Sammy was still there to hold her hand.

Wishing that *Mia* was here instead of her, like she should have been.

The rest of the girls went in – and came straight back out and disappeared. One girl, however, rejoined Michelle on the seats. But she didn't look confused; she looked cool and confident, as if she already had this job in the bag. And Michelle was sure that she probably had, because she had that certain *some*thing about her that Mia had: that sparkle of absolute self-belief in her eyes, and all the poise of a true working model.

Ten minutes later, one of the men from the panel popped his head out. Smiling, he said, 'Sorry for the delay, ladies, but it looks like this may take a while. Go get yourselves something to eat while you're waiting – and make sure you tell them to add whatever you order to our tab. Okay?'

Returning his smile, the other girl rose to her feet, saying, 'Sure, babes. Ciao for now.'

Unable to do anything except smile as the girl slinked out sexily, Michelle jumped up and rushed out to look for her mum and Sammy. Finding them in the restaurant, where they were sharing their third pot of coffee, she slumped down in a chair and buried her face in her hands.

Immediately guessing that she'd failed the audition, Sammy reached across and rubbed her shoulder. 'Now, now, my love . . . there's no need to get upset. You did your best, and that's all we expected of you.'

Flooded with disappointment, although she'd secretly never expected any different outcome, Kim repeated what Sammy had already said, adding, 'You're a good girl, and we know how hard this was for you, but you got in there and gave it a shot, and you've really done us proud. It's not your fault you're not cut out for this; it's *Mia*'s for letting us all down.'

'Thanks, mum,' Michelle murmured, truly glad that she was here, because she needed her support more than ever right now.

'Right, well, at least it's out of the way now, so you can relax,' Sammy said, giving Michelle an encouraging smile as he sat back to let her know that she shouldn't feel bad. 'Let's get you something to eat, and then we really should think about heading back. The traffic will be horrendous before too long.'

'I've, er, got to wait,' Michelle told him, biting her lip nervously. 'I think I might be in trouble,' she added quietly, glancing around to make sure nobody was listening. 'I think they might have realised that I'm not Mia.'

Sammy asked her to explain. His bushy eyebrows rose when he heard what had happened. Chuckling softly when she'd finished, and had pointed out the other girl, he said, 'Ah . . . how interesting.'

A glint of excitement in his eyes now, he looped his hands together on the table top and quietly told Michelle that the other girl was the one he had pinpointed as being her only real competition when they had arrived.

'The fact that they asked you both to wait,' he added, 'is a very good sign indeed. I knew they were in a hurry, but I had no idea they were going to make a decision today. I imagined that they might hold a few more auditions first. But that's the Americans for you, I suppose . . . they know what they want, and they make sure they do all the groundwork beforehand so as to waste as little time and money as possible.'

'So what are you saying?' Kim asked, sensing that it was good but wanting him to spell it out so that she didn't get it wrong.

'I'm saying that it looks like this has become a two-horse race,' Sammy told her. 'And *that*,' he added to Michelle, 'is incredible, considering this is only the second time you've ever done anything like this.' Shaking his head now, as if even he couldn't believe it, he said, 'This is certainly something to celebrate, and I think I'm going to have to invest in a large bottle of champagne – *whatever* the result.'

The photographer's assistant was sent down to collect the girls. Unable to face eating because her stomach was churning, Michelle had been sipping on a glass of water for the past hour. Face drained of colour now, she told her mum and Sammy that she'd see them in a bit and prepared to follow the assistant back up to the panel room. But the assistant told her that she was sure nobody would mind if she brought them along – which Michelle took to mean that she would probably need their support, because she was about to be told that she hadn't got the job.

She was wrong.

As soon as the other girl was told the bad news and released, Michelle, Sammy and Kim were invited into the room.

'Congratulations, Mia,' the woman told her, smiling warmly as she stood to kiss each of Michelle's cheeks. 'You're the new face of Blaze UK.'

In an absolute daze, because she couldn't believe that she had managed to pull it off, Michelle listened without understanding a single word as Sammy and the Blaze executives discussed the details of the proposed schedule. Then, after signing her name on the contract, and having her hand pumped and more kisses planted on her cheeks, she drifted out between her mum and Sammy as if she were on a cloud.

Wearing his intelligent agent's face all the way down to the underground car park, Sammy waited until they were alone before showing how ecstatic he really was. Yelling a jubilant '*Yippee!*' which made both Michelle and Kim burst out laughing because it sounded so preposterous coming from such a fat old man, he grabbed Kim and waltzed her around on the concrete floor. Then, turning to Michelle, he pulled her into an enormous bear-hug, telling her how fantastically well she'd done, and how very, very proud he was of her.

'And you thought you couldn't do it,' he scoffed, leading them to the car now. 'Should have listened to Uncle Sammy, 'cos I *told* you!'

Still laughing, Kim said, 'Er, excuse me, *Uncle* Sammy, but I seem to remember that you were just as convinced as me and her that she'd fluff it. You didn't even want to let her do it; it was my idea.'

Holding up his hand, Sammy said, 'Ah, now you're quite wrong about that, my dear. While I admit that I had my reservations, they were based purely on Michelle's inexperience. But I've never doubted that she had the right look. And, I might add, that's not just because she is her sister's double. This young lady –' he swept a hand out to indicate Michelle '– has her very own look. And I don't know if either of you were listening back there, but the Blaze guys were raving about her.'

'So why did it take so long for them to decide between her and that other lass?' Kim wanted to know, climbing into the front seat when Sammy stopped talking for long enough to open the car doors.

Sammy explained that the two girls had lent an entirely different look to the product. Blaze hadn't planned to aim at girly-girls; they wanted to tap into the young, trendy, sexy, independent-woman market. And while the other girl had been the exact personification of that, Michelle had come along and thrown a big old spanner in the works.

'The general consensus,' he concluded, 'was that while Michelle gives off a far softer, more vulnerable impression than the vibrant, hot young chick they had envisaged as the face of Blaze, she's got something so mesmerising about her eyes on film that they just couldn't ignore it.'

'Christ,' Kim murmured. 'Who'd have thought it?'

'It's nothing I hadn't already told you,' Sammy reminded Michelle, grinning at her in the rear-view mirror as he pulled out of the car park and onto the road. 'Remember last time? The producer specifically mentioned your eyes, and I told you to try and remember whatever was going through your mind that day, because it obviously worked. Well, it's happened again. Only this time you didn't let the nerves get to you. You, young lady, are a natural.'

Still reeling from the shock of it all, Michelle felt herself slowly coming back down to earth as they headed home. And the closer she came to landing, the more she knew that she couldn't take any of the credit for what had happened today. This was all down to Mia. *She* was the one who had created the look that Michelle had emulated today; and it was her expression and mannerisms that Michelle had been copying. She was the true model; Michelle was just a good imitator – and the sooner Mia came back, the better, because there was no way Michelle would be able to keep it up for ever. Before long the Blaze people would start to realise what a mistake they had made.

PART THREE

23

Steve's face was calm but his mind was working overtime, wondering how the hell to get rid of some of his money without actually losing it.

That was the problem with powders: the more you could afford at one time, the less it cost, and the larger the profits. And it was a constantly growing market, so there was always somebody waiting to snatch it out of your hands as soon as it came in. So the business snowballed, and you found yourself rolling in even more of it.

Great stuff, but where the fuck was he supposed to stash it without attracting unwanted attention? He couldn't keep it here in the safe because, much as he trusted his guys, every last one of them would torch the place with him in it if they thought he had that kind of money lying around waiting to be lifted. Same with his apartment – or anywhere that was connected with him. And even if they didn't get at it, he'd be thinking that they were *trying* to, which would send him crazy.

And banks were just as bad – if not worse. It had been easy once upon a time to distribute it around multiple accounts in multiple banks, but since the crafty bastards had started merging and sharing information which was previously secure, all it would take was for some computer nerd to start playing dot to dot and they would soon have the full picture of exactly who had what and where.

And he couldn't do the usual Mr Big trick of splashing

out on cars, mansions, yachts and ridiculously ugly and expensive artwork, because that was too noticeable, so it was guaranteed to bring the authorities down on him like a swarm of bees. And they weren't stupid; they knew there was only so much money to be made from a tiny lap-dancing club in a grotty little backstreet.

Any which way you looked at it, he was fucked, because the more you had, the more at risk you were of losing it – and of going to prison for a very long time. And with the crash of so many markets recently, the less other people had, the more noticeable his wealth became. But what was he supposed to do? Stop dealing and start trying to scrape by on the pitiful club profits? He'd be broke within a month!

Looking up when Vern popped his head around the door, he said, 'What's up?'

'Davy's here.'

Sighing, Steve said, 'Bring him up.'

Davy Boyd was smiling when he strolled in a few seconds later. He reached across the desk and shook Steve's hand. Flopping down onto the visitor's chair, he took a dimped spliff from behind his ear and lit up as Steve poured a couple of shots of the white rum that Davy favoured.

'So, you got it?' Davy asked, taking his glass and settling back in his seat.

Taking a package out of his drawer, Steve tossed it over to him. 'Same batch as that last lot from a few months back.'

Shaking it, Davy peered at the packet closely. 'Cool, man. My boys were all over me for more of that shit, but I had to tell them they'd seen the last of it when you said you couldn't get hold of any more. How much you got?'

'More than enough to keep you happy,' Steve replied, grinning slyly.

Easing a corner of the package open, Davy sniffed at the

powder, then tested it with the tip of his tongue. His spliff-reddened eyes were testament to his own preferred high, but he still liked to know the shit he was passing on to his customers. Murmuring, 'Nice, nice' now, he nodded his approval and resealed the bag. 'So, how much?'

'Seven an ounce.'

'Fuck,' Davy spluttered, his eyebrows shooting up in disbelief. 'That's gone a bit rocket-fuel, ain't it? It was only five and a half last time.'

'Hey, I've had a major hassle shipping this lot in,' Steve told him, not in the least worried because he knew that Davy would take it whatever the price. 'Came over in a shitload of straws weaved into rugs, so I've had the ball-ache of extracting it and getting it packaged. And now I've got hundreds of fucking rag-rugs rotting away in a lock-up to get rid of.'

Peering at him thoughtfully, Davy said, 'How much you want for them?'

Laughing, Steve took a swig of his drink. 'You joking, or what?'

'Nah, for real,' Davy insisted. 'My bird, Vivienne – she's into all that arty-farty shite. She needs something to keep her occupied before she drives me nuts with her yakking, and this could be it. Set her up with a stall on some market – let her flog the shit so she thinks she's still got her independence. You know what birds are like.'

'Not my birds,' Steve quipped. 'They prefer being kept. And that suits me, 'cos you can't trust any bitch when she starts running around thinking she's earning her own money.'

'Seen,' Davy drawled, grinning slyly.

'Anyhow,' Steve said, getting back to business. 'I'll do you a deal. You take the gear for seven an ounce, and I'll throw the rugs in for nothing.'

Mulling it over, Davy said, 'Six-fifty, and I won't charge you for ridding you of them.'

Steve held his hand across the desk. Davy shook it, finished his drink and shoved his glass forward for a refill. 'So, how's the house?' he asked as Steve obliged. 'Managed to get shut yet?'

'Have I fuck,' Steve snorted, screwing the lid back on the bottle and restashing it in the drawer in case Davy thought they were making a day of it. 'And I don't want to think about it, so drop it, 'cos you're the one who suggested the fucking property market in the first place.'

'The ripper got ripped, eh?' Davy joked.

'Believe me, I'm not ripping you,' Steve assured him. 'That gear is so pure you'll have to cut it to fuck just to make it safe for the knob-heads you deal to. You'll quadruple your money, easy.'

Saying, 'I'll hold you to that,' Davy reached for his second drink and took a long swallow. Sighing with satisfaction as the warm liquor soothed his hash-charred pipes, he pursed his lips thoughtfully. 'Talking about the investment shit . . . I was talking to one of my old boys the other night. He's not long come out of the Strange, and he's set himself up dealing diamonds. Now, I know that's probably not something you've thought about or you'd have mentioned it. But I reckon it could be worth looking into.'

'Oh yeah?' Steve sat back.

'Yeah, see, diamonds don't depreciate like other shit. Cars drop by a third as soon as you drive them two inches; and – as you know – houses fluctuate depending on the market. But diamonds don't just hold their value, they *rise*.'

An amused smile played on his lips as he listened, then Steve said, 'Since when have you been such an expert?'

'Not me,' Davy told him. 'My mate. And he's straight as a die, so if you got talking to him and decided it was something you wanted to get into, you'd have no worries about getting stuck with anything you couldn't get rid of – not like all them scamming bastards on the net.' Shrugging now, he said, 'He's a good kid, and it'd help him out to get a customer like you with money to burn. And it'd help *you* out, too. Fully legit, and no one questions the profits, 'cos everyone knows diamonds go up not down.'

Eyes narrowed thoughtfully, Steve sipped at his drink. He had never even thought about diamonds as an investment opportunity, but now that Davy had mentioned it he could see the sense in it. Small, so no storage overheads; plenty of available buyers, so no worries about being lumbered with shit you didn't want; and prices increasing rather than decreasing.

'This mate of yours,' he said after thinking it over for some time. 'When can I meet him?'

24

When the plane taxied to a stop, Liam got up, slipped on his jacket and reached into the overhead compartment for his small case and rucksack.

Standing by the door, thanking the disembarking passengers for flying with them and wishing them a safe journey to their next destinations, the pretty flight attendant gave him a coy smile as he approached.

'Goodbye, Mr Grant . . . I trust everything was satisfactory?'

'Absolutely, you're an angel,' Liam said, looping the rucksack over his shoulder and setting off down the steps. He was aware that she was still watching him. But, cute as she was, he wasn't in the mood. He'd had an early start that morning, and he just wanted to get to the hotel, grab some dinner, and get some sleep.

The chill air that always seemed so much more vicious in Manchester than anywhere else hit him full in the face as he stepped onto the tarmac. Shivering, he pulled his collar up around his ears and made a dash for the terminal.

Reaching the arrivals lounge to find that Davy hadn't arrived yet, he headed to the news kiosk to get a pack of cigarettes. Reaching it just as the scrolling poster unit attached to the wall rolled over, he stopped in his tracks, his stomach flipping when he found himself staring into Michelle's eyes.

As quickly as the feeling had come over him, it was replaced by the bitter taste of resentment when he remembered that it was *Mia* he was looking at, not Michelle – Mia, the cold bitch whose attempts to steal him from her own sister had led to him going to prison.

Although he had to admit that if he hadn't known it was her, he would have been fooled. There was a time when he'd thought that he would easily know the difference between them if he saw them again because of the difference in their eyes, but Mia had obviously found a way of mimicking Michelle's soulfulness because her eyes were incredible in this picture.

Still, no amount of acting ability, or whatever digital wizardry had produced the luminosity her eyes now possessed, could ever make him overlook the rotten core beneath the façade.

After buying his cigarettes when Mia rolled out of view to be replaced by a perfume bottle, he made his way to the coffee shop and, sitting at a corner table from where he could see the door, sipped at a steaming latte.

This was the first time he'd been back to Manchester in months, and it felt good to be here. As Gina had predicted, he'd gone straight back to Ireland after getting out – although, contrary to what she'd thought, he hadn't gone back intending to settle and start again but simply to attend his father's funeral.

Released early on compassionate grounds, he'd flown straight over to Galway, where his father had demanded to be buried alongside *his* own father – a man whom Liam had met only a few times but remembered as being as much of a nasty cunt as his son had turned out to be, which made it fitting that they should spend the rest of eternity together in the hell they had created for everyone else along the way.

Liam hadn't attended the funeral out of any sense of loyalty or respect – he'd merely wanted to see for himself that the old bastard really was dead. His Aunt Ruth had turned up pissed and spoiling for a fight, but he'd completely blanked her.

And it had only been respect for the priest, who had been so kindly, that had prevented him from fulfilling his promise to his father and spitting in his face when he'd viewed him in the open casket.

Proud of himself for maintaining his dignity, unlike the remainder of his father's foul family who had gone from the graveside to the pub for a good old scrap – with each other, and whichever poor innocent locals happened to get in the way – he'd gone over to Dublin straight after the funeral, to visit his one remaining aunt on his mother's side.

That visit had extended well beyond the intended time – as visits so often did when you were around people who genuinely cared about you. Refreshed and relaxed after a few weeks, he had decided that it was time to put his future plans into action.

The idea had come to him during his last three months in prison, when an old diamond trader called Harry Bell had come in on a fifteen stretch. Harry had told him how lucrative a market it could be – especially if the dealer had the nous to really gen up on the product. Any fool could buy and sell rocks, he'd said, but it took someone special to recognise the subtle differences of these utterly unique gems.

Naturally curious, Liam had quickly become infected by Harry's passion and, under his tutelage, had come out with a respectable knowledge of cuts, grades, points and prices. Armed with that, and with the money he'd managed to save while inside – which Davy's screw had smuggled out and deposited in his account – it wasn't long before he got rolling.

And, so far, he'd been doing quite well, although he'd probably have been a damn sight richer by now if he'd embraced the internet as a trading tool. But he wanted to do things the old-fashioned way: handling his goods, and meeting his clients face to face. Anyway, the internet was a playground for criminals, and he had no intention of going down the same road as poor old Harry; getting suckered by a smuggling cartel who, after lulling him into a false sense of security with several above-board deals, had used his credentials to ship containers of cocaine over to Britain.

Harry had no idea how many had got through before the last one was intercepted, but it had been done so skilfully, leaving only his details as a trail, that he'd found himself completely unable to prove his innocence at the trial. And Liam had no intention of allowing himself to be suckered like that, so he'd concentrated on building up his physical contacts, using his instincts to weed out the suspect ones – of which, he quickly learned, there were far more than there were honest ones.

Which was exactly what he intended to do at the meeting he'd come over for now, the one that Davy had set up for him. He'd assured Liam that the guy was trustworthy, but Liam wasn't fool enough to go by another man's word. Grateful as he was for the way that Davy had looked after him, he couldn't overlook the fact that Davy was a dangerous skunk-head who could switch in an instant. So, yes, he would meet the guy as arranged, but he would make up his own mind about whether or not he wanted to do business with him.

Almost falling asleep to the strains of the soft classical music that was floating out through the coffee-shop speakers, Liam jumped when Davy's distinctive voice bellowed out across the almost empty arrivals lounge.

'Yo, motherfucker! Long time no see!'

Grinning, he stood up to greet him. They had kept in sporadic touch by phone since Liam had gone back to Ireland, but this was the first time they'd actually seen each other since before his arrest. And the years between had narrowed the gap, so Liam now felt they were meeting as equals for the first time.

'Hey, gimme a hug,' Davy demanded, laughing as he added, 'Or is that too queer for you now you've gone all IRA on us?'

Giving him a back-clapping hug, Liam asked if he wanted anything to drink. Looking at the greasy dregs of coffee in the bottom of the cup, Davy shuddered. 'Nah, man, that's nasty. Anyway, the motor's on a tow zone, so we'd best clip.'

Picking up his bags, Liam followed Davy out to where the old black Mercedes was parked haphazardly across a *No Waiting* sign painted in huge letters on the ground.

He climbed into the back and touched fists with Davy's man Faz who was in the front passenger seat.

'So how's tricks?' he asked when Davy climbed into the driver's seat. 'Everything still cool with you and Vivienne?'

'She's certifiable,' Davy told him, firing the engine.

'What, worse than Ruth?' Liam asked, settling back in his seat as they set off.

'You kidding me? Ruth's *gone*, man. Didn't you see her when she went to send your dad off?' Davy stared at him in the rear-view mirror – narrowly missing a man who was in the middle of a pedestrian crossing.

'I didn't talk to her, to be honest,' Liam replied, wincing at the near-collision. 'She was kaylied, so I left her to it.'

'Just as well,' Davy chuckled, taking the spliff that Faz handed to him. 'Always said you shouldn't mess with them mad Irish bitches. Should have seen her when she caught me and Vivienne at it – near enough tore the poor cow's fucking head off. But when she tried ripping my bollocks off with them false fucking nails of hers, I thought, nah, man . . . I'm not having this. Enough's enough.'

'So you left?'

'So I left.' Grinning now, Davy sucked deeply on the spliff. 'Best fucking move I ever made.'

'Told you to do it years ago,' Liam reminded him, lighting

a straight to keep his head clear as the car filled up with the strong weed smoke.

'Yeah, well, some of us need a bullet in the head before we see sense,' Davy laughed. 'Anyhow, never mind her. How's it going with you? Made your first million yet?'

'You asked me that yesterday when you rang,' Liam reminded him, hoping that Davy had a sharper grasp on his driving than he did on remembering things. 'And, like I said then, far from it. But I'm doing okay – thanks to you.'

'Oi, pack it in with the soppy shit,' Davy scolded. 'You sound like you'll be after a shag in a minute, and I don't do blokes.'

Smiling, Liam covered a yawn with his hand. Knackered as he was, it was good to be back. And it was really good to see Davy after so long. He hadn't been sure about him when they'd first met, but he'd proved himself to be a good mate, setting Liam up with that room when he'd needed somewhere to live, and looking after him when he'd been sent down.

Glancing at him in the mirror, Davy said, 'Oi, don't be falling asleep. I can't be carrying you round like a baby – not with my old back. We'll be there in ten, so open the window and wake yourself up.'

'I'll be all right when I get to the hotel,' Liam told him. 'A good kip and something to eat, I'll be right as rain.'

'Sorry, forgot to tell you, there's been a change of plan,' Davy told him. 'Steve rang when we were on our way over. Apparently, some out-of-town business has popped up, so he asked if we could go straight over.'

'Oh, right,' Liam murmured, wishing he'd known, because he didn't like taking gems along on a first meet. He liked to make his assessment first, decide whether the guy could be trusted, or if he even wanted to do business with him.

'Chill,' Davy said, guessing what he was thinking from his

expression. 'He don't trouble no one 'less they trouble him. Anyhow, me and him have got too good an arrangement for him to risk pulling any shit on one of mine. Plus he ain't gonna risk fucking things up with you 'cos he really needs to start offloading money, and you're the way forward for him. So relax – yeah?'

Liam nodded, but that didn't mean he was taking Davy's word.

Steve was at the bar when Vern let Davy, Faz and Liam in, sipping on a large Bacardi and idly flipping through a newspaper. Closing it now, he shook Davy's hand and nodded at Faz. Then, extending his hand to Liam, he said, 'Good to meet you. What can I get you?'

Liam swung up onto a stool and asked for a JD. Clicking his fingers at a four-foot-nothing Oriental woman who was drying glasses behind the bar, Steve ordered their drinks. Then, lighting a cigarette, he squinted at Liam through the smoke. 'So, Davy tells me you're a diamond merchant?'

'Wouldn't really class myself in that league,' Liam told him honestly.

'But he's doing real good,' Davy chipped in, resting his elbow on the counter-top as Faz wandered over to sit at a table to ogle two girls who were practising their pole techniques on the stage.

'I'm doing okay,' Liam said, flashing a hooded glance at Davy. 'Anyway,' he said to Steve now, 'he tells me you're looking to make some investments?'

'That's right. Can I take it you've brought something to show me?'

'A few bits,' Liam said cagily, letting it be known that he wasn't carrying enough to warrant any thoughts of robbery.

Picking up on it, Steve smiled. 'Don't worry, I'm not after a one-off deal. If I like what I hear price-wise, and you can guarantee a steady supply, with certificates and what have you, we could be talking long-term.'

'So long as you're not planning to go into it full time and sack off the other stuff,' Davy said, concerned about his own business, because Steve was the biggest supplier – with the best gear – in Manchester.

'Behave,' Steve shot back brusquely.

'Relax,' Davy drawled, putting together some Rizlas. 'Liam's my boy, and he knows the score every which way. He used to work for me, and then he went down for me, which puts him right up there for me – you gets me?'

'Could you do me a favour and take that over there,' Steve asked, jerking his head in Faz's direction. 'Just so me and Liam can have a quick chat and see what we think of each other.'

Nodding, Davy carried his half-loaded spliff to the table.

'So, you took a rap for him?' Steve asked, still eyeing Davy

Shrugging, Liam took a swig of his drink. He didn't really appreciate having had his business broadcast like that, because he'd made a vow to go straight, and he'd been sticking to it. The last thing he wanted was for people to think that he was dodgy, because dodgy attracted dodgy, and before you knew it you were being sucked into shit you didn't need to be involved in.

Looking at Liam intently now, Steve nodded thoughtfully. He too worked on instinct, and his instincts told him that this man was not only loyal – as he'd obviously already proved by taking a rap for Davy – but also trustworthy.

'Want to show me what you got?' he asked.

'That go all right?' Davy asked when they left the club half an hour later.

'Yeah, cool,' Liam told him, climbing into the back of the car. 'We'll be getting together again in a few days.'

'Nice, nice,' Davy drawled, starting the engine. 'So, where to now? Hotel, or back to mine?'

'Think I'd best get my head down.' Liam yawned loudly. 'I overdid it at a mate's stag do last night, then I was up and out by six this morning, and it's really starting to catch up on me.'

'Lightweight,' Davy scoffed, grinning at him in the mirror as they set off.

After ordering himself a bottle of JD from room service, Liam took a shower. Lying on the bed with the towel wrapped around his waist after his order had arrived a short time later, he poured himself a large drink and gazed at the screen. An old episode of *Columbo* was showing, which didn't help keep him awake. Feeling his eyes growing heavier, he finished his drink and reached for the remote – just as the adverts came on. He found himself looking at Mia's face for the second time that day.

Gritting his teeth when she smiled, and softly purred, '*Let Blaze bring out the goddess in you . . .*' he pressed his finger firmly down on the off button, dissolving her treacherous face.

Having used his charms to extract the room number from the receptionist, Davy rode the lift up to the fifth floor and hammered on Liam's door until he opened it.

'I thought I said I'd ring,' Liam grumbled, rubbing sleep from his eyes as Davy walked into the room. 'I was flat out, man.'

'How old are you?' Davy snorted. 'I've got ten years on you, and I'm a stone-head, but you don't catch *me* sleeping before five a.m. It's only eleven, man. You got fucking narcolepsy, or something?'

'No, and you've got *twenty* years on me – at least,' Liam shot back, his humour returning as he began to wake up.

Saying, 'Shut the fuck up and get dressed, you tosser,' Davy poured himself a large drink and sat at the small breakfast table by the window, glancing around the room. 'How much this shit costing you?'

'Seventy-five a night,' Liam told him as he pulled on a fresh pair of jeans.

Davy's jaw dropped in disbelief. 'You pulling my plonker?'

'That's not that bad.'

'Jeezus, I'm in the wrong line,' Davy muttered, shaking his head. 'I wasn't even charging that for a *week* in my place.'

'That's different. This is luxury, that's a shit-hole.'

'*Was* a shit-hole,' Davy corrected him.

'Don't tell me you've finally put your hand in your pocket and shelled out for repairs?'

'As if! Nah, didn't I tell you what happened?'

Shaking his head, Liam sat on the edge of the bed to tie his laces.

'It blew up,' Davy told him, grinning gleefully as he made an explosive gesture with his hands. '*Kaboom!*'

'Christ, was anyone hurt?'

'Well, not hurt exactly,' Davy replied nonchalantly. 'The old alkie and the junkie died straight off, so I doubt they felt anything. But the girls had already left by then, and that strange kid was out. Some kind of gas leak, according to the report. Nowt to do with me.'

'That's terrible.' Liam shook his head.

'No, it ain't, it's wicked,' Davy countered happily. 'The dump's been levelled without me having to fork out for scaffolding, and planning permission's just been granted to shove up a block of flats, so I'll be quids in once I get shot of it.'

Liam gave him a suspicious look and said, 'And when did you start planning that – before or after the explosion?'

Smiling slyly, Davy said, 'Fucking hell, it's a good job you weren't on the investigating team or I'd have been well rumbled, eh?' He got up and headed for the door. 'Anyhow, come on. You've held me up long enough with your poncing about. There's liquor going to waste out there.'

'Where we going?' Liam asked as he kicked his case under the bed and followed him out.

'To a pussy club,' Davy told him, rubbing his hands together. 'Only don't tell Viv, or she'll chop me nuts off.'

Davy's so-called pussy club was actually a dark little jazz club on a backstreet behind the university, where live bands played the kind of experimental shit that Davy was secretly into but which very few other people seemed to be able to make any sense of. His main boys were sitting at a table off to the side of the stage, and Liam was surprised to see Darren Mitchell among them.

Davy introduced the guys that Liam hadn't met before – and reintroduced a couple that he had in case he'd forgotten their names – before he ordered drinks all round. Then, getting down to his real reason for meeting up here, he passed under the table to each of them a bag of the white heroin, which he'd cut liberally with bicarb and weighed out to the gram.

Business out of the way, the boys were free either to go or to stay and socialise with the boss. And, Davy being a generous man who kept the alcohol flowing, most of them stayed.

Uninterested in the seemingly made-up-on-the-spot noise that the three weirdy-beardy musicians were producing up on the stage, Liam found himself glancing at his watch every few minutes, thinking that there had to be a better way to spend his first night back in Manchester. Now that he was properly awake, he'd have preferred to do a tour of the city-centre clubs. Dublin was amazing for nightlife, but there was no beating a good Mancunian DJ spinning the latest tunes.

Darren caught his eye after a while from across the table and jerked his head, mouthing, 'Coming for a smoke?'

Glad of an excuse to get away from the music, Liam got up and followed him out onto a tiny balcony at the rear of the club.

'Christ, this place is shit,' Darren complained as soon as they were alone.

'So why did you come?' Liam asked, sticking his hands into his pockets and leaning back against the flimsy wrought-iron guard rail.

''Cos this is where Davy likes to meet up to hand out the gear,' Darren told him, lighting the spliff he'd rolled. '*He* sorts us, and *we* deal with the streets. I suppose this is his way of keeping us tight.' Exhaling his smoke now, he said, 'Didn't know *you* knew him?'

'Yeah, been mates for years,' Liam said, thinking it best not to mention that Davy was part of the reason why he'd been inside, otherwise Darren might get jumpy. 'How come you got involved with him, though?'

'There was nothing else going for me after I got out.' Darren shrugged. 'I'm not knocking Davy, 'cos he's been safe, and at least I've got regular money coming in. But dealing fiver bags of smack to idiots ain't exactly my idea of fun. I really thought I'd be doing something better with myself by now, but you know how it is.'

Liam accepted the spliff when Darren offered it to him and took a deep drag. He was surprised. Having been celled up with Darren for several months, he'd kind of dismissed him as a no-hoper. Partly because of the bullshit he'd come out with when he'd first gone down – although Liam was aware that that was a defensive mechanism most guys employed to let the others know not to mess with them. And partly because he'd spent every free minute in the gym pumping iron, then every night flexing and admiring his muscles – which had been a major irritation for Liam. But mainly it had been Darren's obsession with Mia and all the pictures he'd insisted on pinning up of her that had made Liam dismiss him as a knob.

In hindsight, he supposed that Darren couldn't have known what Liam's problem was, seeing as Liam never actually mentioned his own connection with Mia so he shouldn't really have held it against him. And he seemed perfectly all right now – as long as he didn't start banging on about her again.

He did.

'Remember the girl I had all the pictures of when we were on lock-down?' Darren said, taking the spliff back. 'Mia Delaney – the model.'

Liam sighed heavily and nodded. 'What about her?'

'She's well famous now,' Darren said proudly. 'There's posters of her all over, and she's on TV as well, in an advert for some make-up.'

Liam muttered a bored-sounding, 'Really?' and tried to change the subject. 'So, how long have you been working for Davy?'

'Months,' Darren told him dismissively. 'Anyhow, remember how I told you I used to go out with Mia? Well, I met up with her again after I got out.'

'Good for you.'

Looking suddenly wistful, Darren gazed down into the club's dark backyard. He'd spent months telling anyone who'd listen that he and Mia had picked up right where they'd left off, but somehow he couldn't bring himself to lie to Liam. The guy had been moody when they'd been banged up together, but there was something about him that commanded respect.

'Actually, it wasn't that good,' Darren admitted, saying out loud the words which he hadn't even wanted to think in private. Sighing, he took another deep pull on the smoke. 'I thought she still felt something, 'cos we had one of them eye-to-eye moments – you know? But she'd got herself hooked up with some rich twat, and his minder caught me off guard and gave me a right going-over.' He paused briefly, a glint of anger leaping into his eyes as he remembered that night. Then he went on. 'Anyway, it all went a bit balls-up after that, 'cos my mate's bird – who used to be *her* best mate – took pictures of her snorting coke in the loos and sold them to the papers.'

'Really?' Liam gave him a disbelieving look. Bad as Mia had been, she hadn't struck him as the kind of girl who'd get into coke. But then, she'd play-acted her way through their entire 'relationship', so who knew *what* she was really into?

'It was a bit weird the way it turned out, actually,' Darren went on, frowning now. 'After Laura's story came out, Mia did an interview saying it was her twin sister in the pictures and not her. But Laura reckoned it couldn't have been, 'cos Michelle wasn't like that. It *was* the sister, though. I'd really thought it was Mia at the time, but it made sense after I found out, 'cos she'd been well too skinny, and she'd acted dead weird with me. Anyway, their mam said it was Michelle, so you can't argue with that, can you? And Mia's still fit as hell in her adverts, so . . .' Trailing off, he exhaled wearily.

Feeling sorry for him, because he obviously had it bad, Liam said, 'I take it you haven't seen her since?'

'Yeah, I've *seen* her a few times, going in and out of the house. But she's always with her mam and some fat bloke, so you can't get anywhere near her.'

'And what happened to her sister?' Liam asked, making it sound casual.

'Well, I know she went into rehab for a while, 'cos it was all over the papers about Mia taking time out from her modelling to support her. But nobody's heard much since then. There was a rumour that her mum had locked her in her bedroom 'cos she'd caught her at it again, but you just don't know, do you?'

Saddened, because he remembered Michelle as being intelligent and gentle, and it sounded as if she'd completely screwed her life up, Liam shook his head.

'So, what you been up to since you got out?' Darren asked, able to talk about something else now that he'd got Mia off his chest.

'This and that,' Liam told him evasively, glad that Darren didn't already know, because at least that meant that Davy hadn't been broadcasting his business to everyone even though he'd told Steve Dawson. And the fewer people who knew that he was in town carrying diamonds, the better. Darren seemed to have matured but that didn't mean he could be trusted. He was a smack dealer, after all.

'It's shit when you've got a record, isn't it?' Darren murmured regretfully. 'You don't think when you're a kid. You just do what you're doing and fuck the consequences. But soon as people hear you've been banged up, forget it. You ain't going nowhere.'

'There's something out there for everyone,' Liam assured him. 'You've just got to decide what you want and go for it.'

'That what you did?' Darren gave him a look that was part respect, part envy.

Nodding, Liam watched as he flicked the little red-tipped roach into the yard. 'Ready to go back in?'

'Yeah, best had.' Subconsciously hanging back to let Liam lead the way, Darren trailed in behind, saying, 'Do us a favour . . . don't tell Davy and the guys any of the shit I just told you about Mia. Only I've done a fair bit of bragging about her, and I wouldn't want them to know the real score. You know how it is.'

Liam told him that his secret was safe and went back to the table. After sticking it out for another half-hour he decided that he'd had enough. He'd only come along to spend a bit of time with Davy, but Davy seemed quite happy playing

Big Daddy to his crew so he doubted he'd be too put out if Liam left. Liam made his excuses and promised to hook up again with Davy soon.

He walked along aimlessly when he hit the street, not knowing or really caring where he was headed, mulling everything over. It had been good to come back because it had opened his eyes to some stuff that he hadn't been conscious of. He hadn't thought that he'd brought any preconceptions or expectations along with him on this visit, but it was clear to him now that he *had* expected to find that people had moved on, as he himself had. And the fact that they hadn't depressed him.

Like Davy, stuck in the centre of the little universe he'd created around himself; a world with a shifting population of misfit boys, all thinking they were tough, yet drawn to their king like moths to a flame; craving the stability he seemed to offer, and finding a purpose in life by doing his dirty work and lining his pockets.

And Liam wasn't knocking Davy for that, because he performed as big a service for the boys as they did for him. There had been a time when Liam himself had thought that Davy was the man, and he was undoubtedly dangerous because he could inflict real damage when he cut loose – like when he'd given Kedga that going-over and put him in hospital. But Davy was getting too old for all that shit and one day someone was going to spot a weakness and destroy him. Yet, instead of planning ahead and turning his attention to other, safer businesses while he still had the chance to walk out of the life he was in, Davy stayed put. Like that plot where the old house had stood – Liam would have already sold it by now, but the way Davy was going it would still be sitting there in another five years.

Still, Davy's life was Davy's life, and he was going to live it as he saw fit. He was a good mate – but only because he'd decided to take Liam into his heart. If he hadn't, Liam had no doubt that he could be his worst enemy.

Pushing Davy out of his mind, Liam found himself thinking about the conversation he'd just had with Darren. The lad had surprised him, because he obviously had a yen to do something with his life. The depressing thing was that it would probably never happen – because of Davy. Dealing for someone else was a mug's game; you made enough money to keep yourself going, but rarely enough to be able to step up a level and become your own boss – or step out of it and take a chance on something else, like Liam had done.

Still deep in thought, Liam didn't realise he'd been heading towards Michelle's house until he suddenly found himself standing opposite it. Frowning, he gazed up at the bedroom window, wondering if Michelle really *was* locked in there, like Darren had said: tied to the bed to protect her from herself, dreaming about the drugs she could no longer get her hands on while her famous sister and their mum lived the high life around her.

Liam shook his head to clear the depressing thoughts and headed round onto the Princess Parkway to look for a cab. As soon as he'd concluded his business with Steve Dawson in a few days, he was getting on a plane and going home. Manchester would always hold a special place in his heart, but right now he needed out of here because there were too many ghosts dragging him down.

25

Steve had just come back from Dover, and he wasn't in the best of moods. Seven young Kosovan girls had been smuggled in and he had no idea what he was supposed to do with them. He'd specifically ordered Thai, because that was what sold best, but the fuckwit driver had been panicking so much about the fact that he'd nearly been rumbled in Calais that he'd flat-out refused to keep them. They were Steve's problem, he'd said, and if Steve tried to get heavy about it he was going to hand himself in to the police and tell them exactly what he'd done – and who for.

With the driver safely out of the way now, bobbing headlessly out to sea on a stream of fast-moving sewage, Steve still had the problem of the girls – most of whom couldn't even speak English. He could have kept them all, he supposed, but he just couldn't be arsed trying to find places for them. And it didn't help that some of them looked diseased, because the last thing his customers wanted was girls coughing death into their faces while they were fucking them.

Steve made a snap decision and picked the two prettiest, most healthy-looking ones and told Vern to put them in the car. Then, shoving a bunch of money into the hands of the other girls, he clapped his hands and sent them scurrying to freedom in the dark.

Back at the club after the long drive back, he'd had Tiny, his minuscule Chinese bar-and-girl-manager, feed and bathe

the two he'd kept. Then, after giving them a little something to relax them, he'd locked them in their new rooms, leaving two of his men to listen out for them.

After taking a shower to wash the stench of them off him, Steve went into the windowless office that could only be accessed through the lounge that he and his men used for their private meetings and video viewings. Here he rang a select few of his clients to let them know that he had some new meat on the menu.

Relaxed by the time the club opened for business, Steve took up his seat at the bar, figuring that maybe it hadn't worked out so bad after all. The bitches he'd released didn't know anything about him, so he was in no danger of them grassing him up. And the ones he'd kept had caused more interest among his clients than he'd anticipated, so they would soon be earning their keep.

When Liam arrived a couple of hours later Steve felt firmly back in control and gave his visitor a questioning smile.

'Hope you don't mind me calling in out of the blue,' Liam said as he sat down on the neighbouring stool. 'But something's come up and I'm going home sooner than I expected. I thought I'd best come and see you before I go, though – see if you're still interested in that stuff we were talking about.'

Steve told Liam that he would have informed him if he'd changed his mind. Then he offered him a drink and, jerking his chin at Liam's case, said, 'You got the new lot, then?'

Liam murmured, 'Some of it,' and glanced cautiously around. The club was packed and, although most of the guys already looked wrecked, he didn't want to talk business around them.

Steve waited until they had their drinks, then stood up and led Liam to the back of the club, putting him out of his misery.

Liam followed Steve out through a claustrophobic little

maze of locked black-painted steel doors into what appeared to be a private kitchen area. He frowned when Steve opened a door which led to a flight of narrow stairs and the sound of muted weeping floated down to them.

'You sure this is all right?' he asked, wondering if it was Steve's woman and they'd had an argument or something.

Assuring him that everything was absolutely fine, Steve relocked the door behind them. The weeping was coming from behind one of the locked doors at this end of the long corridor. As they passed, Steve kicked it and yelled, 'Shut the fuck up, you stupid cow!'

Because it wasn't his business, Liam said nothing and followed him into a room at the far end. Two burly men were sprawled on chairs in there, drinking from a bottle of whisky which stood open on the coffee table and watching a blue movie on a small plasma TV in the corner.

Barking, 'What have I fucking told you about watching this one without asking me first?' Steve snatched up the remote to switch the film off.

Before the screen went blank Liam caught a glimpse of the face of the girl in the film who was being gang-banged by three men. The hairs stood up on the back of his neck. The picture had been crystal clear, and the camera-work was obviously of professional quality so there was no mistaking that it had been Michelle. And she looked every bit as drugged-up and skinny as Darren had said.

As he noticed the look on Liam's face, Steve's expression switched from anger to its usual unreadable neutrality. 'Something wrong, mate?'

Liam's instincts told him that something definitely wasn't right about this set-up, but he didn't know Steve Dawson well enough to start asking questions. So, shaking his head, he said, 'No. I just thought I'd seen that girl somewhere before, that's all.'

Steve took him into the office, locked the door behind them and took his seat at the desk. After waving for Liam to take the seat opposite, he peered at him in silence for several long moments. The guy had obviously recognised Mia and that wasn't good, because things had been going really smoothly until now.

Mia had told him all about the little stunt they'd pulled when they'd pretended that her sister Michelle was her in order to keep Mia's name clean when the coke pictures had come out. She'd told him in the mistaken belief that he would release her once he knew and would let her go back to the wonderful life she'd actually thought she should be allowed to live without him. And the *tears* when she'd realised that he'd meant what he'd said about him owning her . . .

But if Mia had thought that her mum would be worried enough to start up an international manhunt to save her she was mistaken again, because mommy dearest, obviously assuming that Mia had disappeared of her own free will, had simply replaced her with her sister again – giving Steve the perfect cover to hold her for as long as he liked.

And he *did* like.

But now that this guy had recognised her, if he said the wrong thing to the wrong person he could turn everything on its head. Which left Steve in an awkward position. Did he kill him, and give himself the hassle of having a body to dispose of – which he could really do without right now? Or should he let Vern and the boys give him a physical talking-to, in which case – if Liam was anything like Steve, and Steve suspected that he was – he'd probably go away and start digging until he found the bone? Or should he just spin him a line, and hope he accepted it and let the matter drop?

Having already sensed that Liam was the kind of man who – unless he was provoked – kept himself to himself and didn't bandy other people's business around willy-nilly, Steve decided on the third option.

'You probably *have* seen that girl before,' he told Liam now, adding, 'Or, should I say, you *think* you have. You see, her sister's a model, and there's pictures of her all over the place just now.'

'Oh, right,' Liam murmured, trying not to sound as sick as he felt.

'My girl prefers the *private* kind of modelling,' Steve went on. 'Only she doesn't want to wreck her sister's career so we've decided not to release any of her films just yet. You understand what I'm saying?'

Getting the point loud and clear, Liam nodded. He'd seen something that he hadn't been supposed to see, and now he was being warned to keep his mouth shut.

'I hope so,' Steve said darkly, linking his hands together on the desktop. 'Because foolish talk costs lives.'

Unfazed by the threat behind what was obviously Steve's favourite phrase – although Liam personally thought it made him sound like a knob – Liam casually laid his case down on the desk, saying, 'Whatever you and your girl have got going on is *your* business, and I'm not interested in anything except my own. So, if you're ready to take a look . . . ?'

Smiling slowly, sure that they understood each other perfectly, Steve nodded.

Steve opened his concealed safe twenty minutes later, counted out the agreed amount of money and handed it to Liam in exchange for the diamonds wrapped in their black velvet cloth.

'So when will you have the rest?' he asked, already deciding that he'd made the right decision by moving into this line, because there was something awesome about actually handling the stones instead of just talking about them. As soon as you saw them in reality, you knew that you were dealing with something that had the power to hypnotise money out of pockets. And they seemed to have a physical energy when you touched them, which made you want more of them.

'I'm not sure,' Liam told him, smiling as he locked the money into the case.

He'd listened to Steve's explanation about Michelle and it had sounded feasible, but his instincts were still telling him that there was something more sinister to it. He might not have known Michelle for long, but he knew that she'd been far too reserved and shy to go into this line of work. Obviously the drugs would have changed her. But, in his experience, people who were so deep into drugs that they would sink to the level of doing porn didn't give a flying fuck about anyone else, so why would she have been so concerned about protecting Mia's career? That didn't make sense.

Liam knew that he wasn't going to get any answers here and now but he was determined to find out what was going on. And to do that he would have to make Steve trust him and want to keep in touch.

'My guy never gives me any warning,' he said now, setting the bait. 'He just calls and tells you he's at such and such a place, and if you want what he's got you'd best come *now*.'

'And what if you can't?' Steve asked as he took a bag of coke out of the drawer.

'You make sure you *can*,' Liam said simply. 'Even if you have to jump off whoever you're fucking and jump straight on a plane. See, his stuff is the best of the best, and if you don't get it someone else will snatch it out of his hands.' Smiling conspiratorially now, he added, 'And I'm not missing out on the stuff he's bringing over this time, because I've heard rumours that he's got hold of something pretty special that all the other dealers are desperate to get their hands on. But that baby is *mine*.'

'How much?' Steve asked, immediately wanting it just because everybody else did.

'Oh, I don't think I'll be selling this one just yet,' Liam told him, smiling regretfully. 'This is what we call a keeper. It's a rare one, and the value goes through the roof when you sit on them for a bit. Maybe in a year or two.'

'Everything has its price,' Steve said confidently, laying out two thick lines on a mirror. Pushing the mirror towards Liam, he held his gaze as he handed him a gold straw. 'Name yours.'

Liam snorted the line to let Steve see that he was one of the lads and so had nothing to fear from him. Then he sat back and wiped his nose.

'I'll call in and see you when I get it,' he said. 'And we'll talk about it then.'

'Ring first,' Steve told him, leaning down to snort his own line. 'I've got a lot on at the moment so I'll be in and out of town for the next week or so.'

'Give me some dates when you're going to be away,' Liam said. 'Only I've got a load of shit of my own to deal with back home, so I'll only be flying back over here to pick the stuff up and I'm not hanging around waiting for you.'

Steve respected the guy for refusing to leap to his tune like everyone else did and told him what he needed to know.

Liam left the club a short time later and walked down to the end of the road to find a cab. After telling the driver to take him to the hotel, he took out his phone.

'Darren . . . it's Liam. I need to talk to you; can you come to my hotel a.s.a.p?'

26

'Fucking hell,' Darren muttered, his expression grave when he'd heard what Liam had to say. 'Didn't realise she was that bad. No wonder Mia don't want to talk about it. They must be well ashamed. But how come you're so bothered about it?' he asked then, frowning at Liam across the table.

Liam breathed in deeply and said, 'Remember how pissed off I used to get whenever you went on about Mia when we were banged up? Well, it's because *I* used to date Michelle, and . . .' Trailing off, thinking it best not to mention specifics, he shrugged before saying, 'Well, let's just say we didn't finish too good, and it used to piss me off to have to see her face all the time.'

'But that was Mia, not Michelle,' Darren reminded him.

'Identical twins,' Liam reminded *him*.

'Yeah, I see what you mean,' Darren said, reaching for the drink that Liam had just poured. 'So, you and Michelle, me and Mia, eh? Small world, or what?'

'Yeah, and that's why I've come to you with this,' Liam said, his voice serious. 'I didn't really know what you were about when we were padded up together, but talking to you the other night I got the impression you've quit arsing about.'

'Look, I know I'm a cunt,' Darren admitted bluntly. 'Always have been, probably always will be – that's just who I am. There's tons of shit I've done that I'm not proud of, but when I came out I knew I never wanted to go back inside, so I decided to buckle down and make something of myself.'

He twisted his lip in a self-deprecating sneer and took a swig of his drink before continuing. 'Not done too good so far, I know, but I was thinking about what you said the other night and I reckon I just need one big job to get me some decent money, then I'm off.'

'Off where?'

'Anywhere but here.' Sighing, Darren sat back in his seat. 'Anyhow, that's my problem. This stuff with Michelle . . . what do you think's really going on?'

'I don't know,' Liam murmured, pursing his lips and gazing thoughtfully into his glass. 'It just doesn't feel right. And that place . . .' He paused and looked Darren in the eye. 'Can I trust you not to tell Davy what I'm saying?'

Darren snorted softly and said, 'Believe me, I don't tell Davy nothing. No offence,' he added quickly. 'I know you're old mates, and he's probably sound with you. But me and him aren't on the same level. I'm just one of his joeys, and he'd think nothing of slitting my throat if he thought I was up to anything. So I keep my head down and make my money without saying shit.'

Saying, 'You're smarter than you give yourself credit for,' Liam refilled their glasses. 'Okay, I figure I can trust you,' he said. 'So I'll tell you what I think, and what I need to know. Obviously you know more people round here than I do, so if you can put out a few feelers I'll make it worth your while.'

'Cool,' Darren said, nodding his agreement.

'There's definitely something dodgy about that club of Dawson's,' Liam went on. 'I'm just not sure *what* yet. You ever been there?'

Darren shook his head.

'Well, it's one of those little lap-dancing places,' Liam told him. 'You know the kind – full of dirty old bastards and young dead-eyed girls. But if that's all that's going on there, why all the security? Dawson's got the place set up like Fort

Knox: windows barred, steel doors – the lot. I heard a woman crying when we went up to his office and after seeing the state of Michelle in that video I'm wondering if the club's a front, and he's got some kind of brothel set-up going on. So that's one of the things you can ask around about – see if anyone knows anything.'

'Right you are,' Darren said, mentally storing that one away.

'I know he deals,' Liam went on, ''cos that's where Davy gets his gear from.'

'You sure?' Darren frowned. 'He reckons he gets it from London – drives there every week to pick it up.'

'Yeah, well, that's his business,' Liam replied, kicking himself for having let that slip when normally he was so guarded. The coke was obviously still in control of his mouth. Warning Darren not to go telling Davy or anyone else that he knew any different or they'd both be in the shit, he said, 'Anyway, the club closes at four, so I thought I'd take a trip back over there in a bit to see what happens when they lock up – if anyone stays inside, or if they all leave.'

'So, what, you're thinking about breaking in?' Darren asked, getting excited despite his speech about going straight. They were moving into his territory now; burglary was in his blood.

'If I have to,' Liam told him. 'But not tonight. Dawson's going away for a few days, so I'll probably do it then, when there's no chance of him coming back unexpectedly. He's got some big fuckers working for him and I'm not risking anything kicking off. I know his main man Vern goes everywhere with him, and he looks like the biggest threat, so—'

'Sorry,' Darren interrupted. 'Did you just say Vern?'

'Yeah. Why, do you know him?'

'If it's the same bloke, yeah,' Darren said, his eyes suddenly flashing with anger. 'And that would kind of make sense, come to think of it,' he added thoughtfully. 'Remember I told you about when I saw Mia in that club, and how she'd hooked up with a rich twat and his minder did me in? Well, *his* name was Vern – the minder, that is. I remember her saying it.'

'What did he look like?' Liam asked.

'Big fuck-off black fella,' Darren told him, sneering as he added, 'One of them that all the birds go crazy for: hard as fuck, with a killer smile. Tell you what,' he went on, a hint of longing in his voice now, 'the *dreams* I've had about catching that cunt on his own.'

'Sounds like the same guy,' Liam said. 'And Steve Dawson's definitely loaded. And you said Michelle was with him?'

'Yeah, only at the time I thought it was Mia, obviously. But now we know it's definitely Michelle, and she's still with him. But what a cunt, letting his own bird do shit like that with other blokes.'

'Or *making* her do it,' Liam murmured quietly.

'Maybe,' Darren said, giving him a doubtful look. 'But he wasn't forcing her to do the drugs. She was well into that, you could tell.'

'That's how pimps operate,' Liam told him, still convinced that Michelle would never have gone into this way of life voluntarily. 'Charm them, get them hooked, then the next thing they know, they're out of their heads and being sold to the highest bidder.'

'Yeah, you're right,' Darren muttered, taking another swig of his drink. 'So, what's the plan? You going in there to see if it was her crying, or something?'

'To be honest, I'm not really sure *what* my plan is,' Liam admitted. 'But, now you mention it, I suppose you've got a point. It could have been her, couldn't it?'

'Only one way to find out,' Darren said pointedly. 'And if it is them blokes who went for me, you can count me in. Only I hope they *do* come back unexpectedly, 'cos I've got a score to settle.'

After reiterating that he'd prefer to do it when no one

was around, Liam glanced at his watch. 'Right, well, it's nearly half-three, so I reckon I'd better call a cab and head over there. Want me to drop you back at yours on the way?'

Darren took his car keys out of his pocket and grinned. 'I've got my old man's wheels; I'll take you. Four eyes are better than two, and all that.'

A short time later, parked up a fair distance from the club but still within viewing distance, Liam and Darren stayed low in their seats as men began to drift out of the club and make their drunken or stoned ways home. A good forty minutes later a people carrier pulled up, and the working girls came out and climbed into it. And ten minutes later, three big men came out.

'Liam slid almost onto the car's floor as they passed on the opposite pavement. He hissed, 'That's all of the security guys apart from Vern.'

'So there's just him and his boss in there?' Darren asked, cracking his knuckles as if subconsciously preparing for a fight.

'And the woman who runs the bar,' Liam confirmed. 'I haven't seen her yet.'

Minutes later, Steve's BMW nosed into view from the alley at the side of the club. Seeing just two figures in it, Liam narrowed his eyes as he and Darren carried on watching the door. When nobody else came out after half an hour, he said, 'The bar woman was definitely there earlier, 'cos she served us. And I would have noticed if she'd come out with the girls, because she's like a midget compared to them. So why would she still be in there after everyone else has gone . . . *unless* . . .' Turning to Darren, he said, 'I bet she lives in. But why would you need someone living in a place like that unless you've got something to guard? And if we're talking girls here, you wouldn't need a man to guard them. A woman could do it.'

'Jeezus,' Darren muttered, shaking his head. 'This is starting to sound like that sex-slave shit you hear about.'

'My thoughts exactly,' Liam said quietly.

'So what do you want to do?' Darren asked. 'They've all gone, and I doubt they'll come straight back. If you want to go in, I'm up for it.'

'No, we need to work this out properly,' Liam told him. 'We need to find out if there's any way to get past the doors, for starters. And I don't think it'd be too smart to show our faces, 'cos Dawson's the kind of guy who'd hunt you down.'

'It'd take me two minutes to find a way in,' Darren told him confidently. 'Every ship's got a leak somewhere. And balaclavas are the answer for the other problem – which *ain't* a problem 'cos I've got loads back at my place. And gloves. I've got leather, wool, cotton, surgical – take your pick.'

'Christ, what are you?' Liam asked, amused now. 'A one-man fucking crime wave?'

'*Two*-man,' Darren corrected him, grinning. 'My brother, Pete – remember I told you about him? Well, me and him work together, and he's fast as fuck. Should I say we *used* to work together,' he corrected himself now. ''Cos I've been going straight since I got out. Least, I will be after I've earned enough to sack Davy off.'

'Sometime never, then?' Liam said, chuckling softly.

'Yeah, whatever,' Darren scoffed. Then, starting the car's engine, he said, 'So what's it to be? Back to the hotel, or over to mine to pick up what we need so we can strike while the iron's hot? I mean, what's to think about, really? We'll only have to come back another time and watch until everyone's gone again. And you still won't have any idea what you're actually going to do once you get inside, so what's the difference if we just go ahead and do it now? Before it starts getting too light, though, eh?'

Liam shook his head and raised his hands in a gesture of

surrender. 'All right, let's do it. But you'd best hope that Dawson and his man don't come back 'cos I reckon that could get pretty nasty.'

'Don't you worry about that,' Darren said, setting off.

As he ran down the alley at the side of the club half an hour later, his face concealed by a black balaclava, his hands encased in black leather gloves, Liam was seriously beginning to wonder if he'd lost his mind. This was exactly why he didn't touch coke, because the few times he'd tried it in his youth it had made him do crazy reckless things – like this. And only when it had worn off – like now – did he realise what a mistake he'd made.

But it was too late to call it off now, because Darren and Pete were already scaling up the drainpipes at the rear of the building, checking the bars on the windows for weak points.

Pete was a last-minute addition to the team, one that Liam could really have done without. But Darren had insisted that he was one hundred per cent trustworthy, and Liam had thought *what the hell.* If he was as fast as Darren had said, it would speed things along. And he was every bit as muscular as Darren, which would be a definite bonus if Steve or any of his men *did* come back.

But he wasn't so sure about the knives they had both insisted on bringing along.

Liam spun on his heel when he heard a noise behind him. He held his breath and peered into the shadows. Exhaling nervously when he caught the glint of a cat's eyes as it ran past, he gritted his teeth.

'Psst!' Darren hissed. 'Look!'

As he squinted up towards the silhouetted figure, Liam's heart began to pick up speed when he saw that Darren had managed to open a window.

'It's a bog,' Darren informed them in a whisper. 'I'll climb in, then you two follow. And try not to make any noise, 'cos I can hear a telly.'

Watching as Darren disappeared, to be quickly replaced at the window by his brother, Liam took a deep breath and climbed up the pipe to join them.

Darren, who had slipped into the role of leader, placed a finger against his balaclava'd lips when they were all crammed in the tiny space together and pushed the door handle down slowly. When he found the hallway on the other side in darkness, he eased his way out.

There was a slash of light along the bottom of the door of the room in which Liam had earlier seen the video of Michelle. Darren took his knife out of his pocket and flicked it open silently. Taking this as a cue, Pete did the same. Thinking *oh, fuck!*, Liam had no choice but to follow as they tiptoed towards the door.

After putting his ear against it for a moment, Darren whispered, 'You say the chairs face the TV?'

Nodding, Liam said, 'Yeah, but take it easy. It'll be the woman, don't forget.'

Easing this door handle down now, Darren slowly opened the door – and found himself looking down the barrel of the gun that was being pointed at him by the smallest woman he'd ever seen in his life. She obviously didn't really know how to use it, though, because she'd put herself way too close to her target, and Darren was able to kick it out of her hand before she could even think about pulling the trigger.

As Pete made a dive for the gun Darren laughed, and said, 'What the fuck am I supposed to do with *this*?'

Pete pushed him out of the way, grabbed Tiny by the hair and brought his face right down to hers. Then, shoving the gun beneath her chin, he said, 'You speakee Eenglish?'

Understanding him perfectly, Tiny shook her head.

'Like fucking hell she doesn't!' Darren snorted. 'Otherwise

she wouldn't have known what you just said. Here, let me deal with her.'

Tiny shrank back when Darren pushed his face into hers. She pursed her lips and glared at him defiantly.

'Don't bother trying to pull any of that Ma-Triad-defending-her-boys-to-the-death shit on me,' Darren told her. 'We know you've got a girl locked up in here, and we want the keys – *NOW*!'

Tiny raised her chin, clamped her lips tightly shut and stood her ground. Whatever they did to her, it would be nothing compared to what Mr Dawson would do if he thought she'd given in without a fight.

'These what we're looking for?' Pete said, finding a set of keys hanging on the wall behind the door.

Grinning when he saw the flicker of *Oh, shit!* in the midget woman's eyes, Darren said, 'I reckon they are, yeah.'

Taking the keys from Pete, Liam went back out in the corridor. He unlocked the first door, pushed it open and felt around for a light switch on the wall.

'Jeezus,' he muttered when he saw the girl on the bed. 'Guys . . . look at this.'

Darren dragged Tiny along by her hair in case she got any funny ideas about locking them out of the room and calling the troops in. His eyes widened when he saw what Liam had found. The room was bare apart from the double bed that the girl was lying on and a single chair in the corner. In another corner, a small video camera was set up on a tripod facing the bed. But there was no red light on, so filming had obviously stopped for the night.

'Yo!' Pete hissed, picking up a small wastepaper bin with several used condoms in it and showing it to the others.

Shaking his head in disgust as he approached the bed, Liam squatted down beside the girl. She only looked about fifteen, in his estimation, and she was definitely foreign – although not Oriental, like most of the girls downstairs. She looked Eastern European; maybe Russian.

Liam picked her hand up and felt for her pulse. 'Well, at least she's alive,' he said, having feared from her pallor and the coldness of her skin that she wasn't.

'Look at that,' Pete said quietly, pointing at the crook of her elbow where, in the middle of a livid bruise, two pinprick holes were clearly visible.

'You do that?' Darren demanded, shaking Tiny roughly. 'Yeah, I bet you fucking *did*, you evil twat,' he barked when she said nothing.

Liam got up, rushed back out into the corridor and opened the door of the next room. Finding an almost identical girl in there, in the same condition, he opened the third door. This time the girl was Oriental. Pausing only long enough to wonder why she was up here instead of down on the club floor with her sisters, he opened up the last room.

Michelle lay inert on the bed, her face as grey as dish-water. The freckles that Liam had thought so cute stood out like spots of dried blood against her skin. Her lips were dry and cracked, and the skin around her eyes was crusted with yellow gunk. But unlike the pinpricks on the arms of the European girls, her arms were laced with heavy track-marks, indicating that she had been here for far longer than they had.

'Bastards!' Liam hissed. 'You dirty fucking *bastards*!'

'Yo, someone's coming,' Pete whispered, putting his ear against the door at the end of the corridor. He could hear footsteps climbing the stairs.

Darren felt Tiny's head jerk back and he looked down just as she opened her mouth. He clamped his hand over it, knowing that she'd been about to scream, swept her up off her feet and carried her quietly back to the first room. There, after punching her and knocking her out, he tossed her onto the floor behind the door and dashed back out to switch off the lights that they'd turned on. Surprise was the best element of a successful attack: let whoever was coming in have to step into darkness, then take them out before they realised what was happening.

Tensing at the sound of a key turning in the lock, Liam felt the shroud of calmness that he hadn't known in a long, long time descend over him. Whatever happened in the next few seconds, he knew that he would be taking Michelle out of here – and if somebody tried to get in his way, so be it.

'I knew we shouldn't have left her on her own with the two new girls,' he heard Steve saying, sounding as if he was angry as he opened the second lock.

'It's quiet,' Vern's deeper voice pointed out, as if Steve couldn't hear that for himself.

'Yeah, well, thanks for that, *Einstein*,' Steve shot back sarcastically.

'I just meant that she might have pressed the alarm by mistake and didn't realise she'd done it,' Vern said calmly.

'I'll tell you what, if she has, I'll fucking kill her,' Steve growled, pushing the door open now. 'Dragging me back round here at this time of the fucking night, like I've got nothing better t—'

Silenced by Liam's vicious punch which caught him flush in the mouth, splitting his lip and chipping his tooth, Steve slammed back against Vern. Shoving Steve back to his feet, Vern reached into his pocket for his gun. Seeing the movement, Darren planted his foot on the other man's chest and sent him sprawling down the stairs. Vern landed in a heap at the bottom and started firing random shots up the stairwell, most of which embedded themselves in the wall.

Darren snatched the gun that Pete had taken from Tiny and was still holding as Liam and Steve started fighting in the corridor behind him. He squatted down at the side of the door and, reaching his arm round it, fired back at Vern. Hearing a thud when one round hit its target and the shots from downstairs stopped, he peeped around the door, feeling sick when he heard the big man gasping for breath.

'Fucking hell, man!' Pete muttered when he heard the same thing. 'This is bad shit! What d'y' do that for?'

'Oh, what . . .' Darren retorted defensively. ''Cos I should have just let him carry on trying to shoot us instead, yeah?'

'No, I'm not saying that.'

'Just shut up!' Darren barked, feeling bad enough already without Pete making it worse. He might have been dreaming about giving the man a kicking, but he'd never meant to *kill* him.

Darren turned to tell Liam that they had to get the fuck out of there and winced when he saw him kicking Steve over and over as the man lay unconscious on the floor at his feet. He jumped up, ran at Liam and pulled him away, hissing, 'That's enough, man! You're gonna kill him – pack it in!'

Breathing deeply, Liam said, 'All right, all right, I've stopped. Get off me.'

Darren let him go and glanced sideways into the first bedroom they had opened. 'What we gonna do?' he whispered urgently. 'We've got to get out of here, but we can't carry them all out.'

'Leave them,' Liam said, turning and marching back to Michelle's room. 'We'll take her, and ring the police when we get away – tell them to fetch an ambulance.'

'Fuck that!' Darren squawked. 'I've just *killed* someone!'

'The little bird's prints are on the gun, not yours,' Pete reminded him. 'We're all wearing gloves, remember? Just shove it in her hand and they'll think she did it.'

'You reckon?' Darren looked at him uncertainly.

'Yeah, man! Just do it.'

'Fast,' Liam added as he scooped Michelle up off the bed

with the sheet around her. 'I'll take her down to the car. Check in his pockets for keys.' He jerked his head towards Steve. 'He'll have locked the outside door, knowing him.'

Pete found the keys as Darren stepped over Steve and went into the lounge room. He tossed them down the corridor.

'*I* can't do it,' Liam pointed out irritably, his arms full of Michelle.

Sucking his teeth quietly, Pete tugged Steve's wallet out of his coat and emptied it. Jerking his head at Darren who was just coming out of the lounge, he snatched up the keys he'd thrown and led the way down the stairs.

Pete stepped over Vern's body at the bottom and inhaled sharply when he saw all the blood. Darren did the same, but Liam was too busy trying to keep his grip on Michelle. Steve had indeed relocked the outside door. Finding the right key after several attempts, Pete let the others out ahead of him.

'What you doing that for?' Darren demanded as his brother closed the door and started locking it. 'The police won't be able to get in.'

'No, but the staff will in the morning, then it'll be their problem, not ours,' Pete hissed. 'And now we know what they're running here, they ain't gonna want the pigs sniffing round, are they? They'll just get rid of the body and clean everything up.'

'And what about the girls?'

'Not our problem,' Pete reiterated firmly.

'I think it is,' Darren retorted, snatching the keys out of his brother's hand and reopening the door.

'Are you off your fucking head?' Pete snapped. 'We've got to *go*, man!'

'Just fetch the car round,' Darren told him. 'I'll bring them out by myself if you don't want to help me.'

'And do what with them?' Pete asked exasperatedly. 'There's already four of us. You gonna put the rest in the boot?'

'If I have to, yeah.'

'Get a grip!' Pete said, dragging Darren away from the door. 'Leave it open then. At least they'll be able to do a runner when they wake up, eh?'

Grudgingly accepting this, Darren ran after him to the car.

'Where to?' Darren asked, firing the engine when they were all in.

Liam hadn't even thought about that, but he knew that he definitely couldn't take Michelle back to his hotel while she was in this condition. And Darren's place was out of the question, because he and Pete lived with their parents. And he couldn't go to Davy's, either, because he didn't want Davy to know that he'd had anything to do with this, given Davy's connection with Steve.

It was starting to get light by now and they pulled their balaclavas off as they turned out of the street and onto the main road. Darren said, 'You'd best think of somewhere quick, man. We can't just drive around all day with her in that state.'

'And you were gonna try and cram another three in!' Pete reminded him, lighting a cigarette. 'See what I meant now, do you?'

'Shut your mouth,' Darren snapped, snatching the cigarette, forcing Pete to light another one.

When he turned to offer Liam one as an afterthought, Pete saw the expression on his face as he stroked Michelle's hair with her head in his lap. He nudged Darren, who shook his head when he looked at the couple in the rear-view. Then, a thought occurring to him, Darren said, 'I know where you can take her.'

'Oh?' Liam gave him a hopeful look. 'Where?'

'Me grandad's place.'

'Nah, man,' Pete protested. 'He's only been dead two fucking weeks, and mam's talking about going round any day to clear it out.'

'Leave mam to me,' Darren told him. 'I'll tell her I saw the old man's ghost – that'll keep her away for a few more weeks. And you'll have found somewhere by then, won't you?' This last he directed at Liam.

'Yeah, course,' Liam agreed, thinking that anywhere would do right now. As long as he had somewhere to lay Michelle down and take care of her, he'd worry about where to go from there later.

27

Steve was stiff and in agony when he came to. When he saw all the open doors, he remembered what had happened and sat up. A whimpering noise was coming from the lounge. Spitting out a shard of broken tooth, he got up and went in to see who it was.

Tiny was curled in a ball behind the door, the gun lying beside her as she rocked to and fro. Steve squatted painfully down beside her and raised her chin with his finger. Her jaw was badly swollen on one side, and there was dried blood caked around her mouth, and down her chin and neck.

'Jeezus,' he croaked. 'You all right?'

She nodded. Then her lips turned down as the tears began to fall. 'I tink Vern dead.'

'Stay there,' Steve told her. Going back out into the hall, he kicked his empty wallet aside and glanced into the bedrooms. The two new girls were still flat out; unused to the heroin, they would probably take a few more hours to come round properly. But the Thai girl was gone, and so was Mia – which brought a flaming ball of fiery anger rising up from Steve's gut to his head. The rest were just cattle, as far as he was concerned; there to serve a function, and easily replaceable when they had outlived their usefulness. But Mia was personal – and he wanted her back.

Vern was in a heap at the bottom of the stairs. The Thai girl was on top of him, her legs stretched back on the stairs, her head twisted grotesquely around.

Grimacing as he gazed down at her open lifeless eyes, Steve tensed when he heard the squeak of the downstairs back door being pushed open slowly.

'Steve . . . Vern? You in there?'

'Noel, thank fuck it's you!' Steve called back when he heard the voice. 'Get up here quick – we've got a problem!'

'Shit on a stick!' Noel blurted out when he saw the girl. Then, after glancing at Vern, his gaze shot to Steve.

Shaking his head, Steve said, 'We need to get rid.'

'What the fuck happened?' Noel asked, staring at the girl again, whose legs were splayed wide. Shuddering at the sight of knickerless corpse-pussy, he looked away. 'And how come the door was unlocked?'

'No idea,' Steve admitted. 'Me and Vern were at the casino and Tiny pushed the alarm, so we came back over to see what was up. We thought she'd done it by mistake, because the door was still locked and it was all quiet up here. But some fuckers were waiting in the dark; I got lamped, and Vern got shot.'

'Must have been some fucking battle,' Noel commented, his gaze bouncing from one to other of the numerous bullet holes in the wall behind Steve's head. 'How many of them were there?'

'Don't have a clue,' Steve said darkly. 'It happened too fast, and they caught us off guard. I'll ask Tiny; she was here.'

'What were they after?' Noel asked. 'Anything missing?'

'Yeah, my fucking money,' Steve told him angrily. 'One of the cunts must have mugged me on the way out.'

'What about the safe?'

'Haven't had a chance to look yet.'

'The other girls?' Noel asked now, still studiously not looking at the one who was lying right in front of him.

'New ones are still out of it,' Steve told him. 'But my one's gone.'

'Oh, right,' Noel said gravely. 'Any idea where?'

'No, but if she escaped at the same time *that* one tried to, she could be anywhere by now.' Shaking his head again, Steve gritted his teeth. 'Where's Tommy?'

'Should be here in a minute,' Noel told him, glancing at his watch. 'Want me to get the others rounded up?'

'Yeah, we need to do a clean-up soon as,' Steve said, turning to go back to Tiny. When he saw the room keys still dangling from the lock of Mia's room he yanked them out.

'Tiny . . . ?' He marched up the hallway, went into the lounge and looked down at her where she was huddled on one of the chairs now. 'Did you leave the doors unlocked?'

'No me, man,' she said, pointing at the wall where the keys had been taken from. 'I hang there, he take.'

'How many men were there?' Steve asked. 'And how did they get in?'

'Tree.' Tiny held up three fingers. 'All black.' She stroked her hands down over her face to indicate the balaclavas they had been wearing, items for which she had no word.

Misinterpreting the statement to mean that the men, not their headgear, had been black, Steve cast a hooded glance at Noel, who was standing in the doorway. Nodding to indicate that he understood that Steve was telling him to get on the phone and get the guys to start putting out feelers for three black men who might have pulled the job, Noel went out into the hall to make his calls.

'How did they get in?' Steve asked Tiny again.

'Bat' room,' she croaked, pointing out along the corridor to the small toilet which was situated between the Kosovan girls' and the Thai girl's rooms. 'Window no bar in dere,' she reminded him.

'And what happened when they came in?' Steve wanted to know. 'Did they say anything? Touch anything?'

'I have gun, but man kick it out of hand,' she said. 'Then

man pull hair, say, "We know you got girl lock up, keys – *NOW*!"'

Steve's eyes narrowed as she mimicked the male voice. He said, 'Girl? You sure he said girl, not *girls*?'

'No, *girl*,' Tiny insisted. Then, frowning, she said, 'I tink.'

'All right, we'll go over it again later,' Steve said, seeing that it was painful for her to talk. 'Did they go into the office?'

'No.' Tiny shook her head. 'Just here. Then see girls.'

'What did they say when they saw them?'

'"Fucky hell",' Tiny told him, mimicking a man's voice again. 'And man call me dirty name for . . .' Unable to think of the words for giving an injection, she mimed the action on her own arm. 'Then you come, and *boom*!' She mimed a punch in her own face.

Steve nodded and told her to stop talking. Deep in thought, he went back out into the hall and relocked the two remaining girls' doors while Noel spoke quietly on the phone. He didn't like this; there was something personal about it. If it had just been a random break-in, whoever had done it would probably have tried the doors first. But they'd gone straight for the only window that didn't have bars.

And they had specifically mentioned the girls to Tiny, which they could only have known about if at least one of them had been a customer at some point. But none of the black guys who came to the club had ever used the upstairs girls. Much as they enjoyed their little lap-dances, they wouldn't be caught dead dirtying their cocks in whore pussy.

Anyway, the whores weren't advertised to the club's clientele; they were purely for the entertainment of Steve's business colleagues, who liked to have themselves videoed doing the deed so they could buy the DVDs and wank over them in privacy. But if Tiny had been right first time, and the men had said 'girl' instead of 'girls', did that mean that they had come to get one girl in particular? If so, the only one who could possibly be worth anything to anyone was Mia. But had she been taken, or had she simply escaped, as the Thai girl almost had?

Steve would find out, one way or another, but right now he had to get this mess cleaned up because the police could be here at any minute.

Spurred into action when his men began to arrive, he had two of them take Vern's and the Thai girl's corpses to the incinerator. Another drove Tiny over to Rochdale to see a doctor that Steve used whenever someone had got hurt and he didn't want the police sniffing round.

The fact that the Kosovan girls were still alive posed a bigger problem, but Steve decided to dump them out in the sticks while they were still unconscious. They had no clue where they had been, so they couldn't lead anybody back to him. And dumping them was easier than killing them, given the mess he was already in right now.

With the upper floor cleared, Steve got his cleaners to give it a thorough going-over to rid it of any evidence of foul play. Then, relaxed, knowing that even if the police came they would find nothing, he waited until it was dark before heading out to visit Mia's mum's house – where he presumed she would have run to if she had escaped, like the idiot that she was.

28

'Michelle? Are you awake?'

Mia forced her eyes open and winced in the light. She blinked slowly as the hovering face wavered just out of focus and frowned deeply. It wasn't Steve, she was sure of that; or Vern, or Noel, or the other one – Tommy. So was it a punter?

'Michelle?'

'Mia,' she corrected the voice. Her own was croaky and raw.

'Mia's fine,' Liam assured her, guessing that she was confused. He smiled and reached for the glass of water that was sitting on the cabinet beside the bed. 'Do you want a drink?'

Mia's eyes cleared a little and she blinked rapidly as Liam's face began to take form. '*You?*' she gasped. 'But how—?'

'Sshhh,' Liam told her, gently lifting her so that she could sip at the water. 'We'll talk later.'

Mia gagged when the cold water touched her lips and she began to shiver violently. Liam laid her back down and pulled the blankets up around her. She was suffering withdrawal symptoms; he hadn't accounted for that. As he gazed down at her concernedly when she began to moan, he knew that there was no way he could put her through the torture of cold turkey because she'd already suffered more than enough. Anyway, there was no telling how much heroin Steve Dawson had been giving her while she'd been locked in that room, and if Liam tried to make her stop abruptly there was a strong possibility that she could die of shock.

Telling her that he'd be back in a minute, Liam ran downstairs and rang Darren, asking him to bring round a couple of wraps of the gear that Davy had supplied him with. He was loath to do it, but it was the only way of weaning her off the stuff since he couldn't risk taking her to a doctor and getting her on a methadone programme. But there was no way he was injecting her – on that he was adamant. Her veins were already fucked, so she would have to smoke or snort it instead.

29

Michelle and Kim were singing their heads off as Sammy turned the car onto their road. They'd just come back from Prague and they were all still buzzing because it had been Michelle's first catwalk show and she had performed fantastically.

Sammy couldn't stop telling her how proud he was of her, and Kim was really chuffed that she had not only been invited along but had been treated like a queen – which had made a lovely change from Mia's shows where, more often than not, she was either banned from going or hidden away in a corner like a dirty secret.

Kim had seen a whole new side to Michelle since Mia had done a runner, and she had really been enjoying her company. As a child, Michelle had always been pushed into the background by Mia and Kim felt guilty when she thought about it, because she knew that she could and *should* have done more to even the playing field between them. But it was true what they said about the one who shouted loudest getting all the attention. Mia had found her mouth at a very young age, and by *God* had she used it; demanding this, demanding that – and putting Kim on a guilt trip if she dared to say no. And Kim had found it easier to give in than to argue, because Mia never gave up. If she wanted something, she'd just keep banging on and on until she got it. Whereas Michelle had been the exact opposite: never demanding, and therefore usually not getting.

After pulling up outside the house, Sammy jumped out to get their cases out of the boot while Michelle nipped down to the shops to get the milk they'd forgotten to stop for on their way back. Kim went inside to put the kettle on.

Sammy had also been enjoying Michelle's company. Now that she was gaining confidence she was proving to be an absolute natural – which was great from a professional point of view, because the work offers were flooding in. But her character was so different from Mia's that she was an absolute joy to work with; never stroppy, or difficult, always polite and willing to go the extra mile and then some to get the best shot – which was earning her a good reputation and a lot of support from within the industry. In the short time that she had been 'Mia', Michelle had made a more positive impact than her sister had made in two years – and she hadn't had to pull any stunts to achieve it; she'd just been her natural, warm, beautiful self.

As he reached the door with the cases Sammy heard Kim shouting. He dropped them on the step and ran inside.

'What's the matter?' he asked, holding out his arms to cushion their collision when she barrelled out of the kitchen and ran straight into him.

'Look!' she squawked, waving her arm in an arc to indicate the mess. 'We've been burgled!'

'Oh, good lord. Is anything missing?'

'Don't think so,' Kim muttered, her eyes darting from this to that. 'Looks like they just came in to trash it. Oh, me *telly* – they didn't have to do that!'

The TV was lying screen down on the floor beneath the window, surrounded by glittering shards of glass. Sammy shook his head. With that, and the couch and chair cushions scattered around with their stuffing bulging out through large knife-slash holes, and ornaments lying broken where they'd landed after being swept off shelves and ledges, the damage did seem rather wanton.

'How did they get in?' he asked.

'Back door's been booted in,' Kim told him as she headed out into the hall to go and see what damage had been done upstairs.

Sammy followed and put his arm around her when she went into her bedroom and burst into tears. It was just as much a mess in there as it was downstairs: mirror smashed, everything that had been on the dressing table now broken on the floor. But it was the state of Kim's bedding that really upset her. Looking as if it had been torn apart by somebody's hands, it was an irreparable mess.

'I only got that out of the catalogue three weeks ago,' she sobbed, slumping down onto the quilt and stroking it. 'It cost seventy-five quid, and I haven't even started paying for it yet.'

Telling her not to worry, that he would personally replace it, Sammy glanced up when he heard Michelle coming in through the front door below. She was still humming the song that they had been singing so happily just a few short minutes ago. Then she stopped abruptly, and Sammy heard her gasp when she saw the mess in the living room.

'Mum?' she called out, sounding shocked and panic-stricken. 'Mum, where are you?'

'Up here,' Sammy called back.

Michelle ran up the stairs and came into Kim's bedroom. 'Oh, no,' she moaned. 'Your lovely bedspread.' She sat beside her mother and put her arm around her. 'Don't cry, mum. We'll get you a new one.'

Sniffling back her tears, embarrassed because she wasn't a natural crier, Kim said, 'Don't worry about me, I'm just being soft. You'd best check your own room, love.'

Michelle nodded, got up and went to check, not surprised to find her bedroom in just as much of a mess as the rest of the house, with ripped clothes strewn everywhere and everything fragile smashed.

'I'm going to see if Pam heard anything,' Kim said. She went back down the stairs with a thunderous look on her face.

When she'd gone, Sammy scratched his head and looked at Michelle. 'I think you'd best come and stay with me again.'

Picking up on the undertone of worry in his voice, Michelle said, 'I don't think they'll come back. They don't usually; not once they realise there's nothing of value to steal. It was probably just local kids who found out the house was empty.'

'I hope so,' Sammy replied quietly. 'But all the same, I think I'd feel happier if you stayed with me – just until we're sure this wasn't a targeted attack.'

'Targeted?' Michelle repeated. 'Why would anyone target us? We're nobody, and we've got nothing – everyone knows that round here.'

'My dear, are you forgetting that you're really rather famous now?'

'That's Mia, not me,' Michelle replied without hesitation. 'And she's not even here, so why would anyone target . . .' Trailing off when she realised what she'd said, she smiled sheepishly.

'Exactly,' Sammy said.

Kim came back just then, already shouting as she pounded her way up the stairs. 'You know what, she is one spiteful cow, her next door! She heard everything – the door getting booted in, the house getting ransacked – the lot. And she just sat on her fat arse and left them to it.'

'Didn't she call the police?'

'Did she hell!' Kim blurted out. 'Like I said – *spiteful*!' Looking at Sammy now, the indignation sparking in her eyes, she said, 'You'd never guess me and her used to be best mates. We used to be in and out of each other's houses all the time – didn't we, Shell? Went everywhere together: bingo, shopping, the pub – *every*where. Then she got on one when I said

I needed my Christmas club money back for our Mia's photos, and she's been a cow ever since. Jealous, that's what she is. Bitter, twisted, and jealous as hell.'

'I see,' Sammy said, exchanging a semi-amused glance with Michelle.

'I wouldn't mind so much,' Kim ranted on obliviously. 'But she's the one who did the dirty on me, but she goes on like *I*'ve done something to *her*.'

'Mum,' Michelle interrupted softly. 'Shut up, you're giving us a headache.'

Kim gaped at her. Then, seeing the laughter in her and Sammy's eyes, she tutted and gave them a sheepish grin. 'Was I going on with myself?'

'Er, *yeah*.'

'Sorry. She just does my head in.'

'Anyway,' Sammy said forcefully, to prevent her from starting again. 'Michelle and I have been talking, and we think it's best if you both come to stay with me for a while.'

'Oh, there's no need for that,' Kim argued. 'Thanks for the thought, but I doubt they'll come back – whoever it was. And it won't take long to clean up.' Shrugging, she added, 'Might miss the telly, but at least I've still got the portable in me room, so we'll have something to watch.'

'I'd really rather you came to my place,' Sammy insisted. 'So, could you at least humour an old man?'

Kim grinned at Michelle and shook her head. 'What's he like?' Then, spreading her hands, she said, 'Okay. I suppose it can't hurt. And at least we've already got our bags packed.'

'Oh, lord, the bags,' Sammy said, remembering that he'd dropped them on the doorstep. He rushed back downstairs.

30

Liam eased the bedroom door open and smiled when he saw that she was awake. He carried the cup of tea that he'd made over to the bed, handed it to her and sat down on the edge of the mattress. 'Feeling any better today?'

Nodding, Mia sipped at the tea. Incredibly, she *was* feeling better, and it was all thanks to him. It was three long weeks since he'd rescued her, and he'd looked after her with the patience of a saint: washing her, feeding her, mopping up her sick, and comforting her when the withdrawal pains and the awful itching and shivering had threatened to drive her crazy. And throughout it all he'd talked to her, telling her all about his childhood and how he'd ended up in Manchester, and about being in prison, and how he'd been working to turn his life around since getting out.

And Mia had loved it, soaking up every word and lapping up his gentle attentions. The only downside being that, just like the last time, he thought she was Michelle. But Mia didn't care. *She* was the one being held in the arms of the only man she had ever loved, and as long as nobody took that away from her, she didn't care how many times she had to hear him calling her by *that* name. He might *think* that he was in love with Michelle, but in reality Mia was the one he'd revealed his innermost thoughts to – and had made love to. And he might not yet have made love to her *this* time around but he soon would, she was sure. He was too much of a gentleman to take advantage of her while she was ill, but when he knew that she was fully recovered he would take her in his arms and tell her that he never wanted to be without her again.

'You've got some of your colour back,' Liam told her as he stroked her hair back from her face. 'You're starting to look like your old self again.'

'Thanks to you,' she murmured, closing her eyes and pressing her face into his hand, savouring the feel of his skin against hers.

'You've been really strong,' he reminded her, not wanting to take all the credit. She'd made an enormous effort to kick the drugs. And it hadn't been easy, because she'd really suffered at times. But she'd been determined. For days now she hadn't even asked for any of the gear that he'd got from Darren, which was a fantastic sign. And if she carried on like this Liam was sure that she'd be up and about in no time.

'Have you thought about contacting your mum yet?' he asked, broaching the subject which always seemed to dampen her spirits but which he knew needed to be raised. 'You know she must be worried sick about you.'

'She won't be,' Mia said quietly, taking another sip of her tea. She wished that Liam wouldn't keep trying to talk about this because it reminded her of the outside world and she didn't want to think about that. She wanted to stay here for ever, just the two of them.

But that wasn't going to happen.

Aside from the fact that the house they were staying in belonged to a dead man whose daughter could walk in at any time to clear out his belongings, Liam had to go back to Ireland soon because there were things that needed to be sorted out over there. He'd be coming straight back, though, because now that he'd been given a second chance with Michelle he was determined to make it work. And, in light of the threat that Steve still posed, he'd actually been considering asking her to move over to Dublin with him. But for them to be truly happy in the future she needed to reconnect with her family first – especially with her mum. No matter how badly she might have been treated in the past, or how much she'd been pushed aside in favour of Mia, Liam knew that she would regret it if she left it too late.

'Do you want me to call her?' he asked now, thinking that maybe she just didn't feel strong enough for the inevitable barrage of questions.

'No!' Mia blurted out. 'Please, Liam, stop pushing me. I'll do it in my own time.'

'You keep saying that,' he persisted gently. 'And I know you; you'll just let it slide, and before you know it, ten years will have passed.'

'And we'll be married with eight babies, and that'll be all the family we need,' Mia giggled, reaching for Liam's hand and linking her fingers with his.

Liam smiled fondly down at her and kissed her on the forehead. 'You're ringing her,' he said firmly, standing up. 'I'll give you two days, and if you still can't face it I'll do it for you. Because she needs to be told that you're okay.' Glancing at his watch, he said, 'Anyway, I've got to nip out to get some shopping. Is there anything you want me to get for you?'

Telling him that she needed cigarettes, and wouldn't mind a drink now that she was feeling better, Mia looked up at him mock-sulkily, adding, 'When can I get up? I'm sick of lying here on my own all day.'

'Your clothes are over there,' Liam told her, nodding towards an armchair in the corner on which he'd placed a neatly folded pile containing jeans, T-shirt, a pair of trainers, and a set of underwear – although the bra had been a guess, because he had no idea about sizes of stuff like that.

Uttering a surprised 'Oh' because she hadn't even noticed them, Mia gave him a grateful smile. 'Thanks. I'll try them on while you're at the shops.'

Liam winked at her and went out. When she heard the front door open and close a few moments later, Mia pushed the bed covers off and lowered her feet to the floor. Feeling like a little old woman because her legs seemed so weak, she walked slowly out onto the landing and along to the bathroom. The only time she'd been out of bed in the entire time she'd been here had been to go to and from the toilet. As she ran a bath now, she decided to explore the second bedroom and see where Liam had been sleeping while he'd been refusing to take advantage of her.

His bed was neatly made, his clothes folded and laid on top of his rucksack – as if he thought he might need to pack them in a hurry. His green army jacket which he only ever wore with jeans was hanging on the back of the door. Resting her head against it, Mia inhaled the scent of him before sliding her hand into a pocket. Disappointed to find it as empty as the rest of his pockets, both in that jacket and his suit coat, which was hanging on the door of the old wardrobe, she switched her attention to his rucksack. Finding nothing in that, and unable to get into his Samsonite case because it was locked, she glanced around the room itself.

Mia pulled a disdainful face at all the old man's things that were lying around, then spotted a stack of newspapers and magazines sticking out from on top of the wardrobe. Thinking that it would be nice to have something to read while she was soaking in the bath, she stood on her tiptoes and reached for them, but they spilled over as she was pulling them towards her and fell messily onto the floor around her. Cursing under her breath, she squatted down to scoop them up. But, just as she was about to pick up a magazine which had fallen open, she hesitated when she saw her own face smiling up at her.

Snatching it up, she looked at the cover, frowning when she saw that it was a *TV Quick* from a couple of months earlier.

And the frown deepened when she went back to the picture inside, because it was part of an advert for a company called Blaze Cosmetics, and she didn't remember doing a shoot for them.

But she must have, because there she was.

Either that, or it had been taken from a reel of unused shots from a different campaign and sold on without her permission.

Staring intensely at the picture now, Mia scrutinised her hair and her make-up, trying to remember when she'd been made up exactly like that in the past. People thought that you always looked the same when you were made up, but it wasn't true. A shade of eyeshadow or lipstick, or just the angle of the eyeliner tail could change the entire look of your face. And Mia knew her face in every form better than anybody, but she just didn't recognise this shot. And that surprised her, because it was really good, so she should have done.

Liam had arrived back from the shops, but she'd been so busy concentrating on the picture that she hadn't heard him. She jumped when he came into the room to tell her that he'd turned the taps off because the bath had been about to overflow and spun around with the magazine still in her hand.

Laughing at her expression, Liam came towards her. 'Sorry, didn't mean to frighten you. I shouted twice, but you mustn't have heard me.' He glanced at the magazine and said, 'What's that you're reading?'

Mia opened her mouth, about to tell him that she'd been trying to remember the shoot this picture had been taken at. Then she remembered that she was supposed to be Michelle and clamped her lips shut again.

When he saw the picture for himself, Liam murmured, 'Ah . . . your sister.' Sitting down on the bed now, he said, 'I've actually seen that picture loads of times, but I didn't want to mention it in case it upset you. I thought you might think they were just getting on with their lives without you, or something. But I'm sure it's not like that. Mia's probably just got commitments she can't get out of.' Snorting softly now, oblivious to the raging fire of jealousy that his words were igniting in her, he went on, 'I must admit I was pissed off when I saw her on the TV the first night I was back in Manchester. But she's your sister, so I can't hold all that old shit against her for ever, can I? Anyway, we're back together now and nothing's ever going to get between us again, so I think we should just let it go and be happy for her.'

Mia couldn't speak. She desperately wanted to be with Liam, but at the same time she desperately didn't want Michelle taking her place in the limelight. It was Mia's face they wanted, not her sister's. And it was Mia who had worked her backside off to get her name known, so why the hell should that ugly bitch be allowed to walk in and steal the glory from her? It wasn't fair!

Sensing that she needed to be left alone to put her thoughts in order, Liam stood up, saying, 'I'll get you a clean towel for your bath. Oh, and I got some cooked chicken from the deli; thought we could just have butties – if that's okay?'

Mia nodded, then waited until he'd gone out of the room before standing up. Still clutching the magazine, she went into the bathroom, dropped her dressing gown and stepped into the water.

Soothed by the heat of the bath and the sheer luxury of just soaking after weeks of Liam wiping her face, arms and legs with a soapy flannel, she exhaled long and slowly to release the tension, and came to a decision as she stared at the picture.

Liam was buttering bread on the kitchen ledge when she came downstairs. Turning, he smiled when he saw that she was dressed. She'd been naked when he'd rescued her, and he'd carried her out wrapped in the sheet from the bed she'd been imprisoned on. And she'd been wearing Darren's late grandmother's dressing gown since she'd been here.

'You look good,' he said. 'I guess I didn't do too bad on the sizes after all, huh?'

'They're perfect,' Mia told him, pulling a chair out and sitting down at the small table. 'There's, er, something we need to talk about,' she said now, picking nervously at a crumb that had caught her eye. 'I've decided to go and see my mum.'

'Really?' Tilting his head to one side, Liam gave her a questioning look. 'You sure you're ready for that? You don't want to start with a phone call?'

Mia shook her head and smiled sadly up at him. She needed to reclaim her life before Michelle started to think it belonged to her. But, at the same time, she really didn't want to lose Liam.

Silently chiding himself for asking the question, because he knew deep down that it hadn't been out of concern for her but because of his own selfish desire to keep her to himself for a little longer, Liam nodded, and said, 'Of course you should go home. I'll make the arrangements soon as I've done this.'

'We need to talk first,' Mia repeated.

'We'll have plenty of time for that later,' Liam told her, wanting to keep her focused on seeing her family in case she changed her mind again. 'And if you're worried about me,' he went on, placing her sandwich in front of her, 'don't be, because I'm not going anywhere. Well, actually, that's not strictly true,' he corrected himself, grinning sheepishly. 'I have got to go back to Ireland. But if you're going home, I might as well arrange it around that. Give you a bit of time on your own with your folks before I get back.'

'You *are* coming back, though, aren't you?' The panic was stark in Mia's eyes. 'You promise you won't just go and leave me?'

'Never,' Liam assured her, raising her hand to his lips and kissing it. 'Now, eat that. I'll be back in a minute; I've just got to make a call.'

As she picked at the sandwich while he went out to make his call, Mia rehearsed what she had to tell him – praying that he would understand that she hadn't done it deliberately this time; that it had been *his* assumption, and she'd been too ill too correct him.

But she didn't get a chance to say anything when Liam came back, because, sitting down opposite her, he reached for her hand and launched into the speech that *he* had just been rehearsing.

'I know you're scared of what will happen when we leave here, Michelle, but I never dreamt that I'd get a chance to be with you again. And now that I have, I'm not going to walk away from you.' His beautiful green eyes twinkling with sincerity, he went on, 'I know I've done most of the talking since we got here, so you probably think I don't really know the real *you*, but I remember everything about you from the first time we met. When I knocked you over in the park that night, and you got all uppity with me 'cos I was being a gentleman and you thought I was patronising you. And outside the library: the *look* you gave me when I got your book wet. And then when you saw me with the crew that night and thought they were hassling me. You were so sweet, and I knew then that I wanted you.' Eyes darkening now, he squeezed her hand. 'All that shit with your sister was just a terrible mistake, and I've regretted it ever since. But, believe me, it could *never* happen again. I love you, and I want you to be well again so that we can get to know each other as the adults we are now, and not as the kids that we were then. Okay?'

Tears were streaming down Mia's cheeks, but she couldn't speak. What was there to say? If she went ahead and told him who she was as she'd planned to, she knew exactly what his reaction would be.

Sitting back now, relieved that he'd had the chance to tell her how he felt about her before they went their separate ways – albeit temporarily – Liam winked at her.

'Don't cry, gorgeous. Everything's going to be great from now on – you'll see.' Then, glancing at his watch, he said, 'Anyway, hurry up and eat 'cos the car will be here in fifteen, and I need to straighten the place up.'

'I don't want to go,' Mia blurted out, knowing that as soon as she did this would be the end.

'You're just nervous,' Liam said, getting up and giving her a hug. 'But don't be, 'cos I'll be right behind you every step of the way.'

Unable to eat, Mia tossed the sandwich into the bin when Liam went upstairs to pack their things. She lit a cigarette and chewed on her nails, her mind reeling. She had to find a way to make him see that it was her that he really loved – but how?

Still no clearer about what she was going to do when the car arrived to pick them up, Mia dragged her feet as Liam ushered her towards the door. But when he opened it and she came face to face with Darren Mitchell, she froze.

'This is my mate Darren,' Liam told her, touching fists with him. 'I know you don't really know him, but he used to go out with your sister.'

Murmuring 'I know' as the blush flared across her cheeks, Mia looked down at her feet.

Embarrassed, because he was aware that she probably knew all about how badly he'd treated her sister, *and* because of their own last meeting when he'd accidentally exposed her drug habit, Darren said, 'Nice to see you again, Michelle.

You're looking loads better than last time.' Cursing himself for saying that last bit out loud, he shrugged. 'Anyway, best get going. I've only got the motor for a couple of hours. My old man's taking my mam to Blackpool. Sad, I know,' he added, rolling his eyes sheepishly. 'But they're both mad on karaoke, and there's some big competition going on over there that he's convinced he's going to win.'

Shaking his head in amusement, Liam pushed Mia gently out and pulled the door shut behind them. Handing the keys to Darren, he said, 'Cheers for letting us stay here, mate. I don't know what I would have done without you. But I'll see you right.'

Darren took the Samsonite case from him, shrugged, and said, 'No worries. It was the least I could do. Mia's sister, innit?'

In the back of the car Mia gazed out of the window as the two men chatted quietly up front. She had no idea what area they had just been staying in, but her heart began to feel heavy as they left it behind and the unfamiliar streets they drove through gradually started to become familiar. She was feeling almost suicidal by the time they turned off the Princess Parkway onto her road and she closed her eyes tightly, not even wanting to see the house. But seconds later Darren had stopped.

'Michelle?' Liam said quietly, thinking that she'd fallen asleep. 'We're here.'

Inhaling deeply, Mia opened her eyes.

'Don't panic,' Liam said now, reaching through the seats to take her hand, 'but Darren's just told me there's a rumour going round that you've been burgled, and your mum and Mia haven't been staying here for a while. So I want you to stay in the car while we go and check it out – okay?' Nodding when she did, he said, 'Give us your keys. It should only take a minute.'

'I haven't got them,' Mia said, staring up at the house now and wondering – as Liam and Darren just had – if Steve had had anything to do with it.

'Ah,' Liam murmured. 'Of course you haven't. Oh, well, it doesn't matter, I'm sure we'll be able to get in.'

'Round the back,' Darren said, flicking glances at the neighbouring windows. 'They're a right load of beaky gets round here; they'll probably call the pigs if they see us.'

'I don't want to stay here by myself,' Mia squawked as they began to get out of the car. 'I'm coming with you. What if he's got Vern watching – like last time. I'd only been back two minutes and he had me the minute I walked out of the door.'

Liam exchanged a hooded glance with Darren, both of them sure that Vern definitely would *not* be watching, even though there had been no reports of any bodies of shot black males having been found recently. 'All right, come with us,' he said. 'But stay behind me. And if anything happens, *run*.'

As Darren took a screwdriver and a hammer out of the boot, Mia clutched at Liam's arm and cast terrified glances around while they made their way down the alley to the back of the house, petrified of what would happen if Steve got hold of her again.

The door had obviously been kicked in recently, because there were shoe prints all over it, and while it had since been boarded up it was easy for Darren to shoulder it open.

'Shit, what a mess,' he said when he stepped into the kitchen and saw all the debris still littering the floor.

'My clothes!' Mia gasped, heading for the stairs.

Going after her, Liam pushed past her and raced up the stairs to check that nobody was hiding in the bedrooms. He didn't think anybody was there, because when you walked into rooms where somebody had been recently you could still feel the dust settling and hear the phantom sounds of

TVs or conversations which hadn't yet soaked into the carpet. But this house had that still air of abandonment about it – like Darren's grandad's place. Still, it was safer to be sure.

'Oh, no,' Mia cried when she saw her precious designer clothes torn to shreds. She snatched up her favourite Chanel dress and clutched it to her chest. 'This cost two hundred quid! And it's *vintage*. I'll never find another one like it in a million years!'

As he gazed down at Mia while she gathered up the rags, naming the labels and quoting the prices, it flashed through Liam's mind to wonder why it had never occurred to him that she might be as image-conscious as her sister. But the thought went as soon as it came. Girls were like that, so there was nothing funny about it.

'Oh, thank God for that,' Mia exclaimed, spotting the suitcase under the bed. If it hadn't been opened it would still contain all the clothes that she'd had with her when they'd stayed at Sammy's house that time.

Sammy! She'd bet *that* was where her mum and Michelle had gone. And she'd bet that little trickster bitch of a sister of hers had plenty of Mia's nice designer clothes with her, too. And more that she'd probably bought from the money she'd been earning in Mia's name.

'I think I know where my mum might be,' she told Liam now, looking at him as he waited patiently in the doorway. 'I'm not sure of the exact address, but if we can get to the place I'll know it when I see it.'

31

Eyeliner brush poised, Linda, the make-up artist, sighed and gave Michelle a mock-pained look. 'If you don't stop it, you're going to end up looking like Amy Winehouse.'

'Sorry,' Michelle murmured, her nostrils flaring as she sucked her top lip between her teeth to prevent herself from laughing again.

'It's my fault,' Kim admitted, sounding like a guilty little girl as she sat in the chair facing Michelle's, having rollers put into her hair. 'I just get these urges to itch when I'm supposed to sit still. But *you* should control yourself, *Mia*,' she scolded Michelle, no longer having to think before she called her by that name because it felt so natural to her now.

'Oh, right, blame me, why don't you!' Michelle exclaimed indignantly.

'Will you both just *shut up* and let us get on with this before we make a complete mess of it!' Carmel, the hairdresser, chuckled, pulling Kim's head firmly back into position.

Exchanging a *That's told us!* look with Michelle, Kim twisted her head right around when Sammy ambled into the room carrying a tray of coffees.

When he heard Carmel sigh, he said, 'Are they being naughty again?'

'When are they ever not?' Linda asked, raising Michelle's chin to get a better angle on her eyes.

'They're just excited,' Sammy explained, taking his own cup from the tray and sitting down on his chair by the window.

'It's a big thing, this charity do. Great honour to be asked to hand over the cheque to the mayor.'

'I wouldn't know,' Linda murmured, her eyes firmly fixed on the job at hand. 'Us lowly beauticians never get invited to fancy parties – do we, Car?'

'Do we buggery,' Carmel snorted.

'Ah, sorry,' Michelle murmured, trying not to move as she spoke. 'I wish we could take you, but they didn't give us any spare tickets.'

Smiling, knowing that she probably meant it, Linda said, 'We're only teasing, hon. You just make sure you tell us all about it next time we see you, 'cos we've heard there's going to be loads of stars there.'

'Oh, *don't*,' Michelle groaned, feeling her stomach do a little flip. 'I'm already nervous.'

'What have you got to be nervous about?' Carmel scoffed. 'You're just as famous as them.'

'I don't *think* so,' Michelle retorted modestly.

Smiling, Sammy crossed his legs and looked on proudly as Michelle and Kim's pampering session continued. They were beginning to feel more like family to him than client and mother of client, and he absolutely loved the life they had brought into his house.

It had been nice the last time they had stayed, and the silence after they had gone home had been unbearable. But this time there had been none of the strained atmosphere; it had been fun and laughter all the way, and they'd had some lovely talks in the evenings. And the living room was a mess right now, with all the clothes they'd been trying on throughout the day strewn everywhere. But Michelle would soon put it back to rights because she actually enjoyed cleaning up.

'There we go,' Linda said after a while, stepping back to scrutinise her handiwork. 'What do you think, Sammy?'

Bobbing his head to see around her, Sammy nodded. 'Oh yes, very nice.'

'*Nice*,' Linda repeated, tutting softly. 'Typical bloody man! Nice, indeed. She's *gorgeous*.'

'Aw, leave him alone,' Kim said protectively. 'He can't help it.'

Sipping on his coffee, Sammy stared at the blank TV screen and reminded himself that Kim had only spoken up for him like that because they were friends – nothing more. And just because he might wish that there was a little more to it than that, that didn't mean that he would ever be presumptuous enough to cross the boundaries and raise the subject with her. She was an enigmatic woman in many ways, and on the face of it she might seem common or uneducated. Maybe the latter was even true, because she herself freely admitted that her schooling hadn't been of the highest standard. Nevertheless, despite the fact that she could be very literal, forcing precision in the way you worded things to ensure that she took it as you'd intended, she had a very sharp mind and seemed to enjoy a debate on whatever subject might crop up. Still, whatever label others might apply to her, Sammy found her stimulating. And since she'd begun to relax, free of the stresses that she'd always seemed to be under in the earlier period of their relationship, she was also proving to be quite funny and warm-hearted.

After gathering the equipment together, Linda and Carmel sat down on the big comfortable couch to drink their coffees before leaving.

'I love this house,' Carmel commented, gazing around the spacious lounge. 'It feels really big, but homely at the same time.'

'It's gorgeous, isn't it?' Kim agreed. 'Really relaxing. I love sitting in here in the morning, 'cos you can hear all the birds singing. Not like at our place, eh, Mia?'

Michelle smiled, and shook her head. 'No, it's usually dogs barking and people coughing up phlegm round our way in the morning.'

'Mmm,' Kim murmured, gazing off into space. She loved it here; wouldn't care if she never saw her own house again. But she'd have to before too long, because they couldn't just keep abusing Sammy's hospitality like this. They'd now been here even longer than the last time.

'Ah, well, we'd best make a move before we take root,' Linda said, struggling up from the comfortable cushions. 'Thanks for the coffee, Sammy. And ladies, it was a pleasure – as always. Have a wonderful night tonight, and we'll see you next time.'

Sammy paid them, then showed them out and wandered down to the gate to guide Linda out as she reversed her small car onto the road.

Mia twisted her head as they passed the gates. Her stomach churned when she spotted Sammy. He had his back to them and was waving his arms, but no one else was that fat, and his grey curls, which seemed only to spring out from the back of his head, were unmistakable.

'That was it,' she told Darren, lurching forward and almost banging her nose on the back of his seat when he slammed his foot on the brake.

Cursing under his breath when somebody drove up behind him, preventing him from reversing back, Darren shoved the car back into first gear and drove forward until he found a little space to pull into. They'd driven up and down this road three times now, and Mia hadn't recognised any of the houses. But he hoped she'd got it right, because he really had to be heading home soon to give his dad the car or there would be ructions.

'Are you sure?' Liam asked her.

She nodded, and unbuckled her seat belt before getting out of the car.

'And you're positive you don't want us to come in with you?'

'*No!*' Mia smiled weakly and shook her head. 'Sorry, but no – I think I should do this on my own. It's going to shock them enough as it is.'

'In a nice way,' Liam added confidently. He got out of the car and gave her a hug, saying, 'You've got my number, so ring me when you can and let me know what's happening. And don't forget to let me know *your* number when you get a new phone. I'll be back in a few days. Okay?'

Mia nodded again and rested her head against his chest, wishing she could stay like that for ever.

'Sorry, mate, I've really got to shift it,' Darren called out through the open door. He smiled when Liam climbed back into the car, and said, 'See you later, Michelle. Hope everything goes all right. And, er, say hi to Mia for me when you see her.'

Promising that she would pass the message on, Mia waved as they set off. Then, shaking her head to get rid of the lovey-dovey emotion, she headed off across the road to confront her sister.

Sammy had just closed the front door and was about to go back into the lounge where he could hear Michelle and Kim chuckling over something or other. He turned on his heel when the doorbell rang and went back to the door, thinking that it would be Linda or Carmel coming back for something that they'd forgotten.

Taken aback when he saw Mia on the doorstep, he didn't speak for several seconds.

'Hello, Sammy,' Mia said at last, her eyes glinting when she heard the laughter coming from the lounge. 'Somebody having a party?'

Snapping out of the shock, he said, 'Good lord. Um, sorry – *no*, not a party. They're, um, well . . . Come in, come in.' He waved her over the threshold. As he closed the door behind her, he was unsure whether or not to hug her – she had a strange look on her face. Deciding against it, he waved her towards the lounge instead.

'You should hear what she just said,' Kim laughed, turning towards the door when she heard Sammy coming back into the room. 'We were talking ab—' Rendered momentarily speechless when she saw who was standing there, it took her several seconds to get her bearings. Then her eyes widened and she held out her arms and rushed towards Mia, saying, 'Oh, my God! You're back! I've missed you so much!'

Sidestepping her mother to avoid the embrace, Mia narrowed her eyes as she peered from Kim to Michelle. 'Doesn't look like you've been missing me all that much,' she said snappily. 'Looks like you've been having a *great* time without me.'

'That's not true,' Sammy told her, his heart sinking because their lovely, all-too-brief holiday from Mia was over. She was safe, and obviously clean of drugs judging by how well she looked, and that was good. But she'd obviously lost none of her caustic attitude, which definitely *wasn't* good.

'So what's the occasion?' Mia demanded, folding her arms defiantly and glaring at Michelle as if Sammy hadn't even spoken.

Michelle dropped her gaze. She suddenly felt overwhelmed by guilt, as if she'd been caught red-handed stealing something – which, in fact, she kind of had.

'Michelle's been asked to present a cheque to the mayor at a charity do,' Kim told her, nervously wringing her hands.

Sammy picked up her cigarettes from the coffee table and

handed them to her, sure that she must need one at a time like this. Giving him a grateful smile, she lit up, her hands visibly shaking.

'*Michelle*'s been asked?' Mia repeated, her words dripping with venom. 'Don't you mean *I*'ve been asked? Or have you all forgotten that *I*'m Mia?'

Irritated that Mia was making this out to be something that it wasn't, Kim went and stood beside Michelle. 'Look, Mia, none of this is our fault. You're the one who took off as soon as we got home, so what were we supposed to do – cancel all your bookings and let your career go to the wall? Yeah, I bet you would have loved that, wouldn't you? Imagine what you'd be like if you'd come back and everything was over, eh? You'd be kicking off good style by now.'

A nasty smirk on her lips, Mia said, 'Good speech, mum. Been rehearsing that for long, have you?' Flicking a dirty look over the pair of them, she added, 'And since when have you two been so buddy-buddy?'

'Oi!' Kim snapped, pointing the cigarette at her. 'You're the one in the wrong here, lady! Shell's done you a massive bloody favour by standing in for you. And I'll tell you what, she's done a bloody good job of it, an' all. She's been on telly, and everything.'

Mia clapped slowly and sneered. 'Well, whoopdy-doo. She's finally gone and done what she's been trying to do all her life – turned herself into me. But it's over now, sweetheart.' She directed this at Michelle. 'I'm back, so you can get your giant cuckoo feet out of my shoes.'

'You'd best pack in talking to her like that,' Kim said defensively. But Michelle touched her mother's arm to quieten her before she could say any more.

'She's right. This is her life, and she's back now, so I don't need to keep on standing in for her.' Literally stepping out of her sister's shoes now and holding them in one hand, she gathered up the long skirt of the dress with the other and walked over to Mia. 'Here.'

'You don't really think I'm going to touch the filthy things, do you?' Mia snorted.

'Well, they're the ones that suit the dress best,' Michelle told her evenly. 'Anyway, I'm glad you're back. Just give me a minute to get changed, and your life's all yours again.'

'Now let's not be too hasty about this,' Sammy protested. 'Mia's nowhere near ready to pick up the helm just yet. This is too important a function. She's not prepared.'

'So it was all right for *her* to stand in for *me* at the drop of a hat,' Mia reminded him frostily. 'But now *I*'m not ready to be myself again. Don't make me laugh!'

'She's right,' Michelle told him. 'This is her night, not mine. I'll get changed.'

As she walked out into the hall her heart sank when she heard her mum immediately start arguing with Mia. This wasn't supposed to be happening. Mia was home and they should be rejoicing, not throwing daggers at each other.

Two steps up the staircase, she hesitated when the doorbell rang. It didn't feel right to answer somebody else's door when you were a guest in their home, but when Sammy didn't come out after a few moments she had no choice. It was either that or go back into the room and annoy Mia again.

Liam had his back turned when she opened the door, and because he was the very last person she would ever have expected to see here, Michelle didn't recognise him. She said 'Excuse me,' and was smiling when he turned round. But the smile slid from her lips as soon as she saw his face.

Embarrassed to see her, because he'd hoped that he wouldn't have to, Liam said, 'Hello, Mia . . . Sorry to disturb you, and don't worry, I'm not stopping.' Holding up the small suitcase that the real Mia had left in the boot of

Darren's car, he said, 'Michelle forgot this. Could you give it to her, please?'

At that precise moment, Mia marched out into the hall, her voice angry as she yelled at her mum, 'Don't even bother trying to deny it! I can see exactly what's been going on while I've been away. You and that fucking bitch have stitched me up good and proper! But if you think she's—' Gasping when she saw Liam staring in at her through the open front door her mouth opened and closed silently. 'Liam,' she managed to whisper after a moment. 'This isn't what it looks like.'

Speechless, because his head felt like it was being crushed, Liam looked from her to Michelle and back again.

Feeling bad for him because she could see the confusion in his eyes, although she had no idea what was going on herself, Michelle said, 'Are you all right?'

Just that one short, caringly spoken sentence told Liam everything he needed to know. Looking up at her, his eyes filled with regret and pain and anger, he said, 'She's done it again, hasn't she?'

Rushing forward now, Mia pushed Michelle out of the way and ran out to him. Clutching at the front of the jacket as genuine tears gushed from her eyes, she said, 'I didn't do anything this time, Liam . . . I swear I didn't lie to you. I tried to tell you who I was, I *remember*. But you didn't believe me.'

'No, you're right, I thought you were delirious,' Liam conceded. 'But if I'd known I wouldn't have bothered. Because you're poison.'

'I'm *not*!' Mia sobbed. 'You've spent the last three weeks telling me how much you love me, so how can you suddenly say I'm poison? I'm the same person now as I was then.'

'I was telling *Michelle* I love her, not *you*,' Liam reminded her, gritting his teeth as he tried to pull her hands off him without hurting her. 'Didn't you hear *any* of what I said to you before we set off this morning? I said I know we haven't really got to know each other yet this time around, but I loved you for who you were when we first met.'

'Yes, but I was the one you were closest to even then,' Mia countered passionately. 'You never made love to her. You never took her to your flat and made her coffee, and sat talking to her for hours – that was all *me*.'

'And you know what I was thinking when I was doing all that?' Liam came back at her angrily. 'I was wondering why you'd changed – yes, even then. Why's she suddenly acting like a slut? I kept asking myself. Why's she making nasty little comments, then pretending she was only joking?'

'You're lying,' Mia sobbed. 'If you thought that, why did you carry on sleeping with me?'

'Because I was holding on to the memory of the sweet girl – the one I hoped would come back to me if I put up with the other side of her for long enough. Call me stupid – I probably am – but you were *never* the one I wanted. I was always wishing you'd turn back into her.' Liam pointed his finger at Michelle, who was still standing in the doorway with tears trickling slowly down her cheeks. Yanking Mia off him now, he turned to Michelle, and said, 'I'm so sorry . . . I had no idea.'

'Look, do you think we could take this inside and calm everything down?' Sammy asked. 'Only we have a very important function tonight, and we really can't—'

Liam shook his head, held up his hands and started to walk backwards down the path.

'*LIAAAMM!*' Mia screamed, collapsing to her knees.

Sammy told Kim to get Mia inside and went off down the path after Liam, calling, 'Just a minute . . . I need to talk to you.'

'I'm sorry,' Liam said, glancing out along the road for Darren who should have found somewhere to turn around by now. 'I just can't, mate. My head's battered.'

'Could you at least tell me what happened to Mia?' Sammy persisted. 'You see, we haven't seen her in some time, and now she's turned up out of the blue we need to know if she's . . . well, to put it bluntly, is she clean, or is she still taking drugs? Can we trust her?'

'You'll have to ask *her* what's really going on,' Liam told him wearily. ''Cos I thought I was rescuing Michelle. I mean, I saw all the pictures of Mia everywhere,' he went on, total confusion in his eyes now. 'So how could it have been anyone else *but* Michelle locked in that room. It doesn't make sense. And I wouldn't even believe it *now* if I hadn't just seen them together. I just . . .' Trailing off, he threw his hands up in a gesture of despair. 'Am I going mad, or something?'

'It's a long story,' Sammy told him. 'And that's just *our* side of it. But may I ask what you meant about her being locked in a room?'

Liam sighed and said, 'Look, I can't say too much, because this is a dangerous situation, and the less you know, the better off you'll be. But she – *Mia* – was being drugged and kept prisoner, so me and my mates went and got her. She's been with me for the past few weeks, and I can guarantee she hasn't touched anything in days, so she should be totally unhooked by now.'

Sammy licked his lips and glanced nervously around before asking, 'Was Steve Dawson involved in any of this? I only ask because if he was, or is, then I need to think about moving these ladies somewhere safer before he finds them – as you just did.'

'We only found you because Mia directed us here,' Liam reassured him. 'But, yes, he was involved. So, if it makes you feel safer, do what you've got to do.'

Respecting him for his honesty, Sammy extended his hand. But just as Liam was about to shake it a police car drove past, and he groaned when he saw Darren on the back seat.

'A friend of yours?' Sammy asked.

Liam ran his hands through his hair as he watched the car disappear, and said, 'And my lift back into Manchester. His dad's going to kill him if he doesn't get the car back. He's supposed to be taking his mum to Blackpool tonight for some big competition.' Laughing without humour, he added, 'How ironic is that . . . ? The poor sod only went out of his way to drop Michelle down here because he's so obsessed with Mia, but he had *Mia* in the car the whole time!'

Sammy shook his head. 'Well, I suppose the very least I can do after you've put yourself to so much trouble is offer you a lift. If you'd just come inside while I try to think up a life-threatening illness to excuse Mia's – sorry, *Michelle*'s – absence from the charity function, we'll head straight off.'

Liam said, 'Cheers, mate, but I can't handle any more hysterics. I've had my head twisted up enough for one lifetime. I'd best just go see if I can find the car – try and get it back to Darren's dad.'

'This is a long, dark, ridiculously narrow road,' Sammy cautioned. 'Not the kind of place to be caught walking if two cars come along at the same time. Why not let me drive you – see if can spot the car together?'

'Fair enough,' Liam agreed. 'But I'll wait out here, if you don't mind.'

Sammy nodded, and made his way back up to the house.

Kim and Michelle were waiting for him in the lounge, Kim in the armchair she'd claimed as her own, Michelle perched on the arm.

'Shell's going to go ahead with the presentation,' Kim announced, looking more drained after just twenty minutes in Mia's company than Sammy had seen her looking in weeks.

'Are you sure?' Sammy asked.

Nodding, Michelle said, 'Mia's not up to it, so I said I'd stand in for her one last time.'

'Mia will be all right here with me,' Kim went on resignedly. 'I've sent her upstairs to sort herself out. We'll have a drink when you're gone – see if I can get her talking.'

'Oh.' Sammy looked crestfallen. 'So you're not coming?'

'How can I?' Kim asked, sounding wistful because she'd been looking forward to this all week. 'You understand, don't you, love?' She looked up at Michelle now. 'Mee might be the gobbiest, but she's never been as strong as you.'

'It's all right,' Michelle replied without hesitation. 'She's been through a lot; she needs her mum.'

Picking up on Michelle's use of the words *her mum*, not *our* mum, Sammy hoped that this didn't mark the end of the new relationship that had been developing between herself and Kim in Mia's absence. Just as he hoped that it didn't mark the end of her involvement in modelling, although he suspected that once Michelle handed what she saw as Mia's rightful crown back to her she would fade back into the shadows from which she had only recently emerged. And that would be a tragedy, because she had so much potential. But he would talk to her about that on the journey tonight – see if he couldn't persuade her that there was room for them both.

Eyes dark as she sucked on her cigarette, Kim had no doubt that she was in for a long, difficult night. But, not wanting to spoil it for Michelle and Sammy, she forced herself to smile as they got ready to leave. Looking Sammy over, she chuckled softly. 'Bow tie's crooked, Mr Bond.'

Tickled by the 007 reference, Sammy quickly straightened the neckwear. Then, returning her smile, not wanting to show how bitterly disappointed he was that she wouldn't be sitting beside him tonight, he said goodbye.

Michelle turned to kiss her mum before following Sammy out and blushed when Kim held on to her hand and said quietly, 'That Liam's bloody *gorgeous*, and he thinks the world of you by the sound of it. So if you want to go for it, *go* for it. And don't worry about Mia; I'll make sure she stays out of it.'

Michelle hugged her and said, 'Thanks, but we don't really know each other, so it's not worth upsetting Mia over it. Just let him go his way, and we'll go ours.'

Mia shuffled miserably out of the bathroom as the front door closed behind Michelle. She went into the front bedroom and yanked the curtain aside to watch the bitch leave. She'd only agreed to let her sister do this last thing in her place because she knew that she was in no fit state to do it herself. But come tomorrow, she was putting herself *right* back in control. Starting with the bank account – and God help them if they had been helping themselves to her money in her absence. Michelle might have earned it, but only by default.

The car rolled slowly down to the gates. As the vivid red brake lights flared in the darkness, Mia's heart lurched when she saw a figure slide out of the shadows and open the passenger-side door. As the car's interior light came on, clearly highlighting Liam's handsome face, she screamed, '*NOOOO!*'

She almost fell down the stairs in her haste to get out before they got too far and struggled when Kim rushed out to stop her. Far stronger and tougher than her daughter, Kim easily restrained Mia and pulled her into the lounge. Sitting her firmly down on the couch, she took a bottle of brandy from Sammy's alcohol cabinet and poured large slugs into two glasses. She pushed one into Mia's hand and told her to drink it and calm herself down.

'I don't *want* it!' Mia yelled, hurling the glass at the wall. 'I want *Liam*!'

Kim winced when the glass shattered on impact and sprayed shards across Sammy's carpet. She smacked Mia sharply across the cheek. Then, taking her by the arms, she shook her, saying, '*He* don't want *you*, so get over it!'

'I hate you!' Mia gasped, putting a hand to her cheek. 'You lied! You said he'd gone.'

'He did go,' Kim replied truthfully, unaware that Liam had been waiting outside.

'He didn't,' Mia sobbed. 'I just saw him getting in the car with *her*!' She yanked her arms free and tried to get up, her eyes wild with jealousy. 'I'm going after them! Where is this charity thing? I'll call a cab.'

'Mia, just give it up, love,' Kim told her, holding her in her seat. 'He don't want you, he wants her. You heard what he said out there.'

'Why are you taking *her* side?' Mia demanded, tears streaming from her eyes

'I'm not taking anyone's side,' Kim insisted. 'I'm just trying to make you see sense before you get yourself hurt.'

'*Hurt?*' Mia repeated, her voice rising hysterically. 'You haven't got a fucking *clue* what you're talking about, you stupid cow! He *saved* me. Steve had me locked up, and Liam broke in and *saved* me. And he's been looking after me for weeks, while you and that bitch have been pretending I don't exist!'

Pulling Mia into her arms, Kim held her tightly and rocked her. 'Ssshhh . . .' she crooned. 'You're safe now; I won't let anyone hurt you again. And we never forgot about you – we *love* you.'

Peering into the darkness as Sammy drove slowly down the lane, Liam spotted the rear end of Darren's dad's car sticking out of a hedge.

'There!' he said, pointing at it as they passed.

Sammy stopped and glanced back. 'Good lord, he's lucky. There's quite a deep ditch behind that hedge.'

As Michelle watched silently from the back seat, Liam jumped out and shoved the braches apart to get a better look at the angle the car was at. It wasn't too far in, and as luck would have it Sammy had a tow rope in his boot, so they soon had the vehicle back on solid ground. The key was still in the ignition and Liam turned the engine over, grinning at Sammy when it started first time.

Back at the house, Mia had calmed down. As she sipped on her second glass of brandy, her mind was whirring while she watched her mum hoover up the broken glass. Staying with Liam for the last few weeks had been heaven, but in the space of a few short hours she'd been plucked out of their cosy nest and deposited in hell. Liam had looked at her with such disgust and hatred, and then he'd humiliated her in front of them all by telling her that he felt nothing for her – and that was unforgivable.

Mia had tried, she really had. She'd kept her mouth shut and acted the boring lady that she'd thought Liam wanted her to be; and she'd suffered heroin withdrawal for the bastard when every fibre of her being was screaming for a hit. But some people were just too stupid for their own good. The first time she'd ever met Liam she'd wondered if he had mental problems, because what other possible explanation was there for him preferring a boring, ugly bitch like Michelle to *her*? And now, after everything he and Mia had been through together, he *still* claimed to love Michelle. And that bitch, who had already stolen her name, her face and her career, had stood there and lapped it up while Mia's heart was being torn to shreds in front of her – for which they would *both* pay.

Stomach in a knot now as her nerve endings screamed for a fix, Mia finished her drink and put the glass down on the table.

'Feeling better?' Kim yelled over the sound of the vacuum cleaner.

Mia nodded and gave an exaggerated yawn. 'Think I'll just go and have a lie-down.' She got up and gave her mum a guilty smile. 'Sorry for making a mess. I just lost it for a while, but I'm all right now.'

Kim told her not to worry about it and forced herself to return the smile. Glad as she was to have Mia home, her daughter's reappearance had changed everything and it was going to take a lot of readjusting for them all while Mia picked up the reins of her career. They would have to go back to their own house, for starters; and Michelle would probably go back to college, while Kim would be back to being side-lined. But there was nothing she could do about it. It was Mia's life they had been borrowing, and now that she was back she was entitled to do with it as she wished.

'That charity thing they've gone to,' Mia asked, making it sound like a casual enquiry. 'What's it for?'

'Not sure,' Kim told her, trying to downplay it so that Mia didn't get het up again. 'Something to do with Christie's, I think. Definitely cancer, anyway. Nothing major.'

'Where is it?' Mia probed. 'Only I feel bad about holding them up like that. They'll get there in time, won't they?'

'Oh, I should think so,' Kim told her. 'It doesn't start till half-eight. And Sammy says it's not that far. Some country house in Styal, or somewhere like that. Just down the road, he reckons.'

Exhaling as if relieved, Mia said, 'Oh well, that's good. At least I haven't ruined their night.'

'Course you haven't,' Kim lied, switching the vacuum off at last. 'Anyhow, you go get a rest; you look wiped.'

Mia agreed that she was, said goodnight and headed upstairs. Kim put the vacuum away, flopped down into her chair and reached for her drink. But just as she raised it to her lips she noticed the tiny red light glowing on the phone that stood on the table beside Sammy's chair. She knew that this meant that one of the other phones was in use and her instincts bristled. She should have known that Mia was lying; she'd calmed down far too quickly. But who could she possibly be talking to? Kim slipped her shoes off and tiptoed upstairs to find out.

Mia was in Sammy's bedroom. She was speaking quietly but urgently. Kim held her breath and pressed her ear against the door to listen.

'Don't fuck me about, Noel,' Mia was hissing. 'I need to speak to him – *NOW*! Tell him it's Mia; he'll definitely want to talk to me.'

A few seconds later she started talking again, her tone almost wheedling now.

'Hello, Steve, have you missed me? Yeah, I bet you have, but I'm not coming back till you say you're sorry. And you'd best treat me right this time, 'cos I'm about to tell you something you *really* want to know . . .'

Horrified when she heard what Mia was telling Steve Dawson, Kim padded back downstairs on wildly shaking legs.

She snatched her mobile phone out of her handbag and rushed out into the back garden, not caring that her feet were getting soaked as she ran across the grass to distance herself from the house.

'Michelle, don't go to that place,' she blurted out in a loud whisper when her call was answered. 'I've just heard Mia telling Steve he'll find Liam there!'

'We're not with Liam,' Michelle told her. 'He didn't come with us, we just helped him get his car started. He's gone to his friend's to drop it off.'

'You're not talking about Darren Mitchell, are you? Only she told Steve *his* name and address, an' all.'

'Do you know where Darren lives?' Sammy asked, braking hard when Michelle disconnected the call and told him what her mum had said.

She nodded, and peered at him with frightened eyes. 'It's near our house. Why? What are you thinking?'

'Well, unless you've got a phone number for either of them I think we'd better go and warn them.'

Michelle shook her head and clung to the sides of her seat as Sammy swung the car around in a wide arc. 'What about the function?' she gasped.

'To hell with that!'

32

Steve had spent the last few weeks in a state of quiet fury. He'd drawn a complete blank on the identities of the three black guys who'd broken in and attacked him, and Mia had been nowhere in sight when he and his boys had gone round to her house the night after the raid. All their belongings had still been there, but that didn't mean shit, because that was the kind of stunt women pulled when they were on the run – leaving everything behind in order to make people believe they were coming back, giving them time to get as far away as possible.

He'd put feelers out all over the place, but it seemed that Mia's family were as cagey as she was and nobody had a clue where the bitch had gone. Unsure of what she might have said by now, he'd had to clear absolutely everything out in case the police came to do a raid, which was making life increasingly difficult.

If there was one thing Steve hated, it was losing control. But having to stash his gear at odd locations meant that he was always in danger of being ripped off. In addition, he was losing money hand over fist since he'd had to get rid of his upstairs girls. The club girls were having to play it by the book and had stopped giving extras on the spot, so even their earnings were down. And since he'd also had to put a stop to the weed-smoking and small-time dealing that he'd turned a blind eye to in the past, people were finding alternative places to hang out.

Mia was to blame for all that. So when she'd rung just now to tell him who was behind the raid in which she had been freed, he'd been beaten half to death, and Vern had been shot dead, he'd played it cool, letting her believe that he was so grateful for the names she'd given him that he'd be willing to put the past behind them and start again.

And she'd fallen for it, the brain-dead little junkie; even going so far as to tell him where he could pick her up from after he'd done what he had to do.

And could he *please* bring her something nice, because she'd been having *such* a terrible time since those nasty men had snatched her from the loving arms of Steve and his magical gear.

Oh, he'd take her something nice, all right.

'Noel!' he barked now, snatching up his car keys and heading towards the back door. 'Get the guys. We're on!'

Liam parked up outside Darren's house and nodded at Pete when he came rushing out.

'Jeezus, it's a good job you're here,' Pete hissed, jerking his head back towards the house. 'The old man's having a proper paddy in there. Where's our kid?'

'Alderley Edge,' Liam told him taking his bags out of the boot and handing him the car keys. 'He got nicked, but they've let him out, so I'm going to go back for him. I just need a number for a cab company, if you've got one.'

'What's he been nicked for?' Pete asked, frowning as he pulled a thin branch out of the car's radiator grille. 'And what the fuck's he been doing with this?'

Liam chuckled softly and said, 'I found it stuck in a hedge and thought they must have nicked him for driving without insurance, or something. But he rang when I was on my way back and said they'd pulled him for indecency.'

'You what?' Pete screwed up his face.

'Seems he took a corner too fast,' Liam explained. 'So he thought he'd walk back down and get me to come and help him pull the car out. But he stopped for a piss on the way and some old bird saw him and thought he was exposing himself, so she called the cops. They've cautioned him, but he'll have to go back next week to see if they're pressing charges.'

'What a cunt!' Pete burst out laughing.

'Oi, knob-head!' his dad grumbled, coming out of the door just then with a scowl on his face. 'Quit arsing about and get your mam's bag. Only gone and decided she wants to stop in a bleedin' hotel for the night now, hasn't she – like I'm made of bleedin' money.'

Pete rolled his eyes at Liam and said, 'You can afford it, you auld miser. Anyhow, I thought you were a dead cert for winning that grand on the karaoke.'

'I *am* – if I ever get there,' the old man replied, snatching the car keys out of his son's hand. 'But that don't mean I want to waste it on hotels when we've got a perfectly good bed of our own upstairs.'

Pete said, 'Wait up on that cab thing, Liam. I'll come with you,' and headed back into the house to get the bag.

Liam nodded, lit a cigarette and leant back against the car. Getting straight back off when the old man glared at him, he went and sat on the small wall bordering the garden instead. Glancing to his right when another car turned onto the road and slowed down, he frowned when he saw that it was Sammy's Bentley.

Sammy rolled his window down and waved him over.

'What's up?' Liam asked, trying desperately not to look at Michelle.

'We think you might be in danger,' Sammy gabbled nervously. 'Kim – Michelle's mum – just rang to tell us that she overheard Mia telling Steve Dawson where he could find you.'

Giving them a curious look as he came out and placed his mother's suitcase in the boot of the car, Pete wondered what kind of fare Liam thought they'd be paying, booking a bleeding *Bentley* for a cab.

'Is that Darren?' Sammy asked Liam. 'Only Mia's apparently given his name and address to Steve as well.'

Liam shook his head. 'That's his brother Pete. We're just about to call a cab and go back for Darren.'

Sammy told him to hop in, that he would take them. 'And you'd best tell your friend to warn his parents.'

'They're about to head off to spend the night in Blackpool,' Liam told him. 'Just give me a minute.'

He went over to Pete, pulled him aside and told him what he'd just heard. Pete nodded, and turned back to his father.

'Oi, hurry up and piss off, can't you?' he said, somehow managing to act as if nothing was any different than it had been moments earlier. 'Me and Liam are waiting to get the birds round for an orgy.'

Flicking a suspicious glance at Sammy's car, the old man said, 'Oh, aye – picking 'em up in that, are you?'

Darren and Pete's overweight mother wheezed her way over the front doorstep just then, and said, 'You could have bloody helped. It took me ages to get out of that flaming chair.'

'Serves you right for parking your arse in it and leaving me to do your bleedin' packing,' her husband grunted as he took her elbow and guided her to the car. 'I'm signing you up for the gym when we get back,' he grumbled when she got in and the vehicle dropped several inches.

Waiting until they had gone, Pete grabbed Liam's bags and rushed back into the house. Liam followed and didn't object when Pete thrust a balaclava, a pair of gloves, and a heavy flick knife into his hand. Shoving them into his jacket pocket, he said, 'Do us a favour and don't mention any of this to them in the car. They're straights. They don't need to get involved.'

Pete nodded, squatted down and pulled the hall carpet back. He removed a piece of broken floorboard, stuck his hand inside and pulled out a gun.

Again, Liam didn't object. Steve Dawson wouldn't come empty-handed, so they'd be stupid to go unprepared.

Sammy pulled over when Liam pointed out Darren sitting in a bus shelter not far from his house. The fat agent looked at Liam worriedly. 'What are you going to do?'

'Nothing for you to concern yourself about,' Liam told him, not wanting to alarm Michelle who was sitting in the back with Pete now.

'If I may proffer an opinion,' Sammy said quietly. 'I'd hazard a guess that they might be more inclined to strike at the house first. They're already in that vicinity, after all, and will no doubt feel safer on their own territory. Whereas trying to spring a surprise attack at a public venue, where they're likely to be seen by hundreds of witnesses, would be far too risky. Although, if they think that's where *you* are,' he added musingly, 'I suppose they may decide to go there first in order to keep watch, so they can follow when you leave. In which case, you'll have time to get yourselves prepared.'

Nodding, Liam turned to Pete and said, 'We're going to head back to yours.' Then, thanking Sammy, he climbed out of the car.

'How will you get back?' Sammy asked when he came around to the driver's side.

'Cab,' Liam told him, catching Darren's eye and waving him over.

'I'll take you,' Sammy offered without hesitation. 'Just let me drop Michelle off first.'

'No, you've done enough,' Liam insisted. 'Seriously, this is too heavy. Anyway,' he added quietly, casting a hooded glance at Michelle to let Sammy know that he didn't want her to hear this, 'I think you should go and book yourselves into a hotel for the night. Sooner the better – and not the hotel you were doing that charity thing at.'

Fully understanding what he meant – that if Mia had given Steve so much information, she obviously believed that things were all right between them, in which case she was likely to have told him where she was staying in order that he could come for her – Sammy nodded, and said, 'Right you are. I'll book you a cab as soon as I get home and have it pick you up at the bus shelter. Oh, and you'd better take my number – in case something happens that we need to know about.'

'What's going on?' Darren asked, watching as the Bentley drove away.

Liam saved Sammy's mobile number onto his SIM card, slipped his phone into his pocket and set off across the road, telling Darren the situation on the way.

'Wish I'd known we were going straight back,' Pete complained, jumping at every little noise coming from the seemingly endless rows of hedges. 'If the coppers are that hot round here that they're on *him* like a bag of shit for having a wazz, I could end up in proper lumber, tooled up like this.'

Telling him to stay cool, Liam lit a cigarette and peered off into the darkness ahead.

33

'This is bollocks,' Steve snarled, rapping his fingernails agitatedly on the steering wheel. They had been parked up for half an hour now, and he was going cross-eyed with boredom as he stared through the darkness at the gates of the country-house hotel further along the road. And to cap it all, his car stank of sweat and stale fag smoke, thanks to the three bruisers who were crammed in the back.

'You sure it's the right place?' Noel asked, peering out through the windscreen.

'Well, it's the only place holding a function for fucking cancer tonight,' Steve reminded him. 'Unless you ballsed it up when you rang around asking?'

'No, the woman definitely said it was this one,' Noel said quickly. Then, 'What if Mia changed her mind and warned him, and he ain't coming?'

'She's too desperate for a hit,' Steve replied, sliding down in his seat along with the rest of them when a car drove past at speed – unaware that it had contained Sammy, Kim, Michelle, and Mia, who was sobbing as she nursed the black eye that Michelle had just given her. He sat back up when it had passed and yanked a bag of coke out of his pocket, muttering, 'I'm gonna go fucking crazy in a minute.'

'He'll probably go to Mitchell's house when he's done here, so we could go and wait for him there,' Noel suggested, watching nervously as Steve scooped some of the powder out of the bag and shoved it straight up his nose. 'Davy reckons he's got no one else in Manchester to stop with.'

'Yeah, and Davy's an arse-bandit who'd tell you shit was chocolate to protect his little buddy, so why am I gonna believe a word *he*'s got to fucking say?' Steve shot back, sniffing loudly to get all the coke down.

'Well, we know he booked himself out of the hotel he was staying at a while back,' Noel reminded him.

'Yeah, three fucking weeks ago – straight after he fucked *me* over!' Boiling over now, Steve brought his fists down on the wheel and roared like a crazed bear. Then he pulled the mask he'd brought with him over his head and started the engine, yelling, 'Fuck this! I'm going in for him!'

'Aw, Jeezus, calm down, man!' Noel croaked, pulling his own mask on and casting a nervous look back at the others as they scrabbled to do the same. 'You're gonna get us all fucking nicked!'

The receptionist's head shot up when the front doors were kicked open. She instinctively jabbed her foot down on the button that had been fitted on the floor beneath the desk, activating the silent alarm.

'Keep your fucking hands where I can see them!' Steve barked as he ran towards her with his gun aimed at her face. He hit her hard in the side of the head when he reached her, knocking her out cold. Then he swung his arm round in an arc, warning the people who had run out from other rooms to see what was going on to get on the floor.

Leaving one of the bruisers to stand guard over them, Steve ordered the rest to follow him and, barging through a set of double doors behind which he'd heard the sound of applause, he careered through the neatly laid tables inside, indiscriminately slamming the butt of his gun into screaming faces along the way. When he reached the stage, upon which the mayor and a fairly well-known local cricketer who'd been drafted in as a replacement for Michelle were cowering, he fired several shots into the ceiling to shut everybody up before leaping up onto the stage to get a better view of the room.

Scanning the terrified faces as they huddled together, he could hear nothing but the volcanic roar of his own breathing behind the mask. When he realised that his prey wasn't there, he leapt back down and walked backwards through the room with his gun held out in front of him to prevent anyone from trying anything heroic.

Back outside, Steve jumped into the car with his guys in hot pursuit, stuck it into reverse and turned it to face the gates before slamming it into drive, leaving a spray of gravel flying every which way in his wake as he put his foot down.

'You've fucking lost it!' Noel bellowed at him as he skidded out of the gates and headed off into the darkness without switching his lights on. 'Anything could have fucking happened back there!'

Steve ignored him, his eyes wild as he tore down the lane. When he heard the sound of approaching sirens in the distance he yanked the wheel round, slamming into and through a hedge.

'*FUUUCK!*' Noel squealed, throwing his arms over his head to protect it as he waited for them to slam into a wall or some other immoveable object that they couldn't see in the dark.

Steve slammed his foot on the brake, causing the guys in the rear to smash into the backs of the front seats, and glued his eyes to the rear-view mirror. Someone had obviously set off the alarm back at the hotel, but the sirens could only belong to the local plods because there wouldn't have been time for the ARU to have left the city yet. Same with the helicopter.

Counting three sets of blue flashing lights speeding past a minute later, and knowing that there were unlikely to be any more local units in close enough range to follow, Steve waited until the sirens had faded before he reversed back out through the gap he'd made.

He switched his lights on when they reached the slip road onto the motorway a few minutes later and grinned at Noel. 'You need me to stop at a garage on the way back and get you some toilet roll, or what?'

Noel breathed out loudly and shook his head, chuckling, 'You're one fucking crazy bastard, you!'

34

Time was of the essence but Liam was calm. He got the cab driver to drop them in Didsbury, several miles from Darren's house, so that the driver wouldn't link them to anything newsworthy that happened tonight. Then he immediately had another cab pick them up and drop them on the Princess Parkway, from where they were able to run the rest of the way in a few minutes.

On the way they did a quick scout of the surrounding streets to check for any suspicious-looking cars that might indicate that Steve and his crew were already here.

Pete went in first, his gun at the ready. Relaxing when he found the house as they'd left it, he set to work as Darren rang three of his trusted mates and told them to come round to give them back-up, tipping all the empty bottles out of the bottle bin into a blanket and smashing them to pieces. Then, creeping out into the yard, he sprinkled a thick layer of broken glass right the way across the back wall and gate.

Back inside, Darren let his friends in when they arrived. Locking and bolting the front door behind them, he handed out the coke he'd promised them and got them all tooled up and tanked up. Then, when everyone was ready, they crouched in various positions around the ground floor of the darkened house to wait.

'They're here!' Pete hissed from the kitchen some time later, hearing the distinctive crunching sound as creeping feet made contact with his booby trap.

'Wait till they get inside,' Liam whispered back. 'Then we'll know how many we're dealing with.'

'And nobody shoot each other!' Darren warned. 'We stay low and aim at the ones who are still standing.'

'It's too quiet,' Noel muttered, squinting up at the darkened windows for signs of movement.

'That's 'cos there's no one fucking *here*, you thick cunt,' Steve hissed back at him angrily. 'So quit acting like a shit-house and check the back door.'

'It don't feel right,' Noel insisted. 'I feel like we're being watched.'

'Say one more word and it'll be *me* watching you,' Steve warned, ramming the barrel of his gun into Noel's cheek. 'On tomorrow's news, when they find you floating down the fucking Irwell!'

Noel yanked himself free and said, 'You ever threaten me like that again and I'll bang you the fuck out, Steve. I ain't one of your little knob-head dealers, and don't you ever forget that.'

Steve snorted softly and said, 'Just check the fucking door, you paranoid twat.'

'With me foot?'

'Yeah, 'cos we really want every fucker for miles around to hear you kicking it in, don't we?'

'Well, I ain't got no blade.'

'*Jeezus!*' Steve hissed exasperatedly. He spun around and looked at the other goons. 'Anyone got a fucking blade?'

'No,' a voice replied calmly and coldly from the shadows of the alleyway behind them. 'Just this . . .'

'What the *fuck*?' Pete hissed, instinctively covering his head at the distinctive whooshing sound of bullets being fired from a silenced gun out in the yard, followed by the slumping noises of heavy bodies hitting the ground.

'Fucking hell, they're shooting each *other*!' Darren exclaimed in a loud whisper when he saw the momentary blue flashes illuminating the darkness outside the window.

'Stay put!' Liam ordered calmly as he slid across to the hallway door and cocked his head to listen for sounds of movement outside the front door. It could be Steve and his men shooting each other, but it could just as easily be an Armed Response Unit if Sammy had panicked and alerted the police.

When several seconds of heavy silence had passed, Liam whispered to them all to slide their weapons over to him. Then, taking a chance – because he'd go down for life if the police suddenly charged in and caught him in possession of this arsenal – he crawled out into the hall. Remembering where he'd seen Pete take the gun from earlier, he pulled the carpet back and stashed everything beneath the loose floor-board. He crawled back to join the others when he'd done and asked if they'd heard anything.

'Not sure,' Pete said, his ear pressed firmly against the wood of the back door. 'But I think someone's still moving about out there.'

'Well, get back,' Liam advised. 'Just in case the door gets booted in.'

Doing as he was told, Pete joined the rest of them in the small back room. They all held their breath, listened, and waited.

'Right,' Liam whispered decisively after a few minutes. 'We're going to leave by the front. Make it casual, one at a time . . . You guys,' he said to Darren's mates, 'go home and keep your heads down. I'll see you right.' Then, to Darren and Pete, 'We'll go back to Didsbury – find a pub and get ourselves noticed.'

'Why Didsbury?' Pete asked.

''Cos that's where we got dropped off straight after Darren

got released by the Alderley Edge police,' Liam explained patiently. 'Perfect alibi so we don't get roped into whatever just happened out there.'

'Right you are,' Darren and Pete said in unison.

35

'You are one stupid fuck,' Davy whispered, the soft sing-song tone of his voice at complete odds with the glint of madness in his eyes as he stood over Steve in the dark back yard.

'And you're a *dead* fuck,' Steve hissed up at him, gritting his teeth against the searing pain in his thigh from the shot that had sent him down.

'The only dead fucks round here are your lot,' Davy reminded him. 'Which just leaves *you*.'

Squatting down now, he rammed the silencer into Steve's mouth. Hearing the crunch of teeth breaking, he laughed softly.

'You really should have known better than to try and fuck with my boys, Stevie. And fancy ringing *me* to ask where you'd find them – like you really thought I was going to tell you. But like I said – you really are one stupid fuck!'

EPILOGUE

'Are you absolutely sure you don't mind?' Michelle asked. She sounded guilty as she watched her mother sweeping the debris into the corner of the living room.

Kim squinted at her through the smoke curling up from the cigarette clamped between her teeth. 'Don't be daft, you dozy cow. I'm made up for you. Anyhow,' she added, chuckling slyly, 'Sammy's not exactly used to the whole – *you know* – so he probably wouldn't have been very relaxed with you in the next room listening.'

'Mother, I *really* didn't need to hear that,' Michelle said, grimacing.

Sammy came in at that exact moment and looked from one to the other of them questioningly. 'Have I missed something?'

'Just girl talk,' Kim said, winking at Michelle.

'Righto.' Sammy sounded doubtful. Then, rubbing his hands together, he said, 'Well, everything's in the boot, so when you're ready . . .'

'Just need to get this lot in the bin,' Kim said as she flicked ash onto the pile. 'Don't want the likes of Fat Slag next door coming in after I've gone and saying I'm a dirty bitch.'

'Mum, you'll never be coming back here after today,' Michelle reminded her. 'So what does it matter what anyone thinks?'

'I've got my pride,' Kim told her tartly. She scooped the rubbish onto a shovel and dropped it into a bin liner. 'There,' she said, dusting her hands off when she'd finished and looking around with a hint of satisfaction in her eyes. 'Ready for the next one to move right in.'

Michelle shook her head at Sammy and stood up when Liam came in from the kitchen where he'd just taken a phone call.

Kim sighed. 'I suppose that means you're ready for the off?'

Nodding, Michelle swallowed loudly as the tears began to prick at her eyes.

'Don't you bloody dare,' Kim warned her brusquely, pulling her into her arms and hugging her tightly. 'Now, you're absolutely sure about this, aren't you? No second thoughts.'

'No, definitely not.' Bringing herself under control, Michelle took a deep breath to calm herself. 'Modelling was never for me.'

'But you were so good at it,' Kim said wistfully. 'And you seemed really happy doing it.'

'I hated every single second of it,' Michelle told her truthfully. 'The only reason I carried on doing it was because it was the first time I'd ever been able to get close to you without Mia getting in the way.'

'I'm so sorry,' Kim murmured guiltily. 'I never realised you felt like that.'

'Oh, shut up,' Michelle chided softly. 'I wasn't blaming *you*. I know what Mia's like, don't forget. No one gets a look in when she's around. Anyway, I'm just glad we had the chance to really get to know each other,' she went on, smiling slyly as she added, ''cos you're not half as bad as people make out, you know.'

'You cheeky cow,' Kim protested.

'Sorry to interrupt,' Liam said quietly. 'But that was Darren on the phone, and I know you probably don't want to hear this but he said Mia's been seen down by Steve's old club trying to score crack.'

'*Pfft!*' Kim snorted, flapping her hand dismissively. 'Not interested. She's made her choice, and I'm not going to waste any more of my life wiping her backside.'

A flicker of concern in her eyes, Michelle said, 'You won't turn your back on her completely, though, will you, mum? I know she's put you through hell, but if she gets clean and proves she means it . . .'

Kim gave her an incredulous look and shook her head. 'You're a right one, you.'

'I can't help it.' Michelle shrugged. 'She's still my sister.'

'Yes, I know,' Kim said wearily, rolling her eyes in exasperation. 'And, *no*, I won't turn my back on her if she comes back. But she'll have to *really* bloody prove she's changed before I give her any more chances.'

A car pulled up outside just then. Liam glanced out when the horn sounded and said, 'It's Davy.'

Michelle nodded, and gave her mum another hug before turning to Sammy. Closing her eyes when he crushed her to his chest, she said, 'You'd best look after her, or you'll have me to deal with.'

'Don't worry, I intend to,' he replied, kissing the top of her head.

'Too flaming right you will!' Kim scoffed. 'It took you near enough three years to find your tongue; you've got a lot of making up to do.'

'*Mum!*' Michelle groaned.

Feigning shock, Kim said, 'By *God*, you've got a dirty mind, lady! I only meant it's took him that long to ask me out.'

Sammy blushed because he knew exactly what they meant, and ushered them towards the door.

Davy hopped out of the car when the front door opened and unlocked the boot for Liam to put the cases in.

'Got everything?' he asked. 'Tickets? Passports?'

Patting his breast pocket, Liam nodded.

'Man, I'm gonna miss you,' Davy said, his perpetually red eyes clouding with emotion. 'Too many bad men round here; we need more like you.'

'There's still *some* good ones around,' Liam replied quietly, giving him a knowing look as he added, 'Like the ones who cleaned that other lot off the street.'

Davy shrugged as if he didn't know what Liam was talking about. Then, tilting his head to one side, he grinned at Michelle who was standing at the gate with her mum and Sammy. 'Ah . . . here she is – the future Mrs Grant.'

'Leave it out,' Liam hissed, seeing Michelle blushing. 'We're not rushing into anything. And don't you go putting her off, 'cos it's taken ages to persuade her to come over to Dublin and spend a bit of time with me.'

A passing taxi screeched to a halt in the middle of the road just then and the back door flew open. A camp voice yelled out, 'Don't you *dare* get in that car, Mizz Thang!'

Glancing amusedly up at Liam, Michelle shrugged when a pretty, blond, heavily tanned young man, wearing skintight white trousers and a pink T-shirt emblazoned with the words *Killer Queen!* in diamante letters jumped out and marched around to stand in front of her with his hands on his hips.

'So, Ms *Blaze Cosmetics*,' Bruno spat, pursing his lips in mock anger. 'A boy goes away for a few months to find himself a sugar daddy, and a girl can't even be bothered to ring to let him know she's become a fucking *supermodel* in his absence – what's *that* all about?'

'Sorry, that's got nothing to do with me,' she told him. 'You're mistaking me for my sister. My name's Michelle.'

Feeling really good that she was finally able to be herself again, Michelle climbed into the back of Davy's car.

'Is she for real?' Bruno gasped, looking at Kim in disbelief as the car drove away.

'Oh, yes.' Kim beamed, nodding proudly. 'That's my Michelle, all right.'

Looking at Sammy now, Bruno narrowed his eyes and said, 'Don't I know you from somewhere?' Then, clapping a hand over his mouth when it came to him, he said, 'Oh, my God! You're Mia's agent, aren't you? I've been *dying* to meet you. You see, my agent's really, *really* crap, and I need someone who can get me up there, like you did for Mia. I'm really good, and I—'

'Sorry, son,' Sammy interrupted, putting his arm around Kim. 'As of this morning I'm officially retired. So, if you'll excuse us, we have a pressing engagement with a luxury cruise liner. *Kimberley . . .*'

Grinning when he opened the passenger-side door of the Bentley for her, Kim reached behind her and closed her gate for the last time before climbing in – leaving Bruno watching in dismay from the pavement as they drove away, and Pam sick with jealousy as she stared out at them from behind her nets.